THE
CHILDREN
OF
SILENCE

A FRANCES DOUGHTY MYSTERY

THE CHILDREN OF SILENCE

LINDA STRATMANN

The
Mystery
Press

*This book is dedicated to all who suffer from hyperacusis
and those who are working to make their lives better.*

First published 2015

The Mystery Press, an imprint of The History Press
The Mill, Brimscombe Port
Stroud, Gloucestershire, GL5 2QG
www.thehistorypress.co.uk

British Library Cataloguing in Publication Data.
A catalogue record for this book is available from the British Library.

ISBN 978 0 7509 6010 6

Typesetting and origination by The History Press
Printed in Great Britain

CHAPTER ONE

All through the long hot summer of 1880 the thick, dark, greasy waters of the Paddington Canal Basin bubbled with noxious gases. The warehouses and inns that flanked the wharf side were so closely crowded and decayed that each building seemed to be standing only because it could lean on the one beside it. Porters like swollen crows toiled back and forth unloading the barges that brought bricks, coal, timber and cattle to this busy terminus of the Grand Junction Canal. Towering dust hills, hot with decay, were constantly fed by carts piled with rubbish culled from the ashbins of the metropolis, and ragged women crawled over the smoking debris, sifting the rotting material for anything of value. The worst of the stench was by the cattle pens, where animals waiting to be transported to market were crowded into stalls hoof-deep in dung, and the semi-fluid waste swept from the streets of Paddington by scavengers accumulated in overflowing slop pools. Liquid filth drained freely into the stagnant waters of the basin, which also served as a common convenience to the numerous inhabitants of the barges. When warm summer breezes passed over the canal, they carried poison into the homes of Bayswater and flowed like a cloud of infection into the wards of nearby St Mary's Hospital.

Concerned residents had addressed increasingly urgent complaints about the nuisance to the Paddington Vestry, that body of well-meaning gentlemen responsible for the highways and health of the parish, and a report had concluded that widespread sickness and early deaths amongst those employed in the area of the Paddington Basin was due not so much to trade in offensive material but bad air from the miasmic slurry that filled the canal. The Grand Junction Company that managed the waterway had often expressed itself willing to deal with the hazard, but words were cheap and easy, and the task of cleansing the four-hundred-yard-long basin and the canal approach was a monumental and daunting prospect. Admittedly, the waters were only five feet in depth, but at the bottom was a thick layer of clinging foetid mud into which all manner of revolting material had sunk and which when disturbed emitted the suffocating odour of bad eggs.

The protest came to a head in August when a deputation of influential citizens confronted the vestry with a petition signed by over six hundred ratepayers, deploring the filthy and unwholesome state of the Paddington Basin, whose water, according to a professor of hygiene, was 'nothing better than sewage'. Faced with the horrible prospect of a withholding of rates, the vestrymen finally took action and secured an agreement that the basin would be cleansed. The eye-watering stench that hovered over the canal and its environs meant that nothing could be achieved in safety during the heat of summer, but early in November teams of labourers arrived to carry out the unpleasant task.

As the work commenced, thousands of people poured into the area and assembled for the free spectacle of the great canal laid bare. From St Mary's Hospital all the way to Westbourne Park, the murky sulphurous waters were pumped away, and shapeless globs of detritus were slowly revealed. The labourers set to with shovels, and as they worked a grim atmosphere settled over the scene as the men, their clothes, bodies and faces smeared with mud, toiled without speaking. In places the deposits they dug into were two or three feet thick, and from the layers of semi-solid sludge a few recognisable forms began to emerge: bricks, broken and rusted fragments of chain, the metal portions of carts and barrels with some splinters of darkened wood. There were bones, too, of animals fallen or thrown into the canal, or the gnawed remains of meals. Had any of the fragments been human, which was not impossible, they were many years old, long disarticulated and beyond any prospect of knowing to whom they had once belonged and how those lost individuals had died.

There was only one moment when the labourers recoiled and the crowds gasped. Work stopped, and a pail of clean water was brought to better reveal the horror and consider what ought to be done. Protruding from the upper layers of mud was something more recent, a ribcage, and clinging to it some tattered fragments of clothing rotted to a black pulp. It was attached to something grey and glistening, smelling fouler than the mire from which it had emerged. A spine and a cranium, its jawbone fallen away but still with some flesh congealed into a glutinous mass, its shape a perverse travesty of what it had once been: a face.

Seven months later, with the canal imperfectly cleansed and refilled, and the water rather less dangerous than before, the identity of the person – a man, judging from the shape of the skull – whose remains had been found and removed, examined and argued over, was still a mystery.

Frances Doughty, Bayswater's youngest and only lady detective, had not imagined that she would be employed in the case, which seemed to be more appropriate to the mortuary table than the consulting room, but unexpectedly, she was about to receive a visitor who wished to engage her. Many Bayswater ladies came to Frances about matters that concerned their husbands, and she had often observed that the difficulties associated with a deceased husband were as nothing compared to those that attended one who was living. Mrs Harriett Antrobus, however, had a more complicated problem. Some three years ago her husband Edwin had journeyed to Bristol on business and failed to return or communicate with his family and friends. Mrs Antrobus was convinced that he had met with an accident and died, but in law he was alive and could not be declared dead until either a body was found and identified or a total of seven years had elapsed. The situation was compounded by the fact that Edwin Antrobus' will, which could not be proved but existed in a legal limbo, had been drawn up under a misapprehension which had plunged her into grave financial difficulty.

The man whose remains had been found in the Paddington Basin was of about the right age to be Edwin Antrobus, and he could well have died as long as three years ago; moreover, the fragments of fabric found clinging to his bones showed that he had been respectably dressed. It was far from being a complete skeleton; unfortunately, despite the strenuous efforts of the labourers, only the ribs, spine and upper part of the skull had been recovered. The rest of the body, thought to have been torn away by the action of canal traffic, must still lie irretrievably buried in the mud of the basin, since the Canal Company had admitted defeat and abandoned the cleansing work only half-done. It was, however, possible to suggest a cause of death, since the flesh of the corpse's throat, which had been transformed by its long watery immersion into a soap-like material called adipocere, exhibited a deep transverse cut.

Harriett Antrobus had tried to obtain a formal ruling that the body found in the Paddington Basin was that of her husband. It was surmised that he had returned from Bristol, arriving at Paddington Station, which lay close to the canal basin, and on his way home had been waylaid, lured to the wharf side, murdered and robbed. The court proceedings had been widely reported in the *Bayswater Chronicle* and Frances had read them with interest. Mrs Antrobus was unable to give evidence, since she suffered from an affliction that kept her confined indoors, and she was represented by Mr Stephen Wylie, formerly of Bristol and a business associate of her husband's who had been one of the last people to see Edwin Antrobus alive. However, the medical evidence, supplied by Dr Collin who had examined the remains, had, to Mrs Antrobus' great disappointment, proved insufficient to determine identity and the action had failed.

Mr Wylie had written to Frances to make an appointment, enclosing a letter from Mrs Antrobus pleading for assistance, and it was the gentleman who was due to arrive.

'Sounds like she'd rather her husband was dead,' said Sarah, Frances' burly and no-nonsense assistant, 'but who's to say he is? If he made a will that didn't do right by his wife then that marriage was a sour one. Perhaps she drinks. He could be in Bristol right now all alive-o, with a new name, a new business and a new wife.'

'How cruel if he abandoned a wife who was in need of his care and left her unprovided for,' mused Frances.

It was not, she thought, a case that promised easy success, but since a great deal of her work involved investigating light-fingered servants and faithless lovers, she was glad of something that piqued her interest. She awaited her visitor, wondering if, as so often happened in her investigations, she was about to uncover worse things than had ever been found sunken into the slime of the Paddington Canal Basin.

CHAPTER TWO

Stephen Wylie, who arrived promptly to his appointed hour at the apartment Frances shared with Sarah, was a youngish man, that is to say he was not yet middle-aged, perhaps little more than thirty-five, but his youthfulness was obscured by a high forehead lined with worry, from which dark hair was making a stealthy retreat. He brought with him the scent of tobacco, not the stale odour that always clung about the habitual smoker, but the warm fragrance of the freshly rubbed product. He was ushered into the parlour clutching a hat and a document case, and he almost dropped both at the sight of Sarah's imposing bulk and intense, searching gaze. Frances quickly precluded any objections by introducing her companion as a trusted associate. Sarah had never been slight of build, but she had recently been supervising classes in calisthenics for the ladies of Bayswater and looked more confident and powerful than ever. Mr Wylie afforded her a nervous acknowledgement, as if to say that he pitied anyone who might attempt to burgle the premises, and sidled into a chair.

'I have read the reports of the legal action taken by Mrs Antrobus to prove that her husband is deceased, but I find it hard to imagine how I might assist,' began Frances, once they were facing each other across the little round table where she interviewed her clients. 'Nevertheless, if you would start at the beginning I would like you to tell me something of Mr Antrobus and the circumstances of his disappearance.' She opened her notebook and took up a fresh pencil.

'Certainly,' said Wylie, with the demeanour of a man who was embarking on an often-told tale. 'Mr Antrobus and I had been business associates for several years. I was born and raised in Bristol where my family has imported tobacco, snuff and cigars for three generations. Mr Antrobus' business was the manufacture of cigarettes. He and his partner, Mr Luckhurst, have a workshop in Paddington with some thirty employees. Mr Antrobus was very active, he travelled all over the country to see his customers and meet importers of the raw materials. Mr Luckhurst remains in London and attends to the office. It was October of 1877 when Antrobus made his last visit to Bristol, and I had several meetings with him. There was nothing out of the ordinary either in his manner or in the business he conducted. On his last evening there, the 12th, we dined together at his hotel, the George Railway Hotel in Victoria Street not far from the station, and he was his usual self.'

'What was his usual self?' asked Frances.

Wylie's smile expressed a quiet regard for his friend. 'There is little enough to say. He was very much a man of business, reserved in his personal life and with a small circle of acquaintances. I have never known him do a dishonest thing or drink to excess or descend to indelicacy. Some might have found him dull company, but our mutual interests in the tobacco trade kept our conversation alive.'

'What did you discuss on that last occasion?'

'A report in the trade press that a company in Virginia had offered a prize to the man who could invent a machine that would manufacture cigarettes.'

'Such a machine would threaten Mr Antrobus' business, would it not?' Frances observed. 'Was he despondent at the prospect?'

'Far from it!' said Wylie with a laugh. 'We agreed that even if the machine could be built it would be too expensive for anyone to purchase and maintain. In any case, he believed as I do that customers will always prefer the hand-rolled product.'

'There were no financial troubles that you know of before Mr Antrobus disappeared? Did he have any debts?'

'No, none,' Wylie asserted with great conviction, 'and as evidence of that, the business continues to be profitable despite his absence. Mr Luckhurst has employed a man to travel in Antrobus' place, and he has worked very hard to keep everything running as smoothly as possible.' He smiled dolefully. 'I know what inspires your questions as I have been asked them before. There was no reason either for Antrobus to run away or – heaven forbid – lay violent hands upon himself. I should mention,' he added, 'that for the last year I have resided in London, where I hope to expand our family concerns. I have been talking with Mr Luckhurst about a possible merger of interests, and in connection with this he kindly allowed me to examine the books of the company. I have found them entirely satisfactory.'

Frances decided to reserve her opinion on that point. If there should prove to be more than one set of books the business would not be the first to present its investors with accounts that owed more to deliberate concealment than fact. 'Did Mr Antrobus have any business rivals – enemies even – who might have meant him harm?'

'None that I am aware of.'

'When did you discover that he was missing?'

'It was a week after our last meeting. I received a letter from Mrs Antrobus. We had never met or corresponded before but she knew of me and had found my address in her husband's papers. She had been expecting him to return home by the morning train on the 13th, and when he did not she assumed that he had been delayed by business and would write to explain. When she heard nothing further she wrote to Mr Luckhurst who confirmed that her husband had not appeared at the office, and then she wrote to me.'

'Did you make enquiries?' asked Frances.

'I did, immediately. I went to the hotel and was told that Antrobus had vacated his room on the expected day. I spoke to our associates in the tobacco trade but none of them had seen him or received so much as a note. I enquired at the railway station, but a gentleman attired for business looks very much like another unless there is something distinctive about his person, or his manner of dress or his whiskers. Mr Antrobus was not a man who stood out in a crowd. I alerted the railway company in case he had fallen from the train, but they assured me that no remains had been found on the line.' He shook his head. 'Poor Mrs Antrobus was quite distraught at the situation and naturally I said I would do everything I could to help her.'

'She is unable to travel, I understand?'

'Yes, in fact – in fact I was very surprised to hear from her at all. Antrobus had told me almost nothing about his wife's affliction, and I had decided it was best not to pry, but I received the very strong impression that she suffered from a species of hysteria, which is something I have no knowledge of, and was therefore unable to attend to her own affairs. When I received her letter, however, I found her to be intelligent, articulate and not at all disordered in her mind. On better acquaintance I discovered that she is a lady who can only command great sympathy and respect. No, it is a disease of the ears that she suffers from, and which gives her great pain unless she keeps very quiet to herself. A busy street, a noisy carriage or a train would be the most perfect torture to her.'

'I see,' said Frances, who had never heard of such an extraordinary thing. 'So you agreed to act as her agent?'

'Yes, the family had already notified the police, and I engaged a private detective, a Mr Ryan, who was very thorough indeed and submitted a full report. I have it with me.' Wylie patted the document case. 'He spoke to the clerk at the hotel who told him that on the morning of Antrobus' departure he saw him talking to a man in the hallway. He was unable to describe the man but had the distinct impression from their manner that they were not strangers. Then his attention was distracted by the need to attend to another guest, and when he looked again Antrobus and the other man had both gone. They might have departed in each other's company, but it cannot be proved.'

'Tell me about Mr Antrobus' will. According to the newspapers it is very unfavourable to his wife. What is your opinion?'

A grimace creased the visitor's features for a moment. 'Oh, that is a terrible thing!' he said bitterly. 'The will was drawn up several years previously and in the mistaken belief that poor Mrs Antrobus was not competent to manage her affairs. Almost all of the estate is left in trust for the two sons, who are now aged fifteen and twelve and are at school, the trust to be administered by Antrobus' brother Lionel until the boys come of age. Mrs Antrobus was left only a small annuity, presumably on the assumption that her husband had many more years to live – he would be forty-four now if alive – and it must have been envisaged that by the time he passed away the sons would have achieved their majority and be able to care for their mother. But it was not to be. And the cruellest thing is that shortly before his departure he had been

planning to change his will to something altogether more generous. Mrs Antrobus had finally been able to convince her husband
that she was as competent as the next lady – indeed I would say
she is more so – and he had agreed that on his return from Bristol
he would make a new will.'

Frances gazed at him through narrowed eyes. 'Is that not a very
great coincidence, that he went missing at such a critical time?'
she asked pointedly. Sarah made no attempt at concealing a smile
that was almost a smirk. Frances, as she well knew, did not like
coincidences.

'I suppose it is,' Wylie admitted, 'I had just seen it as unfortunate –
the operation of fate. But you think it may be something more?'

'I try to examine every possibility. Is the estate very valuable?'

'I assume so, though it has not as yet been valued. The two
principal assets are his half share in the cigarette manufacturing
business and the house. Antrobus inherited the property from
a maternal uncle, and it is his quite unencumbered. He and his
brother also jointly own the tobacconist's shop previously run
by their late father and of which Mr Lionel is manager. Antrobus
was always a prudent man with money and there are safe investments that produce an interest.' He paused. 'I say "was" since
I feel sure that he is deceased, although in law he is still alive.'

'Of course I understand that the will cannot be proved or, I suppose, even contested until it is shown that its author is deceased,
and that this places Mrs Antrobus in a very difficult position,'
Frances observed, 'but does her brother-in-law, knowing about
the change in intentions, not do what he can to assist her in her
very unfortunate situation?'

Wylie heaved a long sigh. 'Mr Lionel Antrobus is —' he hesitated,
unsure of how to express himself – 'a difficult man. He believes
that he is doing his duty by adhering to the letter of the will and is
undoubtedly concerned for the welfare of the boys, but I believe
that he has always been jealous of his brother's fortune, and there
is no doubt that he heartily dislikes Mrs Antrobus and will do all
he can not to give in to her wishes.'

Large estates and family rivalry, thought Frances, a combination
fraught with unpleasant and highly interesting possibilities. 'Please
explain further.'

'They are actually half-brothers. Mr Edwin is the younger, the son of their father's second wife. He was a great favourite of his mother's brother, a Mr Henderson, and so received a handsome legacy from him. Mr Lionel has received no such additional legacy, only a share of what their father left, and that was divided equally between the brothers. Mr Lionel has always felt that he should have had a larger share from his father as his younger brother enjoyed his uncle's fortune. And he continues, despite all entreaties, to believe that Mrs Antrobus is suffering from hysteria. He thinks that an ailment he cannot see cannot exist.'

Frances frowned. 'That is a very blinkered view. What of deafness, for example? That is not a malady one can see in the sufferer. Does he believe that that does not exist?'

'Oh deafness has been with us since antiquity and I think he will allow it, but poor Mrs Antrobus' disease he will not. He refuses to trust her with a penny more than her husband mentioned in the will and that is little enough. He pays the frugal allowance she would have received, but that is not sufficient to maintain the house. In fact, as soon as he assumed control of the estate he insisted that she should go to live with her sister, Miss Pearce, but that would not have been at all suitable. Miss Pearce was then residing in a small rented apartment, living off a modest annuity, caring for their widowed mother and earning a few extra shillings by giving classes in reading and writing to young children. The mother passed away the following Christmas, and Mr Lionel thought that was the ideal time for Mrs Antrobus to vacate the family home. He wanted to rent the house and place the income in trust for the boys, but Mrs Antrobus needs the peace and quiet the house affords her. It would have been very hard, in fact impossible for her to live in such a small apartment, what with children often present and the constant noise of carriages outside. So they devised a plan to circumvent Mr Lionel's demands. Miss Pearce came to live with Mrs Antrobus. The classes had to be given up, but Miss Pearce found a little outside work as an hourly governess, and that enables them to remain there, if in reduced circumstances, with only one servant. Needless to say Mr Lionel was most annoyed at being thwarted and demanded that Mrs Antrobus and her sister should both leave and place the property under his control. I believe he took legal advice on the matter but he was told that in view of Mrs Antrobus' affliction there might be some difficulty if he attempted to evict her. He has been silent on the issue for a while, but I am sure that he has not given up on the idea. It is a continuing anxiety that adds to the lady's distress. If she was able to prove that her husband is dead, then she might be able to take steps to overturn the will. There are no documents to support what was only a verbal promise to increase her legacy, but any court would at once recognise that as the will stands it is grossly unfair to a blameless lady.'

'The matter must already have been costly,' said Frances, 'and you say that Mrs Antrobus has few resources. How does she meet the legal fees?'

Wylie had the good taste to blush. 'Yes, well, I confess that I have been providing some financial assistance,' he admitted, revealing nothing that Frances had not already suspected, 'and this has not, of course, recommended me to Mr Lionel Antrobus, who had imagined that his sister-in-law was friendless and without the means to oppose him. There is another matter that causes Mrs Antrobus great distress. During her sons' holidays from school they are sent to stay with an aunt in Kent. They are happy enough as there is much in the way of fresh air and recreation but they do not see their mother. She receives letters from them and writes to them but that is all.' He shook his head. 'It is unnecessary for me to say at whose orders that arrangement has been made.'

Frances took some moments to read through her notes. 'When a search was originally conducted for Mr Antrobus, was it carried out in the belief that he had not left Bristol and was therefore centred entirely in that city?'

'That is the case. None of his associates in London have seen him since he last departed for Bristol.'

'But you now wish me to make enquiries on the assumption that he did in fact return to London?'

'I do, yes.'

'But you have no evidence that he did.'

'Oh, but we do!' he exclaimed. 'There are the remains found in the canal.'

'But they prove nothing,' Frances pointed out. 'They may not be his remains.'

'It is our contention, indeed our firm belief that they are the remains of Mr Antrobus. All we require is the removal of others' doubts in the matter.' There was a pleading expression in his eyes, a wet gleam that aroused Frances' suspicion that she was far from being the first detective he had approached for this purpose.

'This is a very interesting commission.' He looked hopeful and opened the document case, which was well stuffed with papers. 'But I regret that I cannot take it.'

'Oh!' His face fell and she could see that it had fallen before. 'I cannot persuade you?' he ventured.

'No. Not on the terms you describe.'

He closed the case and prepared to leave, but she lifted her hand to forestall him.

'You have asked me to start my enquiries by assuming that the remains found in the Paddington Basin are those of Mr Antrobus and with the object of proving that they are. It is quite impossible for me to proceed on that basis. I can gather facts, of course, but what if I uncover facts that show the opposite conclusion? What would you have me do? I can hardly ignore them. I can form theories and test them against the facts, of course, but if the facts do not fit it is time to find another theory. I cannot act as you wish and any detective who does will be taking your money in a spirit of mockery.'

Wylie fidgeted with his hat brim. 'I did, when the remains were first found, engage a London man to make enquiries, and he did very little for a month and then told me that the task could not be achieved and presented me with his bill. And there have been others who refused even to make the attempt. Then I read in the newspapers about your giving evidence at a recent murder trial and was most impressed by the thoroughness of your methods. Someone I spoke to likened you to Jude the Apostle – he said you are the patron saint of lost causes. I am sorry to have troubled you, Miss Doughty.'

'But it is an interesting case.'

He had half risen from his seat but paused, gave her a curious look, and sat down again.

'I want you to be perfectly honest with me,' said Frances. 'I don't think that you yourself are convinced that the remains are those of Mr Antrobus. And if I might venture an opinion, I don't think

Mrs Antrobus believes so either. Both of you are, however, very anxious that the remains are identified as those of Mr Antrobus because if they are he will be declared dead and Mrs Antrobus can try to extricate herself from her financial disarray some years earlier than anticipated. Am I correct?'

He hesitated and then nodded. 'You are correct, of course.'

'On all counts?'

He licked his lips. 'I can only speak for myself, but – yes.'

'And if events should turn out as you wish, Mrs Antrobus would be a widow and free to marry again if she so chooses.'

He said nothing but an embarrassed smile spoke for him.

'Very well,' Frances declared in her best businesslike manner, 'this is how I suggest I proceed. I will start a new enquiry into the disappearance of Mr Antrobus. Since the previous one was conducted only in Bristol, I will see what I can learn in London. I will of course consult with your Bristol agent. But my mission, and I must make this very clear from the outset, will be to find out the truth, whatever that may be. While the remains found in the canal might be those of Mr Antrobus, they could just as well be those of another man. Will that be acceptable?'

'You are very direct, Miss Doughty. I have heard that said of you also.' He thought for a moment. 'I believe we may accept your terms. Let me consult with Mrs Antrobus and I will call again.'

'It will of course be necessary for me to interview Mrs Antrobus.'

'She prefers to communicate by letter with people not familiar with her infirmity.'

'Then you must familiarise me. Mrs Antrobus is most probably the best source of information there is on her husband's character and movements. I must speak with her.' Frances did not add that when conducting interviews she paid great attention to the facial expressions and attitudes of the people she spoke to and some-times learned more from those than from the words spoken. And she would have some potentially embarrassing questions to ask Mrs Antrobus.

'Very well,' he agreed reluctantly. 'I do converse with her, of course, but it is essential that when I do so I speak quietly. Raised voices she cannot abide, not even so much as a sneeze or a cough. Do not wear silk, as it rustles so, neither must you wear shoes with hard soles or open and close a reticule or any case with a fastening where metal snaps against metal. The pain she endures from such sounds are like a knife thrust into her ear. And yet there are some sounds that still give her pleasure – the wind and gentle rain, and voices both soft and low. She plays the piano for relief and her sister has a low melodious voice and sings to her. Silence she finds a great trial as her ears seem to make a noise of their own that never stops by night or day.'

Frances could hardly imagine the misery that must attend such a life, and she looked forward all the more to meeting the lady in question. 'I will write to Mrs Antrobus and make an appointment,' she said. 'I will also interview Mr Antrobus' friends and associates who saw him in the months immediately preceding his disappearance. I need to know all his circumstances: his character, his faults, his ambitions – everything that might provide a clue as to his fate. I must consider whether he has met his death by accident, self-destruction or murder, and also if he might still be alive. I rule out nothing.'

Mr Wylie provided Frances with the Bristol detective's report and the addresses of Mr Luckhurst and Mr Lionel Antrobus, who, Mr Wylie said, knew the missing man better than anyone in London other than his wife. The payment of a handsome advance fee completed the proceedings and he departed.

'What did you think of Mr Wylie?' asked Frances as she and Sarah studied the report and reread the newspapers over a large pot of tea. Frances never ceased to wonder how it was that hot tea, with or without a biscuit, could be so wonderfully warming to the system in the winter, yet so refreshing in the summer. Either way it never failed to stimulate her thoughts.

'Wants to marry the lady, and it's not just the money he's after,' remarked Sarah, 'which is a new one round here. In Bayswater it's money first and love second, if it ever gets a look in which it doesn't often.'

Sarah's robustly cynical view of the world had not been modified by the fact that she was walking out with Professor Pounder, who taught the art of manly self-defence at his Bayswater academy. The Professor was a handsome fellow who cut a fine figure, and it was a matter of some mystification amongst young ladies who prided themselves on their beauty that he should prefer the company of someone so decidedly plain. The Professor, however, was impervious to external show and reserved his admiration for a woman with a stalwart nature and fists that could crack walnuts.

'Yes, but there is more to Mr Wylie than a simpering affection,' observed Frances. 'Perhaps I will learn more when I see Mrs Antrobus. I shall write to Mr Ryan in Bristol. His report is very thorough but it is three years old. Mr Wylie has been kind enough to enclose a portrait of Mr Antrobus, and I can see that he was unremarkable in appearance. He might easily have taken the train to Paddington without anyone at the station noticing him particularly, and there is no feature here that might have helped Dr Collin match him against the remains found in the canal.'

'Will you be speaking to Dr Collin?' asked Sarah. An uncomfortable inference hung in the air.

'I will write to him for an appointment, but he will be as unhelpful as it is possible for him to be.' Dr Collin, while Frances' own family doctor who had known the Doughtys for many years, had never quite forgiven her for revealing that he had once made an error of judgement, something to which no medical man would ever admit unless forced. Dr Collin appeared to believe that the letters MD after his name conferred upon him a pre-eminent place in the estimation of the public, a glow of veneration in which he liked to bask as if it was the summer sun. His manner towards Frances was pure winter.

'One point which was made very forcefully in court,' remarked Frances, 'was that if the remains are not those of Mr Antrobus whose else could they be? No other man of that age has been reported missing in Paddington and, importantly, all the material found with the bones was the remains of good quality gentleman's apparel. There were no coarse fibres as might be expected had a poor man worn a second-hand coat over a rough shirt. He was not a bargeman or porter in his working clothes, killed in a quarrel, but a man of means whose absence would surely have been widely commented on. Even if he was not resident here but a visitor, no other person has come forward to say that a relative has not returned from a visit to Paddington and also laid claim to the remains.'

'I hope you're not going to go off solving murders again,' warned Sarah. 'Remember what happened last time.'

Frances did not have to be reminded of the distressing attack on her person that had occurred during an earlier investigation, and she shuddered. She had not mentioned it to Sarah, but she still sometimes had dreams in which she smelt her assailant's foul breath and felt the pressure of his body crushing against her, only to wake up in alarm and confusion. The miscreant was currently reflecting upon his sins in prison, while the evildoer whose instrument he was, in common with several others whose paths had crossed hers, had recently been found guilty of murder at the Old Bailey and condemned to death. It was a consequence of her profession that occasionally troubled her conscience, but she reminded herself that the law was both firm and just, and she must be the same.

Chapter Three

When Frances commenced a new enquiry and sought meetings at which to gather information, she usually started by assembling the names and addresses she required and wrote letters to secure appointments. It seemed only polite. Sometimes when the ground had been prepared for her by recent events her card or a letter of introduction, together with good manners and a respectable appearance, served just as well. It was at later interviews that she deliberately tried to take people by surprise and prevent them from manufacturing stories to deceive her by arriving without prior warning. There were also times when, stung into a temper by repeated lies, she burst in upon her quarry in a wholly undignified manner, a proceeding which left her feeling a little ashamed of herself but rarely failed to get results. As Frances wrote her first letters in the Antrobus case she wondered whose door she would have to belabour this time.

Within hours of Mr Wylie's visit Frances received a neat little note in Mrs Antrobus' flowing yet legible hand which confirmed that she would be delighted to see Frances the following morning.

June was the herald of summer in Bayswater, and the lifting of winter gloom and passing of a cool spring had given a new lightness to Frances' heart. The fine, warm and above all settled weather had brought out the best in fashion. On every promenade young ladies paraded their newest ensembles in shades of sunny yellow and bright sky blue, with ribbons and bows in their bonnets, ruffles at cuffs and hem, and dainty parasols in their hands.

For over a year Frances had been in mourning both for her brother and father, and while that particular state would, in a sense, never change, she felt that it was time to put off her most sombre attire and adopt a deep pearl grey trimmed with a touch of white. A portrait of her brother with a twist of his hair enclosed in a locket hung about her neck from a black ribbon. The instruction not to wear silk when visiting Mrs Antrobus was an easy one for her to comply with as she had never owned or even worn a silk dress. As she checked her appearance before going out, she realised that she looked like a governess and would probably always do so. A governess, however, did not wave for a cab with such confidence or step lightly aboard with such aplomb as a lady detective.

The dust thrown up by carriage wheels that had once been a choking nuisance to both lungs and pretty fabrics in dry weather was somewhat less of a trial than in previous years. The long needed completion of the wood paving along the length of Westbourne Grove meant that traffic now rumbled over level hardwood sets rather than rattling and shaking over rutted macadam and pebbles, and it was possible for shoppers and strollers to spend more time in front of the windows of Mr William Whiteley's growing emporium, marvelling at the latest trimmings from Paris.

On that bright, light day Frances saw the rotund figure of the proprietor himself standing at the door of his drapery shop, smiling and ushering customers in. He was a jolly fellow, so it was said, until anyone crossed him or owed him money, and then the story was different. Not so long ago he had fought an increasingly acrimonious battle with the Paddington Vestry after buying up some properties on Queens Road to convert them to warehouses and erecting towering hoardings that contravened every building law in the parish. Only the most stringent action by the vestry had succeeded in getting the work halted, but before long Whiteley flouted the court orders and started construction work again until he was made to stop. He had finally succeeded by a process of wearing down the patience and funds of his opponents until the vestrymen capitulated and let him do whatever he wanted.

Harriett Antrobus and her sister lived in an elegant three-storey house on Craven Hill, just far enough away from Paddington Station and the canal basin to avoid all the inconveniences of daily traffic, yet near enough for the man of business to meet his train without risk of delay. Frances rang the doorbell, which, she surmised, must only make itself heard deep within the house, where there was no prospect of it annoying Mrs Antrobus. As she waited she thought about the common noises of daily life that she took for granted. What if they suddenly became intolerable? How could one live? Frances had already consulted her small library of medical books, the legacy of her father who had been a pharmacist, and they made no mention of the malady from which Mrs Antrobus suffered, in fact they said very little about diseases of the ear in general. Perhaps, she reflected, this was an area of knowledge which doctors deemed unfashionable and therefore beneath their notice.

The door was opened by a tall woman of about forty. She was neither plain nor pretty but had the strong square features often described as handsome. She wore a plain dark stuff gown, several seasons old, but an effort had been made to disguise its deficiencies by the addition of woven braid. From her waist there hung not a chain of keys but a bag made of padded fabric, gathered with a cord. On seeing Frances' card her features softened into a welcoming smile. 'Miss Doughty, do come in. I am Charlotte Pearce, Harriett's sister.' She glanced at Frances' shoes.

'I will leave my street shoes in the hall if I may,' said Frances, producing a pair of soft indoor slippers from the basket she carried.

Miss Pearce looked her up and down, took in the quiet dress and lack of clattering jewellery, and nodded her approval. 'That is very kind of you. Harriett will appreciate your thoughtfulness.'

As they passed along the corridor Frances heard a whisper of sound, the deep low notes of a piano, gentle, soft, rippling like waves. It was not a melody, but it resembled the music played in preparation for a melody to arouse the expectation of the listener that higher notes would break in to make a contrast against the underscore; instead, the theme turned full circle and came back again to the start.

On reaching the rear parlour, her guide tapped gently on the door, not with her knuckles but using the pads of her fingertips. She paused and, once the music had ceased, said, 'Harriett, Miss Doughty is here to see you.' In a few moments the door opened soundlessly.

Frances saw a dignified woman perhaps a year or two younger than Miss Pearce. They were clearly, from the similarity of their features, sisters, but in Mrs Antrobus the cast of cheek and brow was more delicate, rounded and refined. While Charlotte might have drawn a gentleman's approving eye she would only have done so if her sister was not present.

In view of her history anyone might imagine that Mrs Antrobus would be bowed down by her cruel situation, but there was a resolution in the lady's expression, and she had the brave and confident face of someone who could meet the strongest adversity with the expectation of triumph. 'Miss Doughty, please do come in,' she said in a voice that was at once soft and harmonious, like her music.

'I will bring some refreshments,' murmured Miss Pearce and slipped quietly away.

Frances entered a small, comfortable parlour, where the floor was deeply carpeted and every hard surface covered by soft drapery. There were no items such as portraits or china ornaments that might inadvertently fall to the floor, but even if there had been and they had fallen they would have been received softly and safely without unpleasant noise. Heavy curtains protected the only window, and the room was bathed in the glow of gas lamps. There was a small pianoforte, the lid of which lay open, and a thick folded shawl rested across the keys, presumably to muffle the sound of the closing lid.

Once both women were comfortably seated Mrs Antrobus smiled warmly, her eyes reflecting the golden light. 'It is a great pleasure to meet you Miss Doughty, I have read so much about you in the newspapers, and I was overjoyed when Mr Wylie informed me that you had agreed to help.'

Frances hoped that Mrs Antrobus had not read the halfpenny stories that were being published in Bayswater about a lady detective called Miss Dauntless who dared do anything a man might do and more, and whose exploits were often confused with her own. The author, who Frances had not yet identified, went under the obvious pseudonym W. Grove. She thought it best not to mention them. 'I cannot promise success, but I will do my very best to find your husband.' She hesitated. 'I am not speaking too loudly for you?'

'Not at all,' Mrs Antrobus reassured her, 'gentle speech without emphasis does not cause me pain.' She handed Frances a paper. 'I have written down the names and addresses of all Edwin's family and associates. There are few enough as you see, he was not a gregarious man and preferred small gatherings to large assemblies.'

'And was he on good terms with all these persons?' asked Frances, studying the list.

'I can scarcely imagine that anyone who knew Edwin might wish him harm. He was the least offensive of men.'

'Nevertheless, people can take offence at even slight causes or sometimes for no obvious cause at all.'

Mrs Antrobus gave the matter some consideration. 'Edwin, as far as I know, has always been honest and fair in business. His partner, Mr Luckhurst, thinks highly of him, as does Mr Wylie. Neither is he a quarrelsome man who might make enemies. People found him courteous and considerate if a little reserved.'

'And yet he made a will that you found harsh. Why was this?'

The bright eyes dimmed with sadness. 'I cannot blame him,' she sighed. 'He thought it best because of the boys. Our doctor had told him that I was suffering from hysteria, and he believed what he was told. I also think that he allowed himself to be influenced by his brother. Lionel has never approved of the marriage. My late father was an assistant in the tobacconist's shop owned by Mr Antrobus senior. Our circumstances were far below what Lionel thought was appropriate. And once I began to suffer with my ears that only hardened his opinion. You know, I suppose, that my sons have been sent away to school and Lionel discourages them from visiting me during the holidays. I miss them constantly.'

'Mr Wylie told me that your husband was about to change his will to something you would find more favourable. Did your brother-in-law know this?'

'He is adamant that he knew nothing of it, but that is not too surprising as it was just a matter of a conversation between Edwin and myself the day before he left for Bristol.'

'How does your brother-in-law benefit under the will as it stands?'

'He receives Edwin's half share in the tobacconist's shop and a sum of money, quite a generous one.'

'And if the will had been changed? What then?'

She ventured a little smile. 'You mean would Lionel's expectations have fallen had mine been advanced? I really can't say. All I know is that Edwin reassured me that he would secure my entitlement to remain in this house for my lifetime and I would receive an income sufficient for its upkeep – rather more than

I have now. He also agreed that in future the boys could come and stay with us during their holidays. That gave me more pleasure than anything.'

'What was your husband's manner shortly before he departed? Did he seem troubled in any way? Was he in full health?'

'As far as I was aware his health was sound and he seemed quite his usual self. If there was anything worrying him I did not know of it.'

Frances wrote in her notebook, but there was little enough to write. She had asked the obvious questions and learned nothing. Either Mr Antrobus' disappearance was the result of some unknown and unanticipated incident, or an aspect of his life she had not yet explored. 'Can you say how it was that you were able to convince your husband to make changes in his will? In fact, before you answer that question, it might help me to know the history of your affliction. How did it arise? What advice were you given?' Frances paused. 'I am sorry if such a question distresses you but it may be of some importance.'

'I understand,' said Mrs Antrobus, 'and I welcome the opportunity to tell another person about my disease. I fear that there may be many others like myself, who are thought to be mad when it is only their ears that are affected.'

Frances allowed her time to collect her thoughts.

'When I married Edwin I was twenty-one and had never suffered a moment's anxiety about my hearing. Not long after Arthur, our youngest, was born, Edwin and I attended a display of fireworks, and there was one that exploded too near to the ground and alarmed everyone. From that time, I found that all noises, but especially those that were sharp and shrill, seemed much louder, and some gave me pain, while other people tolerated the same sounds with equanimity. I took to putting cotton wool in my ears. When that was not enough I used softened wax, but when I removed the wax, the noises seemed even louder and were more painful. The street, a busy shop, these places seemed to be crowded with demons sent to torment me with their screaming. But of course they were not demons and neither did they scream. They were just people, laughing and talking and exclaiming as people do.'

'Were you afraid of becoming deaf?' asked Frances.

Mrs Antrobus exhaled softly through trembling lips, and a tear glimmered at the corner of one eye. 'Oh, Miss Doughty, I would never make light of another's affliction – my own dear late mother was hard of hearing in her final years, and I know what a trial it can be – but sometimes, in my darkest hours, I am ashamed to say that I have prayed to be made deaf. A mother who is deaf will never hear the laughter of her children, but she may still play with them. The voices of small children, even my own beloved boys, cause me the most exquisite pain. Our physician, Dr Collin, said that I needed rest and quiet and prescribed a tonic mixture. But I saw him whisper to Edwin, and later my husband confided in me that Dr Collin believed I was suffering from hysteria, that I had experienced such a fright from the exploding firework that I had started to imagine that all sounds were dangerous, and since – as some doctors believe – there is a connection between the ears and the womb, it resulted in my curious condition.'

'Do you believe that is the case?'

'No, Miss Doughty, I believe it is the kind of nonsense doctors talk when they do not know the answers.'

Frances was unable to restrain herself from a little laugh and was astonished and mortified to see Mrs Antrobus flinch at the sound. 'I am so terribly sorry.'

Mrs Antrobus waved away her alarm. 'Please do not distress yourself,' she said kindly. 'But to complete my story, Edwin truly thought that I was losing my mind and it was for this reason that he made a will which placed his brother in control of his property.'

The door opened admitting Miss Pearce, who brought a tray of tea things. The tray was wooden and lined with a folded cloth while the vessels and plates were of wood as were the spoons, and the teapot was encased in a quilted cover. The tea was poured and the wooden bowls delivered to Frances and Mrs Antrobus, then Miss Pearce departed.

'Do you trust your brother-in-law to act properly under the will?' asked Frances. While it was not possible to know how much Lionel Antrobus might have lost had a later will been made, his current control must, she knew, give him the opportunity to abstract funds if he was so inclined.

'I have no evidence that he is doing anything he should not, but I have no entitlement to see the financial records, and, even if I did, these things may be given a false gloss and I would not see what lay beneath. If Lionel is not acting as he should that will not become apparent until the will is proved. If I cannot show that my husband is deceased that will not be until October 1884.'

Frances sipped her tea. 'So, to return to my earlier question, what was it that made your husband change his mind?'

'I told him that I was not satisfied with Dr Collin's opinion and asked to see other doctors. He agreed, and that was when we learned that my disease was as much a mystery to medical men as it was to us. Each man had a different opinion. One doctor said that there was nothing the matter with me. He said that I was afraid of losing my husband's love and nervous about his absences from home on business and was merely feigning the condition in order to keep him by me. Another suggested that as I had been shocked into it I should be shocked out of it by the loud ringing of bells. The distress that that supposed cure caused me was sufficient to make us abandon the idea very quickly. I was bled with leeches, purged, given some nasty acid to drink and galvanism applied to the nerves of my face. Yet another doctor was obsessed by the idea that he had discovered a disease new to medical science and made a great nuisance of himself, hoping to find fame through my suffering. Then, at long last, we found that I was not mad or deluded or pretending – or even alone; others, both men and women, had had this affliction before, but it was rare and known only to those who make a special study of the ear. Edwin promised that once he returned from Bristol he would change his will. But his mind was very occupied with business matters and it seems he failed to make an appointment to see his solicitor or send him a letter regarding his intentions.'

'Who is your solicitor?' asked Frances, hoping it would be her own advisor, Mr Rawsthorne.

'Mr Marsden. I cannot say I like him a great deal but I have heard he knows his business.'

Frances tried to conceal her disappointment. Mr Marsden regarded her with the kind of derisive contempt he afforded all women who aspired to professions he thought should be reserved for men. At their every meeting he lost no opportunity to belittle her undoubted achievements in the capture of criminals and mention her failure to secure a husband.

'Do you still consult a medical man?'

'No, I believe that medicine has done all it can do for me, which is nothing at all.'

'What I propose to do, Mrs Antrobus,' said Frances, examining the list of names once more, 'is start by speaking to all those people who were your husband's closest associates in the six months before he disappeared. He may have said something to them or they may have noticed something in his manner that could be a valuable clue. I will of course interview his partner, Mr Luckhurst, as well as his brother and Dr Collin. Are there any other names you could suggest? I see that you have not put the names of the other medical men on this list.'

'Oh, I hadn't thought to do so. I suppose I did not think of them either as my husband's friends or associates. Some of them only visited once, and that was several years ago. Let me consult Charlotte and we might be able to recall their names. It was only Dr Goodwin who called more often. He was more kindly than the others.'

'What of the doctor who was such a nuisance?'

She made a tiny grimace. 'Oh, Dr Dromgoole, yes, he caused a great deal of annoyance. He actually suggested that my condition was due to tobacco fumes I had inhaled from my husband's clothing. Quite ridiculous. Edwin was furious with him – in fact I don't believe I have ever seen him so exercised – and told him not to come here again. The man actually wrote to the newspapers proposing this idea but then Dr Goodwin, who is a great expert in these things, wrote to the papers to show what a foolish man Dr Dromgoole was. I saw that Dr Goodwin knew something of my affliction and wrote to him and he agreed to see me. It was he who told Edwin that it was my ears that were affected and not my mind. He was an honest man, and while he brought relief of a kind, he also told me that there was no cure.'

'When did you last see Dr Dromgoole?'

'It was … perhaps four years ago.'

'And Dr Goodwin?'

'I think he last made a professional call about a month before Edwin disappeared. After that I could no longer pay his fees, and in any case there was little more he could do for me. When he heard about Edwin he made a courtesy call, but I have not seen him since.'

Frances added those names to the list. 'What of the servants you employed just before your husband disappeared?'

'We had a parlourmaid, Lizzie, and a cook, Mrs Dean, and Mrs Fisher who came in twice a week to clean. I doubt that they will know anything. There is just one maid-of-all-work now; we engaged her not long after Edwin disappeared, and Charlotte keeps house and cooks. Our means are limited but we do not starve. There are effects that in a household so straitened as ours we might have thought to sell, but of course until Edwin is declared dead and the will overturned they are not mine to dispose of. If I was to sell so much as a teaspoon I am sure Lionel would notice and fly into a perfect rage.'

Mrs Antrobus poured more tea into the wooden cups and Frances took advantage of the pause to compose her next question.

'I feel I must apologise in advance for what I am about to say. In my profession I often see the very worst kinds of behaviour and therefore have a suspicious mind and am obliged to ask about matters which might cause offence.'

'Oh, please do ask,' implored Mrs Antrobus. 'I am so much wrapped in cotton wool I would welcome a little offence.'

'Do you think it at all possible that your husband is still alive and has started a new life elsewhere?'

The lady was not shocked or even upset; she merely nodded. 'I know what you are thinking, and others have hinted the same. I admit that Edwin has found me a great disappointment and a trouble to him. But he would never have deserted me, and he is so proud of our two boys. Even if he tired of my company I cannot imagine that he would not have continued to exert all his energy to secure a good future for our sons. I have written to them and they assure me that he has not communicated with them, and they are truthful and honest.'

As to the truthfulness or honesty of the sons Frances thought that the time might come when she would have to judge for herself, and was Edwin Antrobus really such a paragon of a husband, with no other fault than being a little dull? When Frances thought about it, dullness, represented as such a minor imperfection, was perhaps the last quality she might look for in a husband, even supposing she was looking for one, which she was not.

'Mr Wylie has been a very good friend to you,' she commented.

'He is kindness itself,' said her hostess, warmly. 'I really do not know how I could have remained here without his assistance. You know that my brother-in-law has done everything in his power to make me vacate the house and I am sure that if it was not for Mr Wylie he would have prevailed.'

'Is Mr Wylie a single gentleman?' asked Frances.

'He is, yes.' In the dim light it was hard to see if there was a hint of a blush, but a movement of the eyelids indicated that Mr Wylie's marital status was of some moment to the lady.

'I must once again be forward in my questioning. Has Mr Wylie made any kind of declaration to you, either formal or otherwise?'

Mrs Antrobus smiled. 'How wonderful to be engaged in a profession that permits you to be so inquisitive and find out so many secrets. How much more entertaining than mere parlour gossip. Of course in my current position it would be most improper for Mr Wylie to address me as anything other than a concerned friend, and I can assure you that he has not done so. What may transpire in the future,' she gave a demure look, 'I really could not say.'

'I assume that any papers your husband kept here have already been examined for information which might help find out where he might be.'

'They have, but you may examine them too. I have nothing to hide, and I do not believe he did either.'

When Frances departed an hour later she still felt she knew very little about the missing man. His effects had been kept in good order as if he was expected home from the office at any moment. A desk, which although it had lockable compartments was unlocked, contained accounts from his tailor and shirt maker, all paid, and the usual family papers. There was no evidence of membership of clubs or guilds and nothing at all to suggest a secret second life.

❧

Frances returned home to find that two notes had been delivered in her absence, a terse one from Lionel Antrobus informing her that he could spare her a few minutes of his time on the following day and one from Mr Luckhurst saying it would be his pleasure to assist Frances by any means in his power. He would be in his office all day on Thursday and she could call at any time convenient.

Sarah, who not so long ago had been a servant and knew the ways of servants better than anyone, cheerfully took upon herself the task of visiting all the domestic staff agencies in Bayswater with the object of locating and interviewing Mr Antrobus' former cook, maid and charwoman. It was not an easy task, but there was just a chance that one of them might be keeping a secret for her master.

Frances' afternoon was spent in correspondence and further reading. She liked to study the newspapers, especially the *Bayswater Chronicle*, with some care, and for the last year she had retained copies for reference. She knew that she had seen the name Dr Goodwin mentioned in its pages quite recently and soon confirmed that in February Dr Caleb Goodwin, who since 1860 had been consultant otologist at the Bayswater School for the Deaf and Dumb, had resigned his position and was taking legal action against the school. No further details were available. The Bayswater Directory, an annual publication of extraordinary usefulness, of which Frances owned several editions, revealed that the school was located in Chepstow Crescent, while Dr Goodwin resided in nearby Pembridge Villas. Frances wrote to him requesting an interview.

The troublesome Dr Dromgoole, the only person known to have had some difference with the missing man, proved more difficult. In 1877 he had been residing in Kildare Terrace, but in the current directory the same address was listed as The Bayswater Female Sanatorium, whose supervisor was a Dr Caldecott. Of Dr Dromgoole there was no sign.

CHAPTER FOUR

L ionel Antrobus lived above the family tobacconist's shop on Portobello Road, a location that did not have the fashionable cachet of the emporiums on Westbourne Grove. He was, according to Mr Wylie, jealous of his wealthier brother, but Frances thought that a man whose home was an apartment above his business could hardly fail to be envious of the smart residence in Craven Hill.

Frances was not especially familiar with the district of Kensal New Town and realised as she approached the shop that she had made a misjudgement. Antrobus Tobacconists occupied a corner site close to the grand terraces of Ladbroke Grove, and far from being the small establishment she had expected, was of good size, clean and very well appointed. Lionel Antrobus, since he owned only half the business, was undoubtedly less wealthy than his younger brother, but many men might have envied him an attractive property in such a favourable location.

A notice in bright gilt lettering announced that the shop supplied everything for the smoker of discernment. The window display was mounted on a ladder of shelves, lined with close ranks of decorative tins revealing a bewildering variety of tobacco as well as snuff, cigars, cigarettes, pipes and all the accoutrements that clearly must be essential to the smoker, some of which were very mysterious as to their purpose. A dedicated smoker, Frances thought, might easily spend more on the means to store and enjoy his tobacco than the tobacco itself. Reflecting that many of the medical sundries once sold by her late father's chemist's would have appeared equally mysterious to the uninitiated, she experienced, quite unexpectedly, a sharp pang of loss, the knowledge that a part of her life was gone, never to return. Her father had not been a smoker, saying that it was an occupation for fools with too much money, but he had made a good income from smoker's remedies and would never dissuade anyone from pursuing the habit.

She pushed open the shop door and breathed in an atmosphere suffused with unfamiliar scents, all of them pleasurable. The interior was spotless, the counters and shelves of that deep warm hue of polished wood that mimicked the product, and everything was neatly and tastefully arranged. A youth in his twenties was presenting boxes of cigars for the appreciation of a gentleman while a pale young woman of similar age was weighing and packaging pipe tobacco for another customer. The man who stood behind the counter, casting a critical eye over his staff and the displays, was in his late forties, tall, immaculately dressed and groomed, and with a severe expression. That expression did not soften when he saw Frances. She had met with less friendly receptions and did not flinch but approached him and presented her card. 'Mr Antrobus?' she said. 'I am Frances Doughty. We have an appointment.'

He took the card, surveyed it and nodded curtly. 'You are not the first detective to trouble me on this matter and I suppose you will not be the last. Well, let us have our discussion and be done. Come to my office, we will be private there.'

He conducted Frances to the back of the shop where there was a small room furnished with a desk and two chairs, a small side table, a narrow wooden chest with deep drawers and shelves closely packed with ledgers.

The desk was a marvel of neatness and precision, almost as if laid out for inspection as a model of what a desktop ought to be for the man of tidy mind. One leather-bound book, a notepad and a pen tray were on its surface. On the table were a crystal water carafe and glass and all the necessities of a man who smoked cigars. The room smelt of cigar smoke, warm and light with a little spice, with a contrasting tang of fresh polish.

On the facing wall was a portrait, perhaps ten years old, of the proprietor and his brother Edwin standing behind a seated man of greater age, presumably their father. The portrait bore the legend 'Antrobus Tobacconists'.

Lionel Antrobus was not, thought Frances, as he took his place behind the desk, his shoulders stiffly squared, a man who could ever be at his ease. It was hard to imagine him at his leisure or smiling.

He put Frances' card on the desktop and placed it square to the edge as if it would offend him to lie in any other way. 'So you subscribe to this wild allegation that the remains found in the canal are those of my brother?' he began, abruptly.

'I do not pre-judge,' said Frances. 'It is not impossible, of course, but all I want to discover is the truth.'

He looked unconvinced. 'When Harriett started this foolishness I demanded to see the body, and there was little enough to see but all of it unpleasant. I would have thought that after three years there would be nothing but bones, but I was told that flesh immersed in water can sometimes change into another thing altogether. It did not look like my brother, but then it hardly looked like a man. Of course I wish to end the uncertainty over Edwin's fate, but I could not in all honesty say that the remains were his.' He frowned. 'Is Harriett still claiming that Edwin was about to change his will?'

'She is, yes. And you knew nothing of this?'

'No, and moreover I find it hard to believe. Why would Edwin place all his estate in the hands of a madwoman? You know that she is so obsessed with noise that she hardly ever leaves the house?'

'I have spoken to her,' Frances went on, trying not to be ruffled by his attitude, 'and she struck me as intelligent and more than capable of dealing with her own affairs.'

He gave a brief snort of contempt. 'You have spoken to her once and no doubt she presented herself well on that occasion, but I have known her for many years and beg to disagree. She has made my brother's life intolerable with her strange imaginings.'

'And yet,' Frances reminded him, 'there was one doctor who advised your brother that his wife was not losing her mind but suffered from a disease of the ears.'

'And half a dozen others who thought she should be locked away,' he retorted.

'But Dr Goodwin is a highly regarded expert in these matters, a specialist in his field.'

'Goodwin?' he exclaimed with an expression of great distaste. 'Miss Doughty, if you take my advice, you will keep away from Dr Goodwin. He has a reputation and, in my opinion, is not to be trusted.'

'A reputation?'

'I have no intention of elaborating further,' he snapped.

'Of course I cannot expect you to repeat what may be no more than the slander of a jealous rival, but if I am to pursue my enquiries I must speak to everyone who knew your brother and that must include Dr Goodwin. Do you have any proof of what you say?'

'No,' he admitted, reluctantly, 'but it is well known amongst the medical fraternity and gentlemen's clubs in Bayswater.'

All-male establishments, Frances reflected, no doubt populated by the very men who were always complaining about the female love of gossip. Whatever Dr Goodwin's peccadillos, however, she could not see that they impinged on his medical expertise.

'Very well, I will judge the gentleman for myself. And now, would you be so kind as to show me your brother's will, as requested in my letter.'

He turned to the cabinet, unlocked a drawer and produced the document. 'There, and much may it profit you,' he said, pushing the will across the desk. 'But I am sure you appreciate that if anyone had wanted to make away with Edwin for his fortune they would not have planned to wait seven years for it.'

Frances unfolded the papers.

'If you wish to accuse me of murdering my brother, please do, it has been said before.'

She returned his stare. 'I never make accusations unless I can prove them.'

He tapped his fingers impatiently on the desk as she studied the will. 'This is a strange profession for a woman, Miss Doughty. So much prying into the private business of others, does it give you pleasure?'

'It puts food on my table and pays my rent.' She almost added that it also made her independent of men, a circumstance that seemed doubly attractive to her after only five minutes in the company of Lionel Antrobus.

The will was much as she had expected. There were bequests of twenty pounds each to the servants and a sum of three hundred pounds to a Mrs Davison who resided in Maidstone. To his brother, Lionel, Edwin Antrobus had left three thousand pounds and his half share of the shop and to his partner in the cigarette business, Mr Luckhurst, two thousand pounds. Harriett was to receive only a few personal items. A fund of which she was unable to touch the capital would pay her a small annuity. All the rest of the estate was to be divided equally between the couple's sons, Edwin jnr and Arthur, provision being made to meet the cost of their education if required. A clause included the instruction that if the testator died before his eldest son was of age, the estate was to be administered by Lionel Antrobus and all decisions concerning the two boys were to be taken by him until Edwin jnr's twenty-first birthday.

'Do you think this is a fair will?' she asked.

'I do, yes.'

'And you have examined your brother's financial papers and this is a true description of his estate? There were no debts to reduce the value?'

'None to speak of. The usual tradesmen's bills, which have been settled.'

'He had no rivals or enemies who might have wished him harm?'

'No.'

'I have been told of a Dr Dromgoole whom he found annoying.'

'Oh, that fellow!' he exclaimed contemptuously. 'He made something of a nuisance of himself but then it was shown that he was a fool and a charlatan and his reputation was quite exploded.'

'Did they quarrel?'

'They may have done. In fact – yes, Edwin once told me that Dromgoole had accosted him in the street and been most abusive. The man was almost incoherent. He was probably more of a danger to himself than anyone else.'

'Is he still practising medicine?'

'I don't know. It would not surprise me if he is. I have yet to meet an entirely sane doctor.'

Frances wondered if Dr Dromgoole, having suffered a reversal in his medical career, was currently employed at the Bayswater Female Sanatorium in Kildare Terrace, which had once been his home, and felt sorry for any woman who had recourse to such a place and such an attendant. More importantly, if Dromgoole's prospects had been damaged as a result of his encounter with Edwin Antrobus, it was a possible motive for murder.

She completed her notes and returned the will, which disappeared swiftly into the drawer from whence it had come. 'What do you think happened to your brother? I take it you have heard nothing from him since he last departed for Bristol in 1877?'

'Nothing at all. Edwin and I are half-brothers and while we respected each other we were not close. We did not meet often and when we did our conversation was more of a business than a social nature. But you will want to know his character. Even Harriett will not have him as other than honest and well meaning. I do not think he would have deserted her – he was too honourable for that – although had he done so I would have found it hard to blame him. He would not, however, have voluntarily left his sons without a father. I believe that he must have met with an accident or was taken ill or was the victim of a crime. Either he has died or, if alive, is unable, rather than unwilling, to communicate with his family.'

Frances sensed that despite his protestations Lionel Antrobus did care about his brother's fate, if only because he believed that it was his duty to protect a younger relative.

'From his portrait there is little to distinguish him in appearance from many another gentleman of his age and class. Can you think of any way that he might be identified?'

'He always carried business cards, and there was a signet ring that once belonged to his uncle and which he never removed. But cards may be lost or damaged and rings stolen.'

'When did you last see him?'

'About a week before he went to Bristol.'

'What did you talk about?'

'Tobacco, mainly.'

'He did not mention Mrs Antrobus? Or his will?'

'No. He said his sons were doing well at school and he hoped in time to create positions in the business for them.'

'When did you discover that he was missing?'

'That would have been two or three days after he was expected home. Harriett wrote to ask if I had seen him. I replied that I had not. I assumed at the time that he had been detained on business. It also occurred to me that he might simply be taking the opportunity of spending some additional time from home.'

'Was it unusual for him to take additional time?' asked Frances, wondering if there was some compelling half-life the missing man might have led.

'He was occasionally away for longer than he had planned, but when he was delayed he would write and say so. You may read into that what you wish. I have no further information. When I heard nothing more from Harriett I assumed that Edwin had returned.'

'When did you realise that the matter was a serious one?'

'Some days later I received a letter from his partner, Mr Luckhurst, who said that nothing had been heard from Edwin and his friend Mr Wylie was making enquiries in Bristol on Harriett's behalf. He agreed to send me a telegram as soon as anything was known, but after a week I decided to go to Bristol myself. I spoke to all Edwin's known associates there and the hotel but learned nothing. I went to the house and examined all of Edwin's papers, such as they were, but they furnished no clue as to his whereabouts.'

Frances studied her notes. 'What of the lady to whom your brother left three hundred pounds? Mrs Davison?'

'Edwin's maternal aunt, a respectable widow who lives in Kent near the school. She has a pleasant villa and the boys reside with her during their holidays. I visited the school and spoke to the boys, also their headmaster who knows Edwin by sight, and they have assured me that he has not been there. I also spoke to Mrs Davison but she has not seen or heard from my brother.'

'I have read the report of Mr Ryan the detective employed by Mr Wylie. The hotel where your brother stayed was the George Railway Hotel, the one he always used when in Bristol, and there was no evidence that he had transferred to another. Mr Ryan placed notices in the newspapers in case your brother had taken a room in a lodging house or an apartment, but with no response. None of his friends or associates said they had given him accommodation. Mr Ryan also made enquiries at the telegraph offices but it does not appear that your brother sent any messages. Either he remained in Bristol at some unknown location or returned to London or travelled elsewhere.'

'This I already know,' replied Antrobus, although he appeared impressed with the thoroughness of her approach. He gave a regretful shake of the head. 'It is hard to see what more can be done. The police have all the facts, and I have kept Mr Ryan on a permanent salary to continue his enquiries. Copies of Edwin's portrait have appeared in the newspapers.'

'But until now the investigation has centred on Bristol where he was last seen. Perhaps the answer lies nearer to home. It is this aspect of the enquiry in which I am engaged.'

'Then I wish you success,' he said dryly. 'Oh I do not underestimate you Miss Doughty. I am given to understand that men do so at their peril, nevertheless I do not see what you can possibly achieve.'

'In your opinion,' Frances continued, 'who of all your brother's acquaintances in London knew him the best?'

'Luckhurst, since they worked so closely together.'

'No one else?'

'No.'

'What is your opinion of Mr Wylie?'

'In what respect?'

'In every respect.'

He placed his hands squarely on the desk as a judge might have done before pronouncing sentence. 'Do you mean is it my belief that he wishes to prove my brother is deceased in order to overturn the will and have Harriett come into Edwin's fortune, and then marry her so that he might acquire it for himself?'

'That is a possible sequence of events,' Frances admitted. 'Or he might genuinely esteem and wish to protect her and will offer to marry her in due course, even if she fails to overturn the will.'

'I could never make him out,' mused Antrobus. 'He is effective enough as a man of business, but he is also, or at least appears to be, weak. Whether that is the case or merely a means of disarming suspicion, I do not know. He has never been married, or as far as I am aware wished to be; still I know nothing against his character.'

'He pays Mrs Antrobus' legal fees,' Frances observed, to see how he would respond.

'He does, and I can hardly imagine that my sister-in-law can, in her current position, be such a prize as to be worth his investment. I doubt very much that she has told him all her history. I am certain that she has not told it to you. She comes from tainted stock. Her father may have been honest but she has a cousin who has served several terms in prison for theft. If Wylie secures her,' he added with a note of undisguised satisfaction in his voice, 'he may live to regret it.'

Frances took her leave fearing that she had uncovered only the smallest part of the hatreds and prejudices that existed in the Antrobus family, which bubbled more violently and poisonously than the Paddington basin in summer.

CHAPTER FIVE

ildare Terrace, where Dr Dromgoole had once lived, was a quiet leafy residential street running south from St Stephen's church and terminating in some pleasant gardens, where wooden benches nestled amongst flowering shrubs under the shade of mature trees. Mr William Whiteley, who, whatever his faults, had been instrumental in converting Westbourne Grove from a place where businesses rarely flourished to the Oxford Street of West London had lived at No. 2 for some years.

The weather continued fine, and Frances decided to walk there from Portobello Road. Not long ago her father's parsimony had obliged her to walk almost everywhere whether wet or dry, and by and large she had enjoyed it. She had never felt the need to protect her complexion from the sun as did so many young women who equated pale cheeks with beauty, neither had she worn the kind of gowns that might take damage from a little dust or mud and could not be made good with a stiff brush.

From a distance the sanatorium looked like any other house, apart from the small brass plate beside the door. When examined more closely the sign was smart enough to be recent and read 'Bayswater Female Sanatorium, supervisor Dr T. Caldecott, all enquiries to Mrs Caldecott'. The house itself, however, was in need of substantial repair to the external brickwork, and the window frames were past any hope that might be afforded by a simple coat of paint.

The doorbell was answered by a stout, red-faced maid, who looked fully capable of dealing with any kind of visitor. 'I would like to see Dr Dromgoole if that is possible,' said Frances, presenting her card.

The maid squinted at the card. 'No doctor of that name here.'

'I believe he used to live here. Perhaps Mrs Caldecott might advise me?'

The maid looked at Frances closely, judging her to be respectable and unlikely to create a disturbance. 'Come in then. Wait here.'

Frances entered a narrow hallway where the harsh smell of carbolic was unable to conceal staler less pleasant odours and was shown a door marked 'Visitors'. At the end of the hall a charwoman was kneeling beside a bucket, attacking the tiled floor with a scrubbing brush. There was an abrupt movement of footsteps on the floor above, the banging of a door, a hurried conversation and a loud wailing cry, which went on for some moments and ended with a gulp.

Frances glanced at the maid who seemed unperturbed, 'Oh don't take no notice of that. Some of the ladies here are a bit … well, they get confused about where they are and want to be taken home. I know that one, she'll soon get quietened down.' There was the sound of fresh sobbing and two pairs of running footsteps, followed by a squeal of protest, then another door banged.

'Chloral,' said the maid, cheerfully. 'Don't know what we'd do without it.'

Frances was left alone in the visitors' waiting area while the maid lumbered away. The large square room would once have been a front parlour, but now it was almost bare and most uninviting. A row of old and very worn wooden seats supplied the minimum of comfort and the carpet had long outstayed its usefulness. The fireplace had been swept, but not recently. A slight attempt had been made at decoration by placing a vase of dried flowers on a small table and framed embroideries on the painted wall but they did little to brighten the overall atmosphere of weary gloom. The visitor who was anxious to find something useful to occupy his or her time was provided with a two-page pamphlet about the work of the sanatorium and a week-old copy of the *Chronicle*. Frances examined the pamphlet but it made no mention of the house's former owner.

The woman who arrived to speak to Frances wore a nurse's gown and apron and a welcoming smile. 'Miss Doughty, I am Eliza Caldecott, matron of this establishment. I would so much like to help you. Dr Dromgoole, did you say?'

'Yes, I understand that this was once his home. Who is the current owner of the property?'

'The General Asylum Company. They own the Bayswater Asylum for the Aged and Feeble Insane on Monmouth Road. This house was purchased not from Dr Dromgoole, however, but from his cousin, Mr Malcolm Dromgoole, who was acting for him.' There was something about her tone that said more than the mere words.

'Acting for him because he was unable to act for himself?'

'That is so. If you are interested I suggest you speak to Dr Magrath at the asylum who will have all the details. And I believe that if you go there you will also find Dr Dromgoole.'

'As an employee or a resident?' asked Frances apprehensively.

'A resident, I'm sorry to say. I understand he had a complete breakdown. Were you hoping to interview him?'

'I was – I still am.'

Mrs Caldecott gave her a sympathetic look. 'That may prove difficult.'

'I see that, but I must make the attempt.'

'Might I ask the nature of your enquiry?'

'It concerns the disappearance of Mr Edwin Antrobus in October 1877. Dr Dromgoole had been acquainted with the missing man. I am speaking to everyone who knew him in case they observed anything that could help me trace him.'

'This is about the body found in the Paddington Basin, isn't it? That court case that was in all the newspapers.'

'It is, yes,' admitted Frances.

Mrs Caldecott appeared less comfortable with their conversation. 'From what I read the man found in the canal had been murdered. If you imagine that Dr Dromgoole was responsible for the death of Mr Antrobus or anyone else, I think it most unlikely.'

'Have you met him?' asked Frances hopefully.

'No, but I'm sure he can't be the violent type or he would never have been admitted to the asylum. They don't take those kind there. Dr Magrath will explain, I am sure.'

Frances could see a promising line of enquiry petering into nothing; nevertheless she knew she must pursue it, if only for completeness.

The asylum was barely a minute's walk away. Frances passed through the cool gated gardens, wishing she had the leisure to spend more time there, and found a double fronted property almost hidden in a quiet corner overhung by trees whose dipping branches placed a discreet veil over the establishment. Frances presented her card to the maid and asked if she might see Dr Magrath. She was shown into a carpeted waiting room considerably more comfortable than the one she had just left. It was ringed about with chairs that might have graced a parlour and enhanced by paintings of variable quality, some of which seemed to have been painted by artists afflicted by colour blindness, as there were some unusual choices of hue in the depiction of sky and faces. One artist seemed to be suffering from double vision: all the ladies in his portraits had two noses.

'I see you are admiring the work of some of our residents,' said the man who entered the room. Unlike so many doctors who adopted a dignified air in keeping with the respect that they felt should be due to their professional status, the new arrival had no such pretensions. He advanced rapidly with a broad friendly smile and shook her hand warmly. 'Thomas Magrath. I am sorry to have kept you waiting so long, I was engaged with a patient.'

Frances returned the smile. 'Thank you for agreeing to see me.'

He was holding her card, which he favoured with an openly curious glance. 'Is this a personal matter or connected with your detective work?' He offered her a chair and drew up another to sit facing her, his cheerful manner overlaid by the well-practised concern of a consultant. He was about forty and therefore, thought Frances, in that best part of a man's life, having reached the height of his mental powers but still enjoying the flexibility of youth. Whatever the future might hold in the way of entrenched opinions and weariness with the repetitive round of his daily life was not yet apparent in his address.

'I am making enquiries on behalf of Mrs Harriett Antrobus, whose husband Edwin has been missing for three years.' From Magrath's expression she saw that he knew of the recent court action. 'I am interviewing everyone who knew Mr Antrobus and that includes Dr Dromgoole, who once attended Mrs Antrobus and who had a difference of opinion with her husband.'

'Ah,' said Dr Magrath looking suddenly troubled, but he did not elaborate.

'I appreciate,' Frances went on, 'that Dr Dromgoole's current state of health may mean that there is little of value that he can tell me, but all the same, I would like to see him.'

'Of course, of course, and so you shall.' Magrath thought for a moment, then tucked the card into a pocket, sprang up energetically and rang for the maid. 'You might also like to speak with Mr Fullwood, our senior attendant, who has been concerned with Mr Dromgoole's care and supervision since he was admitted.'

The maid appeared. 'Doris, could you ask Mr Fullwood to prepare Mr Dromgoole to receive a visitor? And please bring me the patient's file.'

'*Mr* Dromgoole?' queried Frances when the maid had gone.

'Yes, yes indeed,' said Dr Magrath. 'He practised medicine in Bayswater for a number of years, but although he had undertaken a course of study at university and I believe was awarded his Bachelor of Medicine he had never taken his M.D., a deception that was not exposed until his contretemps with Dr Goodwin, which I expect you know about. Dromgoole had always been somewhat unstable, but it was that dispute which precipitated his breakdown. He came to a meeting of the Bayswater Medical and Surgical Society and accused all the gentlemen there of plotting against him. They were concerned for his safety and had him restrained and committed to the public asylum. Not at all the place for a man in his situation, of course. His relative arranged for the sale of his property to enable him to be placed in more comfortable circumstances. He is quite a pitiful creature now, weak in the legs and with a mind that wanders and retains very little.'

'Might this relative be able to assist me?'

'He is an invalid and resides in Scotland. All the arrangements were made by his London solicitor, Mr Rawsthorne.'

As Frances digested this information, the maid returned with a folder of papers, which she handed to Dr Magrath. She had the blank composed expression of someone whose remit was to reveal nothing about the inmates of the establishment. 'Mr Fullwood is getting the gentleman ready now,' she said. 'He'll be out on the terrace.' She gave Frances a look that might have been curiosity before she left.

'It would be useful for me to know the dates on which the significant events occurred,' said Frances. She rather hoped that Magrath might allow her to see the documents, but instead he studied them himself and she realised that the contents of the folder would be considered strictly private.

'Yes, he was first brought here on 5 July 1877 after spending a month at the public asylum.'

'So at the time of Mr Antrobus' disappearance in October he was residing here?'

'He was, yes.'

'Are your patients ever allowed to leave the premises?'

Magrath paused. 'I had assumed,' he said cautiously, 'that your interest in Mr Dromgoole related to discovering what information he might have about Mr Antrobus, but I am gathering the impression that you suspect him of being involved in that gentleman's disappearance.'

'I have to examine every possibility,' Frances told him, 'if only to dismiss them and move on. But so far I have found that Mr Dromgoole is the only person known to have had a disagreement with Mr Antrobus, and if, as you say, he is unstable, he might have done him harm.'

Magrath closed the folder and shook his head very emphatically. 'Miss Doughty, our presence here would not be tolerated if we were to admit violent patients. We are an establishment for the very aged and those who are infirm and who, we can assure all the residents hereabouts, are no danger to anyone. Many of our patients are unable to walk unassisted and we take them out from time to time in bath chairs, where people can see for themselves that they are to be pitied and not feared. Mr Dromgoole is not an old man by any means, but he is quite frail. He suffered a serious injury to his head when in the public asylum which further added to his woes – an attack by another patient. He is quite incapable of harming anyone. He is permitted brief excursions when the weather is fine but always in the company of an attendant.'

'Has he ever said anything on the subject of Mr Antrobus?'

'Not that I am aware of.' Magrath gave the question some further thought. 'You say that he was Mrs Antrobus' medical advisor?'

'Very briefly, yes.'

'I remember the heated correspondence in the newspapers between Mr Dromgoole and Dr Goodwin – there would hardly be a medical man in Bayswater who does not – although the patient was never named. And now I think about it I did once receive a letter from Mr Antrobus on the subject of admitting his wife here as a patient. I replied asking for a doctor's report but heard nothing further.'

'Mrs Antrobus, as her husband later understood, has a disorder of the ears and not the mind,' Frances advised him.

'Tinnitus aureum, perhaps?' Magrath suggested. 'Noises in the head which do not come from any outside source. It is often mistaken for insanity, especially when the patient hears voices. Doctors of medicine receive almost no education on these afflictions.'

'I understand that Dr Goodwin is a highly respected man in his field of expertise.'

'Oh, he is! I do not believe he would make such a mistake.'

'I am pleased to hear it.' Frances smiled and left a silence that she hoped would be filled.

Magrath looked thoughtful. 'Although, and I hesitate to say it —' He shook his head. 'Perhaps there are some things best left unsaid.'

'In my experience those are always the things most useful to a detective. Do go on.'

'It may be strong meat for a lady.' Frances waited expectantly, and he went on. 'Before he was admitted here Mr Dromgoole was very insistent that he knew something against Dr Goodwin. Something concerning his personal life, which he believed to be very shocking. I do not know to what extent his allegations may be trusted. His opinions will of course have been coloured by his own state of mind and the quarrel, but, as I am sure you know,' he added with a shrug and a sad smile, 'bad words travel faster than good ones.'

Before Frances could say any more the maid returned to advise them that they could now see Mr Dromgoole, and Magrath led the way to a terrace looking out over a small but nicely laid out garden. Before they stepped outside, Magrath paused. 'It might be best,' he said softly, 'if you were not to mention the names of any of the Bayswater medical men to Mr Dromgoole. It could upset him terribly. He was especially bitter about the correspondence in the *Chronicle*, and any reference to Dr Goodwin would be most distressing.'

The lawn was dotted with bath chairs whose occupants were very aged, shrunken figures hunched against the sunlight. Despite the warm air, their thin forms were wrapped in shawls and blankets, such that it was difficult to see whether they were men or women. A comfortable chair padded with cushions was on the terrace, and as Frances approached she saw that the man who sat there was very much younger than the other patients, perhaps little more than fifty, although it was hard to tell. His dark grey hair and beard were well trimmed and his blue eyes looked clear, but there was something fixed about his expression that did not bode well for the interview. There was a depressed star-shaped scar on the side of his head, suggesting an old fracture beneath. Beside him stood a slightly built man in his thirties, wearing a dark blue suit with embossed buttons and peaked cap, helping the patient drink from a cup of water.

'Mr Fullwood, this is Miss Doughty who wishes to speak to Mr Dromgoole,' advised Magrath.

'Miss Doughty is very welcome to do so,' replied Fullwood, with a polite nod in her direction. 'I think new visitors do him good.' He drew up a chair for Frances beside Dromgoole, and she was seated. The doctor and attendant both remained standing, observing the patient closely.

'Mr Dromgoole?' asked Frances, but there was no reaction. Recalling that he had had pretensions as a Doctor of Medicine, she went on, 'or should I call you Dr Dromgoole?'

After a moment or two he turned his head towards her and slowly a smile spread across his features, a look of joy and hope. 'Adeline?' he said, 'is that you, Adeline?'

Frances was about to explain that she was not Adeline, but then thought she might do better if she pretended she was. 'Yes, I have come to see you.'

'Oh!' he exclaimed, and an expression of great joy lit up his face. He reached out and took one of her hands in both of his.

'Do you remember Mr Antrobus?' asked Frances.

'Oh, Adeline, my Adeline!' he sighed.

'It is a pleasure to see you again,' said Frances wishing she knew who Adeline was. She glanced up at the two men, but they both shook their heads. 'I was hoping you could tell me about Mr Antrobus.'

Dromgoole said nothing but as he smiled, tears welled up in his eyes.

'I think you had a quarrel with Mr Antrobus,' Frances persisted, hoping that repetition of the name might produce some memory. 'Do you recall that?'

The patient began to weep noisily and tried to pull her hand to his lips, but Fullwood came forward and gently disengaged the grasp. 'I'm sorry,' he murmured, 'but I really think you will learn nothing.'

Frances could only agree. Even if Dromgoole could reveal some information she could not vouch for its reliability. 'If he does say anything about Mr Antrobus, I would be grateful if you would write to me and let me know,' she said to Dr Magrath as they returned indoors. 'Who is Adeline?'

'I'm afraid we don't know,' shrugged Magrath. 'Mr Dromgoole was not married and we know of no relative of that name. A childhood sweetheart perhaps or a lady to whose hand he aspired.'

Adeline was not a common name, and Frances thought that if she could find the lady she might learn what concerned Mr Dromgoole.

Frances returned home to find a letter from Dr Goodwin consenting to an appointment the next morning. Sarah had good news: she had located Mrs Dean, the cook who had worked at the Antrobus house at the time of Edwin Antrobus' disappearance, at which time they had employed her for some five years. A cook, especially a good one, was a person of value, and she had not been difficult to find. Ladies often exchanged confidences about their cooks, boasted of good ones or complained about the ones they had just dismissed. Any lady who prided herself on being something in Bayswater society knew where to find the best cook, even if it meant raiding the kitchen of a great friend, and agencies liked to know where they were and whether they were content.

As Frances had anticipated, Sarah reported that Mrs Dean's duties had meant that she had seen little of her master and almost nothing of his wife and therefore had no information to divulge about Mr Antrobus' disposition or state of health. She knew that her mistress had a strange affliction that meant that she kept to herself most of the time and had noticed that Mrs Antrobus liked to play the piano – 'not proper music at all but bits of tunes that repeated over and over again'. They didn't often have visitors to dine – there was Mr Antrobus' business partner, Mr Luckhurst, and his brother, Mr Lionel, and his wife and son, and his mother-in-law, Mrs Pearce, though not so much in the last few years as she had been very unwell. His sister-in-law Miss Pearce called often, though never at the same time as Mr Lionel. The parlourmaid had told her that Mr Lionel and Miss Pearce didn't 'get along' and it was thought better not to have them visit at the same time or there would be what Mr Antrobus called 'an atmosphere', something he wanted to avoid. Mr and Mrs Antrobus had not dined together for some little while. Mrs Antrobus usually took her meals in her parlour, and often Miss Pearce would join her there. Then when they had dined, Mrs Antrobus would play the piano and Miss Pearce sang or hummed songs in a strange deep sort of voice.

The cook was aware that medical men called, but she never saw them and they didn't stay to dine. If Mr Antrobus had quarrelled with anyone she knew nothing about it. She could provide no information that would help locate the present whereabouts of the parlourmaid and the charwoman.

Sarah was not disheartened by this very modest success and felt confident that she would find the other two servants in time. Frances felt similarly confident. When, a year and a half previously, Sarah had asked to be an apprentice to Frances in her new business, the request had come not from a burning desire to be a detective but because she wished to remain loyally at Frances' side. Since then she had not only proved to be a valuable assistant and an indispensable protector of her employer's safety, but she was taking on cases of her own, ones appropriate to her very special talents. She had earned a formidable reputation in Bayswater for meting out justice in a robust manner.

Sarah had recently become the champion of a poor washerwoman who lived separately from her husband and supported four small children. Believing that the earnings of his wife were his own property to enjoy as he pleased, he had a habit of descending upon her when short of beer money, terrorising his family and taking away whatever he could find.

A neighbour of the unfortunate woman, hearing of her plight, suggested she employ Sarah's services. The unhappy washerwoman had pleaded that she had barely enough to feed her children, but the neighbour had gone to Sarah and appealed to her good nature and general distrust of men. Sarah, whose relish at dealing with such a case was payment enough, realised that simply taking the husband to a private location and explaining to him the error of his ways, pleasurable as such a task would be, might not be sufficient. The fact that since 1870 married women had been entitled by law to keep their own earnings was something that had been lost on too many men, who had chosen to ignore the wishes of parliament and continued to cow their wives into submitting to their demands. Sarah decided to engage the services of Tom Smith, a young relative of hers and a junior businessman of extraordinary energy who was running a team of messenger boys he referred to as his 'men'. Tom had the washerwoman's husband followed and as a result, when he was about to raid his wife's home once more, the police were summoned in time to witness the crime and arrest him.

Sarah's only regret was that any respite for the wife would be temporary, and she was considering what to do about this when, to her relief, the husband suffered an attack of *delirium tremens* and was removed from the police cells to the public asylum.

Unusually for Frances, that evening was to be given over entirely to the pursuit of pleasure. She allowed herself not to feel guilty at such an indulgence since it was a special occasion marking the recent return to London of Frances' near neighbour and friend Cedric Garton. Cedric was a dedicated man about town, suave and elegant in his clothing, amusing in his conversation and a great lover of all things artistic. He lived in a beautifully decorated apartment with his devoted manservant Joseph and, though widely considered to be both handsome and eligible, had never shown any inclination to marry.

He had spent the last few months travelling about the Home Counties – he refused to go north of Hertfordshire because of the climate – to give lectures on Classical Art to enthralled audiences of mature ladies and aesthetically minded young men, and he was currently delivering the same delightful treat in London, where he had become all the rage of a set of Chelsea poets.

Cedric had already attended several performances of Messrs Gilbert and Sullivan's acclaimed *Patience* at the Opéra Comique. Having enthused about the delicious greenery-yallery of the decor, Mr George Grossmith's velvet knee-britches and Japanese attitudes and the resplendent uniforms of the Dragoon Guards, he insisted on providing tickets for Frances, Sarah and Professor Pounder for what he promised was the gayest night to be had in London.

Frances was particularly interested since there had been several letters to *The Times* and the *Chronicle* from the minor and uncelebrated Bayswater poet Augustus Mellifloe, insisting that the character of Reginald Bunthorne was modelled upon himself; the fact that the piece was intended to be a satire having entirely escaped him.

'I shall never write poetry,' said Cedric, 'it is far too exhausting. And Mr Mellifloe will never write poetry either, because he cannot.'

Cedric, for all his protestations of idleness and habitually languid manner, was actually a devotee of the manly art of pugilism as taught by Professor Pounder's sporting academy, an exercise to which he brought both energy and finesse. When urgent action was required, he was as vigorous and active as any man in London.

It was a joyous evening, despite the hot and heavy atmosphere produced by the crowded theatre and the gas lamps. To Frances' amusement one of the songs immortalised the skills of a private detective, Ignatius 'Paddington' Pollaky, and Cedric said he hoped that one day she too would be celebrated in song.

Sarah's comment was that she could not see why the twenty lovesick maidens so doted on the namby-pamby poets when they might better have admired the muscular Dragoon Guards, and Cedric could only agree. Professor Pounder said nothing, but then he was a man of few words.

Frances was not very familiar with the world of the theatre but reflected that it was in some ways a miniature of life. Everyone on the stage was an actor pretending to be what he or she was not, and did not everyone do that all the time, including even herself? She tried her best to be honest but it was not always possible.

She still awoke, perspiring, from those horrid nightmares, yet outwardly pretended that the brutal attack which she had only survived unscathed due to the intervention of Sarah's firm fists, but which she seemed doomed to relive again and again, had not shaken her. She professed no more than curiosity about her absent mother, yet it was a constant and consuming mystery.

Frances also observed that the musical piece, though light, included double deceptions: not only was the actor Mr Rutland Barrington pretending to be idyllic poet Archibald Grosvenor but Grosvenor himself, at a moment's notice, threw off what proved to be a pretence of which he had wearied and became what he wanted to be, a 'commonplace young man'. In one very amusing scene the Dragoons donned aesthetic garments in an attempt to win the ladies but thankfully soon reverted to their uniforms. How much might be achieved with costume, Frances thought. How easy it was to put off one set of apparel and don another, and be seen differently by the world, which only took notice of exterior show.

CHAPTER SIX

Frances' appointment with Dr Goodwin was at ten o'clock the next morning and this gave her the opportunity of rising early to visit the offices of the *Bayswater Chronicle*, which, apart from a tendency to sensationalise the commonplace and wallow in the sensational, was one of the more accurate periodicals. The detailed accounts of the arguments that so frequently broke out at meetings of the Paddington Vestry was one of the best guides to matters of public concern, as well as being very amusing. She was often assisted in her endeavours by the paper's most active reporter, Mr Max Gillan, who understood the value of information as an item of commerce and appreciated that it passed in two directions.

On this occasion, Frances was not looking for anything in particular but simply wanted to examine all the newspapers for the few months before and after the disappearance of Mr Edwin Antrobus for any clues that might throw some light on the event. Since the finding of the remains in the canal the entire focus of the investigation had moved from Bristol to Bayswater, and who could tell what gem might be lying in plain sight, unclaimed because no one had looked for it?

Her arrival at the offices of the *Chronicle* always caused a stir of excitement, especially amongst the younger clerks, one of whom, Mr Gillan had once hinted, was 'sweet' on her. If he thought Frances would trouble herself to enquire as to which one then he was fated to be disappointed. In any case, she did not need to ask since a diminutive youth, who looked scarcely old enough to lace his own boots, jumped up as soon as she appeared, carried a small table and a comfortable chair into the storeroom where the volumes of bound papers were kept and volunteered to bring her anything else she needed. As Frances took her seat she explained that she needed a lamp, the 1877 *Chronicle* and solitude, in that order, and he hurried away to oblige. She did not flatter herself that she had aroused the young gentleman's romantic feelings and suspected rather that he thought her peculiar and therefore interesting in a way that only a newsman would appreciate. The youth returned, pink-cheeked under the weight of the bound volume, and then scurried away to fetch the lamp. Before retiring to his desk he said shyly that his name was Ibbitson and if there was anything further she required she had only to ask.

Starting in June of 1877 Frances found the last rumblings of the debate between Dr Goodwin and Mr Dromgoole and was curious enough to go further back through the pages to its beginning. Dromgoole's initial letter published in May was headed 'Warning of the Dangers of Tobacco':

For many years now the medical profession has subscribed to the view that smoking or chewing tobacco is harmful to the health of our nation, especially in the young. Consumption of tobacco, it is well known, affects the heart, the arteries, the teeth, the digestion and even the eyesight. But I have discovered that it can also affect the hearing and that it is not even necessary for the afflicted person to make use of tobacco but only to be in the constant company of a smoker. By inhaling another's smoke, or even the aroma of tobacco that clings to the clothing of a smoker, substances deleterious to health will pass via the Eustachian tube to the middle ear. A gentleman, robust and mature, might not suffer any ill effects, but what of his wife and her more delicate constitution? How will she combat the vile poison nicotine? A case has recently come to my attention, and I am doing no more than my duty as a physician to announce it to the world, of an unfortunate lady married to a gentleman in the tobacco trade, whose organs of hearing are so affected by tobacco that she feels pain from even the smallest noise and cannot undertake many of the duties of a wife. This is, I believe, a new disease in the medical canon, unknown to the ancients and therefore wholly attributable to the effects of tobacco on the female. Women everywhere must ask their husbands to give up this noxious habit.

The letter was signed 'Bayswater M.D.'.

Whatever the medical issues, Frances could see that this theory was unlikely to find favour with the Antrobus family.

A week later came the response from Dr C. Goodwin, M.D., consultant in otology at the Bayswater School for the Deaf and Dumb, and the Central London Throat Nose and Ear Hospital:

> I must correct several errors in the letter signed Bayswater M.D., whose identity, wisely, in my opinion, he has chosen to keep secret. The affliction of the hearing he describes is not a new disease but has been well known to otologists, although not to the general medical practitioner, for many years. It is exhibited by both male and female patients, many of whom also suffer from tinnitus aureum, and is referred to in the literature as hyperacusis. The most usual causes, insofar as causes may be known, are loud noise and injury to the head. It has nothing whatsoever to do with tobacco.

And there a wise man should have quietly withdrawn from the fray, but Dromgoole was not that man. His response was a tart letter pointing out that Dr Goodwin, unlike himself, had not examined the patient in question and was therefore not competent to pronounce on the cause of her suffering.

Dr Goodwin replied, revealing that since the publication of his letter he had had the opportunity to examine the patient and had observed nothing to make him vary his original statement. He added that he had received many letters from other Bayswater physicians, all of whom had been eager to assure him that they were not the authors of the letter signed 'Bayswater M.D.' and suggesting who the actual author might be. All had put forward the same name. He had made enquiries and discovered that while claiming the distinction of the letters M.D. after his name, the individual had not been awarded them by any recognised body. He advised therefore that his correspondent cease to publish his medical opinions and also refrain from annoying the patient with unwanted visits or he would be obliged to make his information public.

The letter was followed by a note from the editor, who informed his readers that for legal reasons the correspondence on that issue was now closed.

Frances' perusal of the papers for the last six months of 1877 revealed that nothing of any great significance had occurred. There were no violent street robberies, no stabbings, just the usual minor thefts, assaults and damage to property carried out while under the influence of drink, two small fires and an omnibus accident. None of these incidents had happened on the day or even the week that Edwin Antrobus returned to London, assuming that he had done so. There were a series of articles about Antrobus' disappearance and appeals for anyone with knowledge of what had happened to him to write to the newspaper, followed by letters from humorists, frauds and people with fantastical imaginations as well as some honest speculation, none of which were remotely helpful.

Leaving the *Chronicle* offices, Frances walked along the busy thoroughfare of Ledbury Road and along Chepstow Crescent, passing the school where Dr Goodwin had once been a consultant and with which he was now in dispute. A tall white-fronted house, it was bounded by a low wall and ornamental gates, the path leading to the front steps flanked by stone urns filled with tumbling masses of colourful flowers. Frances smiled at such a thoughtful touch for children who could not hear, providing pleasure to their other senses. A signboard, still glistening as if freshly painted, announced that the school was now called The Bayswater School for the Deaf and employed the most modern and approved German methods of instruction under the guidance of headmaster J. Eckley, special consultant to the Society for Training Teachers of the Deaf.

The side of the school was close by a narrow lane leading to the cottages of Pembridge Mews, but a turn of the corner brought Frances to the more important properties of Pembridge Villas.

Dr Goodwin's door was opened by a maid in her twenties, neat and smart, with an intelligent look. Frances presented her card, and the maid, who knew of the appointment, at once invited her in. A tall sturdy youth was standing in the rear of the hallway and not by chance: he was obviously curious about the visitor and looked at Frances very carefully. He ventured forward shyly and made a respectful little bow. He was a good-looking boy, with light brown eyes and bronze curls, on a fair way to becoming a handsome man.

'Good morning,' Frances greeted him. He smiled, but made no reply.

The maid turned to the youth and instead of speaking took a little notebook and a pencil from the pocket of her apron, wrote a few words, then showed him the page. He smiled even more broadly and nodded.

'This is Mr Isaac Goodwin, Dr Goodwin's son,' the maid explained. 'He is deaf, so we speak by writing our conversation. He can also speak with signs, and I intend to learn them so as to be more useful.'

Isaac wrote in the maid's notebook.

'He writes that he is very interested to meet you as he has read about you in the newspapers. If you go with him he will show you to his father's study.'

Isaac bowed again, and indicated that Frances should follow him, which she did, feeling strangely tongue-tied. They reached a door and he knocked very deliberately three times. It was clearly a signal, one that he could not hear, but a means of telling the occupant of the room that it was he who was about to enter, no reply being appropriate.

After waiting a few moments, Isaac opened the door and they entered a comfortably furnished study. The gentleman who rose to meet them was about sixty, showing the rounded figure that often came unbidden with age, a pleasing though not handsome face, short whiskers and a ruff of grey hair around a bald pate. Frances, who was more than the usual height for a woman, found herself looking down on him as they shook hands. He did not, she thought, look like a man with what Lionel Antrobus had called 'a reputation' but, she reminded herself, cruel seducers and reprobates could be of any age and appearance. There was a conversation between Isaac and his father, carried out entirely in rapid gestures, before the youth, making another respectful obeisance to Frances, departed.

'You are unfamiliar with the sign language of the deaf, I take it,' observed Goodwin, ushering Frances to a chair and sitting at his ease.

The wall behind the desk was lined with bookshelves closely filled with volumes, some of them, judging by the worn leather of their spines, of considerable age.

'I am, yes. Is this something you have devised?'

'Oh no,' he assured her, 'finger spelling and signs have been used since antiquity as the secret language of spies, and they have been employed for the education of the deaf for hundreds of years. The very youngest children quickly learn to converse and soon become proficient. By the use of signs a teacher can impart the skill of reading, and a complete education may be had.'

'Your maid told me she intends learning the signs, I find that very commendable.'

'Yes, she is a capable girl, who might yet become a valuable assistant.'

Frances approved his unusual insight. It was the habit of too many ladies and gentlemen to either ignore or underestimate their servants and assume a level of understanding less than their own, a capital error in her opinion. An individual from a family of substance might receive the best education money could buy and still be a fool, whereas his servant, who had not been so fortunate, could easily outstrip him in wisdom.

'I see that you are admiring my library of medical works,' smiled Dr Goodwin. 'I have heard that you have some knowledge of medicine yourself.'

'My late father was a pharmacist and taught me many of the skills of that profession. It was my intention at one time to study for the examinations, but it was not to be.' Even as she spoke, Frances remained more than a little distracted by the expression 'secret language of spies', which had created some interesting thoughts. 'Do you have any works on speaking with signs?'

'I not only have them but I am the author of several, as well as volumes on the anatomy and diseases of the ear. It has been the one study of my life,' he added, with some feeling. 'My father was born deaf and my mother became deaf at the age of five after contracting scarlet fever. I owe it to their hard work, their struggle to provide me with schooling they could ill-afford, to do all I can for those similarly placed. Unfortunately the ear and its diseases is a subject largely neglected in the education of medical students. If as much effort was made to inform the medical profession as is expended in peddling the supposed cures of quacks and charlatans, we might have made better progress than we have.'

'And you acted as medical advisor to Mrs Harriett Antrobus, whose husband has been missing for the last three years.'

Goodwin looked a little less easy in his manner and placed his fingers on the letter he had received from Frances, which lay unfolded on his desk. 'I did. I am not sure if I can offer any information that can assist you in your enquiries but I will do my best.'

Frances took out her notebook and pencil. 'Tell me about how you first met Mr and Mrs Antrobus and your impression of them.'

'I expect you have already interviewed Mrs Antrobus.'

'I have.'

He nodded. 'And her brother-in-law, who in my opinion carries wilful ignorance to excessive extremes.'

'Yes.'

He looked at her searchingly as if to try and judge what she thought of those two individuals. His general air of concerned amiability could not conceal a keen mind constantly in use. 'Following some correspondence in the newspapers, I received a letter from Mrs Antrobus, who wrote to me at the Central London Throat, Nose and Ear Hospital appealing for my help. From the description of her symptoms I felt sure that she was suffering from a condition known as hyperacusis, that is she experiences severe pain from everyday sounds, with or without tinnitus aureum, which is noises in the head not of any external causation. That being the case, her medical practitioner had done her a terrible disservice in convincing her family that she was losing her mind. In my very specialist practice it is not, I am afraid, rare to uncover such errors that have been the cause of the unhappy patients being committed to asylums for the insane. I called upon the lady and carried out an examination in the presence of Mr Antrobus, which confirmed my original opinion. I could not offer a cure. There were some treatments it was worth employing and these were tried but they were not successful. My main advice was to tell her not to sit all day in complete silence, which she had been doing, but try to introduce some gentle pleasurable sounds, which might act as a balm to soothe her ears. At my suggestion Mrs Antrobus resumed her study of the piano, which she had previously abandoned, and this has given her some relief.'

'Do you have other patients with the same condition?' asked Frances.

'Oh yes, I have five currently: two used to play in orchestras, two operated heavy machinery and one had suffered an accident resulting in concussion of the brain.'

'Tell me about Mr Antrobus, what kind of a man do you think him?'

'A plain man, a man of business, dull, without imagination, yet a good man, with a sense of duty. He is also, however, the kind of individual who having made up his mind about something it is very hard to sway him. He and his brother were both convinced by the family doctor that Mrs Antrobus' troubles were all in her mind, and it was almost impossible for me to move them from that position. Matters were not helped by the fact that Mrs Antrobus and her brother-in-law entertain a hearty dislike for each other, which colours all their dealings.' He paused, his brow furrowed with anxiety. 'You say that you have spoken to Mr Lionel Antrobus, and I am concerned that he may have made some allegations against me − criticisms of my character.'

'He did not make any direct allegations but referred only to unfounded rumours.'

'Rumours with only one origin, if the truth be known,' Goodwin declared, a sharpness to his voice betraying an indignation that had not diminished with time. 'Mr Dromgoole, the man who wrote such nonsense to the newspapers. Do you know about that?'

'I have read the correspondence.'

'When I wrote to the *Chronicle* I had never met him and was unaware of how unstable he was. Had I known it I might have been more circumspect in my comments. He had the effrontery to write to me privately vowing to effect my ruin. He claimed to know secrets about me.'

'I think everyone, even the most respectable person, has a secret that they would not want to be known, however trivial,' observed Frances, reflecting that her profession largely amounted to the exposure of secrets.

'Undoubtedly,' said Goodwin, robustly. 'I am sure I have many. I do not claim to be a perfect man, though we must all strive for perfection. Mr Dromgoole did his best to uncover some scandal that would put an end to my career and lighted upon the fact that I have a son and yet have never been married. He drew the wholly unwarranted conclusion that Isaac is my natural son born of a shameful connection that I wish to keep hidden and decided to tell the world. Isaac is not in fact my relative by blood. I found him as a waif living wild upon the street. The poor child could not have been more than seven years old. I quickly recognised that he was most profoundly deaf. I took him in; I gave him a name, language, education, religion and formally adopted him. He is eighteen now, and no man could wish for a better son. His devotion has repaid me a thousandfold.'

'You did not try and refute these rumours?' asked Frances. 'If you knew their origin you could have gone to law.'

'No. That would only have drawn attention to them and spread them further.'

'Do you still have Mr Dromgoole's letters?'

'They were the ravings of a lunatic, and I burnt them.'

'That is a pity. Sometimes when a man seeks to condemn another he only succeeds by his manner in condemning himself. I can see that such stories might well have given Mr Antrobus and his brother an excuse to reject your advice. Yet Mrs Antrobus has told me that you did effect a change, in her husband at any rate. At the time of his disappearance he had been about to make a new will that would have been far kinder to her. Did she ever express concerns about her husband's will?'

'No, we talked of her hearing and general health, and she sometimes said how much she missed her sons, but it would have been inappropriate to discuss anything else. I should mention that in all my visits to the house either Mr Antrobus or a maid or her sister were in the room when I saw Mrs Antrobus.'

'Did you ever talk to Mr Antrobus when his wife was not present?'

'Yes,' said Goodwin, heavily. 'There were occasions when he drew me aside for a frank discussion, and it was during those interviews that I formed my opinion of him. He was a hard man to deal with, inflexible in his thinking. I once begged him to allow his sons to visit their mother, something that I thought would cheer her dull existence, but he would not. He never said it in so many words but he thought that they were in danger of being tainted by her disease.'

'It cannot be passed from one person to another, surely?'

'Not at all, and I told him so very frankly, but he would not be convinced.'

'When did you last see him?'

'Ah, I can tell you that exactly.' Goodwin opened a leather bound appointment book on his desk. 'Yes, here it is, 20 September 1877. I had called on Mrs Antrobus as usual. I had been seeing her once every fortnight, sometimes applying gentle galvanism but mainly talking to her about her health. As I was leaving Mr Antrobus asked to speak to me privately. He was concerned that there was no improvement in his wife's condition, and I pointed out that with this disease it was a happy circumstance that it had not become any worse. He was not pleased by my reply. In particular, he refused to believe that the condition had been produced by the noise of fireworks (which was his wife's belief), presumably on the grounds that the display, which they had both attended, had been enjoyed by numerous others who had not been similarly afflicted. I advised him that it was very possible for one person to be affected but not others, but even if it was not the fireworks there are other possible causes. He seemed very disturbed by this idea, and when I asked him to elaborate he did not. I strongly suspected that something had occurred for which he was personally responsible and that he had just realised that he had inadvertently caused his wife's condition.

On the following day he sent me a letter saying that he had decided I should discontinue my visits. He did not think that they were helping his wife and he had determined to seek another opinion.'

'Did he say whose opinion?'

'No.'

'That was more than two weeks before he left for Bristol. Mrs Antrobus is convinced that it was your advice which changed her husband's mind.'

'Understandable, I suppose. But I think not.'

Frances was surprised. Had Edwin Antrobus consulted another doctor before he left for Bristol, and was this what lay behind his change of heart? Frances knew that she must speak to this individual, but when she thought of the number of doctors in London and the columns of advertisements in the newspapers offering certain cures for every known ailment, she despaired.

'Can you think of anything at all you learned about Mr Antrobus which might give me some clue as to how and why he disappeared?'

Dr Goodwin pondered for a while, and a look of sadness passed like a shadow across his face. 'I wish I could help you. I would like nothing better than to shine some light on that mystery.'

'I believe you called upon Mrs Antrobus after that last visit?'

'Yes, when I read in the newspapers that her husband was missing I called upon her as a matter of courtesy to express my sympathy and to ask if there was anything I could do. She told me then that the will had put her wholly into the hands of Lionel Antrobus and she feared for her future. She asked me to speak to him on her behalf and I did so, but he was most unhelpful. Of course she was unable to pay any doctor's fees, and she did not want to trespass on my time, so it was agreed not to resume the treatments. To be honest with you, Miss Doughty, the actual treatment did not improve her condition, but what the lady truly appreciated was conversation with someone who understood that she had a genuine affliction of the ears and was not, as many have suggested, insane. Since then, I understand from the newspapers that she has been fortunate in the company of her sister and the friendship of Mr Wylie.'

'And you have not called upon her since then?'

'No.'

Before she left Frances asked if she might borrow a book on speaking with signs, and Dr Goodwin kindly presented her with a slim, well-illustrated volume. He also supplied a booklet of his own composition entitled *Ear Pain, its Causes and Treatment*. He had a thoughtful expression, and Frances could not help but think that there were other matters on his mind, things he might have imparted but had not.

CHAPTER SEVEN

rances rarely ruled out possible suspects in an enquiry at such an early stage but she thought that Edwin Antrobus' two sons who were at boarding school at the time of their father's disappearance would not have had the opportunity to harm him even if they had wanted to, and the respectable Mrs Davison with her nice villa was unlikely to have come to London and slit her nephew's throat in the hope of inheriting three hundred pounds. Mr Luckhurst, however, who stood to receive two thousand pounds, had a far better motive. Was the cigarette manufacturing business really as profitable as Mr Wylie had suggested? Did Mr Luckhurst have his own financial worries that an inheritance might easily solve?

There was one circumstance, however, which to Frances' mind cast doubt on the assumption that the disappearance and possible murder of Edwin Antrobus had a financial motive. If the victim had been killed for his money then the murderer could not have anticipated that the body would not be found for over three years, if indeed the remains in the canal were those of the missing man. If they were not, then the body was still missing. What efforts of restraint and patience must have been expended by the guilty party in order not to reveal knowledge that would have led to the finding of the body and proof of death? Frances found it hard to believe that anyone who hoped to profit from the demise of Edwin Antrobus had not so far provided even an anonymous hint as to where the body might be.

In order to visit the workshop and office of Antrobus and Luckhurst Fine Tobacco Frances had to venture into Notting Hill, where at the end of a row of lofty houses was a lower almost featureless structure, consisting of two storeys and an attic with no basement. The windows were small and very plain, and there was a drab brown door with a worn handle and a tarnished plate with the company name. By contrast with the residences in the same street, the property was not so much neglected as built and subsequently maintained without any regard to external appearance. Frances glanced through a window which was largely shrouded in grey net and at first saw no more than what appeared to be the outline of seated people, but finding a gap between the curtains, she stooped to peer in and saw a gloomy room with long tables at which girls and women sat working. In front of them were deep basins heaped with mounds of loose tobacco, blocks of paper squares and trays to carry away the finished product. Small fingers moved rapidly, rolling and trimming, while a supervisor, the only male in the room, passed behind them, watching the operation and checking the materials and finished product for quality. The odour of rubbed tobacco was very apparent even through the small amount of ventilation available at the top of the windows.

Frances rang the bell, and after a minute she heard footsteps inside and the door opened. A young man of a clerkly appearance stood in a narrow hallway leading to a flight of stairs.

Frances presented her card. 'I have an appointment with Mr Luckhurst.'

The clerk gave her a critical look, as if she was not the kind of visitor that gentleman usually entertained, but all he said was, 'You are expected. Follow me.' They mounted the echoing wooden staircase at the top of which there was a turn into a short corridor, where there was a door with a narrow brass plate that bore the name G.H. Luckhurst, but the clerk took the other direction, into a suite of offices. The clerk's domain was a small anteroom where a desk sat ringed about with cabinets. In such a trade Frances might have expected that the room would smell of burnt tobacco and there would be a box of cigarettes and an ashtray on the desk, but there was no scent of a smoker and no cigarettes. If the clerk smoked, he did not do so on the premises. He tapped on an adjoining door and a voice bade them enter.

The man who sat at the desk was in his mid-forties, with an unusual set to his shoulders, which seemed to be unnaturally drawn forward. With a cheery smile, he descended from his chair to greet Frances with an odd little hopping movement. She saw

at once that Mr Luckhurst was not a good candidate to commit
a violent crime. He was very slight of build, about five feet two
inches in height, and, since his legs were not the same length, able
to walk only with the assistance of a thick-soled surgical boot.
His back was bent, his chest more concave than convex and the
action of his breathing spoke of cramped lungs. The absence of
tobacco smoke in the office was explained. 'A strange looking
fellow, am I not?' he said, with a little gasping laugh.

'Oh, I am very sorry!' said Frances, embarrassed at the thought
that her expression had offended him. One thing she could now
be sure of: the man who had met Edwin Antrobus at the hotel
in Bristol could not have been Mr Luckhurst or the clerk would
have noted his distinctive appearance.

'Think nothing of it,' he said kindly, 'a look of interest from a
lady is always a pleasure. Please take a seat. How may I assist you?'

'I have been engaged by Mrs Harriett Antrobus to enquire into
the disappearance of her husband,' began Frances, once she was
seated. 'In particular I am examining the evidence that he might
have returned to London from Bristol.'

'Ah, yes, the body in the canal,' said Luckhurst, climbing back
on to his chair with an agility that spoke of long custom. 'Which
it seems is not my partner after all.'

'It cannot be shown to be him. That is not quite the same thing.'

'No, of course not.'

'Did you view the remains?'

'I did, very briefly. It is not a memory I wish to dwell upon.
I did not think it was my partner, neither could I offer any suggestion as to who it might have been.'

'I am trying to learn as much as I can about Mr Antrobus and
any events that might have occurred just before he disappeared,
his state of mind and health at the time, his plans for the future, his
friends and rivals.'

'Yes, of course,' he said readily, 'and I will help you all I can. While
I cannot say that I regarded him as a brother, we were close associates for many years, and I miss both his company and acumen.'

'Has the business suffered though his absence?'

He gave a wheezing sigh. 'Oh, we put a brave face on it, but the
truth is I have been hard-pressed to maintain the trade, and while

I have employed another man to undertake the travelling my partner once did, it is not the same.' Mr Luckhurst looked despondent,
but he did not strike Frances as a man who could be despondent for long. 'You see, it was not just a matter of replacing a man,
finding another who could do the same work. When a partner
in a business vanishes, suppliers become suspicious. They think
the trade will collapse and fear that there are dark secrets about
to come to light. They start to demand immediate payment for
materials. Customers think we cannot be relied upon and look
elsewhere. But we have managed to keep our heads above the
water. I am taking a smaller salary and have postponed improve-
ments to conditions in the workshop.'

'Do you know if Mr Antrobus left you anything in his will?'

He looked surprised by the question. 'I have no knowledge of
that. In any case, he is in law still alive, so it is hardly of any relevance.' He paused and his eyes flickered with realisation. 'Ah, yes,
I think I see the relevance, now. Well it is your right, indeed your
profession to be suspicious. May I assure you that I have neither
the desire nor the motive to do away with my friend and partner.
If he were to walk through the door now I would welcome him
back with joy and relief.' He smiled roguishly. 'I suppose many
murderers have told you the exact same tale before you unmasked
them for the villains they were!'

'I am afraid so,' said Frances, who was warming to Mr Luckhurst's
company. While not a handsome man, his face could light up with
a good humour that was very pleasing. Can you think of anyone
who might have wanted to harm Mr Antrobus?'

'No. He was never involved in any underhand trading as far
as I am aware, indeed I do not think it was in his nature to do
so. Of course there are always petty rivalries in business, but it is
more of a friendly competition. The tobacco trade thrives despite
what doctors say, and there is room enough for us all. If there was
anything wrong in his personal or family life that might have led
to his disappearance or death I do not know of it. I last saw him
the day before he went to Bristol, and there seemed to be nothing
amiss with him in any respect. From that moment I have neither
seen nor heard from him. It is my belief that he met with an
accident and has either lost his memory or, sadly, is dead and his

body not found. I have every sympathy with his family: it is a very trying time for them all. His brother has left no stone unturned to discover the truth, and he has had his own troubles, as I expect you know.'

'I did not know.'

'Mr Lionel Antrobus' wife passed away just over a year ago, after a long and painful illness. It was a very distressing time.'

'I am surprised that he was not therefore more sympathetic to his sister-in-law's affliction,' commented Frances.

'Ah, well, there is no love lost there,' said Luckhurst. 'He was not an easy man to talk to even before he was widowed and less so now. He has seen real bodily suffering and has no patience with anything he thinks is all in the mind.'

'He told me that his brother was too honourable to desert his wife. Do you agree?'

'I do. Many another man has to endure the unhappiness that comes with a wife's delicate health. Some can bear it, others cannot. Antrobus did all that he ought to have done, and it was hard for him as the complaint was so mysterious.'

'Were they a contented couple before Mrs Antrobus' illness?'

'Oh, if ever a couple married for love it was they! Do you know,' added Luckhurst, with the serene expression of a man recalling happy memories, 'I was present on the day they met. In fact it was also the day that I first met them both. There was a gathering at the home of a mutual friend. Miss Harriett Pearce was such a beauty. She is handsome now, but back then she illuminated the room! So enchanting, and with a pretty soft musical voice and dainty manners. A man could not help but fall under her spell. Her father, I was told, was a good, hardworking man who lacked both ambition and fortune, but somehow that mattered nothing. Had I been taller I might have wooed her myself, but it is not the fashion to declare one's admiration for a lady from a footstool. After the ladies retired Antrobus spoke very knowledgeably about the tobacco trade. I thought then that he was a man to watch, and we agreed to meet again and talk business. But when we did all his conversation was of the beautiful young girl who had captured his heart. He saw her constantly and six months later they were engaged to be married, but at the time it looked as if they might have to wait several years before a wedding date could be set. He was impatient to claim his bride, but marriage is an expensive business and a man likes to make his fortune before he has a wife and children to spend it for him. But then his uncle died and left him a handsome legacy, so they were married soon afterwards.'

'And was it a happy marriage?' asked Frances, gently bringing him back to her query.

Luckhurst knew that he had strayed from the point and gave a rueful smile, earning Frances' instant forgiveness. 'I haven't really answered, have I? But there was a purpose to my story. I suppose they were as happy as many other couples. But Edwin once told me that his uncle's death, the very event that had enabled him to marry, weighed heavily upon him. His uncle suffered from terrible headaches that sometimes left him melancholy and, well, it was deemed to be an accident, but those who knew him suspected otherwise. It placed a cloud over the marriage from the beginning, a cloud that only grew darker with his wife's illness.'

'You are more sympathetic to Mrs Antrobus' sufferings than her brother-in-law,' observed Frances, 'and possibly more sympathetic than her husband.'

'I am no expert on diseases of the ear but I can see when someone is in pain. The doctors who suggested she was feigning should be made to endure what she does for just one day and then they would change their tune.' He made no reference to his own health, but Frances felt sure that he was no stranger to pain.

'Mrs Antrobus has provided me with a list of her husband's friends. It was a very short list, I am afraid, and I was hoping you might know of any business associates who could provide me with some information.'

'I will do my best,' he offered, 'but I fear my list will also be short.' He took up pen and paper and wrote down the names of a number of suppliers and customers. 'Not that any of these men would have meant him harm. None would have profited from my partner's absence and most would not have been in either Bristol or London at the time he disappeared.' Frances looked at the list, which included the men the Bristol detective had already interviewed and a few others with businesses in London he had not.

'I understand that Mr Wylie has approached you with a proposal to merge your interests?'

'Yes, he has. We have had a number of discussions on the subject, he has examined our accounts and is pleased with what he has seen.'

'Is this something that might have occurred if Mr Antrobus was still a partner?'

'Hmm,' pondered Luckhurst. 'That is a very good question, and I can't say that I know the answer. I had never met Wylie until a year ago, although Edwin often mentioned him.'

'You never went to Bristol on business?'

'I have never been there for any reason.'

'Did you ever encounter a Mr Dromgoole?'

'No, although the name is familiar. Was he not the doctor who claimed that tobacco was the cause of ear diseases? Antrobus is not a violent man, but even he said that the fellow needed a good whipping. You don't think he may have had something to do with this?'

'No, I am sure he did not; I had hoped he might be able to help me with information, but his mind has become clouded. Do you know a lady called Adeline?'

'I do not. Is she young and pretty?' he added, hopefully.

'I'm afraid I know nothing about her except her name. But if you should hear anything at all that might help me please do let me know at once.'

'It will be my pleasure,' said Luckhurst warmly, and he eased down from his chair as she prepared to leave. He took her fingertips in his with the air of a great gallant. 'And we will speak again, perhaps next time over a cup of tea?'

Frances could not help but find his attentions flattering. 'Delighted.'

'I do not think that Dr Goodwin is a Lothario,' Frances told Sarah over supper as she looked at the list supplied by Mr Luckhurst and decided how she might best visit all those named. 'He has his own secrets and troubles of course – there is a legal dispute with the Bayswater School for the Deaf, which I did not discuss with him – but he was a model of courtesy.'

Sarah was studying the book of signs and made a gesture with her thumb.

'What does that mean?' asked Frances.

'It means I'm very pleased.'

'He said that the signs are much used by spies, who I suppose will want to have conversations that others cannot understand. A detective and her assistant might also find it useful. Shall we see what we can learn?'

Sarah looked through the book and made another sign. 'That means "yes",' she said.

Once Frances had completed her plans, which included a visit to Dr Collin, who had consented to an appointment, there followed a pleasant evening's diversion, after which they had both managed to learn the finger alphabet and some useful signs.

'I can see how a child might learn this very quickly,' said Frances. 'If a teacher makes the sign for a house and shows the child a picture of a house, and then the word "house" written down, then the child has learned to speak and read at the same time. Imagine,' she went on, 'the fate of children born before such a thing was devised. They would live their lives in silence, unable to speak or play a part in the world. How wonderful that there is a school to teach the signs and men like Dr Goodwin.'

Frances spent most of the next day on her round of visits to Edwin Antrobus' London associates. After a succession of stuffy shops and offices she found that his connections in the tobacco trade knew nothing of him as an individual and had not seen or heard from him since his departure for Bristol in October 1877. She also felt that she had inhaled so much tobacco scent that she had almost become a partaker of it herself.

Frances had received a note from Charlotte Pearce with the names that she and her sister had been able to recall of the doctors who had attended Mrs Antrobus. There was some awkwardness about approaching medical men, however, since they all started with the assumption that Frances wanted confidential information about a patient, and she had to take great pains to explain to them that it was the patient's husband about whom she was enquiring. With the exception of Dr Goodwin, all were in general practice, and while even those who had only visited the Antrobus home once easily remembered the unusual case, none was able to supply any useful information about the missing man. All tended to assume that since they had not been asked for a second visit their proposed 'cures' had been successful and that Mrs Antrobus' current condition was due to her failure to follow their advice or an unexpected relapse.

Dr Collin was of greater interest since he was the Antrobus' family practitioner, better acquainted with the missing man, and had also examined the remains found in the canal. The ease with which Frances had secured an interview with him was explained as soon as she entered his consulting room.

Dr Collin was a tall lean man in his fifties with an assured air and a manner of practised kindliness towards his patients. Ladies especially took great comfort from his silver grey hair, which implied wisdom, and the sympathy expressed in his mild eyes. His clarity and confidence made him much sought after as a medical witness at trials and inquests, but Frances was well aware that a tone of certainty in the voice and being correct did not always go hand in hand. She had seen the prideful fallible man under the mask, and he knew it.

'You appreciate that although this is not a medical consultation my time is valuable, and you will receive a bill for my usual fee,' he said brusquely when she had explained her mission.

None of the other doctors had been unkind enough to charge Frances for a brief conversation, but she did not say so. If he was hoping to deter her, he would be disappointed. 'That will be quite in order,' she replied. 'When was the last time you spoke to Mr Edwin Antrobus?'

Dr Collin consulted his appointment diary. 'That would be the last time I saw Mrs Antrobus. It was 5 June 1877.'

'I appreciate that this was over four months before his last journey to Bristol, but did Mr Antrobus say something or was there anything in his manner which you think might have a bearing on his subsequent disappearance?'

Collin snapped the book shut. 'It is easy to look back on the past with the greater wisdom of time and see what one ought to have seen then or perhaps even see what was not there.'

Frances gave him a quizzical look. Was this an olive branch?

'I try not to do so,' he added, firmly. 'It was a professional visit like any other.'

'What was your very first impression when you heard that Mr Antrobus had not returned from his visit to Bristol?'

He nodded. 'A good question. I suppose I thought at first that he must have suffered an accident or been taken ill and would soon be found, but as time passed, I admit that I did start to wonder if he had gone away of his own volition. I surely do not need to say what might have driven him to do so.'

'Did he ever speak to you about the arrangements he had made in the event of his death?'

'Not in so many words, but he was naturally anxious for his family because he felt that his wife was unable to look after either herself or his sons. If there were any legal documents he had prepared he did not discuss them with me.'

'I have been told that shortly before he departed for Bristol he changed his mind and became convinced that Mrs Antrobus should be entrusted with the management of her affairs. He was intending to make a new will to that effect. Do you know anything about that?'

'No. In fact you surprise me considerably by that assertion. Who told you this?'

'Mrs Antrobus.'

Collin gave a short, scornful laugh. 'I would hardly trust her word on the matter.'

'Nevertheless, she believes that her husband had satisfied himself that she was not suffering from an affliction of the mind but the ears. He may have consulted someone shortly before his journey.'

'Not Goodwin?' said Collin, his eyes narrowing with suspicion.

'After his consultation with Dr Goodwin.'

'If he fell into the hands of charlatans who advertise cures for the incurable then I can only feel sorry for him.'

'You can't suggest who he might have gone to?'

'I have nothing to do with such people and would advise anyone else the same.' He folded his arms. 'Is that all?'

'I would like to discuss the remains found in the canal, the ones Mrs Antrobus thought might be those of her husband, since you examined them and gave evidence at the inquest.'

Collin brightened at the recollection. 'Yes, that was extremely interesting. It is not very often that I have the opportunity to examine specimen of adipocere. I actually arranged for a photograph to be taken. I don't suppose,' he suggested, with something approaching a smirk, 'that you will wish to see it.'

It was a challenge and Frances decided to accept. 'I would like to see it very much. It will be most educational.'

He gave a dubious twitch of the eyebrows, hesitated, then reached down an album of pictures from his bookshelf, placed it on the desk and leafed through it. Even seeing it upside down Frances could see that it was entirely composed of medical curiosities: unusual deformities, the results of horrible accidents, massive goitres, bulging hernias and strange births. One page he hastily covered with a sheet of plain paper; presumably it related to the male anatomy and was therefore unsuitable for her eyes. At last he turned the book around so that Frances could view it.

Not so long ago Frances had discovered a body buried in a ditch and it had been badly decomposed, the features not admitting of any identification. She had recently consulted her father's medical books on the subject of adipocere and learned that when a body was immersed in water and not exposed to air, the fatty part of the flesh did not putrefy in the usual way but was transformed into a waxy substance that preserved its shape. Even though she had prepared herself for it, the canal remains were an unpleasant sight. It might have been better if all the head had been there and completely covered with pale flesh, looking more like a man, but the action of passing barges had destroyed so much, broken and torn the body until little remained. The knife slash across the throat was easily visible, however. It was a single deep cut that went down to the bone.

Frances could sense Collin watching her as she studied the picture, which only increased her resolution not to waver. 'The cut was made from the left side of the throat to the right?' she asked.

'Yes. In all probability he was approached from behind by a right-handed man, who clasped him about the head with his left arm, pulling it back quickly before he could defend himself, so exposing the throat, and then drew the knife across once.' Dr Collin mimed the gesture. 'A practiced hand and a firm one. It is a common technique amongst footpads.'

'And you are quite sure that this is not the body of Mr Antrobus?' queried Frances, since it was hard to see who it might have been.

'I cannot be sure one way or the other. Although Mr Antrobus was my patient he never consulted me about his personal health and I never examined him. I was only consulted regarding his wife. I therefore have no special knowledge to offer.'

'There was nothing unusual you observed about his health during your normal conversation which could have assisted the court?'

'Nothing at all. He appeared to be robust and active, in the prime of life, sensible and sane. I never saw any reason to suggest that he required medical attention.'

Frances looked more carefully at the picture. 'I can see no hair or whiskers on the remains. The picture I have of Mr Antrobus shows that he had both.'

'Any hair may have become detached by soaking in water before the adipocere was formed.'

'Was there nothing to be learned from the teeth?'

'The teeth in the upper jaw provided no clues since they had been greatly neglected. I doubt that this man has seen a dentist in many years. But cowards may be of any class. The lower jaw is missing as are most of the long bones.' Collin leaned forward to study the picture closely, his fingertips tracing the spine, the vertebrae held together only by being sunken into fatty tissue. 'The spine shows no deformities, the ribs' – he indicated them with a double sweep of his fingers – 'nothing remarkable.'

Frances did not wish Edwin Antrobus any ill, but perversely, how she might have wished him to have had a small scar on his cheek or an unusual birthmark, or curiously shaped ears, or anything that might have enabled someone who knew him to see these horrible fragments and say yes or no. But it was not to be.

Thankfully for her aching feet, which had borne her many miles on a busy day, she could look forward to Sunday, when she would need to walk no further than St Stephen's church.

CHAPTER EIGHT

Despite her weariness after a taxing day, Frances slept badly, her slumbers disturbed by horrid dreams of being crushed by a powerful evil-smelling figure from whom there was no escape. In church the following morning Sarah twice had to nudge her when it seemed that she was about to slip into a doze. She was far from being the ever-alert Miss Doughty she was sometimes reputed to be and was only sorry that she was not more like the daring Miss Dauntless of the stories who was able to face any challenge by day or night without the need for sleep at all.

Sunday afternoon was a time for reflection on the week past and the week ahead. Frances had learned a great deal about Edwin Antrobus, his business and his family but nothing that suggested to her what his fate might have been. There were still two servants to trace but when that was done she could think of no one else to whom she might speak.

Rereading her notes she was reminded that the missing man's uncle was thought to have died by his own hand, an incident that had cast a shadow over the marriage. She resolved to return to the *Chronicle* offices next morning to read the report of the inquest. Was the family taint on the husband's side and not the wife's? Had Edwin Antrobus managed to show a face of sanity to hide his true madness and melancholy?

There was also a new client to see, a report to write and invoices to dispatch, but more happily, she would be entertaining her uncle Cornelius to tea. With that thought she retired to bed early and thankfully awoke refreshed.

On Monday morning Frances received a letter from Matthew Ryan, the Bristol detective. He had learned nothing new about the disappearance of Edwin Antrobus in the three years since his initial report, but in the light of recent events he was making fresh enquiries. An appeal for information would soon appear in all the Bristol newspapers with a full description and an engraving of the missing man drawn from a photograph, asking most particularly if he had been seen in the company of another man and whether, either alone or accompanied, he had boarded the train to Paddington.

Frances' new client was a lady, a Mrs Reville, youthful, beautiful and refined in her speech and manners, who told Frances that her husband was taking proceedings for divorce on the grounds of infidelity. She protested, with tears in her eyes, that she had always been a true and faithful wife, and he had no proof at all of any wrongdoing but claimed that she had given him a disease he could have contracted in no other way. She had appealed to the family doctor, who had refused to tell her anything about her husband's condition on the grounds of confidentiality and could only conclude that, despite his strident denials, it was her husband who had been faithless and passed the disease to her. This was not grounds for her to divorce him, and in any case she had no wish to do so as she still loved him and forgave him everything, but if she were cast aside then she would never again be permitted to see her four children.

Frances agreed to take the case, but she thought how useless it would be to have either husband or wife followed to discover which one was being truthful as both would be on their guard. The hearing was due to come to court in three weeks, so there was very little time to achieve anything.

At the offices of the *Chronicle*, Frances read the report of the inquest on Edwin Antrobus' maternal uncle, thirty-seven-year-old Mr Charles Henderson, which had taken place in Paddington on 14 September 1863. The principal witness was his nephew, then aged twenty-six, who had found the body. Although the young man had borne himself well in court, the *Chronicle*'s report stated that from time to time he could not refrain from shedding tears and attracted considerable sympathy.

Charles Henderson had died three days earlier at a family gathering at his home on Craven Hill. It had been an informal dinner, attended by a Mr Pearce, who was accompanied by his wife and two daughters and Mr Henderson's elderly aunts. During the course of the evening the party had removed to the drawing room, and there had been some conversation on the subject of ornamental snuffboxes, since Mr Henderson collected them, and he offered to show the company a new acquisition that was in a glass case in his study. The study was locked, and he said he would fetch the key and return shortly. Several minutes passed before one of the aunts commented that her nephew was taking a long time and she thought he must have mislaid the key.

About a minute or two later there was a gunshot that appeared to come from within the house. Edwin Antrobus, telling the rest of the party to remain where they were, went out into the hallway and called up the stairs to his uncle, but there was no reply. He ran up to the study and found the door open, his uncle slumped across the desk and a recently discharged pistol and its polishing cloth on the floor beside him. He had been shot through the temple.

There was a pause in the testimony during which the witness was overcome with grief, and the coroner asked for a glass of water to be brought.

When Antrobus was able to continue he said that as soon as he saw his uncle he knew that the case was hopeless. He had left the study and closed the door behind him, returned to the parlour, quickly ordered that everyone should remain there and sent a servant to fetch a doctor. He then stayed with the other guests until the doctor arrived.

Shown a pistol he agreed that it was the property of his uncle, who usually kept it unloaded and locked in a cabinet in his study, together with a supply of ammunition. His uncle kept it as a sporting item although he rarely used it. He himself had never handled the pistol, in fact he was sure that neither he nor anyone else in the house would have had the slightest idea of how to load and fire it. He had given the matter careful thought and as far as he was aware his uncle must have been alone in the study when the shot was fired as every other person in the house was accounted for.

The question of Mr Henderson's state of mind was of paramount importance. He was an unmarried man of independent means and generally of a cheerful disposition and good health. There had been allegations that he was prone to melancholy but this his nephew firmly refuted. Henderson had sometimes suffered from the migraine, which had required him to retreat to a darkened room – there was a chaise longue in the rear parlour where he liked to recline – but after he had rested he was as well as any other man.

The coroner reviewed the evidence. He saw no reason why Mr Henderson should have taken his own life. It appeared that he had himself unlocked the study door, taken the gun out of its case and polished it, perhaps in order to show it to his guests as it was of unusual design. Although he usually stored the gun unloaded it was possible that he might have mistakenly put it away previously with a bullet still in it, and while being polished, it had accidentally discharged, killing him. The presence of the cloth supported that theory, as did the fact that the study door was found open. In his experience men who retired to their rooms with the intention of ending their lives always did so behind a firmly closed door.

The jury had no difficulty in returning a verdict that Charles Henderson's death had been an accident.

Frances concurred, but she could see why Edwin Antrobus felt that his inheritance had been tainted by blood. Whether the incident and his grief had had anything to do with his disappearance fourteen years later seemed unlikely.

It was always a pleasure for Frances to entertain her uncle Cornelius Martin to tea. The elder brother of her absent mother, Rosetta, his kindness to Frances when she was a child was the best and truest paternal guidance she had ever known. Frances had grown up under the cold and unappreciative eye of her father William, whose energies were largely devoted to the upbringing and education of her brother Frederick, and the firm, practical hand of William's sister, Maude. Valued only for her work in the home and the shop, and given no more schooling than was necessary for those duties, her enquiring mind had sought out further knowledge in her brother's books and her father's library, and it had been fed with stimulating experiences when Cornelius had taken Frederick and herself on outings.

Her uncle was a lonely man, still missing his wife after twelve years of widowerhood. On the death of her father Frances had found that unwise investments had left her almost penniless, and the business had been sold to pay debts. Cornelius had generously offered her a home and a simple but secure life, but the celebrity that had descended upon her when she solved her first murder case had brought unexpected commissions, and she had taken the adventurous step of becoming a private detective. Cornelius had not been offended, simply concerned, and he often called on her to reassure himself that she had not been murdered or, worse still, become a depraved woman.

Frances had long forgiven her uncle for keeping secret the fact that her mother had not, as she had always been told, died when she was three but had deserted her father for another man. She had never been able to discover the identity of that man, or whether her mother still lived, mainly because she had made no determined attempt to do so, from fear that knowing the answers might be worse than ignorance. Sometimes it required a very conscious and deliberate effort on her part not to look for her mother. Such was her extreme restraint in this area that she had done no more than painstakingly scour the registers held in Somerset House for any record of her mother's death or even a bigamous marriage, but she had found nothing. Although she tried to put it from her mind, the mystery still gnawed at her, all the more so because she had discovered that she had a younger brother living, the son of her mother and her unknown lover, the lover who might well be her own natural father. The only clue she held was a letter of her mother's referring to the man as 'V'.

Recently, Frances had re-examined her parents' marriage certificate and seen that while one of the witnesses was her aunt Maude, the other was called Louise Salter, a name with which she was unfamiliar. The Bayswater Directory had no record of any householder of that surname. Frances had no wish either to call upon her aunt Maude or invite her to her home, which would have resulted in a fierce lecture on her inappropriate way of life and an unwanted revival of memories of childhood neglect. A far pleasanter prospect was to speak to her uncle.

Sarah set about preparing a suitable tea. Her powerful arms were able to work miracles of lightness in the kitchen; indeed Professor Pounder had commented recently that her gifts of pastry and puddings had required him to spend additional hours in the gymnasium in order to maintain his correct bodily proportions. Cornelius was not a great trencherman but, like Frances, he enjoyed the occasional treat, and in addition to a plate of thinly cut bread and butter Sarah had made pound cake, scones, gingerbread and fruit tart.

On his arrival, Cornelius made the usual considerate enquiries after Frances' health, and she reassured him that she was very well indeed, adding the answers to his unspoken questions that she was settled and content in her new life. Sarah poured tea from the extra large pot, the one that was only used for visitors or when Frances needed an especially plentiful supply to consume during her deliberations.

Cornelius was in his early fifties, and while always neatly attired, he seemed to be living in the world of fashion that had existed when his wife had been alive. He did his best, but a loving spouse or a dutiful manservant would have seen him more freshly turned out. He had regretted Frances' decision not to accept his offer of accommodation, and she felt sure that while he claimed to be happy in his own company, attended only by an elderly housekeeper whose main virtues were not in the field of conversation, he was actually very lonely. He sipped his tea, glanced from Frances to Sarah and back again, and gave a dejected little sigh but did not elaborate on his thoughts.

'I was wondering,' said Frances lightly, once the first round of eatables had been distributed, 'if you know or once knew a lady by the name of Louise Salter.'

Cornelius paused in the middle of appreciating a slice of fruit tart. Frances watched him carefully, but he did not seem to be disturbed by the question. He dabbed his lips with a napkin. 'That is a name I have not heard in a long while. It sounds familiar but I am not sure I can place it.'

'She was a witness to my parents' wedding.'

'Ah, yes, now I recall. A very good-looking young woman, I think she was a schoolfellow of Rosetta's.'

'Have you seen her since then?' Frances had already visited Somerset House and established that no one named Louise Salter had married or died, so assumed that either Salter was her married name or if single she was still alive. 'Was she a married lady?'

'Hmm,' said Cornelius, helping himself to a scone, 'now you do test my memory. I have the feeling that she was a single young lady, in fact the gentlemen present were all very taken with her and paid her compliments which would have been most inappropriate had she been there with a husband. But I do not think I have seen her since that event.'

'My mother never mentioned her? They must have been close friends.'

He smiled. 'Now I can see where this is tending, Frances.'

'Uncle, I cannot stay in ignorance all my life. I may choose for the moment to do nothing with any information you can give me, but still, I would like to know more.'

He hesitated. 'Yes of course, you have a right to know everything. And now I think about it something does come back to me. About two or three years after the wedding Rosetta became very distressed. She told me that a dear friend had suffered a terrible reversal when her father had been made bankrupt through no fault of his own. I think his business partner had run away with the funds, and as a result the family was ruined. I cannot be sure but I think it might have been Miss Salter to whom she was referring. The family was obliged to leave Bayswater. That is really all I know.'

Frances was disappointed but reflected that even if Louise Salter had moved away several years before her mother's desertion in 1863, she might still know something about the events that had led to it. Rosetta Doughty had given birth to twins in January 1864, one of whom had died, and she had then been living in lodgings in Chelsea. Nothing was known of her later history.

There was a knock at the door that took them by surprise as Frances was not expecting a visitor. Sarah answered it and was told by the housemaid that a Miss Pearce had arrived, very upset, and wanted to see Miss Doughty at once.

Frances put down her teacup. 'I hope you don't mind, uncle, but under the circumstances I feel I ought to see this visitor. I will not disturb the tea-table; if she is content to sit in the kitchen then I can provide her with some refreshment.'

This plan was abandoned, however, when Charlotte Pearce burst into the room in a state that suggested that she had been running all the way. Her face was glowing with warmth and little curls of damp hair had escaped her bonnet.

'Oh, please let me assist!' exclaimed Cornelius, leaping up and helping the distressed lady to a chair. 'If this is a private matter I will of course withdraw, but if there is any errand I can go on, you have only to ask, or if Miss Pearce requires conducting to a doctor I will call a cab at once.'

'Thank you, sir, you are very kind,' breathed Charlotte, leaning on his arm. 'I am so sorry to have intruded, I had not realised that Miss Doughty was receiving company.'

'Oh think nothing of it, we are very informal here,' Frances reassured her gently. Sarah had already poured a steaming cup of tea, with two sugar lumps, and offered it to Charlotte. 'Allow me to introduce my uncle, Mr Cornelius Martin. Uncle this is Miss Charlotte Pearce. Miss Pearce, this is Miss Sarah Smith, my very special assistant.'

Cornelius fetched a small table so that Charlotte could put her teacup down, and Sarah added a plate piled high with bread and butter and cake, to furnish the visitor with everything she needed in the way of restoratives. Cornelius, despite his offer to withdraw, did not do so but stood nearby, watching Charlotte anxiously and awaiting instructions.

Once Charlotte had rested and refreshed herself, she took a paper from her pocket and handed it to Frances. 'Harriett received this letter today. I have already left a note for Mr Wylie, but he is away visiting a factory.'

The letter was on the headed notepaper of Mr Marsden, the sour-faced solicitor who was acting on behalf of Lionel Antrobus. Frances could not imagine two men better suited to each other's company.

'Mr Antrobus claims that he is acting on behalf of his nephews, in accordance with the wishes of his brother,' sighed Charlotte, 'but I cannot help thinking that this is some underhand way of securing an advantage for himself. We thought he had ceased to annoy us, but it seems he has only been biding his time for this very moment, which places him in a much stronger position.'

The letter advised Harriett that when her eldest son Edwin jnr attained the age of sixteen, which event was only four months away, he would, in accordance with the wish often expressed by his father, be leaving boarding school and taking a junior post in the business of Luckhurst and Antrobus Fine Tobacco with the object of progressing in time to a partnership. Lionel Antrobus wished to reaffirm that under the terms of his brother's will he had all rights and management over his brother's estate and a duty of care of his nephews until such time as either Mr Edwin Antrobus reappeared or Edwin jnr achieved his majority. It was his intention at all times to act as his brother would have wanted. To ensure fatherly supervision of the boys, it was proposed that he, Edwin jnr and his brother would, from 1 September 1881, live in the family home at Craven Hill. To comply with Edwin Antrobus' wishes that the boys and their mother should not reside under the same roof, Mrs Harriett Antrobus was therefore instructed to vacate the property before her sons took up residence. Mr Lionel Antrobus had also resolved to make the best use of the property by letting a portion of it, and Miss Pearce might remain if she wished, on the payment of a suitable rent, the proceeds to be invested for the future of Edwin Antrobus' sons.

'It seems to me,' said Frances, reluctantly, 'that he has legal right on his side, in that he is acting in the interests of his nephews. Whether one approves or not, he is only doing what his brother would have wanted.'

'The suggestion that I might remain in the house is a mere pretence to make him appear to be acting reasonably,' Charlotte protested. 'I am quite sure that he will demand a rent I will find impossible, but even if I could pay it, I need to be with Harriett. Has she not endured enough? We do not wish to trespass any further on Mr Wylie's generosity. He cannot give us accommodation as he is in lodgings that we could not with any propriety share. And now it appears that Mr Marsden, who we had thought was acting in our interests, has turned against us. Miss Doughty, I implore you, do all you can to find Edwin or at least discover his fate, and then we will not be living in this agony of uncertainty.'

Frances promised Miss Pearce to redouble her efforts, and when her visitor had rested, Cornelius ordered a cab to conduct her home.

Chapter Nine

Next morning Frances received a short note from Lionel Antrobus saying that he would call to speak to her at 10 a.m. He seemed to assume that this arrangement would be convenient for her, since he did not ask if it was, and the reason for the appointment was not mentioned.

'So you don't like him much, then?' grinned Sarah, after Frances had spent a minute or two expressing her opinion of that gentleman.

'I am not at all convinced that he is acting in the best interests of his family, although he works very hard at appearing to do so. He has the entire trust of his brother, despite the difference in their fortunes, which must surely weigh hard upon him, and all power, both of making decisions and the disposal of income has been placed in his hands. Mrs Antrobus fears that he may be appropriating his brother's fortune for his own use. If Mr Edwin Antrobus is not found then more than three years will go by before anyone will be able to see whether his executor has been as honest as he makes out and, if he is adept at covering his tracks, in all probability not even then.'

Frances had already decided to go to Paddington Green police station that morning to speak to Inspector Sharrock in the slight hope that he was willing to divulge what enquiries had been made in London at the time of Edwin Antrobus' disappearance, and there was just time to do so if she looked sharp. The Inspector's willingness to help her seemed to vary with the state of the weather, but she suspected that it might be due to the amount of peace he obtained at home where his wife had to manage not only him but also their six children. Frances, hoping that erupting teeth and summer colds had not deprived the Inspector of too much sleep, ordered a cab and, after writing to Lionel Antrobus to confirm their appointment, set out.

Sarah was busy with an unusual case presented to her by the Bayswater Women's Suffrage Society. She was an active and valued member, standing guard at the door of meetings to control and eject any disruptive elements. Men who came to make a lot of noise and deride the lady speakers did not do so a second time. The society had recently had some leaflets printed to place in ladies' reading rooms with the intention of attracting members, but to their annoyance there had been errors in the spelling that had served to make the lady suffragists appear ridiculous. The printer had tried to maintain that the errors were in the original written copy, but after a visit from Sarah he had been forced to admit that this was not the case. He next claimed that there had been a trivial mistake in the typesetting and wrote to the society offering to refund half the cost. Sarah was about to pay him another visit, to point out that a mere shift of type would have resulted only in a nonsense and not, as it had in this case, an insult to the appearance of the ladies. She suspected sabotage and wanted to root out the culprit.

Frances did not have a successful visit at Paddington Green as the Inspector had just been summoned away on an urgent matter and no one at the station could tell her anything about the Antrobus case or would permit her to examine the papers. She knew she had no entitlement to see the papers but thought it worth making the request. Unfortunately, young Constable Mayberry, the only policeman she might have been able to pressure into doing as she asked, was with the Inspector. The desk sergeant took great pains to inform her that once she was made an Inspector of police then she could order them all about as she pleased, and Frances departed thinking that that would be a very interesting situation.

From time to time Frances undertook secret work for the government, although she was never asked to do anything that placed either her life or her modesty in danger. She did consequently have the ear of the Prime Minister, but she had never dared to suggest that he should allow women in the police force. Mr Gladstone was no longer a young man and the idea of a female in uniform and wielding a truncheon might have given him apoplexy.

Sarah returned in time for a pot of tea to be made and reported her success. She had discovered that the printer's new assistant, having had a falling out with his wife, had decided to take revenge on all women who dared to voice their opinions. The business that the Suffrage Society conducted with the printer was not so large that loss of its custom was a serious threat; however, Sarah had informed the proprietor that many of the society members were married to men of considerable influence in Bayswater, who, if they had any sense, deferred to their wives' wishes. Matters were concluded to everyone's satisfaction, except that of the printer's assistant.

As Frances anticipated, Lionel Antrobus arrived to the very minute of his appointment. He favoured the apartment with a rapid critical glance, saw nothing that offended him and took a seat. Frances, as usual, introduced her valued assistant, and he gave Sarah a wary look and a curt nod.

'Miss Doughty,' he began, in the manner of a man who had no time to waste, 'I understand that Miss Charlotte Pearce has been to see you following the delivery of Mr Marsden's letter.'

'She has, yes, and she was in considerable distress at its demands.'

He exhibited surprise. 'I really can't see why. She must have known that I would require the house for my nephews' use. She cannot have been ignorant of young Edwin's approaching birthday. I believe that I have been more than generous in permitting Harriett and Miss Pearce to remain in the house for so long, and they have been afforded ample notice to find some other accommodation.'

'But their requirements are very unusual and their means limited,' Frances reminded him.

'Neither their requirements nor their means are any concern of mine,' he declared. 'My only duty is to carry out the wishes of my brother, to take the very course he would have taken had he been here. He had always intended that Edwin and Arthur should enter the business at the age of sixteen, and they will need a London home. I do not wish to part the brothers as they take great comfort from each other's company, so Arthur will henceforward live and be schooled in Bayswater. I can scarcely place them in lodgings when their own father's house is available.'

'That much I understand,' said Frances carefully, 'but is it not also the case that you will reside with them?'

'What are you implying?' he retorted angrily. 'The sole purpose of my living with my nephews is to supply a father's supervision. There is another circumstance it would be only fair to mention. At present I reside above the shop premises with my son and his wife.' Frances realised that he must be referring to the young man and woman she had seen serving in the shop. 'My son has just advised me that in six months I can expect to be a grandfather. Upon that event, a relative of my daughter-in-law will come to live with us as housekeeper and nursemaid. The available accommodation is not suitable for the addition of both a child and a single female.'

'Was it your brother's wish that you live at Craven Hill?' asked Frances.

'You seem to think I am doing this for my own personal profit,' he snapped. 'I can assure you that this is not the case. I only take the place of my absent brother, as is my duty. When residing at Craven Hill, which is not my property and never will be, I will also attend to its upkeep and pay a fair rent into my brother's estate for the good of his sons.'

'But why can they not live with their mother?' pleaded Frances. 'I can understand that when they were boisterous young children it would have been hard for her, but they are older now and must surely appreciate how they must behave in her company.'

'So much is true,' Antrobus admitted, 'but it was Edwin's wish that they should not reside with their mother, for reasons which must be obvious.'

Frances remained stubborn. 'It is not obvious to me. Kindly explain. When did he express this wish to you? It is not in the will.'

'He last spoke of it only a few months before he disappeared. The reasons, Miss Doughty, are very plain, and I am sorry that you are unable to appreciate them. There is bad blood in that family, and I am not talking of their humble beginnings, which anyone with ability and diligence might rise above. I am referring to Harriet's confused brain, which so far I am pleased to see has not revealed itself in her sons, but all the same, Edwin felt that any prolonged contact with their mother might provoke similar imaginings in the boys. Then there is her cousin, a hardened criminal who was forbidden the house. He used to lurk in the street nearby hoping to find a way in so he could beg or steal. He is currently in prison, I believe, but once he is released there will need to be a man in the house to protect the property.'

Frances saw that it was impossible to reason with her visitor and abandoned the attempt. 'I understand your concerns, but I do not know why you have come to see me.'

He paused to collect his thoughts. 'I cannot ask you to simply stop encouraging Harriett in her madness; your profession is your bread, I appreciate that. But you must be warned: you are being drawn into some very dark business. Miss Doughty, would you be prepared to change masters – to be employed by me instead? Only tell me what Wylie is paying you and I will undertake to pay you that sum with an additional ten per cent.'

Frances was about to respond with some asperity that her allegiance could not be bought or sold, or no client would ever trust her, but was prevented by a knock at the door. She had already told the housemaid that she was not to be disturbed when interviewing a client unless it was a matter of importance, so she waited with some interest for the door to be opened.

'Miss Doughty,' said the maid, awkwardly, 'I'm sorry to intrude, but it's a Mr Wylie, and he says it's most urgent.'

Lionel Antrobus rose abruptly to his feet. 'In that case I will take my leave at once. Please consider what I have said.'

'You will not leave, you will stay where you are,' said Frances, who could snap out an order when the occasion demanded.

He stared at her in astonishment.

Sarah, who had been sitting stitching a lace edging to a cap while listening carefully to the conversation, quietly put her sewing aside and flexed her fingers.

'You have not misheard, please sit down.' Frances turned to the maid. 'Please ask Mr Wylie to come in.'

'Have you planned this encounter?' demanded Antrobus.

'I have not. I was not expecting to see Mr Wylie today and am most curious as to what he might have to say, as indeed you must also be.' Antrobus gave a dark frown but made no move either to sit or leave.

Wylie arrived somewhat out of breath and was taken aback to see the other man. 'Antrobus? What are you doing here? Well, no matter, this is something you will want to hear. I have brought the most extraordinary news. The remains of Edwin Antrobus have been found, and this time there can be no doubt!'

Lionel Antrobus drew a deep breath and sat down. He was clearly shaken by the announcement and took some moments to calm himself. Frances realised that Wylie, who could see only what was good in the news he had brought, had been somewhat insensitive in the way he had informed Lionel Antrobus that his brother was dead, perhaps assuming that because of the other man's stony exterior there was no trace of fraternal feeling within.

'Please take a seat Mr Wylie and tell me what has happened.'

Sarah, seeing that there was not, after all, to be a fight, looked more at ease, but she did not take up her sewing and remained keenly observant.

Wylie sat, his face glowing with excitement. 'I received a message from Miss Pearce telling me that a policeman had come to the house. A very noisy policeman, I am afraid. She was able to persuade him that Mrs Antrobus could not be disturbed and spoke to him herself. He informed her that some remains have been found in a brickyard in Shepherd's Bush.'

'What kind of remains and why do they think it might be Edwin's?' asked Lionel Antrobus, more quietly than his usual manner, though his hard tone remained.

'A skeleton, and with it a gentleman's leather travelling bag of the very kind Mr Antrobus carried. The bag was empty, so we must presume a thief took the contents, but there was a small inner pocket he must have missed. It contained Mr Antrobus' business cards.'

Lionel Antrobus remained sceptical. 'That only suggests that the bag might be Edwin's; it does not necessarily identify the skeleton. However, it is progress of a sort.'

'Miss Pearce advised me that she interviewed her sister and conveyed to the policeman some information which might assist in finally establishing the identity of the remains.'

'What information?' demanded Antrobus.

'She did not elaborate, only begged me to come here and inform you of the development at once.'

'What did Harriett have to say? Did you see her?'

'Briefly, but she was too overcome to speak. Naturally there will be an inquest.'

Antrobus rose to his feet. 'Was this policeman from Paddington Green?'

'I believe so, an Inspector Sharrock.'

'Then I will proceed there at once and find out what he knows.'

'I went to see Inspector Sharrock at the police station early this morning,' Frances informed them, 'but he was not there, as he was engaged on an important matter, which might well have been the discovery of the remains.'

'It was,' confirmed Wylie. 'He told Miss Pearce that he had already been to the tobacconist's but Mr Antrobus was not at home, and he was on his way back to the station, so he might be there now.'

Frances rose to leave. 'Then we will all go. Sarah, please secure a cab.'

The two men looked at each other in the unfriendliest manner possible.

'And it is essential, sirs,' she told them sternly, 'that you put aside your differences and address yourselves to your common interest – discovering the truth.' Frances had found that speaking to grown men as if they were schoolboys tended to produce the best results, and this occasion was no different. Both sulkily agreed.

On her way out, Sarah cracked her knuckles, loudly.

There was a grim absence of conversation in the cab as it rumbled down Westbourne Grove. Frances reflected on the relief that would come with the dismissal of uncertainty, even by way of bad news, a relief that Mr Wylie undoubtedly felt but Lionel Antrobus clearly did not. If Edwin Antrobus could finally be laid to rest then a great many things would change – and not all of them to his brother's satisfaction.

Sharrock had only recently returned to the station together with Constable Mayberry, who was quickly dispatched to fetch chairs for the visitors, but Lionel Antrobus was too impatient to wait for chairs. 'Inspector,' he rapped, 'I am Edwin Antrobus' brother and I demand to see the remains at once, together with any other evidence you may have.'

'I can show you the bag that was found but the remains have been sent to the Westminster Hospital for Dr Bond the police surgeon to look at. And you sir?' he asked Wylie.

'I am Stephen Wylie, a business associate of Mr Edwin Antrobus and acting for his unhappy wife. Miss Doughty is employed by myself and Mrs Antrobus to discover the truth about her husband's disappearance.'

Sharrock grunted. 'I suppose both of you are content that the ladies join our discussion. Not that it will make much difference if you aren't, from my experience. Come this way.'

The discomfort in the Inspector's office as they were all seated was due to more than just the overcrowding. Only Sharrock seemed at his ease as he placed a leather bag, creased, scuffed and discoloured, on top of the untidy pile of paperwork on his desk. 'Can either of you gentlemen identify this as the property of Mr Edwin Antrobus?'

Lionel Antrobus examined the bag. 'My brother had purchased a new travelling bag not long before he disappeared. He was thinking of having it stamped with the name of the business but he had not yet done so. This could be the one, assuming it has lain neglected in contact with dirt or rubbish, but it could equally well have nothing to do with him.' He opened it and peered inside.

'It is very like the kind of bag he carried, but more than that I cannot say,' Wylie admitted. 'I was told there were some business cards?'

'Still where we found them,' said the Inspector.

Lionel Antrobus drew a card case from an inner pocket. There was a long silence as he opened it and studied the contents. At last he took a deep breath and nodded. 'This is Edwin's card case, engraved with his initials, and these are his cards.' He paused, then placed them on the desk. 'You will want these for the inquest, I suppose, but in time I would like them returned to me. Of course, this does not even identify the bag, let alone the remains.'

'True, which is why I would like to ask if you know of anything about Mr Antrobus which might serve to establish whether or not the skeleton is his,' said the Inspector.

'There was no clothing or jewellery found with it?'

'The remains were disturbed by the activities of workmen. Small items, like pieces of old clothing, buttons, shoe leather and so on, were all mixed in with the general rubble.'

'I suppose no one was seen disposing of a body there?' asked Frances.

'On the contrary, the remains were deposited in the brickyard by workmen who were demolishing some houses recently purchased by Mr Whiteley. The bricks and other rubbish were all loaded onto wagons and taken to Shepherd's Bush. It was only when a skull turned up in a cartload of material being tipped out that the carriers realised there was a body at all. We got some men to sift through the dust heap, and that was when we found the bag and other bones. No jewellery, but a lot of rags and bits of old shoes that could be anyone's. As far as we can see we have just the one skeleton.'

'Which might just as well be that of a female or any other man,' said Lionel Antrobus dismissively.

'We'll leave that to Dr Bond, shall we sir? The size of the skull does suggest a male, and it's more complete than what was found in the canal, so we have a better chance of making an identification. Can you think of anything that might distinguish the skeleton of your brother from that of another man?'

Antrobus gave the question some thought but after a while shook his head. 'Edwin and I did not spend a great deal of time in each other's company, even as children. If he suffered any accidents or illnesses which might have left their mark he did not mention them to me.'

'You don't know if he attended a dentist?'

'No. In fact he had an aversion to dentists and may have avoided them.'

Sharrock looked disappointed, so much so that Frances felt sure there was some aspect of the teeth that could prove vital in identifying the remains. 'Mrs Antrobus was also unable to help us with that, and we are visiting all the dentists in Bayswater.'

Mr Wylie gave a gentle cough. 'Er – I might be able to suggest something.' Lionel Antrobus gave him a look of withering contempt. 'Some years ago when Antrobus was in Bristol he complained to me of a bad toothache – he thought there was an abscess, and it was giving him some considerable pain. I said he should go to the dentist's at once and not wait until he returned home. He took my advice and later told me he was much better for it. I am afraid I don't know which dentist he went to.'

'Did he have the tooth out?' asked Sharrock.

'Yes, I am sure he did and the abscess drained.' Wylie clutched his hand to his jaw. 'He used to hold his hand to his face like this.'

'The left lower jaw, then?' said Sharrock intently. Frances recalled that the lower jaw of the man in the canal was missing, so that particular clue would not have assisted identification of those remains.

'I think so.' Wylie, now that his information was being questioned, began to look nervous. 'Or it could have been the right. I really can't be sure. But from the way he placed his hand, it was the lower one. A wisdom tooth, I think he said.'

Sharrock had the air of a man who had received some crucial information and was trying to appear nonchalant. He pulled a notebook and pencil from his pocket and made a quick jotting. 'I'll let you know when the inquest will open as both of you will be required to give evidence.'

'When do you expect the report from Dr Bond?' asked Frances.

Sharrock glanced up from his writing. 'I suppose you want to see confidential police records as usual, do you?'

She smiled. 'That would certainly make my work easier.'

'Yes, well, we're not here for your convenience,' he grumbled.

'I am sure,' interjected Wylie, 'that Miss Doughty can be afforded all courtesies and information that you would see fit to allow Mrs Antrobus.'

'Well, we'll see about that,' grunted Sharrock. 'As to the report, I hope to have it in the next two days in time for the inquest, and I really don't think you would like me to show that to Mrs Antrobus. Funny things bones, a man once said that the whole of a person's life is written on them. Don't see it myself.'

'Can you at least tell us the address of the building being demolished?' asked Frances.

'It was one of the set of houses in Queens Road being knocked down to make way for Mr Whiteley's new warehouse. The ones with all those great big hoardings blocking people's windows on either side. We're trying to trace the owners now but the properties have been empty for some time. Before that they were lodging houses. Now then, I'm a busy man and unless any of you intends to make an actual confession to murder I must ask you all to leave.'

There were a great many things Frances wanted to discuss with the Inspector, but the visitors decided to take the hint and depart.

Outside the police station, as everyone prepared to go their separate ways, Wylie turned to Lionel Antrobus but was unable to fully meet his gaze. 'I suggest to you, sir, that any legal action you are currently contemplating should be postponed until we know the outcome of the inquest.'

'I will take whatever action I think necessary, without any advice from you, sir,' replied Antrobus stiffly, but he looked thoughtful, nevertheless.

Frances hired a cab but decided that she and Sarah would go straight to see Harriett Antrobus, who she hoped would tell her more than the Inspector had done.

CHAPTER TEN

harlotte Pearce looked relieved to see Frances on her door-step, with the solid presence of Sarah beside her inspiring quiet confidence. 'Please do come in. I was about to send you a message, and I know Harriett wants to speak to you. Such an unpleasant man, that policeman. It was all I could do to stop him talking at the top of his voice. I could not allow him near Harriett.'

'We have come here straight from speaking to Inspector Sharrock at Paddington Green,' Frances advised her. 'I regret that we are not, therefore, prepared with suitable footwear, but perhaps if we were simply to remove our boots?'

Charlotte willingly agreed and conducted them to the back parlour where they found the occupant at her writing desk, a soft-nibbed pen gliding soundlessly over paper. She rose to greet them with a sad expression, and after a worried glance at Sarah, who looked like someone who could make a great deal of noise, was relieved to hear the burly woman greet her in a husky whisper.

'I suppose you have heard the news,' sighed Mrs Antrobus. 'It has been a shock to me, but I must gather myself and try to face it as best I may. I thought it would help if I prepared a statement of all I know that could be read out at the inquest, which of course I would prefer not to attend. I have done as much as I can to help the police, and we will see what transpires.'

'When I spoke to Inspector Sharrock just now I had the impression that there was information he was keeping close to his chest,' Frances told her. 'We were with Mr Wylie and Mr Lionel Antrobus, and I believe that he did not want to prompt their rec-ollection with anything you that had already divulged.'

Mrs Antrobus nodded, and there was a bleak weariness behind her eyes. 'I have been trying to recall anything that might help either to show that the bones are Edwin's or prove that they are not. Of course nothing would give me greater joy than to see Edwin return to me, but I know that only some terrible fate would have made him abandon his boys. I am prepared for the worst, I suppose I have been for some while now, but – and this may seem strange – it is the not knowing that is the greatest agony. I hope they will permit my statement to be read. I will have it witnessed by a solicitor. Not Mr Marsden, who appears to have deserted me for the enemy camp, presumably for financial reasons.'

'What have you been able to remember?'

'There were two things. Edwin once told me that in his youth he had suffered a bad fall and broken some bones in one leg, but it was so many years ago that I doubt the injury would be apparent now. He would not have mentioned it at all if it had not sometimes troubled him in wet weather. And he also once told me that he had had a tooth out while he was away from home on business, but when or where that occurred I really couldn't say. It seems little enough, and how many hundreds of other men have also fallen and had teeth out?'

'I was told that the remains were originally in a former lodging house on Queens Road and did not come to light until it was being demolished. Did your husband or anyone connected with him ever have reason to visit there?'

'I can think of no reason why Edwin, or indeed anyone I know, would have gone there.'

Frances nodded. 'There is one other matter that has recently been drawn to my attention, and I must apologise if mentioning it causes you pain, but I have been told that you have a cousin who has been in prison.'

Both sisters looked very unhappy and uncomfortable at the introduction of this new subject.

'Is that true?' asked Frances. 'If so, I really should have been told about it before.'

'It is true,' admitted Mrs Antrobus, her face registering a deep sorrow, 'and my unfortunate relative has been a stick that Lionel has used many a time to beat me with. Cannot a family have one such shame without it polluting the whole? But I don't see what this has to do with Edwin.'

'Perhaps nothing, but I must enquire after any individual who was known to your husband and who might conceivably have meant him harm.'

'Of course, yes, I understand.' She drooped so dejectedly that Charlotte rose and fetched her sister a cup of water from a much-swaddled carafe. The visitors were offered refreshment but declined.

Frances opened her notebook. 'What is your cousin's name?'

'Robert Barfield.'

'And his age?'

'He is the same age as me, thirty-eight.'

'I understand that he was in the habit of trying to get into this house to see you so he could borrow or steal money and that your husband forbade him to enter.'

'Yes, Edwin always tried to protect me from Robert. I cannot hide what my cousin has done. He has been in prison several times, always for theft. He is the son of my mother's sister, who died when he was about nine. His father found solace for his misery in intoxicating liquor and died of it a few months later. My parents gave Robert a home, but he was strange and wild, and I was afraid of him. Even then he was a petty thief, and I cannot count the times the police came to our door looking for him, but he was swift of foot and always managed to evade them. I recall one time when he hid by climbing out of a window and hanging there by his fingertips while the police searched the house. When he was twelve he ran away, and I have not seen him since, but I do sometimes read of him in the newspapers. It does not make happy reading. Over the years he became a highly accomplished burglar. Nothing was safe from him – he would climb up drainpipes and enter though bedroom or even attic windows to steal money and jewellery. He earned a vulgar nick-name. 'Spring-heeled Bob', the newspapers called him. It was a relief to me the first time he was caught, I thought that punishment would deter him from a life of crime, but prison did not teach him the error of his ways, and no sooner was he free than he was stealing again.'

'Is he in prison now?'

'It is very probable.' Her voice broke a little, and Charlotte gave a soft whimper of distress and came to sit by her.

'I am sorry to upset you, but —'

Mrs Antrobus made a weak gesture of acceptance. 'No, please, do go on. It is necessary to ask these questions, I know.'

'Where was your cousin at the time your husband disappeared?'

'In prison. That is why I knew he could have had nothing to do with it. He was tried at the Old Bailey for a robbery a year or so earlier and received a sentence of three years.'

'Has he been seen in this vicinity since his release?'

'If he has I have not been told of it.'

Frances could only feel sympathy for the dejected woman, suffering for the misdeeds of another, no part of which could be laid at her door. 'If he should try to call on you again, please let me know. If he is up to no good the police should be informed.'

'Of course. I am sorry for him, since he was not able to make something better of his life, but even though he is related to me by blood, I know it is best that I avoid his company.'

It was not a promising line of enquiry but Frances recorded the details in her notebook. Barfield, like Dromgoole, while not the actual culprit, might yet have some information that could prove useful. 'I think it would be wise to await the outcome of the inquest before I take any further action.'

'Yes, I agree, I would not have you undertake unnecessary work. Of course, even if the bones are shown to be Edwin's, the cause of his death could well remain a mystery.'

This was very true, and Frances could only hope that she would not be asked to look into it.

'How long does it take for a body to rot down to dry bones?' asked Sarah, carving slices off a piece of ham for their supper, while Frances endangered her appetite by studying the subject of decomposition in a medical book.

'That is a hard question and one with no simple answer. Bodies may be buried or left in the open or lie in water, the weather may be hot or cold and the person may be fat or thin, young or old. Then there is the action of insects and vermin. There are so many things to consider. If the remains were simply gathered up with other debris during demolition then carried to the brickyard and tipped onto the ground, that disturbance has destroyed so much that is valuable. We cannot know how much of the other material belongs to it, neither do we know whether the man died in Queens Road or somewhere else.'

Sarah brought bread and pickles to the table. 'When did those big hoardings go up? There's been enough about it in the newspapers.'

Frances laid the book aside. 'It was the autumn of last year. The houses had been standing empty for a while beforehand. Then the work started and has been stopping and starting again for months during all the disputes with the vestry.'

'I bet they weren't empty all that time,' said Sarah, darkly. 'Thieves' dens most like. Somewhere quiet and private to meet and divide up the swag. They might have quarrelled and then one of them got stabbed and left to rot.' She lifted the muslin draping a plate to inspect the remains of yesterday's tea party, of which there was very little since Cornelius had insisted that Charlotte be provided with a parcel of cake to take home.

'That would explain why we have another body and no one else reported as missing,' suggested Frances. 'I think Mrs Antrobus may be disappointed once more. But that does lead me to another thought. Even though her disreputable cousin was in prison at the time of Mr Antrobus' disappearance, he could have had associates who were freed before him. If he wanted to revenge himself against the man who had forbidden him the house, he might have told his friends that Mr Antrobus carried large sums of money or other valuables on his person and so encouraged them to rob and murder him.'

'How can you find out who these friends are?' asked Sarah reasonably.

'If information exists then it can be found. It's just a matter of knowing where to look and who to ask. And in this instance, I know just who to ask.' Despite her earlier resolve to take no action pending the result of the inquest, Frances' curiosity got the better of her, and once supper was done she wrote a letter.

While the case of the missing Mr Antrobus had recently occupied most of Frances' time she could not ignore other clients or turn away new ones. There was one exception. A lady of great wealth, but little judgement, had written to plead with her to do all she could to prove the innocence of a prisoner who was shortly due to expiate his crimes on the scaffold. The lady offered a sum of money so substantial that it amounted to a bribe and hinted that if Frances was to admit that she had made a number of errors in her statements to the police, all might still be well. Frances, well aware that she might be making an enemy by so doing, wrote to decline the commission.

One new client for whom she had made an appointment was Mr Jonathan Eckley, headmaster of the Bayswater School for the Deaf, the very establishment that Dr Goodwin was in the process of suing. Frances had not discussed the legal wrangle with Dr Goodwin as it had no relevance to her search for Edwin Antrobus, but she was naturally curious about the unusual conflict.

Mr Eckley was a slender gentleman of about forty dressed in the dark attire most suitable to his profession, with gold-rimmed spectacles sitting on a sharp nose. He wore a handsome silver watch on a pretty chain that he seemed very proud of, as he liked to consult it at every opportunity, and Frances wondered if it was a treasured heirloom or a gift from a grateful parent. His manner, while formal and precise, was cordial, and when he spoke he was in the habit of making very large movements with his lips as if to emphasise every word.

As Frances took her seat, he closed the watch with a brisk snap and dropped it in his pocket. His card was on the table before her and he leaned forward and pushed it closer with his fingertips, to ensure that she missed not one word printed thereon. 'It is very important, Miss Doughty,' he began, in a voice more suitable to a public meeting than a parlour, 'that I communicate to you a full appreciation of the expertise I bring to my profession, and then you may judge the position in which I find myself.'

Frances thanked him and studied the card, which supplied no more material than was on the sign outside the school. Nevertheless she left it where she might easily refer to it.

'It has been my pleasure, indeed my honour,' he went on, 'to be engaged in the instruction of the deaf for some years. I studied with the Society for Training Teachers of the Deaf, and while I am not a surgeon, and have only a layman's knowledge of the structure of the ear, I believe that I am as much a specialist in my field as any doctor in his.'

Frances felt sure that 'any doctor' was a reference to Dr Goodwin, but she let that pass.

'You will notice, Miss Doughty,' he said, reaching out and tapping the card with an insistent fingertip, 'that the school is referred to as a school for the deaf and not as it was previously called, a school for the deaf and dumb. That is because,' he paused for emphasis, 'we undertake to teach the children to speak.'

Frances smiled and nodded. 'Oh, yes, the signs, I have some familiarity with those.'

'No, I do not refer to the signs,' he said with a hard frown. 'We use the German system. The children learn to read lips and articulate words. Only that system can enable the deaf to become full members of society. When I was appointed headmaster two years ago, the school was offering a combined system, both the oral method and signs, as it was then believed that the two could be used together with advantage. We employed deaf teachers to transmit the signs and additional classes in lip reading and articulation were given by hearing teachers. Dr Goodwin was then a consultant, and his son was working at the school as a general servant and caretaker. The boy is quite deaf and, I believe, not of the highest intelligence. He was, however, proficient in signs and aspired to become an assistant to the teaching staff.'

'But clearly there have been changes. What brought this about?'

'Progress,' he exclaimed proudly. 'There must always be progress. We must be prepared, even though it pains us, to throw out the old methods that have served us well and adopt new ones that will serve us better. And I am not talking of some whim of fashion but the results of years of dedicated work by knowledgeable men.' He tapped the card again. 'Last September matters were finally resolved by a conference which took place in Milan. Many learned papers were presented which showed not only that the German method was by far the best one but that all the difficulties previously associated with it were due to a single cause, the teaching of signs at the same time. I attended that conference and my course became very clear. I presented my case to the school governors and they were in complete agreement. Henceforth the teaching of signs was banned and we now educate the children solely on the "pure oral" system as it is called. Dr Goodwin, who has always been a great advocate of signs, made strong objections, but he was overruled. He resigned as consultant, although if the truth be known, had he remained he would have been told that his advice was no longer required. His son continued in his usual capacity – he knew his work and could undertake it without speech – but under strict instructions that he was no longer to communicate with the children by the use of signs.'

Frances could predict where the conversation was going. 'I assume he did not comply?'

'That is correct. I was obliged to dismiss him. I was sorry to do it, but it was necessary. He is a pleasant boy and was a great favourite with the pupils, but for their own good, he was asked to leave. He was not the only one, as you might imagine. Many of the teachers, in particular those who were deaf, were only able to teach signs, and they too were dismissed and replaced by hearing teachers trained in the German method.'

Frances thought that it was hard that a school for the education of the deaf should have treated its deaf teachers in such a way, but decided not to comment. 'Dr Goodwin is currently suing the school – is this because of his son?'

'Yes, but it goes far deeper than that. He still adheres to the old methods and believes that by airing the matter in court he will achieve publicity for his point of view.'

Frances could see that she was in danger of being made an instrument of an acrimonious professional dispute, something for which she had little inclination. 'This is all very interesting but I cannot see how you wish to employ my services.'

'It has come to my notice,' announced Eckley, 'although I do not have the proof I need, that Mr Isaac Goodwin has been meeting privately with some of the pupils of the school and giving them instruction in signs. This may even include recently arrived pupils who have only ever been taught by the German method. Moreover I believe he is encouraged in this by Dr Goodwin. Very recently I saw one of the younger boys actually conversing with the older ones using signs when they thought I was not looking! This undermines all my teaching.' He looked very hurt, and Frances almost felt sorry for him.

'I have ordered them to stop. I said it makes them look like monkeys, but they just seemed to find that amusing and continued to defy me. Ultimately I was obliged to make them stop by tying their hands together. Sometimes one must be cruel to be kind.'

Frances felt less sympathetic. 'What would you like me to do?'

'I need proof – proof that these damaging classes are taking place, proof that it is Mr Isaac Goodwin conducting them, the place he is using and that Dr Goodwin is complicit. The children are not going to Dr Goodwin's house for classes; that I have been able to establish. Neither are they taking place at the homes of any of the children. Their parents are naturally anxious that their children should learn to speak and would never permit such a thing. It is a secretive hole in the corner affair, and my pupils refuse to admit that it is even happening.'

'Do you intend to take any legal action?' asked Frances, 'because I do not believe that there is a crime being committed.'

Eckley sighed. 'I have no wish to punish anyone; I am only thinking of the good of the children. All I want is to put a stop to a no doubt well-meaning activity that is harming their education. Once I have the information I require I will take out an injunction requiring Mr Isaac Goodwin to desist from teaching. I believe I have every right to do so. He is quite unqualified to teach the deaf whereas I' – he tapped the card again – 'have undertaken years of study. I am sure my point of view will prevail.'

'Do you believe that the injunction, if granted, would strengthen your defence against Dr Goodwin's action?'

'Indubitably.' The speed of his response confirmed what Frances had suspected, that this effect had been uppermost in his thoughts.

Frances was in two minds about how to proceed. She had no expertise with which to judge the argument either for or against the two methods of teaching, and it was not in any case her business to do so but to carry out the wishes of her client. Eckley was probably unaware that she had already had an amicable meeting with Dr Goodwin, and she wondered if there was a less confrontational way of proceeding.

'Supposing,' she ventured, 'I was able to obtain for you written confirmation that these classes have been taking place together with a promise that they will be discontinued. Would that serve your purpose?'

Eckley considered the proposition. 'I suppose it would,' he said reluctantly. 'I have not approached Dr Goodwin myself as I have been advised I must not do so in view of the pending action.'

'It is possible that an injunction might be seen by Dr Goodwin's representatives as unwarranted interference, even harassment, and actually harm your case.' She had no idea if this was so, but it was an argument that might succeed.

He gave the question some thought. 'Perhaps, if you were to act as intermediary, a gentle appeal from a female might prove more persuasive than a demand from a man of law.'

Frances was not sure whether this was a compliment; however, her concerns were allayed and she agreed to act for Mr Eckley. She was able without difficulty to secure an appointment to see Dr Goodwin later the same day.

CHAPTER ELEVEN

Dr Goodwin seemed less happy than at their first meeting and Frances could not tell whether some circumstance unknown to her had caused this or whether it was simply the fact that she had called on him for a second interview. Her visits did sometimes have that effect. He welcomed her wearily but politely and spent a few moments standing at his desk ordering his papers as if that would also order his mind.

Frances waited for a brief while, then decided to interrupt his concentration. 'Dr Goodwin, I am here not on behalf of Mrs Antrobus but Mr Eckley.'

'Dear me, what can he want?' exclaimed Goodwin, his head jerking up in surprise. 'I can well understand his not calling here himself. He does not have the stomach to face me with his arguments.'

'He has informed me that your son was dismissed from his employment at the school because he was instructed not to communicate with the pupils using signs and disobeyed the instruction. Is that the case?'

Goodwin sank back into his chair. 'That is a harsh way to put it, but I suppose so, yes. And it is a terrible state of things, a thoroughly misguided proceeding. Eckley denigrates the signs as nothing more than pantomime; well, little does he know it but he is presiding at a charade. The school, supposedly an exponent of the pernicious "pure oral" system, is actually a hotbed of sign language, since that is the best and most convenient way for the children to converse. I have witnessed these German system classes and,' an expression of great satisfaction lit up his face, 'when the teacher's back is turned the children sign to ask each other what was said and those who are best at lip-reading pass it on.' He chuckled at the thought. 'Now don't mistake me, I have nothing against the practice of lip-reading and encourage the children to acquire it, but signs,' he beat a hand upon the desk for emphasis, 'should be their principal means of learning.'

'I understand that your son's dismissal is the subject of your action against the school.'

'It is. I suppose Eckley has told you that I have taken the proceedings mainly in order to voice my opinions of his methods in court. In that, at least, I do admit that he is correct. Isaac has no need to return to work for the school. He is now employed as my assistant and does very well. Has Eckley engaged you to plead with me to abandon my action? If so, you must disappoint him.'

'It is another matter. Mr Eckley believes that your son is conducting private classes in signs for the pupils of his school.'

Dr Goodwin laughed. 'Does he now? Well if Isaac is doing so, and I don't know that he is, I can only applaud his endeavour.'

'As you may imagine,' Frances went on, 'Mr Eckley is very displeased and would like the classes to stop. In fact he was intending to obtain an injunction to require that they stop. I have managed to persuade him that he might do just as well with a written assurance.'

'Which would of course be ammunition in his defence against my case,' observed Goodwin with a frown. 'Well, if the man wants a fight he shall have one, but I will not allow him to attack me through my son. Really, he can have no shame.'

'I think it would be best for everyone if this particular dispute could be settled as quickly and amicably as possible,' said Frances in her best soothing tone. 'Would you be so kind as to ask your son if he is indeed holding these classes. If he can assure me that he is not, then I will so inform Mr Eckley and hopefully the matter will end there.'

Goodwin gave this suggestion some thought then rose and rang for the maid. 'I will ask him, as you request, but I will neither encourage nor discourage him from making any statement. It is for him to decide.'

The maid was sent to fetch Isaac Goodwin, who appeared in a few minutes and stood in the doorway looking apprehensive. Eckley had suggested to Frances that Isaac was deficient in intelligence, although he had not elaborated on his grounds for that opinion. Frances, aware that Eckley might have had some prejudice in the matter and knowing that a physical defect could sometimes be mistaken for one of the mind, would have liked to be able to judge for herself. Isaac was eighteen, and she remembered, with a sudden catch of emotion, her own dear late brother at that age; while remaining always the dutiful and respectful son, he had thought very much as a man and not a child and stood tall with the confident expectation of the duties and privileges that his majority would bring. Isaac had none of that confidence, and there was something child-like in the way he looked at his father, searching anxiously for support and guidance.

Goodwin beckoned Isaac to come forward and gestured to a seat. Isaac looked warily at Frances and sat clutching his hands tightly together in his lap. As signs were his preferred means of communication it was as though he was deliberately rendering himself mute. Frances wondered if he had already surmised that she knew about his secret classes.

When Dr Goodwin made a series of signs, however, Isaac's demeanour brightened and he quickly signed back. A lively dialogue ensued. Frances had hoped that her recent study would enable her to follow the conversation but the rapidity defeated her. She was able to identify a sign which she thought referred to children, and a flashing sequence of fingerspelling that ended with the distinctive 'y' and was probably the name 'Eckley', but little more.

At length Goodwin nodded. 'Isaac says that he has been meeting and conversing with some of the boys at the school. He says they are his friends. Naturally he uses signs, as that is the only way he may speak to them. He denies that he has been teaching them in any formal sense. He wants to continue seeing them and does not wish to sign a document agreeing not to, as it is a promise he would not keep.'

'Well that is very clear,' said Frances, 'and I will see Mr Eckley and let him know that he has no grounds for any legal action.'

'Please do.' Dr Goodwin had a bitter edge to his voice. He looked fondly down at his son and placed an encouraging hand on the boy's shoulder. 'I have nothing at all to say to him.'

Dr Goodwin's home was not far from the school, and had Frances been a more trusting person, she might have gone there directly to report to Mr Eckley and so end her enquiries, but she did not.

In the past year she had learned to trust no one and realised that there was a sense in which everyone told lies or concealed the truth, although not necessarily for any sinister reason. Since the conversation between Dr Goodwin and his son had taken place in a language she was largely unable to understand, and there were unresolved issues between the doctor and the headmaster which might have coloured the situation, she decided to take the precaution of checking the facts for herself. This would involve having Isaac followed to see what he was actually doing, which was, she knew, a somewhat unsavoury proceeding. She comforted herself with the thought that in the absence of a signed statement Mr Eckley was unlikely to believe Dr Goodwin's verbal assurance, and if she was able to provide him with ocular evidence she might yet be able to prevent any unwarranted legal action.

Frances took herself to Westbourne Grove, where Sarah's young relative Tom Smith had been operating his messenger and delivery business from a small attic room high above the watchmaker's shop of old Mr Beccles. Before reaching Tom's eyrie, the narrow stairs brought visitors to the office and accommodation of The Bayswater Display and Advertising Co. Ltd, which was run by two gentlemen who were generally known as Chas and Barstie. When Frances had first met them they were at a low ebb in their fortunes, deeply in debt and doing their best to avoid a multitude of angry creditors. Their most dangerous enemy was a young man known only as the Filleter, an unscrupulous individual employed by moneylenders to terrify debtors into meeting their obligations.

Chas and Barstie's exhaustive knowledge of the business world had, however, enabled them to get a foothold back into commerce, and after a few faltering attempts, they had been resoundingly rescued by the great flurry of opportunity that had resulted from the calling of a surprise general election in the spring of 1880. They had been growing in affluence ever since and even made steps towards respectability by providing services to the Paddington police in investigating cases of company fraud, a subject in which they had considerable expertise. Barstie, who had been ardently pursuing the hand in marriage of a lady of good family, was especially anxious to appear respectable, and the pair had recently made another important step in that direction.

Mr Beccles had decided to retire from business and join his son and his family in Australia, and Chas and Barstie had taken the lease of the ground floor shop, which was being handsomely refitted and a new sign painted. The rear of the premises was being converted into a neat bachelor apartment for the two proprietors. Business was still actively carried on in their old room, but once the new office opened, the upper floors would be let, and Tom had been promised part of the space for his sole use.

Although Frances' main business was with Tom, she decided to call on Chas and Barstie in case they had anything to impart on the Antrobus businesses, and avoiding the worst of plaster, paint and dust, she rapped smartly on their office door. The room was never vacant, since some form of commerce was being carried out around the clock, and until their new residence was completed, also served as accommodation.

'Come in!' came Chas' unmistakably loud and exuberant voice. Frances entered and, to her astonishment, saw the very last individual she might have expected to find there. Chas was leaning back in his chair, his feet propped on the desk which was littered with greasy paper wrappings and half-eaten buns. Facing him was his partner, Barstie, his portion of the desk clear of all material, even the coins he so loved to count. He was looking more solemn than usual, which was understandable because in the third chair slouched the Filleter. Thin as a spider, with long unkempt black hair and an evil expression, his name came from the sharp knife he carried and the knowledge that he was always willing to use it. When Frances had first encountered him he had carried the smell of things long rotted and worse, and while there was no longer a stink that would make even a gravedigger recoil, he still exuded a repellent sourness. He shifted uncomfortably in stained black clothing that seemed only to be held together by sweat and dirt, and the things that crawled in and on it. Chas and Barstie had formerly been so petrified of him that the mere mention of his name would send them running hotfoot as far from Bayswater as they could go. With the improvement in their fortunes, however, differences had been temporarily settled and an uneasy truce had been the result. That much had been a relief to Frances, but to see the three of them actually in company could not, she was sure, be a good thing.

The Filleter said nothing to Frances; he merely scowled, sucked on his discoloured teeth and turned his head away.

Chas had been just about to stuff a piece of cheese into his mouth, but as soon as he saw Frances he leaped to his feet, dropped the cheese onto the desk and wiped his hands on his coat. 'Miss Doughty! What a pleasure! As you see,' he gestured towards the Filleter, 'we have a new business associate – I am happy to say that all our previous troubles are forgotten. Is that not the case Mr — er — ?'

With one swift, easy movement, the Filleter rose to his feet and walked out without a word or a backward glance.

Barstie was visibly relieved but Chas simply shrugged, his good humour unabated. 'A busy fellow, and now we know him better, a useful ally.'

Frances declined to comment, but she felt sure that her face revealed her opinions. If the partners were actually employing this man to collect debts for them the result could only be trouble, but nothing she could say would deter them.

She quickly explained to Chas and Barstie the nature of her current enquiry saying that she would be interested to know of any rumours in the business world that could throw light on Edwin Antrobus' disappearance. She then climbed the stairs to the attic office of Tom Smith's thriving agency.

Tom, who could hardly be thirteen yet, had once been the delivery boy for the Doughty chemist's, but he had shown an early talent both for making extra money and scrounging food so as to live off almost nothing. After the chemist's business was sold Tom had worked for Mr Jacobs, the new owner, but recently he had appointed one of his army of 'men' in his place, in order to devote all his attention to his multiple enterprises. The idea that Mr Jacobs might have thought it his prerogative to make that arrangement had not seemed to occur to Tom, and since the substitution of another boy equally keen and hardworking had been satisfactory to all concerned, the chemist had merely looked surprised and raised no objections.

The new delivery boy was also detailed to inform Tom whenever the chemist's niece, the dainty Pearl Montague, was about to pay a visit so Tom could arrange to be in the vicinity. The young lady was, unbeknown to her or any member of her family, Tom's future bride, and it wanted only for him to make a great fortune and her to attain the age of sixteen for that destiny to be achieved. Frances had seen Miss Montague just once and found her to be a little miracle of golden curls and pink frills, resembling something made of sugar paste. Tom had never so much as spoken to her, but her image, which to him was the pinnacle of female perfection, was constantly before his eyes.

Frances could not help but reflect on how both Tom and Barstie were spurred on in their ambitions by the prospect of marriage, while her work was simply inspired by the need for a home, clothing and nourishment. It was not so very long since Chas had intimated that once he had made enough money to marry then Frances, whose financial acumen he admired, might receive a proposal, but she had never taken this seriously. As Chas' fortunes had grown so her value to him as a helpmeet had declined, and she believed that he was currently taking an interest in a foreign lady with a large estate. Frances knew that her hand would never be sought by a man wanting a rich wife or a pretty wife, or even a loving wife, but only a useful wife. Being useful to one's husband was an essential part of marriage, but was she expecting too much to want to be loved as well?

As she reached Tom's door it flew open and two boys hurried out as if on missions of grave urgency. Pausing only to make a respectful little bow in her direction, they pounded down the stairs. Since neither of them was carrying a message or parcel, she wondered if they were engaged in following suspicious characters or looking for roaming animals. During the last year Frances had quite inadvertently established a reputation in Bayswater as a finder of missing pets, whether four-legged or winged, and she had been grateful to turn over that entire area of her business to Tom, who was able to be in all places at once.

Tom's office had everything that was needful for the young businessman; a broken desk with one leg supported by a half brick, a chair bound about with string, a pile of old wrapping papers torn into squares and some pencil stubs for the composition of messages, a money box with a stout key, a tea kettle and a basket of bread. In winter there would be a roaring fire fed with any combustible rubbish that could be found, and the boys would come here for a warm and some tea between errands. Some of the refreshments they enjoyed often looked suspiciously like the leftovers from her table.

That morning Tom was doing something very unusual, for him at least: he was reading a book. Tom had never been a great reader, he had learned his letters at a parish school and could write well enough for messages. He had later refined his skills for business purposes but had never aspired to reading for pleasure. Frances saw that he was deep in a volume of *Oliver Twist*, which was costing him some physical as well as mental effort, judging by the contortions of his face and the movements of his lips. He had been raking his hands through his hair, which stood up in spikes as if horrified by the unfolding story. Nevertheless he was pursuing the book by sheer dogged determination, as he did everything.

When Frances entered he put the book down and wiped his sleeve across his forehead with a smile. 'You ever read this, Miss Doughty? The Parish Boy's Progress, it says, an' I'll be very sorry if Oliver don't make good at the end.'

'I have, it is a very salutary story,' said Frances.

'I like the Dodger, but that Bill Sykes is a bad'un through and through, an' if you ask me, Nancy ain't no better'n she oughter be.'

'So why have you suddenly taken up literature, Tom?'

'Mr Chas and Mr Barstie said I need to learn the Queen's Hinglish, and I was told that Mr Dickens wrote the best Queen's Hinglish there ever was. An' if I do learn it then they might take me into partnership when I'm old enough.'

'That's quite an ambition,' smiled Frances, 'but I have every confidence you will succeed.'

'Yeh, but I'd rather buy 'em out and be my own master.' He grinned. 'So what's the job, then?'

Frances explained that she wanted to discover whether Isaac Goodwin was actually teaching sign language to the schoolboys or just meeting his friends. 'Could you also find out for me about the properties in Queens Road, the ones being demolished?' she asked. 'Have they really been quite empty since they were sold, or were they frequented by thieves and beggars?'

'Thieves, beggars an' all the rubbish of the streets,' said Tom, cheerfully, 'an' anyone who wanted to do somethin' secret. They all like empty houses. Don't know about them in Queens Road, though, Mr Whiteley's 'ad 'em locked up tighter 'n a drum since he bought 'em.'

'Some bones have been found there – those of a man, together with Mr Edwin Antrobus' travelling bag. The bones might be his or those of a thief who robbed him. Can you suggest whose they might be?'

Tom shrugged. 'Name any man out of a thousand. Beggars an' tramps an' that sort, they drop dead every day or kill each other an' no one misses 'em. But I'll see what I can find out.'

'I always thought Bayswater was such a respectable place,' sighed Frances.

'It's like the Queen's own castle compared with Stepney,' said Tom. 'Murderers jus' use knives 'n poison round 'ere.'

Frances decided not to ask for further elaboration.

That evening a message arrived for Sarah to advise that her diligent enquiries had finally located Lizzie, the parlourmaid who had been in service at the Antrobus home at the time of its master's disappearance. Sarah decided to go and see her the next morning. When she had an object in her sights she was an alarming prospect, and Frances knew that if there was anything to be learned, her assistant would discover it.

CHAPTER TWELVE

Next morning the inquest on the skeletal remains found in the brickyard at Shepherd's Bush opened at Providence Hall, Paddington, under the careful eye of coroner Dr George Danford Thomas, the youthful successor of Dr William Hardwicke who had died very suddenly the previous April. Frances had grown to respect Dr Hardwicke, who was wise and fair and knew how to be gentle with a nervous witness. She hoped the new man would fill his shoes with credit.

The jurymen were inspecting the items laid out on the exhibits table: a box of bones, the leather travelling bag and business cards, and other assorted fragments of clothing that might or might not have been associated with the deceased. There was also, Frances noticed, a coal sack, printed with the name of 'Geo Bates', a local supplier. It was morning, and the little hall was illuminated by sunlight flooding in through the windows, but even in the absence of gas the hall was uncomfortably warm and getting warmer by the minute. The odour of the material on the table, which resembled the contents of a refuse bin, was very apparent, and Frances hoped the proceedings would not last long.

Mr Wylie and Charlotte Pearce, who was heavily veiled, though easily distinguishable to anyone who knew her by her height and clothing, arrived together accompanied by their new solicitor Mr Rawsthorne, who had been appointed to watch the case in view of what was regarded as their betrayal by Mr Marsden. They greeted Frances and all expressed the hope that the day's proceedings would result in important progress.

Mr Marsden, his face fixed in a permanent sneer, arrived in company with Lionel Antrobus. The latter gentleman, though serious as ever, took a moment from conversation with his solicitor to favour Frances with a sharp nod, and Marsden, seeing the action, made a whispered comment to his client which was undoubtedly not to her credit.

Inspector Sharrock had been obliged to take time from his busy day to attend the inquest, a circumstance that clearly did not please him, since he fidgeted constantly and obviously wanted to be somewhere else. The press was also there in force since the public always enjoyed stories that involved a skeleton, and there was the usual throng of the idle and curious.

Mr Luckhurst, walking with a bravely energetic limp, arrived unaccompanied, greeted Frances with as much of a smile as was appropriate under the circumstances and invited her to sit beside him, which she did.

Mr Gillan of the *Chronicle* came late, hurrying from another assignment, and, thwarted by Mr Luckhurst from finding a seat next to Frances, looked disappointed and lurked as near to her as he could, with a suspicious lean to his posture that suggested he was trying to eavesdrop.

'I know this can hardly be called a social occasion,' Luckhurst confided, 'but even so, when in company one always looks for some intelligent conversation, and if it comes from a handsome young lady then so much the better.' Frances was about to commiserate with him for having to manage with her society and not the hoped for beauty, when Dr Thomas announced the opening of the proceedings, and the jurymen took their places.

The coroner began by advising the jury that the nature of the remains meant that there was more than the usual difficulty in establishing the identity of the deceased. They would hear a number of witnesses on that point and must pay them close attention and consider what they said very carefully before making a decision.

The newspapermen awaited the evidence with rapt expectation and sharpened pencils.

The first witness to be called was a waggoner who testified to discovering the bones amongst the builder's debris in the brickyard, having seen them partially spilling out of the coal sack. The bones and the sack were, he was sure, the same items currently displayed on the evidence table, and he also thought the pieces of cloth and leather were those he had seen at the site. He was followed by the foreman of the demolition men who said that he often saw animal bones, sacks and pieces of old clothing in houses being demolished and never thought anything of it. He had seen coal sacks in the cellars of the Queens Road houses before work had begun. Some of them had smelled bad, and he had assumed they held dead dogs or rubbish. He was as sure as it was possible to be that everything was put on the wagon with the rest of the rubble. It was not a part of his men's duties to sift through rubbish.

Inspector Sharrock testified to supervising the team of policemen who had searched through the heap of rubble in the brickyard and extracted the remains, which he had taken charge of and passed to Dr Bond of the Westminster Hospital.

The coroner then notified the jury that the owners and landladies of the lodging houses had yet to be traced and called Dr Bond to give evidence.

Dr Bond, lecturer on forensic medicine and assistant surgeon at the Westminster Hospital, was a dignified and gentlemanly looking man of about forty, with a luxuriant and firmly pointed moustache. He stated that he had received from Inspector Sharrock a number of bones, together with a coal sack and some fragments of rotted clothing, all of which he had been told had been extracted from the same heap on the Shepherd's Bush brickfield. 'Apart from a few very small bones, which I believe to be those of rats, all the remains were human. When I laid them out in their correct positions I saw that I had most of the larger bones of a skeleton, and there were no duplicates. In other words there was no evidence that I was dealing with more than one skeleton.

The size of the bones was compatible with them all belonging to the same individual. The deceased was undoubtedly male, about five feet six to eight inches in height and aged between thirty-five and forty-five. There was no evidence of any disease. There was a healed fracture of the right tibia.'

'How long before death would you say this injury occurred?' asked Dr Thomas.

'I am afraid the condition of the remains makes that very hard to determine. I would not at this stage wish to provide an estimate. I have, however, received some more bone fragments from the police this morning, which, if they are part of the same skeleton, could enable me to do so.'

'After the injury was healed, would the man have continued to suffer pain?'

'That is possible. Even a healed fracture may cause pain many years later, especially in inclement weather.'

'What can you tell the court about your examination of the teeth?'

'The dentition was poor, and many of the teeth were decayed. This man only rarely attended a dentist. On the left side of the lower jaw there were signs that there had once been an abscess that had necessitated removal of the wisdom tooth. The upper wisdom teeth had been extracted many years previously, but I believe the lower left was operated on more recently. The lower right was very much decayed but still in place. There were a number of other teeth missing. These might have been old extractions or, more likely, simply worked loose during the lifetime of the deceased.'

Mr Luckhurst, who had been listening to the evidence with great concentration, suddenly looked very thoughtful. Frances looked at him quizzically, but he said nothing, only took a notebook and pencil from his pocket and began to write.

'Were you able to arrive at a cause of death?' asked the coroner.

'Not conclusively,' said Dr Bond, 'but there was damage to the vertebrae that suggested to me that the deceased may have suffered a broken neck. Whether that was due to accident or a deliberate injury it is impossible to determine, but some considerable force was involved.'

'What kind of accident or injury could have produced this?'

'A fall down a flight of hard steps is one possible cause, or external violence with a strong twisting of the neck.'

'When do you believe death took place?'

'If the body was not buried, and I see no evidence that it has ever been, it would have been exposed to the action of the elements, together with insects and vermin, which would have broken down the tissues more rapidly than if it had been sealed in a coffin. The bones were dry; there was no flesh or connective tissue. This person has been dead for a minimum of two years and more likely longer.'

'Did you find anything that was incompatible with the remains being those of Edwin Antrobus?'

'No, neither did I find incontrovertible proof that they are.'

'Did you draw any conclusions from examining the coal sack and other debris?'

'The clothing fabric I saw was much rotted, probably from contact with the fluids of decomposition. It was not possible to determine if the fragments had any connection with the remains. The fragments were incomplete – I could not account for all of a suit of clothing or gentleman's linen. I think that the staining on the outer surface of the leather bag was from contact with body fluids. The interior of the coal sack was dirty, as one might expect. I do not believe that a fresh human body was ever placed in the sack. The bones were soiled from contact with the inner surface of the sack, and would have been placed in it after the body was reduced to a skeleton.'

As Dr Bond resumed his seat, Frances whispered to Mr Luckhurst, 'I can see you noticed something that interested you.'

'Surprised me,' he said, 'but I will listen to what the other witnesses have to say before I decide what to do.'

There was a short pause for the note-takers to complete their work. The next witness was Mr Rawsthorne, who said that he was acting on behalf of Mrs Harriett Antrobus, who was too unwell to come to court but had signed a statement in his presence, which he would like to read. Dr Thomas assented and Rawsthorne proceeded to read aloud:

> I, Harriett Antrobus, wife of Edwin Antrobus, wish to attest the following in the hope that it will assist the coroner's jury in their deliberations on the remains recently discovered together with my husband's travelling bag. My husband once told me that as a young man he suffered an accident in which he broke some bones. The injury was to a leg, and although it healed it pained him from time to time. He did not, as far as I know, ever visit a dentist in London, but he did once inform me that while absent from home on business he was obliged to have a tooth extracted. I regret that I cannot recall the date of this occurrence or which city he was visiting.

There were no questions for Mr Rawsthorne, who resumed his seat and patted Miss Pearce's hand in a kindly fashion.

Mr Wylie was the next witness and recounted the same story he had told at the police station. However, he said that on further reflection he had become quite certain that the tooth his associate had had extracted was a wisdom tooth from the left lower jaw. He also recalled seeing his friend experience some pain on walking and when he had asked about it Antrobus had simply said it was an old injury that occasionally troubled him.

As Wylie resumed his place, Mr Luckhurst, with an intensely serious expression, rose to his feet and went to speak to the coroner's officer. There was a brief conversation and then Luckhurst wrote in his notebook, tore out the page, handed the paper to the officer and limped back to his seat. Frances glanced at him, and Mr Gillan leaned closer, but Luckhurst simply allowed a flicker of the eyebrows and said nothing.

Lionel Antrobus was called next. Asked if he could corroborate the evidence concerning his brother's leg injury he said he could not. If his brother had broken any bones he was unaware of it.

'A broken leg is not a trivial injury,' observed Dr Thomas. 'The deceased could have been incapacitated for some time. Family and business associates would not have been unaware of it.' The jurymen nodded in agreement.

'I agree,' said Lionel Antrobus. 'For that reason I do not believe the remains can be those of my brother.'

He also had no recollection of being told about a tooth extraction, although he was obliged to admit that he and his brother had not been close. Before Edwin's entry into the tobacco trade they had met only infrequently, and afterwards most of their conversation had been on business matters.

As Lionel Antrobus returned to his seat with a grim expression, the coroner was in the process of announcing that there were no further witnesses to call, when he was handed Mr Luckhurst's message. He perused it without a change in demeanour and then said, 'There is one last witness.'

The officer beckoned Luckhurst to the seat by the coroner's table. As the little man lurched up to the chair, Frances wondered for a moment why he did not employ a walking cane, but then reflected that it might be a matter of pride that he could do very well without one. As he took his place he smiled at the onlookers as if to say 'Look your fill, do! Aren't I a sight to behold?'

'Please give your full name to the court and the reasons why you have volunteered to give evidence.'

'My name is George Henry Luckhurst and I am Mr Edwin Antrobus' business partner. I believe I know him better than anyone present in this court. I was first introduced to him by a mutual friend in 1863, shortly after he returned from America, where he had spent two years studying the tobacco industry.'

Frances wondered if the significance of this information was as apparent to others as it was to her. It meant that Edwin Antrobus had been far from home at a time that could have coincided with a leg injury. If he did not want to worry his family he might not have mentioned it at all in letters home, which explained why no one knew of it.

'Three years later we went into business partnership as Luckhurst and Antrobus Fine Tobacco.'

'Did Mr Antrobus ever tell you about an accident in which he had broken bones?' asked the coroner.

'No, he never mentioned it to me.'

'Did he ever tell you that he had had a wisdom tooth extracted while on a business trip?'

'No, he did not.'

'Did he ever say that he was suffering pain from an abscess in the jaw?'

'No. He was a very reserved man. He rarely discussed personal matters and almost never alluded to his state of health. He wished to appear robust and strong, especially in view of the active nature of his work that necessitated a great deal of travelling. He did not like to admit to any weaknesses.' Luckhurst paused, and for a moment the only sound in the court was pencils on paper.

'I do have one thing of importance to convey in that respect,' he added, and his tone carried such seriousness it was enough to cause the scribblers to pause and raise their heads. 'Some years ago I was suffering considerable discomfort from a wisdom tooth and thinking of going to a dentist. I asked Antrobus if he could recommend a man, and he said he could not as by and large he detested dentists and only went to them when it was strictly necessary. He also volunteered the opinion that wisdom teeth were more trouble than they were worth. He told me that he had had all of his removed in America when he was twenty-five and, while it had been an unpleasant experience requiring substantial doses of ether and whisky, he had never regretted it.'

There was a brief silence in the court followed by a burst of excited chatter, which the coroner quickly quelled.

'Mr Luckhurst,' Dr Thomas leaned forward intently and everyone waited in anticipation to hear what would be said next. 'I want to be quite clear on this. Mr Antrobus told you that he had had all of his wisdom teeth removed as a young man?'

'He did.'

'I assume that you simply took his word for it.'

'I did not look into his mouth to check, no,' said Luckhurst with a smile.

Dr Thomas addressed the jury. 'I wish to remind you, gentlemen, that Dr Bond has testified that the remains before you have one wisdom tooth still in place.' He turned to Luckhurst again. 'Is there anything else you can tell me?'

'No, that is all.'

As Luckhurst returned to his seat Frances looked about her and saw Mr Wylie very shocked and unhappy, Mr Rawsthorne displeased and Marsden with an unashamed smirk of triumph. Lionel Antrobus, his evidence now vindicated, his control of his brother's property unchallenged, did not, despite everything, appear content. The burden of duty and the uncertainty remained. Mr Gillan and the ranks of newsmen were clearly delighted, their pencils speeding over paper in a tangle of hooks and whirls, their eyes shining at the prospect of a column headed 'Exciting scenes in court.'

'That is all the witnesses we have today,' announced Dr Thomas, staring keenly around the room as if challenging anyone else to appear, but the assembled company held its collective peace and he nodded. He then addressed the jurors, who exhibited that look of anxiety that always appears on the faces of men confronting the prospect of returning a decision they do not feel competent to make. 'I propose adjourning the proceedings for one week to enable further witnesses to be found.' There was audible evidence of relief.

The pressmen rose as a body and scrambled for the door.

Frances turned to Mr Luckhurst. 'On your honour, sir, that was true?'

'As I live and breathe,' he assured her. 'Whatever the outcome to myself, even if I am his sole heir, which I most strongly doubt, I could not sit by and see Antrobus declared dead on a mistake.'

Frances looked at her notes again. Harriett Antrobus had told her that her husband had had a tooth out while on a business trip but she had not been able to state where or when this had taken place or even what tooth it had been. The suggestion that it was a wisdom tooth had come solely from Mr Wylie. 'Perhaps it was not a mistake.' She looked quickly about her and saw Mr Wylie in conversation with Mr Rawsthorne.

'Some red faces, I fear,' said Luckhurst, rising to his feet. 'But business calls me. I will write to you very soon and look forward to making your better acquaintance.'

Frances wished him farewell and sought out Mr Wylie, whose embarrassment as he saw her approach was manifest.

'Miss Doughty,' greeted Rawsthorne, 'at the very centre of things as usual! I am told that you are acting for Mrs Antrobus.'

'I am, and I had imagined that all would be completed today, but it seems not.'

'Mr Wylie has just told me that he is very sorry for his mistake. It appears that his memory did not serve him well.'

Frances turned to Wylie, who was trying to avoid her gaze. 'And yet, I recall that you volunteered the information about the lost tooth before Mrs Antrobus had written her statement and before the remains were examined. Now how can that be?'

Wylie gave a helpless shrug and a nervous laugh. 'I can only apologise.'

'I do not want an apology,' Frances told him, 'I want an explanation. When you came to inform me that the remains had been found you said that when you saw Mrs Antrobus she was too overcome to speak, but I am now wondering whether that was entirely true. Perhaps you did speak to her briefly and she told you as much as she could recall about the tooth extraction: the information she later included in her statement. But it was little enough and so you thought you would help her with a made up story to corroborate what she had said. I assume you paid careful attention to Dr Bond's statement just now?'

He squirmed like a man in pain. 'I – do not have the stomach for such details, but – yes.'

'And you added a further refinement to your evidence to match what he had found. Is that not the case?'

'Mr Wylie,' warned Rawsthorne sternly, 'I would advise you to say nothing. Miss Doughty has just alleged that you perjured yourself to a coroner's jury, which is an extremely serious matter.'

Wylie gave a little gasp and wiped his face with a handkerchief. It was warm and oppressive in the court but he was perspiring even more than could be attributable to the climate. 'I must abide by the advice of Mr Rawsthorne,' he muttered weakly.

Frances favoured him with an unforgiving stare. 'Of course you must.'

She left Mr Wylie to his uncomfortable thoughts and went to speak to Lionel Antrobus, but as she did so she saw a young woman, who had been sitting at the back of the court with a half veiled bonnet, make for the exit. There was something a little familiar about the dress and the neat quick movement, and Frances hurried after her for a closer look, quickly realising that she was Dr Goodwin's maidservant.

Was this simple curiosity, wondered Frances, or had the maid been sent by Dr Goodwin to observe the proceedings on his behalf, and if the latter, why, after his interest in Mrs Antrobus' case had ended several years ago, was he still concerned?

Lionel Antrobus and Mr Marsden were in close conversation when Frances approached them boldly. 'Sirs, I am sorry to interrupt, but I hope I might have a word.'

Marsden offered a sly smile. 'What brings you here, Miss Doughty? Looking for stories for your sensational tales?'

'I am sure I don't know what you mean,' replied Frances with a dignified air.

'Neither do I,' said Antrobus.

'Oh this young lady is a prolific writer of halfpenny tales, all about a silly girl detective called Miss Dauntless,' taunted the solicitor. 'Half of Bayswater thinks the stories are true!'

'I am not the author of the stories and I don't know who is,' Frances retorted sharply.

'She writes under the name W. Grove, but I know better,' insinuated Marsden with a sneer.

'You know nothing, sir. But my business is not with you. I was about to ask Mr Antrobus if he knows where his brother was employed when in America.'

Marsden wrinkled his nose in distaste. 'I don't know about you, Mr Antrobus, but I find the word "business" on the lips of a female particularly unpleasant.'

'And yet I see that there is a point to the question,' observed Antrobus, thoughtfully. 'I will look into it,' he promised.

As Frances thanked him, she saw that Inspector Sharrock, who had been talking to the coroner, was just about to depart and quickly bid them 'Good-day' and hurried after him. Behind her she could hear Marsden give a laugh of derision.

'Inspector, if I might have a word with you!' Frances called.

Sharrock rolled his eyes, but he paused. 'I'm a busy man, but I know better than to put you off, as it will only make twice the nuisance later on. One word, that is all I have time for!' They left the hall and walked on down Church Street together, Frances' long legs and youth enabling her to easily match the Inspector's impatient stride.

'I have been hoping to speak to you about the enquiries that were originally made into the disappearance of Mr Antrobus in 1877. I know that it was thought that he had vanished while in Bristol, but I can't believe that you would not have made some enquiries too.'

'We were in consultation with the Bristol police and gave them such information as we had, yes. And they won't be at all happy when they hear about this. They've been asking round all the dentists in Bristol to see if any of them remembers a Mr Antrobus and his wisdom tooth. I've a mind to arrest that Wylie for wasting police time!'

'Did you ever consider at the time that Mr Antrobus might have returned to London or decided to leave his family?'

'The police are not stupid, Miss Doughty,' he said irritably, 'we know the sort of things people get up to.'

'I am sorry, I didn't mean to imply any failing on your part, but I know you and your men are very hard-pressed and there was no actual evidence in this case that a crime had actually taken place.'

'That is true, and there still isn't. You know about the wife, of course. Men have walked off for less than that.'

'But there are the sons.'

'Yes, and he was a good father by all accounts, but they haven't had so much as a letter from him. One of the Kent police went to the school and had some words with them. They are two very unhappy boys, missing their father, there's no dissembling there. There's an aunt too, respectable type. The constable paid her a visit, and if she's hiding Mr Antrobus there was no sign of it.'

He darted away, and Frances let him go.

Frances returned to her empty rooms to reflect on what she had learned. As Harriett Antrobus herself had said, many men suffered falls and where was the man who had not lost a tooth? The only thing that connected the second skeleton to Edwin Antrobus was the bag and its contents, and a thief could have abandoned it at any time. The one thing of which she was sure was that Mr Wylie, from his anxiety to have matters resolved, had lied to the court.

CHAPTER THIRTEEN

Frances' reflections were enlivened when Sarah bustled back, full of news. She had interviewed the Antrobus' former parlourmaid, Lizzie, who had said she knew of no reason for her master not to return home from Bristol, there having been nothing unusual in his manner or state of health before he disappeared. Edwin Antrobus, she declared, had been neither better nor worse than any master she had worked for previously or since, and his conduct had been perfectly proper at all times. Mrs Antrobus' affliction, which had required her to creep about the house like a mouse, she had thought very strange, but it was not for her to question the arrangements. Mr Antrobus was very sad about the unfortunate position but bore up well. As far as she was aware there had been no disagreements between husband and wife, although had there been any they would have been conducted almost in whispers.

Few visitors had come to the house. Mr Luckhurst was sometimes there. Mr Lionel Antrobus and his family called, Miss Pearce came once a week to see her sister and there were any number of medical men. The only person with whom she had ever seen Edwin Antrobus have an altercation was a poor man who had repeatedly come to the house and was very persistent in his appeals for money. He didn't look like someone who had been living on the street, only someone very ill-clad who had not attended to his toilet as often as he should. On the first occasion he had actually dared to come to the front door and asked to see the lady of the house. Lizzie had directed him to the servant's entrance, but he had refused to go, saying he had as much right as anyone to come in through the front door. The maid, naturally not wanting to let him in, had shut the door, leaving him standing on the doorstep while she fetched Mr Antrobus.

Her master, when told of the visitor, had been very relieved that the man had not been allowed into the house. He had hurried to the door and found the man still waiting outside. There had been a sharp exchange of words ending with Mr Antrobus angrily ordering the man away and telling him never to return. Later he told the maid that the caller was a thief and a beggar, and she had done right not to admit him.

'Could she describe him?' asked Frances, thinking that this was another person who might have set upon Edwin Antrobus in the street.

'Between thirty and forty. Hungry looking, with long dirty whiskers. After that he came to the back door a number of times, but he was always turned away. The charwoman also told the maid that she'd seen a poor man peering through the back windows and trying to get into the house through the servants' entrance, but it was obvious that he was up to no good and she shooed him away. Once she even saw him trying to squeeze through a bedroom window that was part open to air the room and saw him off with a broomstick. Might have been the same man as came to the front door, but as far as they knew he never actually entered the house. They didn't see him again after that.'

'How long ago was this?'

'It was a few years before Mr Antrobus went missing. She couldn't be exact.'

'I suspect he wasn't a beggar at all but Mrs Antrobus' cousin, the burglar who seems to spend so much of his life in prison. If he didn't return it was probably because he was in custody again.'

The maid had also confirmed that Mrs Antrobus almost never went out, except very occasionally when she and Miss Pearce hired a closed cab and went to visit their father's grave at All Souls' in Kensal Green, or sometimes on very quiet mornings they liked to walk in Hyde Park. On those occasions Mrs Antrobus was so muffled against any sound, it was an extraordinary sight to behold.

Lizzie remembered very well Mrs Antrobus' distress and confusion when her husband did not return from his business trip, and Miss Pearce had been sent for to comfort her. There had been a number of callers to discuss the dreadful situation: Mr Luckhurst, Mr Lionel Antrobus, some policemen and one or two other men who she thought were lawyers or detectives.

The servants had stayed on for a month after Mr Antrobus disappeared but left when the lady of the house confessed that she was no longer able to pay their wages.

There remained one more servant to trace, the charlady, a Mrs Fisher, who had been quite elderly. Lizzie thought that she had probably given up heavy work and gone to live with her married daughter, whose name she didn't know.

'I'll find her, though,' said Sarah.

Next day Frances received a visit from Tom's most trusted 'man' who, in default of knowing his real name, was usually called Ratty. He had been living on the street making a living by his wits when Tom offered him the only home and regular employment he had ever known. Ratty had proved himself to be fast on his feet and highly observant, able to follow and spy upon anyone without their noticing he was there and with an excellent memory for faces. His recent work for Frances had led to a sudden ambition to become a detective.

Some months ago Ratty had supplied information that had helped to solve a murder for which Professor Pounder had briefly been a suspect, and Frances had rewarded the boy with a suit of clothes to replace the assortment of ill-fitting rags he usually wore. As far as she was aware he had only worn the suit once, when he was invited to a tea party hosted by Cedric Garton to celebrate Frances' success and his sparring master's freedom. Frances had assumed that the suit had gone to the pawnshop, but when Ratty arrived that morning he was wearing it, and she realised that, as the best article of clothing he had ever owned, he had been preserving it for a suitable occasion. The effect was a little curious since, being at the age when boys suddenly grow almost in front of one's eyes, he was several inches taller than he had been only six months ago, and his clothes were too short both in the leg and body, revealing an unsavoury looking torn grey shirt underneath. He had made an attempt at washing his face but had not yet learnt that for completeness he should extend his efforts to reach his ears. A boy's round hat was perched oddly on the side of his head.

'Well, you are looking smart today,' said Frances.

He struck a jaunty pose. 'Bein' a 'tective, I thort I should look like one! Won' get no customers less I got the togs! 'N Tom is showin' me 'bout letters an' writin' and all that kind 'v thing.'

'Perhaps you should join the police force,' Frances suggested. 'You'll soon be tall enough.'

He pulled a face. 'Don' like coppers, Miss. Never did, never will.' He looked about him. 'Any tea?'

'There's always tea,' she reassured him, 'and Sarah has made jam tarts.'

Ratty grinned.

Over tea and pastry Ratty reported that, as per Frances' instructions, both the school for the deaf and Isaac Goodwin had been under close observation. No pupils boarded at the school, and most lived in Bayswater. A few arrived by carriage every weekday morning from further afield and were taken home the same way, and there was a family of three girls who were brought by a nursemaid and collected by her in the afternoon. Two small boys were taken to and from the school by a parent. None of these children ever conversed with Isaac Goodwin. There remained three boys aged between twelve and fifteen, two of whom were brothers, who lived near Porchester Gardens and walked from their homes to the school and back unaccompanied. During the luncheon period, they would sneak out of the school and dart into the nearby mews to engage in a very active conversation in sign language, and they conversed in the same manner all the way home.

Mr Eckley, who thought it beneath his dignity to go spying on his pupils himself, had occasionally emerged from the school and sauntered about the street in a manner that suggested he was looking for the supposed secret classes but was carefully trying not to appear to be doing so. He had a strutting manner of promenading and disdained to break into a run, which meant that the boys could easily evade him.

Frances fetched a street map and Ratty pointed out the narrow alley just around the corner from the school in Chepstow Crescent leading to the stables and coach houses of Pembridge Mews.

'They din't wanter be seen,' reported Ratty. 'They kep' a sharp lookout in case anyone saw 'em. They saw me, orlright but I jus'

walked in and out like I 'ad bus'niss there and they took no mind
'v me 'n I went into a stable 'n watched 'em from in there. What's
wrong wiv all that hand langwidge any 'ow?'

'Maybe nothing, but the school has banned it. I don't intend
to report the boys: that isn't my concern. Did Mr Isaac Goodwin
meet them?'

'Yeh, las' night, 'e did, 'n they all went inter the Mews t' talk.
It weren't jus' a normal talk, neither, 'e was very upset about some-
fin', d'no what, 'v course.'

'But it was just a conversation? He was not teaching them signs?'

'Far as I c'd see they was jus' talkin' – well, silent talkin' anyway.
'E kep' doin' this –' Ratty demonstrated grasping his left wrist with
two fingers uppermost and his thumb beneath, 'then –' Ratty
made fists of both his hands and put one on top of the other.

Frances got the booklet Dr Goodwin had given her but she
felt sure she understood. The second sign was, she already knew,
the letter G and the first was like the action of a doctor in taking
a pulse. The book confirmed it. Isaac had been making the signs
for Dr Goodwin.

Ratty studied the pictures. 'An' this one!' He stabbed the book
with a grubby finger. The sign was for 'teacher'.

Frances wondered what that could mean – was Isaac referring to Mr Eckley the headmaster or his own wish to teach?
Presumably it was Frances' recent visit and Mr Eckley's threats
that had upset him.

''E did this one, too,' added Ratty making both his hands
into claws and drawing them apart across his chest, almost like a
monkey in the zoo scratching itself. 'D'no what that is.'

Frances leafed through the book but could see nothing illustrated that might help her. ''N then 'e did this.' Ratty put the
thumbs and forefingers of both hands together and drew them
apart in a curve, like opening a miniature curtain. ''N they did
it back.'

'How mysterious! I think you should continue to watch
Mr Goodwin for another week at least. He may have discontinued teaching for the moment but start again when he thinks
it is safe to do so.' Frances secretly hoped that Isaac would provide her with nothing to suggest that he was likely to fall foul of

Mr Eckley's righteous wrath and the whole matter could be settled without any legal action.

While waiting for developments Frances addressed herself to her other cases and conducted an interview with a Mrs Lowy, who thankfully had nothing at all to do with skeletons.

Mrs Lowy was a lady of middle years, tastefully clad, although Frances observed that her gown was not the current season's but last year's; she had not, as a younger woman might have done, applied artful embellishments to make it seem new.

Frances happened to know that Mrs Lowy's husband, Ferdinand, a purveyor of fine furnishings, was not as prosperous as he would like to appear. Chas and Barstie liked to drop the occasional private hint as to which businesses in Bayswater were experiencing difficulties and which individuals were struggling with debt, and Mr Lowy's name had been mentioned several times recently. She wondered how much of this was known to his wife.

There were wives who took an interest in their husbands' commercial life, providing sage advice and assistance, and others who might have done so had they been given the opportunity but were deliberately or thoughtlessly left in ignorance. Still others agreed with their husbands that trade was a man's world and women were merely an unnecessary and distracting intrusion into a sphere of life for which they were not suited. Frances had seen more than one distraught victim who had known nothing of an approaching catastrophe before it descended upon her and her children like a thunderclap.

Had there been a subtle suggestion from Mr Lowy that his wife might like to delay ordering her new gown? There was a time when Frances would simply have observed and felt sympathy, allowing her mind to pass on to other matters, another's private hardships not being her business. Now they were her business, and she took no comfort from the fact. Occasionally her enquiries had uncovered the hiding places of debtors and, more importantly, where they had concealed their funds. Most of the time, however, there was nothing to be done.

Mrs Lowy, Frances knew from local gossip, had a very specific problem, the theft of a valuable family heirloom, a necklace that had belonged to her grandmother. Her client explained that she had kept it in a jewel case on her dressing table and rarely wore it because it was rather ugly and unfashionable. Nevertheless she was upset at its disappearance, because of a purely sentimental attachment. Mrs Lowy brought a portrait showing her wearing the necklace and Frances could only agree, although she did not say so, that it was indeed ugly, with festoons of heavy chains, clusters of jewels like overblown flowers and a central pendant with a cameo of a fierce looking man and his supercilious wife.

'It is – a very distinctive piece.'

'It is,' said Mrs Lowy. 'No one could sell it as it is or even pawn it without attracting attention. Any thief would have to break it up and sell the stones. I would be so upset if that was to happen. And the cameo – my grandparents' portrait – will I ever see it again?'

'The jewel box was unlocked?'

'Yes, I suppose that was careless of me but I never imagined anyone would steal it. My maid has been with me for twenty-five years and is a thoroughly good woman. The housemaid was on her half-day holiday the day it went missing. The only other person who ever enters the room is Ferdinand.'

'Is the necklace insured?' asked Frances, although she could predict the answer.

'Oh yes, for far more than any thief could make from it, but I don't care about the money, I just want the necklace,' she finished plaintively.

'And you shall have it,' said Frances confidently. 'I am often asked to find stolen jewellery and on many occasions I have found that it was not stolen at all but simply mislaid. Sometimes it has simply been moved to another place in order for it to be cleaned or valued or matched with a gown.'

'I am sure I did not move it, and no one in the house admits having done so,' protested Mrs Lowy.

Frances smiled in a manner she hoped would calm and reassure her client. 'Nevertheless, a busy person can so easily forget these things. You would be surprised at how often it happens. I am sure that you have looked everywhere for it, but I have an associate, a Miss Smith, who is an expert at finding things that are lost. This is what we will do. Miss Smith will visit you this very evening and she will undertake a thorough search. Will your husband be at home?'

'Yes, he returns at seven and dines at eight.'

'Then it is essential that you make sure he knows the instant he returns that Miss Smith will be at your house promptly at nine to look for the necklace. I would not want him to be alarmed.'

Mrs Lowy looked surprised, but she agreed.

Frances called on Tom and explained that she wanted one of his 'men' to wait outside Mr and Mrs Lowy's home and when Mr Lowy returned from his office, to see if he went out again, follow him to his destination and then report to her at once.

'What you wanted to know about them houses up at Queens Road,' said Tom. 'Locked up and boarded tight ever since they were sold. Only opened up to let the workmen go in. Mr Whiteley's not a gent to let the grass grow. Lots 'v argyments about the hoardings as they was too high. Vestry wanted 'em taken down; Mr Whiteley took no notice; big palaver.'

'Might someone have been able to climb in?'

'Not less he was a monkey with arms six foot long and hands on the end of his legs.'

Frances thought that Mr Poe might have made something of that, but she was certain that there was no escaped orang-utan in Bayswater or she would have been asked to look for it.

'Was one thing, though,' added Tom. 'Someone did try and break in a few months ago, only they didn't get nowhere. I mean they pulled some of the boards apart, but there was only about enough space for a cat to get in, or someone very thin if they wriggled a bit.'

That evening Frances received a visit from one of Tom's 'men' she had not encountered before, a mouse-like boy of about ten called

Dunnock, who said that within minutes of arriving home from his office Mr Lowy had rushed out of the house carrying a small parcel and gone to an address. This address, Frances was able to ascertain from her directory, was the home of his brother.

Frances at once proceeded to the home of Mr and Mrs Lowy and engaged in a brief private interview with the gentleman of the house to say that a search would no longer be needed as she had located the missing necklace in the safekeeping of his brother. She added that she hoped he had not yet pursued a claim with his insurance company, whose directors might find it hard to believe that he had made an innocent error. He thanked her gratefully, paid her a handsome fee and hurried to tell his wife the good news.

Frances had found the task she had carried out for Mr Eckley somewhat distasteful and was relieved when she felt able to report after a few more days of observation that she was satisfied that Isaac Goodwin was not teaching sign language to the pupils of the school. She went to see Eckley in his study, and he listened to what she told him with a serious expression.

'My conclusion is that you have no grounds for action against Mr Goodwin.' Frances produced an envelope from her reticule. 'My invoice. I require settlement in thirty days.' Frances did not usually provide an invoice quite so promptly but she wanted to end that particular association as soon as possible.

'But he was seen using signs to the boys?'

'In conversation only. How else might he speak to his friends?'

'Hmph! He can read and write.'

Frances was losing all patience with the man. 'Do you really intend to try and dictate how Mr Goodwin converses with his friends? I do not think you have any legal means of enforcing your wishes.'

Eckley polished his spectacles and gave this some thought. 'Very well, you may desist from your observations for the moment. I must confess I am disappointed that they are meeting in Pembridge Mews. I had them chased out of there some months ago. I shall write a letter to the boys' parents to advise that they will be expelled if caught loitering there again. But I do have another commission for you. Is it part of your business to look into people's antecedents?'

'Certainly.'

'Then I wish you to discover the antecedents of Mr Isaac Goodwin. In particular his parentage.'

Frances had been about to make a note of his requirements but stopped, immediately suspicious. 'This is something I often do for prospective employers, business partners and fathers-in-law. You do not appear to fall into any such category.'

He resumed his spectacles, through which he gave her a hard look. 'If I engage you to do this it should not matter to you why I ask for the information.'

'Excuse me, but I think it does.'

Mr Eckley was not a gentleman who was used to having his actions questioned by anyone, least of all a young woman. He pushed out his chest as if to assert his authority. Frances remained unimpressed both by his authority and his chest.

'I must bid you good day,' she said, preparing to leave.

'Oh very well, if you insist,' he said reluctantly. 'I assume that you are unfamiliar with the paper I gave to the Milan conference on the teaching of the deaf last September?'

'I am.'

'In describing the many advantages of the German system I pointed out that deaf children who only learn to speak with signs are necessarily restricted to the society of other deaf children. When they are of an age to marry they will probably marry within that society. The result of an intermarriage of two deaf persons you may imagine.' He paused. 'Surely I do not need to explain?'

'You do not. But your theory may not be a good one. Dr Goodwin, for example, is the son of two deaf parents and is not himself deaf.' A thought occurred to her. 'Did you know that when you presented your paper?'

'I did not, but it has been pointed out to me several times since,' he said with marked irritation. 'My response is that it is true that he is not deaf now, but who knows that he may not become so in future?'

Frances could see why Dr Goodwin might find Mr Eckley's position on this question somewhat insulting, adding an extra barb to his legal action. 'And of course Mr Isaac Goodwin is not a blood relation of the doctor but adopted.'

Eckley smiled unpleasantly. 'So Dr Goodwin would have us all believe.'

'I am aware that there are rumours and unkind gossip regarding the parentage of Mr Isaac Goodwin, which appears to have emanated from a person who was not in his right mind,' Frances advised him. 'I am surprised that you take notice of such things.'

Eckley shrugged. 'If the rumours are false then Dr Goodwin should thank me for proving that they are so; if true, they will support my theory.'

'You claim scientific disinterest on the subject?'

'I do.'

Frances placed her invoice on the desk, put her notebook and pencil in her reticule, snapped it shut and rose to her feet. 'Mr Eckley, I will have nothing to do with this. It is very apparent to me that your true motive is to discover something dishonourable about Dr Goodwin, which you will then either use in your defence in the coming court case or, worse still, as blackmail to persuade him to drop the action. That would make me an accessory to a crime.'

He opened his mouth with an expression of hurt pride, an angry denial on his lips and then gave a little laugh of embarrassment. 'You see through me, of course,' he conceded. 'I had heard that you are a perceptive young lady. Would you accept my guarantee that if you carried out the work your name would not be mentioned?'

'No, Mr Eckley. I will accept my fee for what I have done so far and no more. And if I were you I would abandon this mode of attacking Dr Goodwin. Whether you win or lose it will reflect badly upon you.'

Frances gave him no further opportunity to pursue his arguments and left.

CHAPTER FOURTEEN

The resumed inquest on the bones found in the builders' rubble provided little that was helpful. The owners and landladies of the demolished houses had been traced and stated that they had never observed anything that had aroused suspicion. All were adamant that they took care to check the contents of the cellar every time there was a delivery of coal, and not only had there not been a sack marked Geo Bates, all had purchased their coal from another supplier. The houses had been vacated in September 1880 and had then been securely locked. No tenants had gone missing during their term of occupation in the previous five years, and those who had departed paid their rent and left in good health.

It had been hoped to conclude the proceedings at the second hearing but Dr Bond, a man in constant demand, had been called away on another case and had not completed his detailed examination of the remains, so the inquest was adjourned for another week.

Later that same day Frances interviewed a new client, Mr Wren, manufacturer of neckerchiefs, handkerchiefs, cravats and cummerbunds. Mr Wren was a highly nervous and very angry man. His eyes flickered about the room as he explained his business, his fingertips constantly rubbed against each other and his shoulders occasionally gave a sudden twitch. It had come to Mr Wren's notice that a business rival, a Mr Cork, had been placing advertisements in the *Chronicle* which had not only claimed health-giving benefits for his own products but made veiled suggestions that articles produced by Mr Wren were deleterious to the male economy. He had already instructed his solicitor to send a letter to Mr Cork ordering him to stop the offending advertisements, and publish a retraction, but the disappointing response was that nothing had been done contrary to the law. Frustrated by this, Mr Wren was determined to find something with which to attack his rival and therefore wanted Frances to examine old copies of the *Chronicle* to see if anything had been done in the past that was actionable. He would do it himself, he said, but it was a tedious undertaking and he did not relish the prospect, neither could he spare his clerk.

Frances did not relish it either, but it was paid work.

Sarah departed soon afterwards to pay a visit to the sender of an obscene letter to Miss Gilbert and Miss John, devoted companions and founders of the Bayswater Ladies Suffrage Society. The sender was not expecting a visit from Sarah, a fact that only added to her pleasurable anticipation. It never ceased to amaze Frances that a person could put a disgusting letter in the post and feel safe that their crime would not find them out. It had taken very little wit to track the miscreant to her home address, and the whole unpleasant episode would quickly be put to rest with a few well-chosen words. Miss Gilbert and Miss John, who declared themselves very shocked at the allegations, saying they had never heard of such a thing, preferred not to prosecute.

Frances dispatched a hurried luncheon of bread and jam, and then went to the offices of the *Chronicle* to look for Mr Cork's advertisements.

It was, as Frances had anticipated, an exceedingly dull way to spend an afternoon. She was rapidly coming to the conclusion that Mr Wren and his hated rival were as bad as each other and that it was her client who was the guiltier of the two. After a few hours staring at small print, and with a headache threatening, she was obliged to refresh herself at a nearby teashop.

While undertaking the commission, she had taken the opportunity to read about the Old Bailey trial of Mrs Antrobus' cousin Robert Barfield, which had taken place in February 1876. The servant of a respectable lady had left a door unfastened for a just few moments while taking rubbish out to the ash bin, and Barfield, who had been lurking in the neighbourhood looking for opportunities, had seized his chance, crept into the parlour and stolen a watch. He was arrested an hour later since his manner while trying to sell the watch had aroused the suspicions of the jeweller, who had delayed the transaction long enough to send his assistant for a policeman. Initially Barfield had claimed that he had inherited the watch from an uncle, but when the engraving showed that this was untrue and the rightful owner arrived to claim her property, he changed his story and said he had bought it from a man in the street whose name he did not know. The jury had no difficulty in recognising an incorrigible liar and he was convicted. In view of his known criminal history, he was sentenced to three years in prison. Had he actually broken into the house the sentence would have been considerably longer.

Frances returned to the newspaper office to continue her thankless task and was visited by Mr Gillan, who made sympathetic noises. 'All you need to know is that Wren and Cork used to be in business together. Cork thinks Wren stole his patterns and Wren thinks Cork stole his ladylove. If you settle one argument then they'll just think up another one.'

Frances had just discovered a rich vein of furious correspondence, the authors of which published under pseudonyms but were almost certainly the two rivals. 'I am surprised the *Chronicle* publishes letters like these.'

'We usually have the measure of our men and how far they will go, and our readers like a good joust. If you think those letters are a bit strong, you should see the ones we don't dare publish.'

Frances was struck by a sudden thought. 'The last time I came here I was reading in the 1877 editions the dispute between Dr Goodwin and a man calling himself "Bayswater M.D.", to which the editor called a halt, presumably on the grounds that the debate was becoming heated and possibly libellous. If there were other letters which were not published, would you still have them?'

'I'll send Ibbitson to look them out,' said Gillan with a grin. 'Obliging lad; ambitious to be something in the newspaper world. He could go far.' If Gillan was hoping to stimulate a romance he had failed, but a helpful newsboy with a promising future was, thought Frances, someone a detective should cultivate.

Young Ibbitson quickly provided Frances with a folder of unpublished letters from a number of sources covering the debate between Dr Goodwin and 'Bayswater M.D.'. Several were from medical men who had correctly surmised that the latter was actually Mr Dromgoole and expressed the opinion that his friends should have him 'looked after', a polite expression for what had actually occurred soon afterwards. Others said the same thing but rather less politely.

There was also a long letter from Dromgoole, which did nothing to make Frances disagree with the general estimation of his state of mind.

'Dr Goodwin, a gentleman who is supposed to be so knowledgeable and virtuous as to inspire confidence in the public should look to his reputation,' Dromgoole had written, his excitement increasingly obvious as his handwriting snaked wildly across the page, ink splashing from the deep stabbing strokes of an angry pen. There were prominent and unnecessary capital letters, the whole interlarded with multiple exclamation marks:

> Here is a man who cannot even acknowledge his own natural SON!! And WHY does he maintain this fiction that the unfortunate simpleton boy is not a relative? Is he ashamed of him? NO!! Dr Goodwin is ashamed of Himself!! First he conducts an Intrigue with a Married Woman – I will not say Lady – a deaf person who is his own Patient! How horrible!! He woos her with his sinister Signs making disgusting protestations of illicit love under the very nose of her trusting husband who cannot understand that he is being cruelly duped! If it were not so base it would be better played as a Farce upon the popular stage. And Goodwin prevails upon the weak faithless wife, becoming her Paramour, assuming all the privileges of a husband, a role Wholly Unsuited to a respectable Englishman. And when finally the foolish husband's eyes are opened and his wife confesses her Treason, the unhappy man is moved by pity to agree not to Divorce her if the Child, the fruit of their illicit dealings, is sent away. This feeble infant is minded by persons of the VILEST kind, only to be later passed off by his own natural Father as adopted in the name of charity!!
>
> If this is not unspeakable enough, Dr Goodwin continues to have assignations with his Mistress, who is now masquerading as a respectable Widow, a fact of which I am sure her family is unaware but which I have witnessed with my Own Eyes. Their place of assignation is actually a holy place, a fact that can only cause the gorge to rise with Disgust!! I thank

God that I am not married, or I would be obliged to keep my wife indoors all the time, lest whenever she left the house she met secretly with such Dishonourable men as Dr Goodwin. I do not write the name of his Inamorata, but I would be prepared to announce it in public if required.

Frances wondered how much of this poisonous material had been spread across Bayswater and how many who heard it had actually believed it. Did Dr Goodwin know the full extent of Mr Dromgoole's venomous attack? Goodwin had admitted knowing of the rumours that Isaac was his natural son but had felt sure that no one would attach any credit to the ravings of a madman. His stance of remaining silent had seemed to be the most dignified way of dealing with them.

The unpublished letter was altogether more damaging. If true, the allegation that Dr Goodwin had seduced his own patient would put an end to his medical career, and the mere suspicion, even if unsupported, would be highly dangerous for him. The only thing in Dr Goodwin's favour was that the story emanated from a highly untrustworthy source, but so few people who took pleasure in scandals ever troubled themselves to look into them and weigh up their value before passing them on.

Following the dispute with the school, the old rumours that Dr Goodwin thought forgotten were playing right into the hands of its headmaster. Frances was now even more pleased that she had declined to act further for Mr Eckley. She had no respect for a man who allowed an academic disagreement to degenerate into a sordid personal attack.

Frances looked at her notes again and wondered who the alleged mistress of Dr Goodwin and mother of Isaac Goodwin might be. Could she be the mysterious Adeline? Was jealous love the reason for Dromgoole's anger? Or was the entire story, including the lady herself, merely a figment of the accuser's fevered imagination?

Later that day Frances was surprised to receive an unexpected visit from Dr Goodwin, who arrived with a deeply furrowed brow.

'Miss Doughty, I am sorry to intrude upon you unannounced, but I have some very serious questions to ask,' he began, removing his hat and passing a hand across his forehead.

'I will endeavour to help you in any way I can,' said Frances, offering him a seat at her little parlour table.

He sat but looked uncomfortable and distracted. 'Have you or any of your agents been making secret enquiries about me or my son?'

Frances took a deep breath. 'I will be open with you, Dr Goodwin. Initially I interviewed you with the object of learning more about Mr Antrobus, since I am acting on behalf of Mrs Antrobus, but subsequently, as you know, I examined the allegations made by Mr Eckley that your son is teaching signs to the pupils of his school. For the purpose of that enquiry I engaged one of my associates to keep a watch on your son's movements, and he did observe him having a conversation with some of the pupils of the school.' Goodwin frowned with displeasure but was silent. Frances continued: 'My associate was, however, entirely satisfied that it was merely a conversation and your son was not conducting classes in sign language, in which, you will be pleased to hear, the boys already appeared to be most adept. I was therefore able to report to Mr Eckley that I could find no evidence of any classes taking place, and there the matter was closed.'

'I can scarcely credit what you are telling me,' he said with evident disgust. 'A young woman involved in such underhand affairs! If I had a daughter who acted as you do I would feel ashamed!' Frances said nothing. 'And do you still work for Eckley?'

'I do not.'

'I want the truth! It has recently come to my notice that in the last few days someone has been going about Bayswater asking questions about me, and all the old unpleasant rumours that I thought had been forgotten long ago are being talked about openly again. Fortunately I have friends who know me to be an honest man and have warned me about it. Has Eckley employed you to spread these terrible slanders?'

'I know that my profession is distasteful to you, but I too am interested in the truth. I would never act in such a way.'

'But do you know who is responsible?'

Frances hesitated.

'You do, don't you!' he cried, clenching both hands into fists. 'You must tell me!'

'I do not know for a fact, but one may always suspect, as I am sure you do yourself,' she replied cautiously. Just because Mr Eckley had asked her to undertake the task did not necessarily mean that following her refusal he had approached another agent, although it did look very probable, but to point the finger at him without better evidence would, in Goodwin's current mood, be inadvisable.

'Oh, I suspect, I certainly suspect!' he cried, with bitter energy.

'I ought to mention,' added Frances, 'that I have just discovered some letters sent to the *Chronicle* in 1877 but which fortunately were never published, one of which was from Mr Dromgoole, consisting largely of a personal attack on your character. The material was highly defamatory but clearly the work of a very disturbed brain. I have not shown it or even mentioned it to anyone, of course, but it is very possible that Mr Dromgoole wrote to other periodicals with the same allegations and discussed them with his friends. However, I have also found that Mr Dromgoole suffered a complete collapse in his health and is currently being cared for in a private establishment. I went to see him, and he hardly even knows himself. Not only is he in no position to act against you, but his circumstances mean that any proceedings launched by another on the basis of his statements would be bound to fail.'

'I had thought that would be his ultimate fate,' said Goodwin. 'I never met the man, but his letters told me all I needed to know. But I do not suspect Dromgoole, it is that charlatan Eckley, I am sure of it. It is he, is it not, who sent his spies all over London to ask about me and my son?' To Frances' relief he did not pause for an answer and went on, 'That scoundrel is bent on ruining me – it is not enough that he harms the education of those unfortunate children, dooming them to a life of silence in his misguided efforts to make them speak and takes away the one good means they have of learning – he descends to the very lowest kind of attack. I have asked him to participate in a public academic debate, but he will never agree to it; he knows he would not succeed; no, instead he tries to crush my ideas by crushing me!' He slammed his fist into his palm, leaving Frances in no doubt as to the correct sign language for 'crush'.

'I assume that with the pending legal action it is not advisable for the two of you to meet privately, but perhaps you might arrange a meeting in the presence of your solicitors to clear the air?' she suggested.

'Pistols at dawn might be more effective!' he grunted.

'I hope that was not a serious proposal?' said Frances, with understandable alarm.

'No, of course not!' he gasped, clutching his forehead again. 'And you promise me that you have had nothing to do with this? All I have learned is that the enquiries were made by a man. Is he one of your agents?'

'I do not employ any men. And since I have given you my promise once, I really do not see why you find it necessary to ask me for it again.'

'Very well,' he said, breathing more easily. 'I have heard from all quarters that you are honest and trustworthy and I accept your assurance that this is the work of another. I don't suppose you know of any other detectives working in Bayswater?'

'The only detective I know by name is Mr Pollacky of Paddington Green,' said Frances, recalling the immortalising of that shining star of the detective world in *Patience*. 'I have not met the gentleman but I know he is very highly thought of. But I cannot think that a man of his reputation would stoop to work of this nature.' Frances secretly hoped that Goodwin would not ask her to discover the name of her rival detective as this might take her into some very murky areas and create an enemy who would make her own work very hard in future. 'In any case, it is not counter to the law to simply ask questions.'

'No, of course not, and whoever he is, he has his bread to earn like anyone else and may not have the luxury of choosing his clients. It is the fountainhead of the campaign against me that I seek, the man who pays for my persecution, and I suppose even if I found his underling he would not give up the name of his employer.'

'If you are so certain that it is Mr Eckley I must once again suggest that you consult with your solicitor,' Frances advised. 'A simple letter may be all that is necessary.'

Goodwin took his leave, shaking his head very unhappily.

Frances, although she had resolved the enquiry concerning Isaac's supposed classes, decided that the school should remain the subject of occasional observation for a few more days in case Mr Eckley undertook any threatening action against Dr Goodwin, and she sent a note to Tom.

CHAPTER FIFTEEN

'My dear Miss Doughty!' announced Chas, arriving next morning with Barstie to make his report, displaying all the panache of a Micawber, only rather more pecunious, 'We have the honour to present our conclusions!'

The two partners made the most of the simple comforts offered by Frances' parlour, and Sarah went to get tea.

'We have employed every resource at our disposal, alerted all our agents, sent our spies hither and thither and consulted our informants.'

Barstie said nothing, but he looked at Chas as if to say that the vast army of minions being conjured up was actually a great deal less numerous than implied.

Chas and Barstie had often hinted that there was a wealth of unpublished information circulating in the business world, known only to those gentlemen who took the trouble to be kept informed. There were clubs where, during murmured conversations misted in clouds of cigar smoke and lubricated with brandy, business could be done, agreements made and reputations destroyed. Documents were never signed in such places. The legal force of ink on paper could not be denied, but a verbal agreement between gentlemen was a matter of honour, a currency more valuable than gold, which once lost was far harder to regain.

There was also, Frances felt sure, at a much deeper level of secrecy, information that never passed outside the doors of private offices without payment or the exchange of favours of equal value. Whether the supply of information by these methods was a part of Chas and Barstie's services Frances did not know and preferred not to find out, since the legality of such measures was questionable, and she had probably already profited by them.

'The result of our endeavours,' Chas went on, 'is that we feel confident that both Antrobus and Luckhurst Fine Tobaccos and

Antrobus Tobacconists are as honest as any establishment in London. They do not owe more than is usual, they settle their debts in good time and their business accounts are well prepared. The disappearance of Mr Edwin Antrobus was undoubtedly a setback for the partnership, but it is recovering both its trade and its reputation, principally through the hard work of Mr Luckhurst.'

Sarah brought the refreshments and there was an appreciative pause in the proceedings during which attention was diverted from the business in hand by the appearance of bread, fresh butter and preserves.

'Then there is the question of personalities,' said Barstie eventually, regarding the scattering of crumbs on his tea plate with a world of sadness. 'Mr Edwin Antrobus is generally stated to be a worthy fellow.'

'For worthy, read dull,' interposed Chas. 'No one likes to speak ill of the dead. And even though he is still by the strict letter of the law, alive, everyone believes that he is actually dead and so they speak of him accordingly.'

'He appears to be a man without vices,' observed Frances, 'if there is such a thing.' It was an odd thought, but it occurred to her that she would not like to marry a man who was wholly without vices. In the few novels she had read, young women liked to be admired by men with vices because the situation carried a certain piquancy, but they usually married the worthy earnest fellow and settled to the life of contented domesticity which the author felt was appropriate.

'If he had any vices he kept them a close secret,' said Barstie. 'As to Mr Lionel Antrobus, he has more quills than a porcupine, and you approach him at your peril. Yet if he says he will do a thing you can count upon him doing it, and if he were to oppose you he would do so in an honest fashion.'

'Has he ever been known to act in an underhand or dishonest manner?' asked Frances.

Chas shook his head, wonderingly. 'Far from it, sticks to proper principles even if he was to suffer by it himself. Known for it. Respected, very highly respected, but not liked at all.'

Barstie looked hopefully at his empty teacup and brightened as Sarah freshened the pot with hot water. 'Now the real Don Juan is Mr Luckhurst. There are females in the case – several, I believe, and all very demanding on his purse. Luckhurst is a bachelor who lives alone and very simply in rooms above the cigarette workshop, but there is a well-appointed little apartment in Notting Hill he likes to visit.'

'Which he is entitled to do as he pays for it,' said Chas.

Frances had received a letter from Mr Luckhurst that very day inviting her to take tea with him, and she was suddenly very relieved that she had not yet written to accept. Sarah gave a low chuckle and Frances was unable to meet her eyes. She took a deep draught of tea to calm herself. 'Is he in debt?' she asked Chas.

'No, but he runs it a very close thing.'

'So Mr Antrobus' legacy would have been unusually welcome. Mr Luckhurst was left two thousand pounds in the will. He claims not to know about it, but his partner might have hinted as much. If Mr Antrobus had died under circumstances that did not arouse suspicion Mr Luckhurst would have gained substantially and the business would not have been harmed. His partner's disappearance, however, went badly for the business, and he was obliged to take a smaller salary to meet the expenses.'

Chas drained his cup and smacked his lips. 'Thus reducing the number in his personal harem from three to two.'

Frances was not sure if she required so much detail, since she hardly liked to imagine Mr Luckhurst, or any man for that matter, reclining on a couch of silken luxury, attended by extravagantly bejewelled sirens.

'I cannot see Mr Luckhurst as a murderer,' Frances observed to Sarah after the visitors had left, 'whatever the provocation.'

'You didn't see him as a ladies man. You've been wrong before.'

'True, but judging by Dr Collin's account, I don't think Mr Luckhurst is tall or strong enough to have murdered the man found in the canal, neither do I think him capable of breaking the other man's neck.'

'Do you still think Mr Antrobus is dead and not run off with another woman? He's been to America; he might go there again. He could be farming tobacco as he knows so much about it.'

'I would never deny a possibility. If he was murdered soon after he was last seen, anyone who stood to benefit by his death has been remarkably patient. We have two bodies of about the right age to be Mr Antrobus, both dead for about the right amount of time, and there is so much uncertainty and so many conflicting tales that I cannot rule out either being him. But both were found purely by chance.'

'All the more reason to think he's alive and doesn't want to be found.'

'Except that he hasn't contacted his sons.' There was a long period of silent reflection. Frances' own mother had abandoned her for a man and had never contacted her once in all the years that her family had maintained the fiction that she was dead. Perhaps in her mother's case the shame of betrayal was a worse blow than death. Edwin Antrobus too might have something to conceal that would be crueller to his sons than his absence.

Sarah made another pot of tea, but even this did not help clarify Frances' thoughts.

Later that day Frances had only just bid farewell to another new client, a gentleman who suspected his business partner of under-taking competing trade behind his back, when there was an urgent rapping on the front door. It was not the heavy thump of fists that usually announced the arrival of Inspector Sharrock but the quick smart sound made by the head of a silver-topped walking cane. Frances peered out of the window and saw Cedric Garton. There was a carriage waiting, which at once alerted Frances' attention. 'I think we are wanted,' she told Sarah. Cedric's manner on the doorstep was sheer impatience, and when the maid answered his knock, he darted past her with great energy.

By the time he had reached their door Frances and Sarah were ready to go out. Since neither was a lady of fashion to whom prepa-ration to face the admiring world was the work of at least an hour, it took only moments for their wraps and bonnets to be put in place.

'Dear ladies!' exclaimed Cedric, as he appeared at their door. 'If you are planning to go anywhere at all I beg you to abandon the idea at once and come with me! I have a carriage ready.'

'Of course!' said Frances as they followed him downstairs through a delicate waft of gentleman's cologne. 'But tell me what is the matter?'

'It's young Ratty, I'm afraid; he's just been arrested. I was fortunate just now to see him being taken away, and he called out to me to fetch you.'

They all leaped into the cab, and Cedric told the driver to ride like the wind to Paddington Green police station. 'I hardly recognised the lad at first he has grown so, but I am very glad he saw me.'

'Do you know why he has been arrested?' asked Frances.

'No, but he was very distressed and might even be injured, though not badly as far as I could see, at least he was wriggling and yelling enough.'

Frances shook her head. 'He will not like being in the hands of the police, whatever the matter might be. Poor boy, I will do whatever I can for him. Where did you see him?'

'Pembridge Villas, being dragged into a cab by two burly boys in blue and screaming fit to burst. Then off they went in the direction of the police station. There were other police about too, and a hand ambulance was being wheeled away with something on it, covered up.'

Frances suffered a growing sense of dread and guilt. 'I hope I have not been responsible for this. Ratty has been doing some work for me, and it might have led him into danger and perhaps even caused someone's death.'

'Now you can't know that,' said Cedric reasonably. 'What was the lad doing?'

Frances explained about the meetings in Pembridge Mews, and all the way to the station Cedric made reassuring noises about the terrible things that could go on in narrow alleyways that might have nothing at all to do with her enquiries.

At the station, Frances and Sarah ignored the protestations of the desk sergeant and hurried towards Inspector Sharrock's room, where loud howls told them that Ratty was being questioned. The sergeant abandoned his post and placed his wide form in their way, spreading out his arms with an expression of fierce determination.

'Stand back or there'll be trouble!' he bellowed, but Cedric merely leaned forward and said a few whispered words in his ear.

The sergeant turned bright red, said nothing more and went back to his desk.

'You can't just barge in like that!' cried the Inspector as Frances and Sarah walked into his office, closely followed by Cedric. 'Oh no, of course, forgive me, you are Miss "goes wherever she pleases" aren't you? Well you can't come in here, I've got a murder suspect and he's very dangerous!'

Ratty looked anything but dangerous. The assured would-be detective who had been trying to look older than his years was now a very scared boy, sitting hunched over in a chair, his arms wrapped tightly about him, pale as a ghost and sobbing loudly.

'Nonsense!' retorted Frances, confronting Sharrock. 'Inspector, how could you? You have young children of your own, would you want them to be treated like this?'

'My boys wouldn't go around carving people up,' protested Sharrock.

'I din't, I din't!' Ratty wailed, and Frances pulled up a chair and sat beside him.

'It's all right,' she soothed, 'I'm here now.' She took a handkerchief and mopped tears and snivel from Ratty's face.

'And they wouldn't go lurking about alleys up to no good!' added Sharrock.

Frances gave him a hard look. 'He is working for me. If he was "lurking" as you say, then he was doing it on my behalf. And I can't believe that he has carved up anyone.'

'Oh really? Well you ought to pick your people a bit better. He won't even give me his proper name. Just says he's called Ratty. What sort of a name is that?'

Frances made an effort to stay calm. 'It is what he is always called. He doesn't know his proper name.' A fresh torrent of tears was assisting her in the cleaning of Ratty's face which was beginning to blossom into bruises, and there was a cut on his head. His forearms were still pressed tight across his narrow chest, the hands clutching at his upper arms were clotted with drying blood, and his suit was also smeared with red.

'I din't 'urt no one!' gulped Ratty. 'The gent wuz dead when I saw 'im.'

Frances tried to unlock Ratty's grasp, without success. 'I hope the policemen didn't hurt you.'

'Hah!' exclaimed Sharrock. 'Where did he get that suit, just tell me that? Stole it I expect!'

'I gave it to him,' said Frances steadily. Sharrock scowled but was silent.

'Inspector,' Cedric addressed him, stepping forward, 'I would stake my reputation on the boy being honest.'

Sharrock looked him up and down and narrowed his eyes. 'I wouldn't recommend that, sir.'

Ratty wiped his nose on his shoulder, an action that improved the condition of neither. 'Coppers din't 'urt that much. It wuz the murderer in the alley; 'e comes rushin' out an' knocked me over, an' I think I banged me 'ead, 'cos the nex' thing I wuz on the ground 'n then I went to look at the gent, but 'e wuz dead. There wuz blood all over! So I went to get 'elp 'n then the copper comes. C'n I go 'ome, Miss?'

'Yes, of course you can,' Frances reassured him, carefully avoiding looking at the Inspector, although she could hear him growling, 'but if there is anything you know that might help catch the criminal, you must say what it is first.'

A constable came in and Sharrock took him aside for a muttered conversation, then grunted and nodded.

Sarah had gone to get a basin of water and a cloth and managed to persuade Ratty to let her bathe his face and hands and examine his bruises. 'He's been knifed!' she called out suddenly as she removed the coat to show that Ratty had been slashed across one arm. His clutching hand had stopped the worst of the bleeding, but it was still oozing badly. Sarah quickly pressed her large fist about the wound.

Sharrock ran out and roared for someone to fetch a surgeon. 'Soon have him stitched back up again,' he said as he came back into the room. He gave a loud sniff. 'Looks like the lad might be telling the truth after all,' he admitted. 'No knife on him, and no knife in the alley, just a dead man stabbed in the stomach. Nasty business.'

'Do you know who it is?' asked Frances, hoping that the incident might be the result of an altercation between a pair of dangerous criminals.

'We do, and if you hadn't come rushing in just now I'd have paid you a visit. He had one of your invoices in his pocket. He's the headmaster of the deaf school, Mr Eckley. Any idea who might want him dead?'

'Oh dear!' Frances thought of the dispute with Dr Goodwin, the pursuit of Isaac Goodwin, the dismissal of the deaf teachers and the children whose hands had been tied in class. 'He was not a popular man, I am afraid, but I can't imagine anyone going so far as to murder him.'

Once Ratty's injuries had been dressed, a process he bore like a man, or perhaps a boy unusually accustomed to pain, and he had been supplied with hot tea, a plate of bread and sausage, and a promise from Cedric that he would be measured for a new suit of clothes at the first opportunity, the transformation from suspect to valued witness was complete.

Calmer now, Ratty regaled the Inspector with the story of his observation of both the school and Isaac Goodwin, with Frances providing explanations.

Pembridge Mews was a location well suited to all kinds of unusual activity. A narrow cut between two walled gardens opened out into an enclosure of stables and cottages, the dwellings of domestic coachmen, servants and their families, then a sharp turn to the right provided further accommodation and also a location completely hidden from the main thoroughfare. There was no suggestion that the occupants of the Mews were anything other than respectable, but as a secluded spot it saw a great deal of coming and going, especially after dark. There were gas lamps in the Mews, but since these were not as good as the ones in the street, there were any number of dull, dark shadows.

That evening Ratty had seen Mr Eckley going into the Mews and had followed him out of curiosity. Eckley had been alone when he walked down the alleyway, crossed the Mews and turned the corner. No one else had been about, but Eckley had the businesslike look of someone on his way to an appointment, consulting his watch and carrying what looked like a letter. Ratty had hovered nearby hoping to hear a conversation, but there had only been an exclamation and the sound of a falling body. He had been about to peer around the corner when a running figure had collided with him, knocking him over. The next thing he knew he was lying on the cobbles and his head was aching. He had the impression that the running figure was taller, heavier and wider than he, but that was all he could remember.

'You didn't get a look at his face?'

There was a long silence, and then Ratty turned frightened eyes up to the Inspector. "E dint 'ave no face!'

'Hmm,' mused Sharrock, 'perhaps he wore a mask for disguise. Common amongst burglars and the like. And you are quite sure that when you saw Mr Eckley coming out of the school he had a silver watch and chain?'

Ratty took a mouthful of bread and nodded emphatically.

Frances was about to ask if the watch was missing from the body, but Sharrock hurried on into another question.

'So what else did you see when you were keeping lookout before? Thieves and gamblers and drunkards I expect?'

Ratty swallowed and licked his lips. 'Yes, 'n gents wiv doxies, which was very interestin', and gents wiv soldiers, which I din't understand at all. An' the gent what wuz killed, 'e was there too, yest'rday, meetin' another gent. Only not for what the gents wiv soldiers did.'

Sharrock remained impassive. 'Can you describe the other gent?'

'Old, short, bald 'ead. Dressed like a good'un.'

Sharrock pulled a battered notebook from his pocket and scrawled on a page.

'An' 'e were called Dr Goodwin, 'cos that's what Mr Eckerley called 'im. 'N 'e called 'im lots 'v other words too, what weren't polite, 'n then they 'ad a big argumentation.'

'Oh dear!' said Frances again.

Sharrock gave a deep sigh. 'What do you know about this, Miss Doughty?'

'You must have seen it in the newspapers; Dr Goodwin is currently suing the school since they dismissed his son from his appointment. But there is more to it than that: Mr Eckley insulted Dr Goodwin by saying that deaf people should not marry and Dr Goodwin is the son of deaf parents. The men are also in hot disagreement about how deaf children should be taught. Dr Goodwin wanted the matter aired in court, and I am afraid Mr Eckley has been attempting to make it a personal affair by trying to discover something to damage Dr Goodwin's reputation. He wanted to engage me and I refused, but it seems he found another detective, and Dr Goodwin recently learned that someone was asking about him in the hopes of uncovering a scandal. I recommended that they try to settle the matter amicably through their solicitors. They should not have been meeting in private at all.'

'Did you hear what they said?' Sharrock asked Ratty.

'The doc, 'e wanted t' know what Eckerly wuz doin' of, and tole 'im t' stop or else, and Eckerly laughed and said the doc dare not take it to law or 'e w'd be found out.'

'Was there any violence between the men?'

'Nah.'

'Or threats of violence?'

'The doc, 'e shook 'is fist 'n said Ecklerly was not attackin' 'im 'cos 'e 'ad nothing to be ashamed of, but there wuz a lady involved and that was a bad thing.'

Frances thought back to Mr Dromgoole's letter and wondered if the woman he had accused of being Dr Goodwin's paramour did actually exist; not that this was in itself any evidence of wrongdoing.

'Well it all sounds a bit unsavoury to me.' Sharrock shook his head. 'I know what goes on round here, and these respectable types they think it's all the lowlifes who gets up to things but they're all as bad as each other. Just some of them hide it better and make more of a noise about how proper they are.' He raked his hands through his brush of hair. 'I prefer the lowlifes, you know where you are with them, but these doctors and professors and all their prancing about don't impress me. If Goodwin has an alibi, all the better for him, but if not, he's going to have to answer some hard questions.'

Cedric arranged for a cab to take them all home. Frances was pleased to see that Ratty, who was regarding Sarah like the mother he had probably never known, had recovered from his ordeal. 'Why do gents always quarrel about ladies?' he asked.

'A gentleman, if he is a true gentleman, will always protect the honour of a lady,' Cedric advised.

'Even doxies?' queried Ratty.

'A doxy may be a good woman too, perhaps even better than some ladies I have known. But surely Dr Goodwin and Mr Eckley were not at loggerheads over a doxy?'

'D'no,' said Ratty. 'She were called Mrs Pearce, that's all I 'eard.'

'Pearce?' exclaimed Frances, startled. 'You are sure it was Mrs and not Miss?'

'Yeh. 'Cos the doc said she were a spectable widder.'

Was it possible, wondered Frances, that this Mrs Pearce was the late mother of Harriett Antrobus and Charlotte Pearce? Could she have been the married woman mentioned in Dromgoole's letter, the deaf lady and patient of Dr Goodwin who was also supposedly his mistress and the mother of Isaac Goodwin? If Dromgoole had made this accusation to Edwin Antrobus' face, then it was another reason for a bitter quarrel. 'I cannot believe that Dr Goodwin is a murderer,' she concluded.

'If he is not then we must hope he has a good alibi,' said Cedric. 'And thanks to young Ratty here we know the exact time of the murder to the minute.'

There was one small matter Frances wished to resolve. 'What did you say to the desk sergeant that shocked him so?'

Cedric smiled. 'Only that I knew his little secret.'

'And do you?'

'No, but all men have them, why would he be any different?'

Frances realised that in the absence of further information there was nothing she could, or indeed should, do. If Dr Goodwin was cleared then all was well. The next day, however, she returned to Paddington Green, hoping to learn more, and was told by Constable Mayberry that Dr Goodwin did not have an alibi for the time of the murder and was in custody, being questioned.

After less than a year in the force Mayberry, a slender youth of about eighteen, with no pretensions to brains or imagination, was becoming a competent young officer under the steely eye of Inspector Sharrock. The main qualities Sharrock looked for in a constable were sobriety, obedience and energy, all of which Mayberry was able to demonstrate, and as a result, whenever Sharrock wanted a constable to accompany him to the scene of a crime, Mayberry was his first choice. The constable had witnessed both the lady detectives' methods of exposing the misdeeds of criminals and consequently was always respectful to Frances and terrified of Sarah. 'It was all very strange here last night,' Mayberry revealed, 'what with Dr Goodwin being brought in and then a minute afterwards his son arrived, and him being deaf as a post and not able to speak, and very upset, we had a fine time. But he was brought pen and paper, and next thing he had written out a confession to the murder. Said he did it because Mr Eckley was trying to ruin his father.'

Frances tried unsuccessfully to reconcile the anxious boy with a knife-wielding murderer. 'Has he been charged?'

'No, because when the Inspector asked him some questions it turned out he didn't know the first thing about it. Then the maid-servant came in and she said he was at home all the time, but the doctor was out. I think he just said it to save his father.'

'I am glad to hear that. It was a terribly misguided thing to do. I hope the Inspector wasn't too hard on Mr Goodwin.'

'No, well, he saw it was family feeling and let him off. Gave him a stiff talking-to first, mind. Not that the son could hear it but I think the Inspector made himself very clear.'

'Where is Mr Goodwin now?'

'The Inspector sent him home with the maid.'

Frances, hopeful that this strand of the enquiry would be dropped without her intervention, decided to await develop-ments and returned to her apartment. There she found Mr Gillan waiting for her, anticipating a sensational story for the *Chronicle*.

'The whole of Bayswater is awash with rumour!' chortled Gillan excitedly. 'Some say Dr Goodwin has been murdering all his patients for the last twenty years, some say he has been seduc-ing every female he sees. What do you say, Miss Doughty?' He poised a pencil over a page in his notebook.

'I say that people should watch their tongues,' replied Frances.

'The word on the street and in the shops and parlours is that Mr Isaac Goodwin is the natural son of the doctor by one of his own patients. Do you know anything about that?'

'My understanding is that his son is adopted and not a blood relation. It is no business of mine to enquire further. Besides, all the allegations in the world cannot prove the point. You had best take care or your editor will find himself in court again.'

'Ah, well, I have been told that the lady concerned is deceased and cannot be hurt by it now. But it seems that she was hard of hearing and attended a hospital where she saw Dr Goodwin.'

'May a doctor not see a patient without being slandered?'

He smiled knowingly. 'All I can say is that someone knows something, and it is getting about.'

Frances firmly refused to be drawn into saying anything about the matter, but her earlier suspicions that the *Chronicle* had not been the only recipient of Mr Dromgoole's furious outpourings were confirmed. She decided that she ought to speak to Mrs Antrobus if only to warn her about the rumours. Harriett's main sources of information were the newspapers, correspondence, her sister and Mr Wylie, but she might well have been protected from unpleasant stories about her mother being passed around over rattling teacups.

CHAPTER SIXTEEN

When Frances called at Craven Hill, Harriett Antrobus and her sister looked composed and untroubled. Charlotte went to fetch some refreshments, and Frances opened the discussion with the usual polite enquiries after Mrs Antrobus' wellbeing.

Harriett smiled. 'I live my life as I must, of course. I have not been disturbed by the police again, which is both a good and a bad thing. I had hoped to be brought more news but it seems there is none to be had. Have you learned anything?'

'I regret that I have nothing new as regards the identity of the remains found in Queens Road. I will attend the adjourned inquest and can only hope that Dr Bond can throw new light on the unfortunate business. You do know, I suppose, that Mr Wylie overstepped what was wise in his evidence?'

Mrs Antrobus gave a soft little laugh. 'Oh, the silly man! He confessed all to me and was quite ashamed of himself, as he should have been. But he is kind and well meaning, and thought he was acting for the best. I have been very firm with him and said he must do nothing of the sort again. To be found out in such inadvisable behaviour could only harm our prospects. I do, however, have one happy piece of news. You know of course that your uncle, Mr Martin, was good enough to conduct my sister home when she was so distressed after my brother-in-law's recent threats. We persuaded him to stay for tea and found him a very gentlemanly and pleasant visitor. He has expressed an interest in renting part of the house – at least,' she smiled, 'he says it is the house he is interested in – and has called again several times since. Charlotte has shown him the accommodation and she told me he is very pleased indeed with what he has seen.'

The implication in her tone was very clear, and Frances hardly knew what to say.

'But I may be running ahead of myself,' admitted Harriett. 'My sister has known very little happiness, and her selfless devotion to our dear late mother and to me have been the enemy of her chances in life, although no word of complaint has ever passed her lips.'

Frances, though surprised, found herself content with the thought of Cornelius and Charlotte making a match. Late marriages, when the tastes and character of both parties were settled, and neither had any illusions about the realities of domesticity, could be very happy.

'I wish them both well,' she said warmly. 'But to turn to other matters: have you heard anything more from Mr Marsden?'

'I am thankful that I have not. Mr Rawsthorne has called and says he is keeping him at bay while the inquest is undecided. After that – I do not know.'

Charlotte brought tea and served it out with some thin slices of sponge cake, which, Harriett made a great point of mentioning, her sister had made with her very own hands. Charlotte joined them and smiled a little bashfully at Frances.

'I do not enjoy being the bearer of some distressing news,' continued Frances, uncomfortably, putting down her little wooden tea bowl, 'but I am afraid it is necessary, and as a consequence I do need to ask you some questions.'

'Oh, poor Harriett,' murmured Charlotte, and she leaned across and patted her sister's hand, comfortingly.

Mrs Antrobus tried to remain calm and resolute, but even so, she trembled slightly. 'Do not spare me, Miss Doughty. I must know all, however unfortunate.'

'Have you been told that Dr Goodwin is being questioned by the police about a murder?'

There was a sharp intake of breath. 'A murder? I can hardly believe it! Surely not! Oh, but you must mean as a witness; he cannot be a suspect!'

'I am afraid he is currently suspected. I am not engaged to act for him and can only hope that he is released soon.'

'There must be a mistake,' protested Charlotte.

Mrs Antrobus nodded emphatically. 'I agree. A man such as Dr Goodwin would not, could not do such a thing! But who is dead?'

Frances was unsure whether either sister knew the victim and watched them both carefully as she spoke. 'The murdered man is Mr Eckley, the headmaster of the Bayswater School for the Deaf.' Mrs Antrobus expressed only great surprise, but Charlotte was momentarily appalled and recovered her composure with an effort. 'I agree that Dr Goodwin cannot be responsible,' continued Frances. 'You will have read in the newspapers that he has a legal dispute with Mr Eckley. Unfortunately the law alone was not enough for Mr Eckley who attempted an assault on the character of Dr Goodwin, one that threatened his reputation and professional standing. I believe this is the main reason for the police's suspicion. I know nothing against Dr Goodwin, and I am sure that the attack was ill founded. But the result was that a great many rumours which arose as a result of the quarrel with Mr Dromgoole have been re-awakened, and I fear that they may touch upon your family.'

'On our family?' Mrs Antrobus looked mystified. 'I don't understand. How can that be?'

'Mr Eckley, in a misguided attempt to strengthen his case, employed a detective – not myself – to uncover anything that might harm Dr Goodwin. He found an old story, a slander: the suggestion that Mr Isaac Goodwin, who is the doctor's adopted son, is actually his natural son. The lady who has been named as the mother was a patient of Dr Goodwin's, a Mrs Pearce.'

The sisters looked at each other, appalled, and Harriett gave a little moan.

'Was your mother a patient of Dr Goodwin? If not then the rumours must concern another lady entirely.'

There was a miserable silence, during which the two women clasped each other's hands for support. 'Our mother,' began Charlotte, at long last, 'was hard of hearing, and towards the end of her life she was almost completely deaf. Over the years she was attended by a number of doctors, although many were so long ago we could not tell you all their names. I do think – yes, I believe she did consult Dr Goodwin at the hospital. But I hardly need to tell you that these terrible rumours are quite false, indeed unthinkable and impossible.'

'Mr Dromgoole wrote a letter to the *Chronicle* in the summer of 1877, which the newspaper very wisely did not publish, alleging that Dr Goodwin was still conducting secret meetings with the lady in question.'

'Where are these meetings supposed to have taken place?' asked Charlotte.

'He said it was a holy place, I imagine he was referring to a church.'

'Our mother passed away in December 1877 and was an invalid for the last year of her life. She had a weak heart and could not walk more than a few steps without assistance. Dr Goodwin did not come to our home and mother was unable to leave it without my help. She conducted her prayers privately. Even if Mr Dromgoole was not inventing or imagining his story, which I think is most probably the case, he was undoubtedly mistaken.'

'May I ask your mother's age when she passed away?' asked Frances, hoping that this would at once disprove the allegations against her.

'She was fifty-five.'

Frances calculated that Mrs Pearce would have been forty-one at the time of Isaac Goodwin's birth. It was possible. 'I think it would be wise to instruct Mr Rawsthorne to watch the matter for you. I do not believe an action for slander can be taken in the case of a deceased person, but there might be a way he can require anyone spreading this story to desist. It would help him to know that Mr Dromgoole is currently confined to an asylum for the insane. Also cast your memories back to eighteen years ago, since that is Mr Isaac Goodwin's age. You may recall something which will help your case.'

After a brief pause for thought, Charlotte spoke. 'That was the year before Harriett was married. We were then living in an apartment near the tobacconist's shop where our father was employed. My parents, Harriett and myself. There were only four rooms.'

'Then your case is strong,' Frances reassured the sisters. 'My interest, however, is not the rumours themselves but that they might have been a factor in Mr Dromgoole's quarrel with Mr Edwin Antrobus.'

Charlotte shook her head. 'I can certainly see that such a terrible accusation could have led to an altercation, and perhaps the threat of prosecution, but I do not think it would have ended in any violent act. Of course if Mr Dromgoole is of doubtful sanity …' She sighed. 'Do you think he might have harmed Edwin?'

'No, because he was confined to the asylum at the time Mr Antrobus disappeared, but he was the last man known to have quarrelled with him, and I had been hoping he might have some information which could assist me. I have seen him, however, and his mind is sadly clouded.'

The following morning the inquest on Mr Eckley was formally opened and closed again to permit medical reports to be completed.

To celebrate the fact that a long-term customer had finally settled her account Frances thought that she and Sarah could permit themselves a little greediness in the matter of strawberries. A basket of plump fruits was procured, and Sarah sliced them into a pretty dish, strewed them with sugar and added a generous libation of cream. There were, Frances felt sure, lords and ladies who could eat the best strawberries every day during the season, but none could have enjoyed them so much as she did this rare pleasure. Sitting in the parlour, trying to feel just a little guilty with each spoonful, she allowed her mind to reflect on the cases in hand. Even if Mr Dromgoole could recall nothing now, where were the letters he had sent to other newspapers and periodicals, which were unpublished because of their content? Had he made any threats against Mr Antrobus which might provide a clue to his fate? Frances realised that she might have to visit the offices of a great many publications in the hope that they still retained the material, and it was not a pleasing prospect.

Had Dromgoole written to his cousin in Dundee about his obsessions? She didn't even know if the two had been in contact at the time of Dromgoole's dispute with Edwin Antrobus. There might have been diaries or unsent letters in Dromgoole's house – if so they had probably been consigned to the rubbish heap when the property was cleared after it was sold, but it might be worth asking Dr Magrath if he had retained any of his patient's papers or sent them to Mr Dromgoole's cousin.

Sarah, with much smacking of lips over the strawberries, was amusing herself by reading out the death notices from the *Chronicle*. She preferred the death notices to the births and marriages since she thought that at least half of them were murders, whereas the births and marriages were only a preparation for later murders. As Sarah read, a familiar name cut through Frances' thoughts and made her sit up suddenly. 'Could you read that last one out again?'

'Dixon?'

'Yes.'

'Mr John Dixon, 52, formerly of Edgware Road, on the 3rd inst, after a short illness. With Adeline at last.'

'Is that all?'

'Yes.'

It was, thought Frances, the slenderest of chances, but the Adeline mentioned in the notice might be the same Adeline of whom Mr Dromgoole had spoken so feelingly, perhaps an old friend, relation or sweetheart. Clearly, from the contents of the notice, the lady was deceased, but there might be some advantage in speaking to her friends or family. Supposing Mr Dromgoole had revealed something to her about the disappearance of Edwin Antrobus, secrets that she had then confided to others?

Frances savoured the last of the sugared cream on her spoon, left Sarah to lick the dish and went to the offices of the *Chronicle*. Mr Gillan, with a significant wink, imparted that 'young Ibbitson' who attended to the birth, marriage and death notices would be able to assist her. He signalled to the lad, who bounded over to her like a pet dog, then winked again and went back to his desk. She did not know if it was a coincidence, but since their last meeting the youth had been making valiant and unsuccessful attempts to grow a moustache.

'What can you tell me about the notice for Mr Dixon?' she asked, showing him the newspaper. 'Who reported the death?'

'That was his brother, Mr Fred Dixon,' said Ibbitson. He was fully six inches shorter than Frances, and being obliged to gaze up at her only increased his resemblance to a trusting puppy.

'Did he say who Adeline was?'

'No, he just gave me what he wanted printed.'

'Do you have an address for him?'

Ibbitson looked mortified, as if the lack was his own fault. 'I'm very sorry, Miss Doughty, he just came here and handed me a bit of paper and his fee. That's mostly what they do.'

'I don't suppose the address is needed if you already have the payment,' she said kindly. 'Do you still have the note?'

'Oh yes, we keep them for a few weeks in case they come back grumbling.' Ibbitson searched through some drawers, found the sheet of paper and handed it to her, but it was the bare words of the notice. Frances hoped she might be able to locate Mr Dixon in the Bayswater Directory. The task of finding a death notice for Adeline when she did not have a surname or know when or where she had died was a daunting prospect.

Mr Gillan chanced by, or perhaps it was not chance. 'Keeping the lad busy, Miss Doughty?' he taunted, slyly. 'He's very keen, you know.'

Frances ignored the insinuation. 'Perhaps you might be able to help me. Do you recall the death of a lady called Adeline? It is possible that her surname might have been Dixon.'

'Since you mention it, yes, I do,' said Gillan, readily. 'I saw her husband passed away very recently. That was an unfortunate business. I was at the inquest and the trial.'

'An inquest and a trial? Please tell me more.'

'Now you know how this works,' smiled Gillan. 'I would welcome something in return about why you find the lady so fascinating.'

'It may be nothing; in fact I could be mistaken, in which case there is no story for you.'

Gillan chuckled. 'No story yet, but I know you Miss Doughty, and when you follow a case there is always a story for me in the end.'

'It is just possible that there may be a connection with a Mr Dromgoole, who once practised as a surgeon in Bayswater and had an altercation with Mr Antrobus whose disappearance I am investigating. Mr Dromgoole is too unwell to be questioned and unlikely to improve, but when he was in better health, he might have said something to a friend or relative, and I believe that he was very close to a lady called Adeline.'

Gillan shook his head. 'Well, I don't know about any connection with Mr Dromgoole, but Mrs Adeline Dixon was killed in a very serious accident some years ago. Two omnibus drivers were said to have been racing each other, the result being that one of the omnibuses drove up over the kerb, and Mrs Dixon, who was walking past, suffered dreadful injuries and died about a week later.

Her husband got a nasty crack on the head and was never right again. I think he was put in an asylum.'

A chilling possibility presented itself to Frances. 'An asylum? You don't happen to know which one?'

'I'm afraid not.'

'An injury to his head, you say?'

'Yes, poor fellow.' Gillan tapped his right temple. 'The drivers were tried for manslaughter and he was brought to court, but he couldn't recall enough to give evidence. Kept asking after his Adeline. Every lady he saw he thought was his wife. I don't think he knew she was dead.'

Frances thanked him for the information, but as she left the office and walked out onto the sunny Grove, the clear skies brought her no pleasure, and the chattering strollers, the street vendors, the carriage customers who swept by in their smart equipages, all seemed to have only one topic of interest on their minds, the fact that Frances Doughty, the renowned Bayswater detective, had been taken for a fool. Even the whinnying horses seemed to be mocking her as they trotted past.

CHAPTER SEVENTEEN

As Frances walked to the Bayswater Asylum for the Aged and Feeble Insane she wondered how best to proceed, but the matter was resolved when she saw a uniformed attendant approaching the institution, wheeling an elderly patient in a bath chair. As the attendant turned to manoeuvre the chair down the side alley that led to the garden, Frances lengthened her stride and caught up with him.

'Excuse me, sir, but I was wondering if you might help me?' she asked, hoping that he was the kind of man always ready to assist a female. She had adopted what she hoped was a tone of anxiety, trying not to let it descend too far into agitation.

He paused and looked up with a willing expression.'Certainly, Miss.'

'I am looking for a relative, a Mr John Dixon, who I have only just learned might be a patient here. Is that correct?'

The attendant hesitated, his cheerful smile replaced by a more serious look.'I think you ought to speak to the supervisor, Dr Magrath. Just wait for me to settle my patient and I'll let him know you are here.'

'But Mr Dixon is a patient here? I have not mistaken the place?'

'You are not mistaken,' he confirmed gently.

'I had wondered about that. It was my impression that this establishment is for the very elderly, and Mr Dixon is only fifty-two. Do you have many patients in their middle years?'

'No, he was —' the attendant winced and made a quick recovery. 'I mean, he is the only one. He was admitted following an accident.'

'Oh dear!' Frances gasped.'I hope he is not too disfigured! Is he very frightful to look at?'

'No, no, not at all, it was just a scar on his temple, nothing to distress yourself about, I am sure.'

Frances did not press the attendant further as she thought she had learned all that she could from him without arousing his suspicion. She thanked him and followed him to the garden, where he called a servant to conduct her to the visitors' room to await Dr Magrath. Frances said nothing about the purpose of her visit, only provided her card.

Dr Magrath arrived barely a minute later. He was not, as she had anticipated, pleased to see her. A man who thinks he has disposed of all his business on a single visit is always unnerved by a second one.

'Miss Doughty, how may I assist you?' he asked cautiously.

'Since our last meeting I have thought of another question I would like to ask Mr Dromgoole,' she explained. 'It will only take a moment or two. Might I see him again?'

His expression would have sat well on the face of an undertaker. 'I fear that that will not be possible.'

'Really? Perhaps you might like to consider why I do not find your answer surprising. The fact is that I have recently discovered that you practised a deception on me at our last meeting.'

Magrath tried to conceal his alarm by forcing an overly bright nervous smile but only succeeded in radiating a guilty conscience. He laughed unconvincingly. 'Surely not.'

'It is a matter of great disappointment to me that a respected man of medicine should do such a thing,' Frances went on. 'Kindly redeem yourself by explaining your reasons for presenting another man to me as Mr Dromgoole and let me have your solemn promise to be truthful in future.'

'Ah,' said Magrath, the smile vanishing.

'Your patient was actually a Mr John Dixon, who was admitted here after suffering a serious accident in which his wife, Adeline, was killed. Is that true?'

Dr Magrath appeared to be considering his options. A denial rose to his lips but died unspoken. His fingers fidgeted and his gaze travelled about the room as if seeking inspiration from the strange portraits on its walls.

'Is that true?' Frances repeated, more firmly this time, in a tone that made it quite plain that she knew it was.

He gave up the struggle and made a helpless gesture. 'Er – yes – I am really very sorry.'

'You chose him because out of all the residents here he is the only man near to Mr Dromgoole's age. You could not have deceived me with any other patient. Was that why you told me not to mention Dr Goodwin to him? Was Mr Dixon a patient of his? Did he suffer with his ears after the accident?'

He gave her a rueful glance. 'You have a good memory.'

'So – where is Mr Dromgoole, and what is the reason for the ridiculous masquerade at our earlier meeting?'

There was a long silence, a refuge of time, which Magrath employed pacing in a circle, making an earnest inspection of the carpet. 'Miss Doughty,' he said looking up at last, 'please believe me that I acted with the best of intentions, and I do not think – at least I hope – that I have done nothing against the law.'

Frances' expression suggested that this was something of which she had yet to be convinced. 'Please go on,' she said, coldly.

'You will appreciate that in an establishment such as this, our patients are either very aged or in frail health, but when he was admitted, Mr Dromgoole was neither.'

'Then why was he here?' Frances looked at her notes. 'Is this something to do with the asylum company's purchase of the house in Kildare Terrace from his cousin, Mr Malcolm Dromgoole, because it appears to me that there has been a very underhand arrangement.'

'Oh no, please believe me, it was all fully legal. Our solicitor Mr Rawsthorne drew up the papers. That house is now, as I expect you know, a female sanatorium.'

'But was it a condition of the purchase that the asylum cared for Mr Dromgoole?'

'It was.' Magrath drew up a chair and sat to face her. 'Mr Dromgoole was originally placed in the public asylum by his medical friends. His cousin was most distressed by this, and having acquired legal control over his estate, he hoped that he might be able to rent the house in Kildare Terrace to pay for him to be better accommodated, but the property was very dilapidated and there were no funds for its repair. Even if he had been able to sell it as it was, the amount raised would have been swallowed up in a few years and Mr Dromgoole would then have had to be returned to the public asylum. So we came to an agreement. The ownership of the house would be transferred to the General Asylum Company gratis and in return the company agreed to accommodate Mr Dromgoole.

'Unfortunately this proved to be more difficult than we had anticipated. As I have already mentioned, an establishment such as ours would not be tolerated in this neighbourhood unless the public was assured that our residents pose no threat to their safety. But Mr Dromgoole was erratic, not of great age and far from feeble. He made more than one attempt to escape, saying that he would take vengeance on the men who had destroyed him. We were therefore obliged to transfer him to a place where he could be more securely housed. I had not expected anyone to call asking for him but his attendant Mr Fullwood and I had already agreed that if that was ever to occur, a harmless deception would be required.'

'Harmless,' repeated Frances in a tone that left Dr Magrath in no doubt as to her opinion on that point. 'I see. And what did his cousin have to say about Mr Dromgoole being moved from here?'

Dr Magrath faltered.

'You failed to mention it to him, I take it?'

'Er – yes – I am afraid so.'

'Deliberately.'

Magrath could only nod.

'What did you intend to do had Mr Dromgoole's cousin come to visit? You could not have deceived him, surely? Harmlessly or otherwise.'

'We thought a visit from him unlikely as he lives in Dundee and does not travel. But had he done so we would undoubtedly have had sufficient advance notice to return Mr Dromgoole here for a brief period. But I do not feel that we have strayed from the essence of the original agreement, as we promised to provide suitable care and accommodation and that is what we have done, albeit in a different location. It was unforeseen circumstances which demanded that Mr Dromgoole was an unsuitable resident for this house.' Magrath, having explained everything to his satisfaction, was relieved enough to venture a smile again.

Frances was not convinced that Dr Magrath did believe he had complied with the agreement or he would have been open with her from the beginning. Underneath his disarming manner there was something else he was concealing, though whether this had anything to do with her enquiries she did not know.

'When was Mr Dromgoole moved?" she asked.

'He was here for about two months.'

Frances looked at her notes. 'He was admitted on 5 July 1877, and if that is correct he left before Mr Antrobus' disappearance and has been securely confined ever since.'

'Yes, so he could not have been in any way responsible for whatever happened to Mr Antrobus.'

'Even so, Mr Dromgoole may have information which I would find useful, so I would like you to tell me where he is.'

Magrath was startled. 'What do you mean?'

'I want to speak to him, which is what I had hoped to do when I came here first.'

'But, his mind has quite gone. You will learn nothing from him.'

'That is as maybe, but I will judge that.'

He hesitated.

'Please let me have the address, and I will travel there today.' Frances sat with her pencil poised over her notebook in anticipation.

After a brief pause, Magrath leaned back in his chair and folded his arms firmly across his chest. 'I am sorry, but that information is confidential.'

'Is it?'

'I am afraid so. There is a very strict limit on what I can reveal to someone who is not a blood relative of the patient.'

Frances had met with worse opposition and was not perturbed. 'You put me to a great deal of trouble, Dr Magrath. I want the information and I will have it, one way or another.'

'It would be detrimental to the health of Mr Dromgoole to undergo questioning, and you have no power to force me to open a confidential file.'

'As to the first, you must forgive me if I do not believe you, and I have more power than you think.'

He remained obstinate. 'I doubt it.'

'Very well, I will write to Mr Malcolm Dromgoole and obtain an order from him for you to open the file. He will no doubt be extremely interested to hear of the change in arrangements. I do not at present have his address, and I am sure that you will refuse to supply it, but I would not be any kind of a detective if I could not have that information in my hands before the end of the day.'

Magrath tried to conceal his alarm but failed.

'Or you could save us both time and trouble and let me know now where Mr Dromgoole is currently located.'

He hesitated. 'I shouldn't, of course.'

'I think you should.' Frances poised her pencil once more.

'It will be a long journey,' he objected.

'Then I had better start at once. So, if you please, the name of the asylum, its addresss and the name of the supervisor.'

Magrath stared at her with growing discomfort.

'I also intend to speak to Mr Rawsthorne, as he will need to check that the agreement he drew up is still being complied with. I should mention that Mr Rawsthorne is an old friend of my family and has been a great help to me in many of my cases.'

Magrath threw up his hands. 'Oh, you may safely leave that with me!' he exclaimed.

'Why does that assurance not inspire me with confidence?' said Frances dryly. 'Now then, the information.' She waited. 'Unless of course the story of Mr Dromgoole being moved is just another lie.' Another wait. 'Yes?'

He groaned. 'I really – I am so sorry. I am afraid that you cannot see Mr Dromgoole – in fact no one can. He is dead.'

There was a long silence during which Frances favoured Dr Magrath with a look that had made many a stronger man quail. 'Where is the record of his death?' she asked. 'Where is his grave? Forgive me for doubting you but I think I have good reason.'

'No record and no grave,' said Magrath, miserably.

'No proof, in other words. If this is yet another lie I shall be very displeased.'

'I wish it was not true but it is.' After further thought, and with an air of extreme reluctance, he rose and rang for the maid. They waited in silence until Doris arrived and was sent to fetch the senior attendant without delay.

'Mr Fullwood will tell you all you need to know, as he was present at the death,' said Magrath.

'When did it take place?'

'I don't recall the exact day. Dromgoole had been here for just over two months.'

'The date on which, according to your file, he was transferred from here, in other words some weeks before Mr Antrobus disappeared.' It seemed that that line of enquiry was now over, assuming that Frances could now trust what Dr Magrath said, although she was a long way from doing so.

Fullwood arrived and Magrath waved him to a seat. 'Mr Fullwood, it seems that Miss Doughty has lived up to her formidable reputation and discovered our deception concerning Mr Dromgoole. Much as I know it will pain us both, I feel that we have no alternative but to tell her the entire truth.'

Fullwood looked uncomfortable. 'We've done nothing against the law,' he muttered defensively.

Frances doubted that very much, since Dromgoole's death, assuming that he was indeed dead, had never been reported or registered. No one who worked in an institution where most of the residents were of advanced age could fail to know the obligation to report a death to the Registrar, an omission that was at the very least a punishable misdemeanour. She decided to wait for Mr Fullwood's story before she voiced an opinion.

'He was always a difficult patient,' Fullwood began. 'I saw from the start that he would need watching, since he was so much younger than the others and with no bodily infirmities.'

'But he was never violent,' Magrath interrupted. 'He made no attempt to attack any of the other patients or the attendants.'

'No, he didn't. He made threats against the other doctors, the ones who'd had him committed, but it was never to do them actual hurt. He said he knew things against them and he would write to the *Chronicle*, and *The Times* and the *Lancet* and the Royal College of Physicians, and when he did they'd be sorry for what they'd done to him. I rather thought he didn't know anything and it was all wild fanciful talk – one man was supposed to be charging his patients twice over, one had been negligent and yet another was romancing a married lady – I thought it best not take note of any names. We didn't allow him to send letters, but I don't think he wrote any. After he had been here a few weeks his mood changed, and he stopped talking about the other doctors, and he cried and said he was a prisoner and couldn't breathe properly. He said he would like to go for a walk and I thought —' he paused.

'We both thought,' said Magrath, charitably, 'that as long as it was quiet and there were not too many people about it would be safe to allow it. We didn't want to risk him bumping into one of the other doctors he knew or having him get lost in a crowd or confused by the noise.'

Fullwood nodded. 'So it was in the evening, fine and warm, as I recall. As soon as we agreed to take him out he became very calm. I should have been suspicious then, but I suppose I was just relieved that he seemed happier. I was careful to keep away from the main thoroughfares, and we walked for a while and he talked almost normally about his family and his life.'

'Did he mention Mr Antrobus?' asked Frances.

'Not that I remember.'

'Go on.'

'Well the conversation was quite interesting and he seemed calm and cheerful, so we walked a little further than I had planned, and I was just about to suggest we return when he said he would like to go and see the canal as he always enjoyed watching the barges. He said it reminded him of when he was a boy and he felt at peace there. I warned him about the smell, but he said he was a doctor and had smelt worse, which I suppose was true. Then he saw a pile of bricks on the canal path, and he suddenly picked up two or three of them and put them in his pockets. He said he was going to drown himself. I told him he needed to come back with me, and I went to take hold of him, but all of a sudden he pulled out a knife. We found out later he'd stolen it from the kitchen. He said if I called out for help it would be the worse for me. I thought I could talk him out of it, and I started to get closer to try and get the knife off him, which I knew I could do, as I didn't think he really meant me any harm, but then —' Fullwood gulped, 'it all happened so fast. Just as I got close, he – he just drew the blade across his throat. Right across. Just the once. Very deep. He must have been very determined. I went to catch him but he toppled over and into the canal. He didn't try to save himself, he just sank.'

'Did you try to save him?'

'No – I couldn't reach him, and in any case I could see it was hopeless, and if I had gone into the canal there would have been two of us dead and not one.'

'How was he dressed?'

'A suit of clothes as might any man wear.'

'And what did you do? Did you advise Dr Magrath of what had occurred?'

Fullwood glanced at Magrath who nodded. 'Yes, I did.'

Frances turned to Magrath. 'So now the matter was placed under your responsibility.'

'It was,' agreed Magrath, unhappily. He took up the story. 'I decided to wait and see if the body was found. I told the other attendants that Dromgoole had gone to live with relatives for a week or two. But we heard nothing. Then I said that he had been moved to another asylum that was more suitable for his needs. As time passed I suppose we thought that he would never be found or if he were, wouldn't be recognised. There was nothing in his possession that might have identified him. Since then the other attendants who would have remembered him have either left or retired. Fullwood and I are the only ones here who know what happened.'

'And you told no one of the death? You didn't register it?' asked Frances.

'Well, he was alive the last I saw of him,' said Fullwood.

'But only moments away from death,' Frances pointed out. 'I do not think the Registrar would be convinced by your argument. And what of Mr Malcolm Dromgoole? He has a right to know.'

Magrath looked guilty as well he might. 'He was not informed.'

'The body that was found when the canal was drained last year – do you believe that is Mr Dromgoole?'

'It could hardly be anyone else.'

'But you said nothing.'

'No.'

Frances hardened her voice. 'And as a consequence of your silence Mrs Antrobus and her friends suffered substantial expenditure in legal fees, not to mention time and trouble, and underwent great personal distress in order to try and establish that the remains were those of Mr Antrobus.'

Magrath gave a little grimace. 'I am very sorry about that, but once we were in the situation we could not see any way out.'

'The way out was to tell the truth.'

'Yes, yes I see that now. I will write to Mr Malcolm Dromgoole immediately to tell him what has happened and hope that he will understand. And of course I will register the death without any further delay and take the consequences.'

He looked so contrite that Frances decided to trust him. 'I will examine the newspapers with great interest to see the matter reported. There is one other thing you can assist me with. I want to try and trace any correspondence and diaries Mr Dromgoole may have left behind in his house, and also I wish to write to his cousin in case he had any letters from him.'

Dr Magrath, more obliging now that he had nothing further to hide, supplied the Dundee address of Mr Malcolm Dromgoole. 'As to anything found in the house, the only things we retained for our patient were personal effects such as clothing and toilet articles. I don't believe there was anything of value; he lived a very simple life. People do keep so very much about them and we cannot retain our patients' effects or our house would be bursting with them. I think there might have been a few books and papers and if so his solicitor would have sent them to his cousin.'

As Frances rose to leave Dr Magrath said, 'I do have something you might find of interest. I mentioned last time we met that Mr Antrobus had written to me asking about placing his wife in an asylum but I heard no more from him. I looked through my files and located the letter. Would you like to see it?'

'Yes, certainly.'

He was absent for a minute or two and returned with the letter. 'You may take it. Since he did not follow up the enquiry he was never strictly a client. But it might be as well not to show it to Mrs Antrobus, as it might distress her.'

Frances only glanced at the letter but saw that it was in the same handwriting as she had seen in Edwin Antrobus' papers and notebooks. It was not until she arrived home and sat down to read it and realised its import that she knew that, distress or not, she was obliged to show to it Mrs Antrobus.

CHAPTER EIGHTEEN

It was only a day since Frances had visited the Craven Hill house with news of Dr Goodwin's arrest and Mr Dromgoole's insinuations about the late Mrs Pearce. Now she had returned and found it hard to conceal her unhappiness at being once again the bearer of bad tidings. Charlotte was not at home, as she was engaged as a governess for the afternoon, and so Frances sat alone with Mrs Antrobus in her little padded and quilted parlour.

'I am sorry to say,' began Frances after the usual politenesses had been exchanged, 'that I have today found something which will come as a surprise to you, and at the risk of causing you pain I am afraid I have no alternative but to share the information with you and ask for your observations.'

'Very well, I am prepared for almost anything, I think,' replied Mrs Antrobus, calmly.

'It is a letter written by your husband to the Bayswater Asylum for the Aged and Feeble Insane.'

Mrs Antrobus gave a little intake of breath and nodded. 'I can imagine what it is you are about to say. There was a time when Edwin spoke of having me admitted to an asylum. I begged him not to; the noise made by patients of such an establishment would have been torture to me, and I am sure that I would never have seen my boys again. I suppose he must have written to ask if they would admit me.'

'He did, but the disturbing thing about this letter, when one considers its content, is the date it was written and the location.'

'Oh?'

'It was written on the 10th of October 1877 on the notepaper of the George Railway Hotel in Bristol where your husband was staying, only a few days before he disappeared and a few days after you say he told you that he had accepted that your affliction was of the ears and not the mind and that he was going to change his will to some more favourable arrangement.'

There was no doubt that Mrs Antrobus was aghast and appalled. 'But – I don't understand – he told me – he —'

Frances watched as a whole array of conflicting and painful emotions passed across her client's features. At length Mrs Antrobus, too overcome to say more, took a fine kerchief from her sleeve and passed the thin fabric across her brow.

'Do you still maintain that he told you he was going to change his will – that he had become convinced of your sanity – because this letter, which is the only piece of firm evidence I have, contradicts your statement.'

It was a moment or so before Mrs Antrobus' heaving breath had stilled to the point where she was able to speak. 'I would never have thought it of him – he seemed sincere – but it appears that I have been most terribly betrayed!'

Frances poured water into a wooden cup and handed it to the shocked lady, who took it gratefully and gulped it, dabbing her trembling lips. There were tears in her eyes and she looked stricken with sorrow. 'Miss Doughty, I can assure you that before Edwin went to Bristol we had a very long and frank conversation in which he told me that he had come to agree with what Dr Goodwin had said and that he finally realised that I had not, after all, lost my mind. He said he also appreciated that the will he had made was not appropriate to my situation and promised me that as soon as he returned he would make another. That, I can tell you most faithfully, is what he said. But there is, of course, no witness to the conversation. And a matter of days later he wrote this terrible letter. All I can say is that either in the intervening time something occurred to make him change his mind or else' – her eyelashes glimmered with fresh tears – 'he never meant what he said, all the conversation was a lie intended to put a stop to my complaints and make me more amenable to any plans he might make for me.' She shook her head. 'Unwilling as I am to admit it, Lionel has been right all along, on that point at least. He has always maintained that Edwin had no intention of amending his will. I expect' – she shuddered – 'that Edwin would have been kindness itself and perhaps arranged some supposedly pleasurable outing, muffling me against the noise, so that I would not know where I was being taken and then, only too horribly late, I would have found out exactly what fate he had planned for me.' She sobbed quietly.

When Charlotte arrived home Frances left her to soothe her sister's sorrow.

Sometimes Frances was the recipient of plain envelopes that originated from a small office in the heart of London. Some enclosed letters directing her to carry out small but important duties, and once those duties were performed, other envelopes arrived containing banknotes. The plain letter she eagerly opened that day was, she hoped, a reply to her request for information, and she was not disappointed.

Robert Barfield, she learned, had not had many associates during his time in prison, where he had been committed for a three-year term in February 1876, and those few he had were still incarcerated at the time of Edwin Antrobus' disappearance in October 1877. Barfield, however, was not. He had been released on licence in the previous month, and his current whereabouts were unknown.

Harriett Antrobus, Frances realised, was obviously unaware that her light-fingered cousin had been a free man at the time of her husband's disappearance, and he must therefore be considered a strong suspect in any fate that had befallen him. The ragged man who some years before had tried to enter the house and been peremptorily sent on his way by Edwin Antrobus was in all probability none other than Barfield. Frances wondered if he had again attempted to gain entry after being released from prison. Mrs Antrobus, she reflected, had last seen her cousin when he was a beardless boy of twelve. He would now be thirty-eight. What changes had those years wrought? Would she even recognise him if she were to see him again? Had he deliberately altered his appearance and changed his name in order to insinuate himself into the Antrobus circle? Had the 'commonplace young man' transformed himself into an 'idyllic poet' or something else entirely?

Most of Robert Barfield's thefts had been of the particular type that had earned him the soubriquet of Spring-heeled Bob, but there had been no recent robberies in Bayswater that looked like his work. He was also, however, a man of opportunity:

the last crime for which he was known to have been imprisoned happened only because he had noticed an open door and
walked in. Supposing, Frances thought, he was trying to conceal his identity, perhaps as part of a more subtle and lucrative
scheme. He might, if he was sensible enough, consider it unwise
to resume his old tricks and thus leave a recognisable calling
card all over Bayswater.

It was vital that the police should be made aware of the situation and Frances at once wrote a note to Inspector Sharrock.

While Frances awaited the adjourned inquest on the brickyard
skeleton and a reply to the letter she had written to Mr Malcolm
Dromgoole, there were other cases to keep her busy.

The affair of the cheating business partner had been so well
suited to the special talents of Chas and Barstie that she had
turned it over to them at once. As she had anticipated, it had been
settled quickly and resulted in a fragmentation of the concern
that left valuable debris to be picked up by anyone with a sharp
eye and fast on his feet. Frances felt some relief that her friends
had not called upon the very particular services of the Filleter,
or the double-dealer, instead of suffering merely a loss of reputation, might have found himself in an alleyway with his throat cut
as an example to others.

Frances' newest client was a Mr Edgar Candy, a youthful gentleman impeccably groomed and dressed. He brought no documents
with him, only an expression of concern. 'I have come to see you
because I am the victim of a slanderous attack,' he began, 'one
which has had serious consequences since it has destroyed my
prospects of an advantageous marriage.'

Frances opened her notebook. 'Please start from the beginning,
and tell me a little about yourself.'

'Yes, of course.' He paused as if considering what facts might be
of relevance. 'I am twenty-seven, and since coming into an annuity six years ago, I have been of independent means. But I am not
one of these idle fellows who waste their time and dissipate their
fortunes. I believe in making myself useful to society and so I act

as secretary to a number of charities in Bayswater. Some months ago, the death of my grandfather brought me a handsome legacy, and I determined that it was time for me to marry. I consequently sought and won the hand of a young lady, a Miss Digby, of good family and excellent character. We had agreed on a wedding date, and the engagement was to have been formally announced next week. I have seen no indication that my affianced regarded this event other than the way in which any young lady might antici-pate becoming a bride.'

Mr Candy, thought Frances, had said nothing of love or even affection, although that might have been from natural reticence before a stranger. He seemed like a practical young man, who valued only money and reputation. She said nothing and allowed him to continue.

'Two days ago, I called upon Miss Digby to ask her to accom-pany me to a society gathering, with a suitable chaperone of course, and to my great surprise she told me it was not conveni-ent. When I pressed her for an explanation, her manner towards me changed and she begged to be released from our engagement. I asked for her reasons, but she refused to give them. Naturally, as a gentleman I acceded to her wishes, but you can imagine my mys-tification. I decided to speak to her father, wondering if he had influenced her opinion; he assured me that he had not. He sug-gested that his daughter, being very young and of unformed opinions, had simply changed her mind. I could see no obvious reason for her to do so and came to the conclusion that a rival for Miss Digby's hand had traduced me and whispered slanders in her ear. I wish to impress on you, Miss Doughty, that whatever this individual might have said can have no foundation in truth. I have been honest with Mr Digby about my fortune, and there is nothing against my character. But I cannot allow this to continue. Supposing my rival makes an attack on my honesty, my public standing? It is not to be tolerated.'

'I understand your concern. Tell me, when Miss Digby asked to be released, what was her manner towards you?'

'Manner?' he asked, as if that was an expression that required further explanation.

'Yes. Was she calm, or embarrassed, or upset?'

'Oh, I see.' He considered the question. 'I really couldn't say. She is a quiet girl and spoke quietly. Who can tell what occupied her thoughts?'

'Perhaps if I spoke to her she would be willing to express those thoughts to me, but if there is another suitor who has slandered you she is unlikely to give up his name.'

'At the very least I wish to know what has been said about me, in order to show that I am innocent of any charges. If I am able to prove that the slanders are without foundation then my rival is exposed as a liar and Miss Digby may then make up her own mind as to who is the better man.'

Frances agreed to take the commission, and also made a note of the charities for which Mr Candy acted: a home for incurable children, a free dispensary and a fund to assist the families of men injured in the building trade. Mr Candy, she reflected, might be of the opinion that he had nothing with which to reproach himself, but others might not agree.

Frances was easily able to secure an appointment to speak to Miss Digby, but on her arrival was met not by the lady but her father, who had the good grace to look embarrassed.

Mr Digby was a dealer in fine porcelain, with a solidly success-ful business and personal good standing in Bayswater. He knew Frances by reputation and was aware that she was not to be trifled with. He began by reassuring Frances that he knew nothing to Mr Candy's detriment and had been fully in favour of the marriage. No one had indicated either directly or by insinuation that there was anything to impugn either Mr Candy's honesty or character.

'It is a matter of extreme delicacy,' he said awkwardly, with what he hoped was an engaging smile but came out as a sickly grin, 'and I believe that I can trust your discretion. If I was to tell you that my daughter, being fickle by nature, simply changed her mind, would that suffice?'

Frances considered this suggestion. 'What would suffice for the purposes of my client is to be reassured that he was not, as he had thought, the victim of slander, but if there are any circumstances that might emerge in the future that would cast doubt on what you say, it could have further repercussions. It would be as well if you were honest with me on the understanding that I will not reveal any more to Mr Candy than is strictly necessary according to his commission.'

Mr Digby looked resigned. 'You are aware, of course, that the engagement had not yet been announced, and Mr Candy's interest in my daughter has been of a most refined and discreet nature so that it was not widely known in society. My dear girl is a lovely creature, with every art and appearance that would attract a suitor, and she is just nineteen.' He gave an embarrassed cough. 'I have been approached by a young gentleman, the cousin of a baronet, who asked my permission to call upon my daughter. They had already met and conversed, and I saw a lively interest but had not realised its full import. He revealed to me that he had already advised Enid of his intention to speak to me and she had received this news with pleasure. Under the circumstances I asked if I might have time to consider his request and had an urgent conversation with Enid. She told me that she preferred her new suitor, and I admit I could see that the connection would be a very favourable one. We thought it would hurt Mr Candy's feelings if he felt that he had been supplanted by a rival, and we did not want to create any bad blood between him and my future son-in-law and his family, so when Enid asked to be released from the engagement she simply told Mr Candy that she felt she was too young to take such an important step. I have agreed to the new connection but stipulated that the engagement will not be announced for six months at least.'

Frances was satisfied, but before she left, Mr Digby engaged her to enquire into the family of the new suitor to see if he really was the cousin of a baronet.

Frances reported to Mr Candy that his reputation stood unimpeached, and there was no slanderer. He took the news with equanimity and appeared content with the thoroughness of Frances' work, so much so that he asked her to make enquiries into the bona fides of some claims against the injured workmen's charity.

In a single day one commission had somehow transmuted into several, and while she was grateful for the employment, Frances began to wonder if she might soon need another assistant.

It was agreed that Sarah, assisted by Tom and his 'men', would check on the injured workmen, while Frances would pursue the new suitor herself. The Westbourne Grove reading room held a directory of the nobility that would tell her if the titled family mentioned by the suitor actually existed. Should the baronetcy prove genuine that was not the end of her task, since he might not be connected with it. He would have to be followed from his lodgings to find out where he went and who his companions were. Frances did not anticipate with any pleasure being obliged to tell Mr Digby that his daughter had thrown over a respectable suitor for a fraud, but it was better to know the truth before marriage than afterwards.

The day ended on a lively note. Frances and Sarah were practising their sign language skills before retiring for the night when those two bitter rivals Mr Wren and Mr Cork descended upon them in such a froth of anger that they seemed ready to strangle each other with their own cummerbunds. Mr Wren was twitching more violently than ever and Mr Cork, a squat, red-faced man with small staring eyes, looked about to explode. Frances did not know the cause of their new quarrel and did not want to. Sarah had often claimed she could stop any argument by banging together the heads of the persons concerned, and for a moment Frances thought she was about to see the method demonstrated. Instead Sarah dragged the two of them downstairs by their collars and out of the house.

She returned an hour later announcing that the men, now much the worse for alcoholic beverages, had fallen onto each other's necks like long lost brothers and were back in business together again. She predicted a quiet six months before one of them killed the other, it being a matter of debate which way round that transaction would go.

'Now,' said Sarah, resuming her seat and opening the book. 'What's the sign for murder? We might need that one.'

CHAPTER NINETEEN

On Monday morning Frances received a note from Mr Malcolm Dromgoole, cousin of the deceased surgeon, announcing that he had come from Dundee to arrange a funeral for the remains and wished to call and see her that afternoon.

While anticipating that interview with some interest, Frances and Sarah were far from idle and spent the morning gathering information about Miss Digby's new suitor and receiving reports on the applicants to Mr Candy's charities. Tom, Frances discovered, was so busy on her behalf that he was planning to create a new team of 'men' who would devote themselves to the very special kind of work she required, placing Ratty at their head.

After a luncheon of boiled eggs and toast Frances applied herself to correspondence while Sarah departed to teach one of her twice-weekly classes in ladies calisthenics. As Sarah saw it, the purpose of the art was to improve the strength and health of her pupils, with advanced lessons on what to do when insulted by a man in the street.

Mr Malcolm Dromgoole was a tall spare gentleman of about forty but with dull grey features prematurely lined by illness. He arrived leaning heavily on a stout walking stick, and it was apparent that the climb upstairs to Frances' rooms had been a strain on his constitution. When he sat, trying not to show how grateful he was for the rest, it was some minutes before his laboured breathing returned to normal. He rested a leather document case on his knees, and Frances poured him a glass of water from her carafe.

'It appears, Miss Doughty, that I have you to thank for uncovering the deception practiced upon me by Dr Magrath,' he began, in a gentle soft accent like the wind rippling though heather.

'I expect he told you that I was too unwell to travel at the time my poor cousin was first confined to the asylum, and I have not ventured far from home since then or I would undoubtedly have come to London to see him before now. I spoke to Dr Magrath this morning, and it was not a pleasurable visit for either of us but, as you might well imagine, far less so for him than for me.'

'When I last spoke to Dr Magrath he admitted his fault and expressed his sincere regrets for the pain and inconvenience he has caused. I trust,' added Frances hopefully, 'that he has now done all he can to rectify the situation.'

'I can confirm that my cousin's death has now been properly registered and reported to the correct authorities. Magrath will find himself with a fine to pay, but if he imagines he can clear his conscience with a few pounds he is very much mistaken. It will go hard for the reputation of the asylum if the newspapers get wind of it, which I am sure they will.' Dromgoole did not look unduly concerned at the prospect.

He opened the document case and extracted a small flat parcel, which he placed on the table. 'Your letter enquired about my late cousin's papers and diaries. This is all I have; they were sent to me when he was first admitted to the asylum. I have looked at them, and there are some curious ramblings which mean nothing to me, but you may find them of interest.' He took a small card from his pocket and placed it on the parcel. 'I will be residing at this hotel for the next two weeks. Please could you ensure that the papers are returned to me before my departure.'

Frances thanked him. 'And if there is anything further I can do to assist you —'

'You may be invited to tell all you know to my solicitor Mr Rawsthorne. I have an appointment with him later today to examine the details of the agreement he drew up with the asylum.'

Frances had anticipated from Dromgoole's manner, firm as iron under the fragile exterior, that he would take his case further. 'I expect Dr Magrath will maintain that he adhered to the spirit if not the letter of the agreement.'

'He has already made that claim to me, but I disagree. The conditions for transfer of the property were that the asylum would provide proper care of my cousin for the rest of his life. I do not believe that permitting him to steal a knife, escape his attendant and cut his throat constitutes "proper care" and I feel sure that Mr Rawsthorne will concur. I intend to take steps to nullify the agreement and have the property transferred back to my possession.'

'I am sure you know that the house is now a sanatorium.'

He gave a thin smile. 'I do, and a worthy endeavour no doubt, which I will not disturb providing they pay me a suitable rent.'

Frances sometimes felt guilty that many of the establishments she had encountered during the course of her investigations had been obliged to close as a direct consequence of her activities, and she felt quite relieved at this assurance.

When her visitor had departed, Frances prepared a substantial pot of tea and unwrapped the package of papers. There was overwhelming evidence of Dromgoole's failing sanity, with half-completed letters in increasingly erratic penmanship, the words trailing across the page and sometimes ending in an illegible thread. Capital letters and exclamation marks abounded. In better order was a small notebook, which appeared at first to be a diary for the early part of 1877, but as Frances perused it she realised that it was a record of Dromgoole's attempts to follow Dr Goodwin in the hopes of securing evidence against him. Whether or not Goodwin had known about it, Dromgoole had been keeping watch on his home and his journeys to and from the school, and he had made a record of every person Goodwin had spoken to, with additional notes of what he imagined they had said, which usually involved secret plotting against himself. There were two items of especial interest. On a date in May 1877 Dromgoole had succeeded in pursuing Goodwin on a cab ride to Kensal Green cemetery. He had followed Goodwin's walk amongst the tombstones, which had terminated at a location where a heavily cloaked and veiled lady was waiting. The two had spoken for a long time before they went their separate ways. A week later Goodwin had met the same lady in the same location. Dromgoole, suspecting that the tombstone might provide some clues, examined it after the pair had departed and found it to be that of Albert Pearce, 1815–1873, much mourned by his loving wife Maria and daughters Harriett and Charlotte. Was this consecrated ground what Dromgoole had described as 'a holy place' in his letter to the *Chronicle*?

There were, thought Frances, a number of possibilities. The records of these secret meetings could have been the deliberate invention of Mr Dromgoole or products of his imagination. If real, then the location might have been chance. Supposing, however, that Dr Goodwin had been having private meetings with a lady who had good reason to be visiting that very tomb. Who was the veiled lady? The widow, Mrs Pearce, mother of Mrs Antrobus and Charlotte Pearce and reputed mother of Isaac Goodwin? That was not possible for two reasons. In 1877 Mrs Pearce was a frail invalid unable to travel without assistance. She was also deaf, and if Dr Goodwin had conversed with her he would have used sign language or writing and Dromgoole would have observed this and commented on it. Could it have been Harriett Antrobus he met? Or her sister? And what was the purpose of the meetings? Dromgoole was insinuating a criminal connection, but that might not necessarily have been the case. Importantly, did the subject of these meetings have any relevance to the disappearance of Edwin Antrobus?

Frances decided to try and obtain some clarification by interviewing Dr Goodwin, who was, as far as she was aware, still in custody.

Frances took a cab to Paddington Green police station, where the desk sergeant, with a surly look, advised her that Dr Goodwin had been released after questioning but was still under suspicion. Inspector Sharrock was out, having rushed away on another case.

Frances was just about to leave when the sergeant muttered, 'Not looking for a missing ring, are you?'

'No,' replied Frances.

'Oh, then you might have been saved some work, because one has just turned up. Funny thing, that. People usually come in all of a bother to say valuables have been stolen, not when they find them again.' He shook his head, as if the behaviour of other people was destined always to remain a mystery.

There was nothing Frances could do at the station, so she decided to go to Dr Goodwin's home and speak with him. She had descended the steps and was on the pavement looking for a cab when a thought suddenly struck her and she re-entered the station and returned to the sergeant's desk. 'What kind of a ring?' she asked.

The sergeant shrugged. 'Signet ring of some sort. Don't know about the worth. Young man came in very excited saying it was his uncle's.'

Impulsively, Frances reached for his record book.

'Oi! Not so fast! The cheek of it!'

'I am sorry,' said Frances, contritely. 'Please let me know the name of the young man who reported the finding of the ring. It could be important.'

He scowled and thrust his head forward belligerently. 'You ought to be at home, minding your own business.'

'I know what I *ought* to be doing, I am reminded of it very frequently.'

Uttering a throaty grumble, he ran a thick finger down the open page. 'John Antrobus. Isn't that the same name as — ?'

Frances turned and hurried out of the station. She found a cab, hardly knowing where she should be going, then decided it was best to go to the Antrobus Tobacconists shop. All the way to Portobello Road she reread her notes and tried to remember what Lionel Antrobus had told her about his brother's signet ring. It had been at their first meeting when she had asked how his brother's remains might be identified. He had mentioned the business cards and also the ring, the one that had originally belonged to Edwin's maternal uncle who had left him the house, a ring that had never left its new owner's finger. If young John Antrobus had been so excited that he had rushed round to the police station then there could be no mistake, the ring had been found, and it could be the start of a new trail of clues that could lead to the missing man.

Lionel Antrobus and his son were not in the shop, but the young woman Frances had seen earlier, who she assumed was John Antrobus' wife, was minding the premises, and she quickly explained her business.

'I remember your speaking to my father-in-law,' said the timid girl. She seemed to be avoiding Frances' eyes and moved about behind the counter, gently adjusting the position of goods on the shelves to a state of perfection.

'Can you tell me anything about how the ring was found?'

'No, only that John came in after making a delivery, saying he had seen it when passing by a pawnshop. He went in and looked and there was no mistake, it was his uncle's. My father-in-law sent him to tell the police and then went out.'

'Do you know which shop it was?'

'I think it was Mr Taylorson's, on Golbourne Road.' Frances was about to depart when she saw the young woman sway on her feet and rest her hands on a shelf for support.

'Are you feeling unwell?'

'I —' the pale creature looked embarrassed, and there was a light sheen of perspiration on her brow.

'I hope you don't mind my mentioning it, but Mr Antrobus did reveal to me that a happy event was anticipated.' Frances looked more closely. 'You are clearly feeling faint, and I really do think you should sit down.'

'Oh, I am not supposed to use the customers' chair,' the young woman protested.

'I don't see how anyone can object under the circumstances. Come now, I insist.'

Frances passed behind the counter, took the distressed girl firmly by the arm and guided her to a chair, not before time, for she would certainly have fainted if she had remained standing much longer. Frances loosened the collar of her patient's gown, fetched the carafe and glass from the back office, gave her some water to drink and bathed her forehead with a wetted kerchief. While she was thus occupied, the delivery boy arrived. Frances gave him no time to consider whether he should be obeying the orders of a stranger but handed him some coins and instructed him what to fetch from the nearest chemist. He scampered away. Frances was engaged in securing the comfort of the young woman, who was slowly recovering, when John Antrobus arrived.

'Esther?' he exclaimed.

'Your wife is feeling a little faint and nauseous, that is quite usual and to be expected, but she does need to rest. Long hours on her feet will not help her.'

'I will be quite well in a few moments,' said Esther. 'Miss Doughty has been very kind, she knew just what to do.'

'And I insist that you lie down and rest for at least an hour,' Frances told her firmly. 'And repeat that whenever you feel tired or faint, as often as is necessary.'

John Antrobus was able to persuade his wife that she should go up to the apartment and proceeded to help her there. Frances promised that she would mind the shop in his absence, and any customers who came in would be asked to wait for his return.

Taking up a position behind the counter, Frances tried to look as if she understood the business and had every right to be there. A gentleman entered and since he knew exactly what he wanted, and was able to point out the item on the shelf, she decided not to ask him to wait, but consulted the price ticket and made the sale. The cash register, which looked like a large iced wedding cake made of brass, was a little daunting, but she had seen such machines operated before, quickly saw what needed to be done and succeeded in entering the price and providing change. Her father, who had never employed anything other than a lockable box, would have been horrified at such an invention. The next customer required an ounce of pipe tobacco. After years of weighing powders and making neat packages in the chemist's shop, Frances' fingers had not lost their skill, and she was handing the gentleman his purchase when Lionel Antrobus and Inspector Sharrock walked in. The customer nodded politely to the astonished shopkeeper as he departed.

'Would you kindly explain exactly what is happening here?' demanded Lionel Antrobus, with a face of fury.

Frances was about to do so when young John returned. 'Father, we should thank Miss Doughty. Esther was taken ill while I was away from the shop, and Miss Doughty was kind enough to send out for medicine and look after her. Esther is resting now, and I am sure she will be well soon.'

For a brief moment Lionel Antrobus was speechless, then he recovered and said. 'I see. Well, naturally I am … grateful.'

'Miss Doughty is a lady of many talents,' observed Inspector Sharrock, 'the main one of which seems to be turning up all over Paddington when I least expect her.'

Frances was content to relinquish the place behind the counter to John Antrobus, his father staring at her with an expression of intense curiosity. 'I came here because the sergeant at Paddington Green told me about the ring being found,' she explained.

'Oh did he now?' said Sharrock. 'I shall have to have a word with him about revealing police secrets.'

'Was it Mr Edwin Antrobus' ring?'

A customer entered the shop. 'Let us go into the office,' suggested Lionel Antrobus, quickly. He stood aside to allow the Inspector and Frances to precede him.

'Not Miss Doughty as well?' complained Sharrock.

'Yes, Miss Doughty as well; she seems to know her business.'

Sharrock gave a snort of protest but gave in.

'Did you receive my message about Mr Barfield?' Frances asked the Inspector.

'I did,' he growled, 'and I won't ask where you got your information from because I might not like the answer. I'm looking into it.'

With three people in it, the little office was overcrowded. Lionel Antrobus offered Frances the visitor's chair, and Sharrock, not even thinking of sitting behind the desk in the proprietor's place, stayed by the door, looking as if he was used to being required to stand, which he probably was.

Lionel Antrobus took the family portrait from the wall of the office and laid it on the desk. 'There are other pictures of my brother, but this is the only one where you can clearly see the ring on his finger.' While Frances and Sharrock studied it, Antrobus took a jewellery box from his pocket and put it on the desk by the picture.

'My brother's ring.' He opened the box. 'It belonged to his maternal uncle Charles Henderson and is engraved with Henderson's initials.' The ring was gold, a plain, heavy-shouldered item set with a carnelian stone carved with the letters 'C.H.' and a spray of oak leaves.

'And he wore it always?' asked Frances.

'He did. He had a great sentimental attachment to it.'

Sharrock nodded thoughtfully. 'That being the case we can now feel sure that Mr Antrobus must have returned to London. It doesn't seem likely that he went missing elsewhere and the ring found its way back here on its own.'

Frances agreed. 'Does the pawnbroker have a record of where and from whom he obtained it? How long has it been in the shop?'

'I always thought it was the police who asked the questions,' said Sharrock.

'Apparently not,' observed Antrobus, dryly. 'Unfortunately Mr Taylorson does not have the individual's name. It was a woman of the poorer class who said she had found it lying in the street, and she brought it to him about two months ago.'

Frances was astonished. 'Only two months?'

'Which does rather leave us with the question of where it has been since it was last seen on Mr Antrobus' finger,' added Sharrock.

'Has the pawnbroker seen the woman since?' asked Frances, 'because I am not at all convinced by her story.'

Sharrock gave a sceptical chuckle. 'I'd like sixpence for every item of value pawned that's said to have been found lying in the street. He hasn't seen her lately, but if she comes back he'll let us know, and the constables will keep their eyes open.'

'I can help the police find her if you wish,' Frances offered. 'If you can supply me with a description, I will ask Tom Smith's men to keep a look out for her.'

'A kind of junior police force that Miss Doughty has at her beck and call,' explained Sharrock to Antrobus. 'Sharp-eyed lads, quick on their feet; when they grow up I could do with some of them in uniform.'

'Very well, I will fund the work, whatever is required,' said Antrobus.

Sharrock consulted his notebook. 'The woman was about fifty years of age, dark dress, brown bonnet, coarse woven flowered shawl, neither stout nor thin, complexion sallow, slight cast in one eye, probably washerwoman or charwoman.'

Frances copied the details into her notebook. 'If she is seen I will make sure that she is followed home and a report made of where she lives.'

Lionel Antrobus had been staring thoughtfully at the ring. 'I think it will be necessary to speak to my sister-in-law about this, difficult as that will be.' He replaced the ring in its box. The Inspector held out his hand, but Antrobus slipped the box into his pocket. 'I will secure a cab.'

The two men hurried outside, walking up towards Ladbroke Grove where there were more cabs to be had. Frances, although uninvited, quickly followed and the Inspector turned to confront her. 'Now then, this is police work! Or do I have to handcuff you to something?'

'Mrs Antrobus is my client,' insisted Frances. 'I am engaged by her to find her husband.'

Sharrock grunted and began to sprint down the street after a cab that stopped as he waved. He stood back to allow Lionel Antrobus to mount the steps first, but Antrobus paused and looked at Frances. 'I rather think the Inspector intends to drive away without you Miss Doughty.'

'I think so too.'

'What is this, musical chairs?' exclaimed the Inspector as Antrobus waved him into the cab then stood aside for Frances to climb in. There was a lurch as Sharrock sank heavily into his seat, and while Frances was safe enough, it was surely only gentlemanly courtesy that led Antrobus to clasp her firmly by the arm to steady her.

Frances thanked him, climbed into the cab and took her seat, her cheeks unnaturally warm. She was still being troubled by the nightmares, experiencing again and again the brutish strength of her attacker, the imprint of his fingertips gripping her shoulder, the foul smell of his breath, the sting of the chloroformed cloth as he tried to press it onto her face. This was different, a man's strong clasp offered as a woman's support and not her danger. She collected herself by making a close examination of her notebook.

'Perhaps, Inspector, you can tell me if there is any news on the murder of Mr Eckley?'

Sharrock scowled. 'I thought we had our man, and we may still do, but there was nothing we could use so we had to release him. I don't mind, I can wait.'

'Are you looking into murder, Miss Doughty?' enquired Lionel Antrobus, disapprovingly.

'I am afraid Mr Eckley was a client of mine,' admitted Frances.

'Do you lose many of them that way?'

'Miss Doughty is not only a danger to herself but all of Paddington,' Sharrock snarled. 'Wherever she goes, companies fail, banks close and buildings come tumbling down. If you employ her, Mr Antrobus, you should be very careful.'

'Inspector, I would prefer you not to undermine my business,' objected Frances, sharply.

'I do it because I don't want you ending up dead in an alleyway as you very nearly did last winter!' thundered Sharrock. There was an uncomfortable silence.

'Is that true?' asked Lionel Antrobus, evenly.

'Not precisely,' said Frances, feeling disinclined to prolong the argument.

Sharrock grunted. 'Luckily her servant was with her and flattened the man's nose for him. He'll live but his mother won't know him again.'

Frances felt unable to meet the gaze of either man.

At Craven Hill all three were admitted to the Antrobus house by Charlotte Pearce, who looked dismayed to see the Inspector and even more so to see her brother-in-law.

'Now then, Miss Pearce,' began Sharrock, 'I want to see Mrs Antrobus, and I won't take no for an answer!'

'Inspector, I beg you to moderate your voice or you will simply be torturing a very ill woman.'

'It is pointless to argue,' Antrobus told him. 'Agree to what she wants so we can hold the meeting.'

With a certain amount of grumbling, the gentlemen submitted to the inconvenience of removing their boots, the Inspector offering a nice display of Mrs Sharrock's neat darning, while Charlotte, having ascertained the reason for the visit, went to speak to her sister to advise her of what had transpired.

'Mr Wylie is with her now,' said Charlotte when she reappeared, 'perhaps in a minute or so —'

Sharrock shook his head. 'No, let him stay, I'll speak to him too.'

'Very well. But please ensure that only one person speaks at a time.'

It was a difficult arrangement. Harriett gazed in alarm at the visitors as her private sanctuary was invaded, and Mr Wylie, rising to his feet in decidedly shaky fashion, looked as if he was afraid of being arrested for perjury.

Charlotte took the signet ring from Lionel Antrobus and handed it to Harriett. 'This was found in a pawnshop. Is it Edwin's?'

Harriett held the ring in her hands and then clasped it tightly. She squeezed her eyes shut and tears rolled unchecked down her face. At length, she wiped her face and looked up at the visitors.

'Yes, I would know it anywhere. A pawnshop, you say? But who brought it there?'

'A woman,' boomed Sharrock abruptly, and Harriett flinched and put her hands over her ears.

'Please Inspector!' Charlotte begged him.

Frances read out the description of the woman who had pawned the ring, but neither Harriett nor Charlotte nor Mr Wylie could suggest who she might be. 'But a careful watch is to be kept and I am sure she will be found,' she added.

The Inspector opened his mouth to speak, and Charlotte placed a warning finger to her lips. 'Really, this is impossible!' he muttered.

'Not impossible, Inspector, it just needs a little care. And however inconvenient it is for you for these few minutes, kindly try and imagine if you had to live like my sister forever.'

Sharrock puffed out his cheeks with frustration. 'Very well,' he went on as quietly as he could. 'Mrs Antrobus, can you tell me if your husband was wearing this ring when you last saw him?'

Harriett nodded. 'I am not sure if I have ever seen him without it since it became his. In fact it was getting a little tight for him, and he might not have been able to remove it even had he wished to.'

Sharrock turned to the still nervous Wylie. 'And you, sir. The truth if you please. When you last saw Mr Edwin Antrobus in Bristol, was he wearing this ring?'

Wylie trembled. 'I hardly like to say: supposing I make a mistake? An honest mistake – it's very easily done. It was a long time ago, and I am not sure if I would even remember such a thing. He might have worn gloves – the weather was quite cold for the time of year, I think – or possibly I might be confusing it with another time, but perhaps —' he shook his head. 'No, no, I really can't say.'

'Well, thank-you Mr Wylie, that is very clear.' Sharrock took a deep breath as if making an effort to moderate his voice. 'The ring, please, Mrs Antrobus.'

'May I not keep it?' asked Harriett, plaintively.

'No, it's evidence. And it isn't your property in any case.'

Reluctantly, Harriett handed it to him.

'When you no longer require it please return it to me,' said Antrobus. 'I will keep it safe for my brother should he return, or for his elder son if he does not.'

Charlotte sat beside Harriett and took her hand. 'Please, everyone, this has been more disturbance than my poor sister can tolerate for one day. I beg you all to go and leave us in peace.'

They obeyed her wishes, Wylie rushing away as fast as he could, clearly wanting to place as much distance between himself and the Inspector as possible. Sharrock headed east to the police station, and Frances and Antrobus briefly and silently shared a cab travelling in the other direction.

'I trust you will not be concerning yourself with any murders, Miss Doughty,' warned Antrobus as she alighted outside the home of Dr Goodwin.

'On the contrary,' she could not resist replying. 'I am about to interview a man suspected of murder.' His shocked expression was reward enough for the discomfort of his company.

CHAPTER TWENTY

rances had not had the opportunity to send a note to Dr Goodwin announcing her visit but she felt that her work had reached that position when speed was more important than custom, so she rang the doorbell and presented her card to the maid. As she expected, the doctor bowed to the inevitable and agreed to see her.

Dr Goodwin showed every appearance of a man living a nightmare. He was clearly trying to go through his daily routine in a vain attempt to delude himself that everything was as before, but his eyes had the dry staring look of a man who had been without sleep, his crescent of grey hair was uncombed, and he was moving about in an uncharacteristically vague and disorganised manner. When Frances was conducted to his study he looked both worried and hopeful. 'Are you looking into Eckley's death?' he asked, waving her to a seat.

'No, that is the concern of the police.' She prepared to take notes. 'I am still pursuing my enquiries on the disappearance of Mr Edwin Antrobus, and to that end I am looking into everything that happened to him and his family and associates in the months before that occurred. Anything out of the ordinary. Rivalries. Arguments.' She paused. 'Secrets.'

Goodwin gave a thoroughly dejected and weary sigh. 'I have already told you all I know.'

'I am not so sure of that.'

He stared at her but uttered no denials.

'First of all I wish to know if Mrs Pearce, the mother of Mrs Antrobus and Miss Charlotte Pearce, was a patient of yours?'

He was surprised by the question but not alarmed. 'Yes, that is not a secret. She had been hard of hearing all her life and had grown increasingly deaf in the years before her death. I did all I could for her.'

'How did she converse?'

'Her speech was not affected. She could lip read some common words, but in the main it was best to communicate in writing.'

'You met with a lady by Mr Pearce's tomb in Kensal Green. That was a secret, I think.'

It was a risk to be so blunt, but Frances knew she had to declare it as a fact and not a rumour, and certainly not as a story emanating from Mr Dromgoole, which could all too easily be denied.

Goodwin was silent for a time. 'A gentleman may meet a lady in full view of any passer-by without there being anything wrong in it,' he said at last.

'You met more than once,' she persisted, 'and I am not implying that anything was wrong, only that others might have thought so and made false allegations which incurred the wrath of Mr Antrobus. Also something might have been discussed at your meetings which could be of importance.'

He shook his head. 'No, nothing.'

'And the lady's identity? The location of these meetings cannot have been chance.'

'How do you know of this?' he suddenly demanded.

'I cannot reveal the source of the information.'

Dr Goodwin stared at the papers on his desk without seeing them and passed his hands over his head, his fingers burrowing down into the fringe of hair at the back. At length he took a deep breath. 'As you have correctly surmised, the lady I met was Mrs Pearce. She was a patient and a friend. Nothing more. She was extremely anxious about the health of her daughter, Mrs Antrobus, and naturally we talked on that subject. Our first encounter at Kensal Green was chance – I had gone to visit the grave of my parents – but after that we agreed to meet from time to time.'

Frances closed her notebook and looked at him keenly. 'In the last year of her life Mrs Pearce was unable to walk more than a few steps unassisted and could not have made the journey to her husband's tomb alone. And you were observed talking to the lady, not passing her writing.'

'What are you saying?'

'I am saying that you are lying to me.'

He looked uncomfortable, even a little afraid.

'I would like the truth now, please,' Frances went on, as if that was the simplest request in the world and not, as she so often found, the hardest.

He took a deep breath and placed his hands firmly palm down on the desk, a gesture of new resolve. 'I apologise. You are correct and I ought to be ashamed of myself, but sometimes it is necessary to tell a harmless lie for the greater good. Very well. You shall have the truth. The lady in question was Mrs Harriett Antrobus, and we met in secret in a quiet place because she wished to talk about her difficulties without her husband or anyone else being present. He was not, I am sorry to say, sympathetic to her hardships, and she wished to speak freely and openly to someone who understood them. Since she is a married lady I attempted to deceive you just now in order to protect her reputation.'

'How often and how many times did you meet there?'

'Not very frequently, perhaps five or six times.'

'How many times after Mr Antrobus disappeared?'

'There was one occasion, which I have already mentioned, when I called at the house as a mark of sympathy. Mrs Antrobus was a patient, nothing more.' He rubbed his eyes. 'I am very weary, Miss Doughty, is that all?'

Frances rose to leave, although she could not help feeling that Dr Goodwin had not told her everything. Recalling the expression Cedric had used to the sergeant at Paddington Green, she approached the desk and leaned forward confidentially. 'I know your secret.'

It was there, the sudden loss of colour from the cheeks, the look of terror behind his eyes. 'I don't know what you mean,' he gasped. 'I did not harm Mr Eckley, the police have found the cabdriver who was conveying me at the time he was killed. I did not conduct an intrigue with either Mrs Pearce or Mrs Antrobus. Isaac is not my natural son, in fact I have no natural children.' He recovered his composure. 'Please leave me now.'

'Very well,' said Frances, more pleasantly. She made to go, but at the door she turned to face him. 'Oh, by the bye, I have read your booklet on the subject of sign language, it is a fascinating art.'

'Yes, indeed it is,' he agreed, looking relieved that the subject of the conversation had changed.

'Some of the signs illustrated are very elegant, and one might almost guess what they are as they mime their subject so well. But I was wondering if you could tell me what this one is? I observed it recently.' She made the sign placing her fingers and thumbs together then drawing her hands apart in a curve.

'Silence.'

'Ah, of course, it indicates a closed mouth. I see it now. And what of this one?' She mimed the motion with clawed hands at her shoulders.

Dr Goodwin looked astonished.

'Perhaps I am not performing it correctly. It looks like the action of a monkey, but I can't see why that would be.'

'Ah, yes, indeed, it can depict a monkey, but so many signs have more than one meaning – this one might also be taken to mean a scamp or a scallywag.' He frowned. 'Where did you see this conversation?'

'I am not at liberty to say.'

When she left him he looked puzzled and very worried.

The following morning's post brought a letter from Matthew Ryan, the Bristol detective, which was so startling that Frances entirely forgot her breakfast, and when Sarah saw it she almost forgot hers too.

Dear Miss Doughty

I have some new information for you, but I don't know what use you can put it to since the informant came to me under a veil of anonymity, refused to give me her name and is most reluctant to appear in court. The best I could do was to suggest that I should put a notice in the newspaper if I wished to speak to her again.

The lady concerned saw the advertisement I placed very recently for any further information relating to the disappearance of Mr Edwin Antrobus. She confessed that in the past, whenever Mr Antrobus was in Bristol on business, he was in the habit of paying her a visit. The lady was at the time married to a sea captain who was often from home. She did not come forward in 1877 for reasons that must be obvious. She has, however, recently been widowed and therefore felt able to reveal what she knows, if with some reservations.

The last time she saw Mr Antrobus is an occasion she remembers well. She had gone to the railway station to meet her sister, who was visiting with her new baby, an event which was eagerly anticipated and which she made a note of in her diary. It was 13 October 1877. She had just arrived at the station when she saw Mr Antrobus, although she did not think it appropriate to greet him. He presented his ticket to the Inspector and passed onto the platform, and she is quite sure it was the platform from which the Paddington train departed. He was not alone but in the company of another man. They were talking, and while not actually quarrelling, they did not appear to be on good terms. The only description she can offer as to the identity of the other man was that he walked with a very pronounced limp.

I am continuing my investigations and will write again if I have anything further to report.

Matthew Ryan

For a few moments Frances was puzzled. The clerk at the George Railway Hotel had not mentioned Edwin Antrobus' mysterious companion walking with a limp. Was this the same man or another? She checked through Mr Ryan's original report and saw that the clerk had seen the men standing talking to each other but had not seen them walk away, so had not had the opportunity to note any unusual gait.

There was only one limping man known to Edwin Antrobus and that was Mr Luckhurst. Had he followed his partner to Bristol and had an altercation with him there? Frances could hardly think he had not been questioned about his movements during the week between his partner's departure and last journey, but a train ride from Paddington to Bristol and back was not a lengthy expedition thanks to Mr Brunel's wonderful railway. Frances was also obliged to consider what credence could now be attached to Mr Luckhurst's important evidence at the inquest if he had in some way been involved in Edwin Antrobus' disappearance. Had he lied to ensure that the remains found in the brickyard were not identified as Edwin Antrobus? And if so, why?

Mr Wylie had lied too, apparently to assist Harriett Antrobus' case, but Frances was obliged to wonder if she had been duped into thinking there was no more sinister motive.

Another possibility was that the skeleton found in the brickyard was that of the limping man last seen with Edwin Antrobus. The witness questioned by Matthew Ryan had stated that the two men had not been on good terms. Supposing they had quarrelled and Edwin Antrobus had murdered his companion and then been obliged to disappear? A man who devoted his life to the wellbeing of his sons might have chosen to leave them fatherless in preference to their suffering the disgrace of their father being hanged for murder. Frances looked at the inquest report but all she could glean was that the dead man had once suffered a leg injury that had healed, which from the description was probably insufficient to produce a noticeable limp.

The obvious thing to do with the new information was take it to Inspector Sharrock.

The Inspector was available, and he readily agreed to see Frances when he saw she was bringing information. She sat facing him across his tumbled desk, resisting the urge to tidy the papers and discover and polish the wood beneath, a surface that had probably not seen daylight in many years.

Judging by the length of time he spent perusing the letter Sharrock must have read it through several times, sniffing and grunting and nodding to himself. He jutted his head forward and squinted at the date. 'Do you mean to say you didn't hold onto this until it was old news? Didn't rush off to Bristol and look into it yourself?'

'I received it this morning and brought it here at once.' Frances might have felt insulted at the suggestion that she sometimes concealed information from the police, if it had not, for excellent reasons, occasionally been true. 'I was thinking —'

'Ladies thinking is a dangerous thing,' interrupted Sharrock, 'and twice as dangerous when you do it.'

'I was thinking,' Frances repeated, 'that there is only one man who matches the description of the man who was seen with Mr Antrobus at Bristol.'

'I got eyes in my head, same as you, but you don't think we forgot to ask Mr Luckhurst to account for his movements do you?'

'I am sure you did ask him, but I have seen Mr Antrobus' will, and it included a legacy of two thousand pounds to Mr Luckhurst. Men have been killed for far less.'

'You have a wicked mind,' growled Sharrock. 'When I was young and innocent I never thought of such things. Took me twenty years to get as cynical as you are now. What will you be like when you're forty? It doesn't bear thinking about.'

'I just wanted —'

'Won't get a husband like that, you know.'

'I'm not looking for a husband,' declared Frances, irritably.

'I was going to introduce you to my brother, but he's just taken up with a widow so you've missed your chance there.'

'Inspector —'

'What about that Mr Lionel Antrobus? He's rich and single. Bit old perhaps, but you could do a lot worse.'

'All I would like to know,' said Frances through gritted teeth, 'is whether Mr Luckhurst had an alibi for when his partner went missing.'

Sharrock leaned back in his chair, which creaked in protest. 'Yes Miss Doughty, he did.' He dived forward abruptly, burrowed under a disorganised pile of papers, and brought out a folder, which he opened. 'At the very moment when Mr Antrobus was leaving his hotel in Bristol, Mr Luckhurst was in the company of two – er – persons. An hour later he was in his office where he attended to business assisted by his clerk, and an hour after that he met a customer by appointment. Four independent witnesses who place him in London for the whole morning. He was not in Bristol when Antrobus left and neither could he have met him at Paddington Station.'

'I must confess I am somewhat relieved to hear it. He did not strike me as a man who would murder his partner for money. Of course that does not mean that he was telling the truth about Mr Antrobus' wisdom teeth.'

'Oh but he was,' revealed Sharrock, triumphantly. 'You haven't got all the answers, you know. The police can do brain-work, too.'

'I never doubted it. But he was said to have had the teeth extracted in America when he was a young man. I am impressed that you were able to make such a discovery after so long a time.'

Sharrock preened himself. 'Ah, well, we have our methods. We found the name of the company in America where Mr Edwin Antrobus spent two years studying the tobacco plant and its cultivation. Very interesting indeed if you like that sort of thing. Turns out the company is still very much in business, and by means of the Atlantic telegraph we were able to learn two things. While Mr Antrobus was there he had his wisdom teeth out. All of them. He was not a brave man in the dentist's chair, but then how many of us are, even under ether? Struggled so much he half-killed the dentist before he went off to sleep. And the whole time he was there he did not suffer any accident with broken bones.'

Frances nodded. 'Then we can be quite sure that the second set of remains are not his, and I am sure the court will come to the same conclusion.'

'At least we now know who the man in the canal was. All credit to you for that one,' the Inspector added reluctantly. 'Dr Magrath has come clean and taken the blame on himself.'

'Does Mrs Antrobus know?'

'Oh yes, Mr Rawsthorne went hotfoot to tell her. He's hoping for new business on behalf of Mr Wylie, suing either Magrath or the Asylum Company or both for all those wasted legal fees.'

The rest of Frances' day was taken up with receiving the last of the reports on behalf of Mr Candy, writing to him with the results and acting on a sudden inspiration on how she might alleviate the troubles of that affectionate yet mistrusting couple Mr and Mrs Reville. She also wrote to Harriett Antrobus to advise her of recent developments, although she decided to omit the detail concerning the unusual friendship between her husband and the lady witness at the railway station. Although Lionel Antrobus was not really her client he was paying for Tom's work to find the woman who pawned the ring, and it seemed only courteous to write to him too.

That evening she and Sarah attended a meeting of the Bayswater Women's Suffrage Society and were accorded the plaudits of the members for their work. Whenever Frances appeared at the meetings there was always a small spate of new clients to follow, and on the way home she reflected that there were bound to be some bad husbands and dishonest servants whose careers would soon come to an end.

Even in Sarah's company Frances still found the night-time streets unsettling, and although it was a warm evening she was unwilling to walk home. They took a cab, thus avoiding the narrow pathway where the attack had taken place. She usually slept well after such a busy day, but this time it was not to be.

There was the stench of unwashed clothing, bad teeth and stale tobacco, the bristly scratch of an unkempt moustache. She fought hard against a horrible strength, the hard muscles of a man so much more powerful than she. All her resources could do nothing against him, the weight and force of a brute. His body pressed violently against hers. He was trying to force a chloroformed pad over her face, and she turned her head aside and fought as hard as she could, dreading the shock of a blow with his fist when she would not give in. Then another figure appeared, a dark presence, tall and strong but not threatening, holding her firmly, taking her to safety, and she smelled the rich warm spice of a cigar.

France awoke, gasping for breath, her whole body shaking convulsively, and found herself enveloped in the warmth of Sarah's massive hug. Some minutes passed before she could or even wanted to speak. It was still night and her room was unlit and very peaceful.

'Another one of them dreams?' asked Sarah.

Frances nodded. She had never told Sarah about them, but somehow was unsurprised that she knew, and she supposed that she must have been crying out. Sarah slept in the adjoining room, and Frances often heard the low rumble of her snores, which was a great comfort. 'I only wish they would stop.'

'They will,' promised Sarah. 'But if you think one might come on, go for a long walk. Walk till you sweat. Sweat hard and then sweat harder.' She was so assured that Frances did not need to ask if she had ever had such dreams herself. 'And you want to come to the ladies' classes,' she added. 'I've got them exercising with a big stick. You can do a lot with a big stick.'

Sarah wiped Frances' brow with a handkerchief and settled her back onto her pillow. 'I would be nothing without your companionship,' smiled Frances, and she soon drifted into a dreamless sleep.

CHAPTER TWENTY-ONE

A t the resumed inquest on Mr Eckley, Ratty appeared in the new suit of clothes, hat and shirt supplied by Cedric, his face scrubbed to a shine. He looked quite the man, albeit a very nervous one.

'Now then, young fellow, if you are to make your way in the world you must have a name,' advised Cedric. 'Even if it is Smith or Jones or Wilkins.'

'I dunno,' said Ratty. He glanced at the door as if tempted to dart through it. 'Ain't got no name 'cept what I get called. It's done all right for me, but the coppers don' like it.'

'When the coroner asks you for your name,' suggested Frances, 'tell him you are called John Smith. I am sure Mr Smith will not mind you borrowing his name for the morning.'

Ratty nodded. 'Will you be 'ere?'

'Of course.'

' 'N you, Mr Garter?'

Cedric smiled at the curious rendition of his name. 'Your first public appearance as a boy detective? I wouldn't miss it for the world!'

Ratty managed a grin, squared his shoulders and stood up straighter.

'If you are very good then Mr W. Grove might write a story about you, and you will be as celebrated as Miss Doughty.'

'Wot, are you Mr Grove?' asked Ratty. 'Tom's bin showin' me the books 'n I c'n read a lot of it now, 'n it's very ixcitin' wot with all the thieves 'n that.'

'Would that I had the talent to write such immortal works of literature!' exclaimed Cedric, with elaborate regret. 'Sadly I must confine my efforts to such tawdry trifles as lectures on art.'

The crowds were beginning to gather. Dr Goodwin did not put in an appearance, which might have been commented upon by the press had he done so, but Mr Wheelock, Mr Rawsthorne's unpleasant clerk, was sitting at the back, sucking ink from his fingernails, and Frances surmised that he had been sent to watch the proceedings on the doctor's behalf.

Frances looked about her to see if there were any faces in the assembled throng that she did not know, but there were not. Even the pressmen were becoming familiar to her by sight. Mr Gillan was there, as she might have expected, and young Ibbitson, who had been permitted to attend his first inquest, sat enthralled by his surroundings. She wondered if the detective employed by Mr Eckley had been traced. If so, he was not present.

The first medical man on the scene had been Dr Collin, who had certified death caused by a single stab wound to the abdomen that had severed the aorta. He could not comment on whether the assailant had been experienced with a knife or not. Some abdominal wounds gave more hope of survival, but the fact that this one had been rapidly fatal could have been mere chance. The knife had been driven to the hilt in a slightly upwards direction, probably when the victim and the attacker were at close quarters. A torn piece of paper, the corner of an envelope, had been found clasped firmly between a forefinger and thumb of the victim. He theorised that Mr Eckley, not believing himself to be in any danger, had been handing the envelope to his attacker when he was stabbed.

The position of the wound suggested that the murderer was neither very much taller nor very much shorter than the victim, who was five feet, nine inches in height. A woman might have done it, but Collin doubted that. The single swift stab showed both courage and resolution; he thought a woman would have been more hesitant, less firm.

Ratty, who had given his name to the coroner's officer as Mr Jonsmith, was called to give his testimony, and Dr Thomas, seeing that underneath his smart exterior the young witness was trembling with fright, spoke to him gently and guided him through the events with careful questions.

'Can you tell the court where you were at about eight o'clock on the evening of Wednesday the 22nd of June?"

'Yes, yer 'ighness, sir, I was near Pembridge Mews up by the deaf school.' The wry smiles of the scribbling pressmen were tempered by close interest when Ratty explained that he had been doing some secret work for 'Miss Doughtery, wot is the best 'tective in Lunnon.'

'And what did you see there?'

'Well there was the dead gent, only 'e weren't dead yet, 'n 'e wen' inter the mews walkin' all smart like, not jus' loafin' about. So I knows summink is goin' on, cos yer don' 'urry inter a mews ter do summink less'n it's ter be kep' secret.'

'Did you follow him?'

'Yes, yer 'ighness sir, 'cos I thort well wot's 'e a doin' of, so I creeps arter 'im all quiet like, wot I am very good at 'cos I'm a 'tective, 'n proper 'tectives are very good at that, sir.'

'Tell me what you saw next.'

'Mr Ecklerley 'e wen' roun' the corner, and I stayed back.'

'No one else came into the mews as you stood there?'

'No sir.'

'Were you able to hear any conversation?'

'No sir, nuthin' I dint even know there was another person there, I thort 'e was waitin' to meet a doxy.'

Sniggers in court.

Dr Thomas ordered silence before continuing the questioning. 'What happened next?'

'Then there was a gaspin' noise like what gents make when they are wiv a doxy sir, an' I 'eard 'im fall over, which they don't usually do, 'n I thort 'e might 'ave been took bad, 'n I wen' to see if I could 'elp but this person came out runnin' and knocked me down an' I banged me 'ead. 'N when I woke up I went ter see if the gent wuz ill, 'n 'e wuz lyin' there with blood all over 'is front. 'N I ran out in the street an' shouted "murder", 'n then the coppers came 'n took me down the nick.'

'Did you see the face of the man who knocked you over?'

'No, yer 'ighness, sir, I din't see nothin' it were all black, not even eyes.'

It was with enormous relief that Ratty was finally able to take a seat beside Frances, and she and Cedric both reassured him that he had done very well.

The next witness was the young man who acted as secretary to the school. On the day of the murder there had been several items of post, three of which had been marked for the personal attention of Mr Eckley, which he had passed to the headmaster unopened, as was usual. Two of the envelopes were addressed in handwriting he recognised, a governor of the school and the parent of a pupil.

The writing on the third he had never to his knowledge seen before. When he tidied Mr Eckley's papers, he had found only the first two letters. Shown the fragment of paper found in the dead man's hand, he said that it looked very like part of the envelope of the third letter. Mr Eckley would usually have gone to his home by eight o'clock, but on that occasion he had intimated that he would work a little later than usual.

The implication was very clear. Mr Eckley had received a letter arranging a meeting in the quiet dusk and had been asked to bring the letter with him. Once he lay helpless on the ground, the killer had removed the evidence. Neither the meeting nor the murder was chance.

Once all the testimony was heard the jury returned the verdict that Mr Eckley had been murdered by a person or persons unknown. The pressmen did not scamper away as usual but sent messages via runners and waited for the next inquest.

'I think the coroner was pleased with you,' Frances reassured Ratty.

He grinned with relief and puffed out his thin chest. 'Mr Jonsmif, 'tective! That's me!'

'Now I had meant to tell you something about the signs you saw when you observed the conversation between Mr Isaac Goodwin and the schoolboys,' Frances went on. 'This one,' she made the gesture as if drawing a closed mouth, 'means silence.'

Ratty nodded. 'Yes, 'e did that 'n then the boys did it too. It was like —' he thought hard. 'Like he wuz askin' 'em to be quiet and they wuz saying "yes".'

'But what about, I wonder? And then there was the sign like this —' she did the clawing movement at her shoulders. 'That means a monkey or, more likely, a scamp or scallywag. Perhaps someone has misbehaved.'

Ratty shook his head. 'It weren't like that, it were like this.' He did the movement but this time Frances saw that the clawed fingers were not at his shoulders but met at his chest and were drawn outwards. 'Is that diff'rent?'

'It looks different,' she agreed. Frances puzzled about it not only because she wanted to know what the gesture meant, but also because she had a feeling that she ought to know what it meant because she had seen it before.

There was a surge of excitement as Dr Bond arrived, which signalled the fact that he had finally concluded his examination of the skeleton that had been deposited in the cellar of Queens Road, and it was hoped that the inquest on the remains could be concluded.

Mr Marsden arrived together with Lionel Antrobus, and on seeing Frances he uttered some words to his client with a sour twist of his mouth. Antrobus' expression was unreadable.

'I wanter go now,' said Ratty, when he saw Inspector Sharrock appear. 'Don' like coppers and don' like him!' he was out of the door before Frances could say another word.

The inquest on the unnamed skeleton resumed, and Dr Bond was called.

'Since the last hearing I have examined additional pieces of bone, pieces of a human fibula, recovered from the site where the earlier remains were found. They are compatible with the conclusion that they are part of the same skeleton. None of the human bones have been duplicated. At the last hearing, and based on the condition of the right tibia, I was of the opinion that the deceased would have made a good recovery from the fracture. The new remains have led me to revise that opinion.'

There was a stir of interest in the court.

'The injury to the fibula was very substantial. I think that the deceased must have twisted the leg and either struck or collided with some hard uneven surface. The bone was shattered into several fragments, some of which would undoubtedly have protruded through the flesh. The process of healing would have been a long one. The fracture was not skilfully set and the bones have not knitted well. There is evidence of a subsequent infection. The deceased would have walked with a noticeable limp. I have also, on the basis of the new evidence and further examination of the tibia, concluded that the injury was suffered less than five years before death. I cannot be more accurate than that.'

'Have you any suggestions to offer concerning the identity of the deceased?'

'I am afraid not.'

Dr Bond stood down, and Lionel Antrobus was called forward to state very emphatically that his brother had walked with an entirely normal gait.

There was no further evidence and the jury could only conclude that the identity of the remains was unproven and the cause
of death was in all probability a broken neck, but whether by accident or design it was impossible to say.

Frances and Sarah discussed the outcome of the inquest over a simple
luncheon of ham and stewed peas, with bread and butter and tea.

'The limping man, whoever he may be, is very probably the same
individual seen in Bristol with Mr Antrobus,' Frances concluded.
'He travelled on the Paddington train, and he could have met with
an accident or been robbed and killed soon after he arrived. But
precisely where that occurred and how and why his remains came
to be at Queens Road no one can say. Why was Mr Antrobus' bag
found with him? Did he steal it? Or did Mr Antrobus, wishing to
disappear, kill his companion and leave his bag by the body in the
hope that when it was found it would be thought to be him?'

'But how would he know when, or even if, the body would be
found?' asked Sarah, reasonably. 'Seems to me that it was just chance.'

'Suppose the man was not killed where he was found. His body
had been left in another place where it had been reduced to a
skeleton and then put in the lodging house quite recently.
The interior of the sack was not stained by decomposition, so the
body was already dry bones. Whoever moved it might have been
frustrated that the body had not been found and, knowing about
the work that was to be done on the properties, put it there so the
workmen would find it.'

'Why not just leave it in plain view?'

Frances could not answer that. She sipped her tea. 'Perhaps I am
looking at this the wrong way about. The body was hidden somewhere where it has lain undiscovered for long enough for it to
become a skeleton, probably several years. It was then, quite recently,
moved to a new location. Perhaps whoever hid it didn't want it found,
and it was in danger of being found if it remained where it was.'

'That house wasn't going to be shut up forever, though. Not
with the way Mr Whiteley goes about his business. They must've
known it was going to be found sooner or later.'

'That is true. So maybe it is not *when* it was found that was important but *where*. The police have been looking into possible connections with the lodging house, which of course is a perfectly correct course of action, but perhaps the one thing we might be certain of is that the individual and the person who hid the body have no connection with the house at all, and the bones were placed there because it was conveniently unoccupied, in order to draw attention away from the original location. The fact that the house was standing empty would have been well known to anyone who passed it by.'

She put her teacup down and inspected the pot, which was empty, and sighed.

'Well, one thing's for sure, it wasn't Mr Antrobus,' said Sarah. Frances had been distracted by the puzzle over the bones but reflected that the fact that they were not the remains of the man for whom she was searching did not necessarily mean his identity was not her concern. Putting a name to the skeleton could lead her directly to Mr Antrobus.

The best clue as to what had happened to the missing man was probably the signet ring, and Frances remained hopeful that the person who pawned it would be found.

Frances and Sarah were busy during the next few days, and their other work was bearing fruit. The new suitor of Miss Digby, who had so coldly spurned young Mr Candy, was shown to be quite genuinely the cousin of a baronet. Ratty had followed him to a gentleman's club, which turned out to be one of the many establishments patronised by Chas and Barstie where they made valuable business associations. The gentleman was known to several of the members, and he had been seen in the company of his noble, if impoverished, cousin. He was handsome, amiable, courteous, single and excellent company. He was also a habitual gambler who had squandered his inheritance and was in desperate need of money. Recently he had assured his creditors that his situation was about to change, and he would soon be able to pay his debts.

Frances called on Mr Digby and imparted the news. He revealed that having given his conditional approval to the match the first thing his prospective son-in-law had done was to borrow five hundred pounds. He wondered if his daughter might reconsider Mr Candy. Frances could not advise him.

There was better news for Mr Candy, as all the men who had made claims against the charity for injured workmen had been shown to be genuine and deserving cases. He appeared satisfied with the information and said that Frances could be sure of getting more assignments from him in future. He made no mention of Miss Digby, and Frances did not raise the subject.

Frances had also managed to resolve the troubles of the respectable Mr and Mrs Reville, neither of whom, it turned out, had been faithless. After studying her father's medical volumes she had had a quiet interview with Mr Reville's widowed mother, who had finally confessed that her husband had not, as she had always maintained, died of a weak heart but from an unspeakable disease which had led to his decline into insanity, a condition which she feared might have been passed to her son. Mr Reville was deeply shocked at this news, delighted that his wife had not been untrue and resigned to the fact that his later years would probably mirror those of his father. The divorce proceedings were abandoned and the family was reunited, Mrs Reville vowing loyally to nurse her stricken husband to the end.

Frances and Sarah were at home the following Saturday when an unexpected visitor was announced, a Mrs Eves, a lady of some sixty years, who arrived clutching a copy of that morning's *Chronicle*. She was plainly dressed in an aged gown that looked as if it had long been doing duty for both summer and winter, and a bonnet of that indeterminate shade which made it hard to imagine what colour it had been when new. She brought with her a stale aroma of dusty carpets and kitchens scoured with old lemons.

At the door of the apartment she stopped, looking almost ashamed. 'Miss Doughty, I'm sorry to trouble you like this, and if you think I am being a silly old woman and send me home I would understand, really I would.'

'Come in,' said Frances, welcomingly. 'How may I help you?'

Mrs Eves crept over the threshold, and looked about her, approvingly. 'You are very comfortable here.'

'Thank you,' smiled Frances, and she offered her a chair.

The visitor sat, both hands still clasping the rolled up paper. 'Do you charge for advice? I can't spare much.'

'Tell me what you need and I will let you know. There is no charge for a simple conversation.'

'Only – I was thinking of talking to the police, but I don't want them round my place searching and upsetting my lodgers or I'd go out of business. I don't think you'd do such a thing, would you?'

Frances and Sarah had once entered a house without being invited in and battered a door down, but the circumstances had been different. 'I promise not to do so unless I believe that a life may be in danger.'

'Oh, no, nothing like that, at least, I shouldn't think so.' Mrs Eves twisted the paper in her fists. Frances waited. 'The thing is, I read in the paper today about the inquest on the bones and the man with a limp.'

'Do you think you might know who he is?'

'I could be wrong, of course, there's lots of men with bad legs. Soldiers, and men who fall off horses, or rickety, or just born crooked.'

Frances could see she needed some encouragement. 'Mrs Eves, if you tell me what you know, I promise I will make no charge at all for a consultation.'

Her face brightened. 'Oh, that's very kind, dear. Well, the thing is I take in lodgers in a house in Moscow Road. I usually have four gentlemen, all hardworking and respectable, and they pay their rent on time and give no trouble at all. But about three or four years ago, there was a man who went away without paying his rent, and I never had any word from him. I didn't think that anything had happened to him, I just thought he had decided to cheat me of my rent money.'

'So you didn't report him as missing,' guessed Frances. Mrs Eves nodded. 'And did he walk with a limp?'

'Yes he did. He told me he had broken his leg in an accident with a carriage.'

'Do you recall when you last saw him?'

Mrs Eves dug into a pocket and produced a small and very worn book. 'It's all here in my rent book. He came to stay on 3 October 1877 and the last rent I had off him was 14 November. A week after that he was gone.'

'What name did he give?'

'John Roberts'

'You had no proof that it was his real name?'

'No, not like actual papers or anything, but I never ask as long as they give me a week's money in advance.'

'Can you describe him to me? His age? His height? How was he dressed? Did he have a travelling bag?'

'Well, as to age, it's always so hard to tell with gentlemen, what with all their whiskers, but he wasn't above forty, I would say. And not specially tall or very short neither. And he wasn't dressed like a labouring man, more like a clerk. When he came he had no bag, just a few things wrapped in paper, but after about a week or two he got himself a nice leather bag, what must have cost a lot. I remember mentioning it and he said business had been good.'

'Did he wear any jewellery?'

'Yes, he'd got himself a nice ring, as well. That's why I didn't expect him to run off, when he had that ring, it showed he had some means, didn't it?'

'Did he get the ring at the same time as the bag or was he wearing it when he first arrived?'

She pulled a face. 'I can't rightly remember. I know the first time I noticed it was after he had got the bag.'

'Can you describe the ring?'

'Gent's signet ring with a stone. I didn't look close.'

Frances went to get the portrait of Edwin Antrobus that Mr Wylie had supplied and showed it to Mrs Eves. 'Is this he?'

She looked at the portrait for a long while. 'I'm not sure. It was a long while back. I'm not so good on faces.'

'Did he ever complain of toothache? Did he visit a dentist and have a tooth out?'

'Not as far as I know. But all my gentlemen have a key and they come and go as they please.'

'Well Mrs Eves, I think you may have some very valuable information, and I suggest you take it to the police at once.'

'Are you sure?'

'I am, and you may even find there is a reward involved.'

Mrs Eves cheered up at the prospect of money, as people usually did. 'All right, I'll go and tell them now.'

'Well,' said Frances when the visitor had gone, 'what can we make of that? On the 3rd of October the limping man did not have a bag. Mr Antrobus went to Bristol on the 8th with his bag and returned carrying it on the 13th. After that the limping man was seen with a new bag and a ring.'

'If he was the man Mr Antrobus was with in Bristol, he must have killed him and taken his bag and ring,' said Sarah.

'Or he could have been Mr Antrobus all along,' suggested Frances. 'Supposing he wanted to disappear and rented the lodgings as a hiding place until he could get away? Then he went to Bristol as himself, met up with the limping man, killed him and then masqueraded as him to throw people off the scent?'

'Hmm.' Sarah looked dubious. 'I can see why he would have kept the bag, as that didn't have any initials on it, but what about the ring?'

'Perhaps he couldn't take it off. Mrs Antrobus said it had been getting very tight.'

'If he couldn't take it off himself then a thief wouldn't have been able to take it off either, unless he cut it off.' Sarah made a gesture like a pair of scissors. 'Did the skeleton in Queens Road have all its finger bones?'

'I'm not sure. There were small bones missing. It would be very unpleasant to steal a ring in that way, but I suppose a desperate man might have done it.' Frances wondered what the world had come to when she and Sarah could sit and talk calmly about people's fingers being cut off.

CHAPTER TWENTY-TWO

The vigilance of Tom Smith and the pawnbroker finally bore fruit several days later, and Tom arrived at Frances' apartments in a state of breathless excitement. 'We've got the woman who pawned the ring!' he announced. 'I was keeping my eye on things up Portobello Road an' Dunnock was watching the pawnshop when Mr Taylorson come out and said somethin' to a poor woman what was lookin' in the window, and 'e must have offered her a good price for somethin' because she went in very eager like, an' then next moment, out come 'is assistant, runnin' as 'ard as 'e could, like Old Scratch isself was arter 'im, to get a constable, only I c'n run quicker, an' I arst 'im an 'e said it was the woman 'oo pawned the ring, so I tole Dunnock to watch the shop an' foller the woman 'ome if she went out, and then I went and tole Mr Antrobus an' I come straight 'ere.'

'Well done!' said Frances. 'Is Dunnock a new man?'

''E is, an' a good 'un. 'Is father's bin in prison lots so 'e really knows all the tricks.'

It was an unusual recommendation, but it clearly impressed Tom.

'Where's Sarah?' Tom looked about him as she usually had some baked treat on hand.

'She is teaching the ladies of Bayswater how to make their husbands more respectful.' Sarah had thoughtfully arranged the ladies' classes to take place during those hours when their menfolk were out and older children at school. Those with infants took it in turns to mind each other's to allow busy mothers to benefit from classes too. Frances had not so far dared to attend the classes although she had several times taken Sarah's advice and gone out for a brisk walk, which had been very beneficial.

'There'll be blood and guts before the day's out then,' said Tom with a grin. 'You'll be wantin' to go up to the station? I got a cab waitin' outside.'

Frances threw on a light wrap and a bonnet, and handed him a shilling.

She arrived at Paddington Green before the prisoner, and when she explained to the sergeant why she had come he sent a constable to go and fetch Inspector Sharrock. 'I suppose there's no point in my telling you to go home now you've carried the message?'

'None at all.'

'I've half a mind to put you in the cells,' he grumbled.

'On what pretext?'

'I've a list of them if you want to see it. There's women serving life done less than you get away with.'

Sharrock bustled in. 'Oh, it's you is it, setting the world to rights again, I see.'

'Only Bayswater,' said Frances with a smile. 'Tell me, did you receive a visit from a Mrs Eves?'

'I did indeed, about the limping man. I'm not so sure about her. We showed her the ring and she thinks it's the same one, but who's to know after all that time? There's another old wife in Redan Place who swears there was a man with a limp and a bad case of toothache lodging with her, only there was no ring and no fancy bag, and he was dressed rough like a man down on his luck.'

'Was this before Mrs Eves' lodger arrived or after?'

'Before.'

Frances thought of the transformation a change of costume could bring. 'It could have been the same man.'

A carriage drew up outside and discharged Lionel Antrobus, a police constable, Mr Taylorson the pawnbroker and a sullen-looking woman.

'Now this might prove interesting,' said Sharrock, rubbing his hands together. 'And before you even try it, Miss Doughty, this time I want to speak to our visitors myself without you poking your nose in.'

The woman was hurried protesting into the cells to consider her position while Sharrock beckoned Mr Taylorson into his room and shut the door.

There was a wooden bench and Frances sat on it. After a moment's hesitation, Lionel Antrobus availed himself of it too.

There was a long silence. 'I believe,' he said at last, 'that due to the present troubled circumstances I failed to adequately thank you for your assistance to my daughter-in-law.'

'Really, no thanks are necessary,' replied Frances. 'I hope she is well?'

'She is, and she adheres to your sound advice.'

'I am happy to hear it.'

There was another long silence.

'Are you intending to remain here to learn how the ring came to be in the pawnshop?' he asked.

'I shall not leave until I do. What is the name of the woman you brought here? Did she say anything?'

'Mrs Unwin, and she said only that she had done nothing wrong. I assume that is usual under such circumstances.'

'Almost invariably.'

'She is a charwoman and goes to many houses to do her work. I imagine that she stole the ring.' There was another brief silence. 'Have you learned any more about the man seen at Bristol railway station with my brother? Are you quite sure he was not Mr Luckhurst?'

'Yes, he has an alibi. There are two landladies who provided lodgings in Bayswater to a limping man at the time of your brother's disappearance. The police are looking into it.'

'So I have been informed. I was told he gave the name John Roberts. Probably false.'

Frances stole a glance at him and thought that behind the stony expression there was sadness and strain. He was not after all unfeeling, but his emotions were so securely locked away as to be unreachable. 'One question I have been asking everyone concerns your brother's state of mind and health at the time he disappeared. Mr Luckhurst told me the circumstances of Mr Charles Henderson's death and I have read the report of the inquest. He said that your brother was greatly affected by it, and though it was many years ago that sorrow remained.'

'I believe that to be true. Edwin never said it in so many words, but he felt a certain guilt about his uncle's death. Perhaps he thought that with the right words at the right time he might have prevented it.'

'Do you believe it was an accident?'

'Yes. Carelessness with a gun. Surprising how many men suffering from headaches are careless with guns.'

The door of Inspector Sharrock's office opened and he emerged, shaking hands with Mr Taylorson. Once the pawnbroker had departed Sharrock ordered a constable to fetch the charwoman from the cells. 'You'll be pleased to know that Mr Taylorson is in no doubt that the woman we have in custody is the one who pawned the ring.'

Lionel Antrobus rose. 'The ring is part of my brother's estate of which I have guardianship. If it has been stolen then it was stolen from me. I am prepared not to press charges against the prisoner if she will reveal where she obtained it.'

'I shall bear that in mind,' replied Sharrock. He paused. 'You have nothing to say, Miss Doughty?'

'Not at present.'

'Then there really is a first time for everything.' The woman was brought from the cells, a constable gripping her firmly by the arm. Sharrock waved them to the dingy side room where he preferred to interview some of the more malodorous prisoners, and hurried in after them.

It took him fifteen minutes to get the information he wanted. The woman was snivelling as she was taken back to the cells.

'Well?' demanded Antrobus. Sharrock beckoned them both into his office.

'Here's a pretty thing. Woman says she found it at one of the places where she cleans and carries coal. Strangely enough it's a place Miss Doughty might have come across recently. The Bayswater School for the Deaf.'

Both Frances and Lionel Antrobus were suitably astonished.

'Whereabouts in the school?' asked Frances.

'In the coal cellar. Now then Mr Antrobus, might I ask if your brother ever had occasion to visit the school?'

'None at all, so far as I am aware.'

'Perhaps Mr Antrobus went to the school for a meeting with Dr Goodwin?'

'It is possible, I suppose. But even if he did, that doesn't explain how his ring, the ring he was unable to remove from his finger, was in the cellar. Was there anything else suspicious found there?'

'I've sent two constables to look into that. But the woman swears blind she saw nothing unusual during the four months she has been working there. No dead bodies, no skeletons, nothing.'

'Skeletons!' exclaimed Frances, suddenly.

The two men looked at her. 'I have had an idea, but – oh dear! It must mean – of course! The Milan conference! It all started with that.'

'Now I don't pretend to understand what goes on in your head, Miss Doughty,' sighed Sharrock, 'all I know is it causes a lot of upset and work, and usually someone ends up in prison. They hanged one only last week, all down to you.'

'Then we must mind our manners,' said Antrobus. He rose. 'I will leave you to your enquiries Inspector. Miss Doughty, if you are not too preoccupied in arranging another hanging I will see you safely home.'

'I will go part of the way – I need to call at Pembridge Villas.'

'There's another poor criminal for it, I can tell,' cried Sharrock. 'Send him along here when you're done.'

Antrobus frowned. 'This is too dangerous a trade for a woman.'

The Inspector gave a short bark of a laugh. 'Don't argue with her, I've tried, it's a fool's game.'

'Where is your servant? Can she not go with you?' Antrobus suggested. 'I'll warrant she is the equal of any male.'

Frances smiled. 'Sarah is my assistant and she is teaching classes in ladies' calisthenics at Professor Pounder's academy.'

Sharrock rolled his eyes. 'Well that's very peculiar, I must say. I wouldn't let my wife do anything like that. She does normal, respectable things at this time of day, like taking the children to see her sister.'

Frances decided it was time to make a very quick departure. She was just out of the door when she heard Sharrock utter a loud roar.

'Who are you going to see?' demanded Antrobus, as if it was some business of his. He hailed a cab and they boarded it.

'I mean to speak to Dr Goodwin on the subject of sign language for the deaf.' She stared down at her hands, spreading the fingers out wide, then brought them together and curved her fingers in so the tips touched. She had seen Dr Collin make a gesture with the fingers of both hands over the picture of the canal remains. Looking down at her hands now she could see how they resembled a ribcage in miniature.

Her companion looked slightly alarmed, as if it was not Frances but Dr Goodwin who should be concerned about personal safety. 'I will accompany you,' he announced.

'You will not,' retorted Frances.

There was a brief argument until he saw that protest was useless, and she descended from the carriage alone.

Dr Goodwin was at home, and after a short wait Frances was conducted into his study. He looked weary, as if sleep had been eluding him for some time, but he made an effort to be both courteous and helpful. 'How may I assist you, Miss Doughty?' he asked.

'It is a question of sign language. During our last conversation I described the sign which you said denoted a monkey or some sort of rascal, but I now think I did not perform it correctly and it was something quite different. Not only that but you knew it at the time; I could see it in your expression, you recognised it, and yet you said nothing.'

He heaved a deep breath. 'This is all surmise. I have nothing to say.'

She pressed on relentlessly. 'I have a reliable witness to a conversation that took place between your son and some pupils of the school. He was in a very agitated state and he made this sign to them.' Frances placed her clawed fingers to her chest, the tips resting together on the breastbone, and drew her hands apart. 'It means skeleton, doesn't it? That conversation took place very soon after the skeleton was discovered in Queens Road. It is not too much of a surmise to conclude that that was the subject of the conversation. He swore them to silence – that much I am sure of, because you yourself told me what the sign meant – and they responded and agreed. And he did this,' Frances made the signs for doctor and the letter G. 'So you were somehow involved.'

Goodwin said nothing but stared at Frances as if looking on the face of doom.

'When your son worked as a caretaker at the school, was it a part of his duties to fetch coal from the cellar?'

Goodwin hesitated as if composing a suitable reply.

'Do not dissemble,' she warned. 'If you do not answer the question, I am sure I can find others who will.'

Reluctantly, Goodwin nodded.

'What did he find there? Or perhaps I should be asking another question. What did he put there?'

As Frances waited for a response she studied the doctor's face. 'I have seen that look before when I ask a question and the person I am asking thinks about how they might manage to tell me as little as possible. I am then obliged to come back again for the information they have been concealing. Why not save us both some time and tell me all?'

Goodwin gave a wry smile. 'Ah, you are very persuasive, Miss Doughty. I can see how you have achieved your reputation.'

'I understand that you feel the need to protect your son; he undoubtedly also feels the need to protect you. You know that he made a confession to the murder of Mr Eckley when you were arrested? Fortunately the police were able to establish very quickly that he knew nothing of the matter. Such efforts are always misguided. I beg you not to attempt the same.'

He gave in. 'You are correct of course, I did recognise that the sign was that for a skeleton. And since I knew you had been looking into Isaac's activities on behalf of Mr Eckley I guessed that it was his conversation you had seen. I spoke to him, and he admitted what had occurred. About three or four years ago there was a visitor to the school, a man who had difficulty walking. He took a wrong turn by chance, stumbled, and fell down the steps of the cellar. His neck was broken and there was nothing Isaac could do. I know he should have gone for help, but he was afraid he would be blamed and so he concealed the body under some wood. Isaac was the only person who went into the cellar, to fetch things from the stores or carry coal. There was some disinfectant he used for the drains and he scattered it on the stairs so no smells would penetrate into the hallway when the door was opened.'

'When did this happen?'

'Isaac can't recall the exact date, but it was towards the end of the year.'

'November 1877?' asked Frances, recalling that Mrs Eves had last seen her limping tenant in that month.

'Possibly.'

'And I suppose the body might have remained there forever if he had not been dismissed from his post as a result of the school's banning of sign language.'

'True. As you may imagine when Isaac realised that another person would be replacing him and going into the cellar, he had to do something quickly. The body had made a meal for flies and vermin, which Isaac had chosen not to discourage, and was by now a skeleton. He burnt most of the clothes in the kitchen range and got a scolding from the cook for his efforts because of the smell. He dared not try to burn the shoes and bones.'

'So he put them in a coal sack and then –' Frances paused. 'But when did this happen? I can guess that these are the remains that were found in the empty house in Queens Road, but if it was after your son knew he had been dismissed the house was boarded up and he could never have got inside.' She thought again. 'Oh, yes of course, I am very unobservant. He asked the children to dispose of the sack.'

'Not asked, precisely. They saw him with it, and he confessed what had happened. He was thinking of putting it in the ash bin, but they persuaded him that it was better concealed somewhere far from the school so if it was found there would be no connection.'

Frances had been quickly leafing through her notes to find the reports she had obtained from Ratty and Tom. 'The boys who walked to and from school would have passed by the house on their way and known about it. And there was some damage done to the hoardings at that time, enough so a child could get through but not an adult.'

'Empty houses have always been a temptation for boys, and there is so much building going on in Bayswater. We warn them of the dangers, of course, but they will seek adventure.'

'You do understand that Isaac has committed a crime in concealing the body?'

Goodwin nodded ruefully. 'I know, I know, and I think it would be wise if he confessed. I shall ask him to do so, and I will be happy to pay any fine that may result. I only hope the boys will not incur too much blame.'

'The boys are just children, and a court might be lenient, in fact it is possible that the police might decline to take any action against them.'

'I hope so.'

'So it only remains to discover who the man was. We have one clue. A ring was found in the cellar by the charlady. That ring was the property of Mr Edwin Antrobus, and it never left his finger.'

Goodwin looked shocked. 'No, no, he wasn't – I mean he can't have been —' he stopped.

Frances raised an eyebrow. 'The visitor wasn't Edwin Antrobus? How do you know?'

'Isaac described him to me,' explained Goodwin weakly.

'Yes?'

'He – he walked with a limp. Edwin Antrobus did not.'

'You did not see the man for yourself?'

'No.'

'I am not convinced.'

'Well – not on that occasion. He might have been the same man who was here once before. He was unknown to me. He had a business proposition that I declined. He must have returned.'

'Describe him.'

'Respectably dressed. Between thirty and forty. He limped. I can recall nothing more.'

'Did he carry a leather travelling bag?'

'I can't be sure.'

'You don't recall whether or not he was wearing a ring?'

'No.'

'Did he give a name?'

'He did but I really can't recall it.'

'And what was the nature of the proposition?'

An expression of pain suffused the doctor's face. 'He was a scoundrel. He had heard all those old rumours about me and thought he could use them for gain.'

'He tried to blackmail you?'

'Yes. I told him to leave. There is nothing that can be proved against me because there is nothing to prove.'

'But a man in your position cannot afford even rumour, however ill founded. Did this concern your meetings with Mrs Antrobus?'

'He had somehow learned of those innocent meetings and made a wholly false assumption. I put him right on the matter.'

'Is that the reason you stopped meeting Mrs Antrobus? Even as a friend? To avoid misunderstandings?'

Goodwin dropped his gaze to his desk, avoiding Frances' eyes. 'Yes, it is.'

'There is more. I need to know it.'

He swallowed uncomfortably on a dry throat and went to get a glass of water. 'Does nothing escape you? Well, you are correct. He accused me of a crime of which I am wholly innocent, a crime which I would not even have thought of committing, let alone actually committed.'

'What crime is this?'

'He supposed that I was love with Mrs Antrobus and that I had killed her husband so as to marry her. He could not have been further from the truth. I do not love the lady and have never aspired to marry. Isaac and my pupils are all the family I could possibly wish for. It seemed wise, however, to protect the lady's reputation by conducting no further meetings with her.'

'Did Isaac know about these threats?'

'No, how could he have done? I certainly didn't tell him.'

'Can you recall the date of that visit?'

'I am sorry, no.'

Frances rose to leave. The question of who the visitor was and how he had come by Edwin Antrobus' ring was still a mystery but one she did not believe Dr Goodwin could help her solve. 'I will leave it to your conscience as to whether you tell the police what has occurred, but I am confident you will do the right thing.'

'You may rely on me for that. It has weighed heavily on my mind ever since Isaac confessed the truth, and I too believe he will not incur too great a penalty.'

She left him to his thoughts.

CHAPTER TWENTY-THREE

On the following morning Sarah at last discovered the Antrobus' former charlady, by a method she was almost ashamed to relate. Realising that the servant might have recommended a relative or friend to the position when she decided to give up the work, Sarah had spoken to the woman currently employed at Craven Hill and found that she was none other than a neighbour of Mrs Fisher, the previous incumbent. Sarah called on Mrs Fisher and, after an interesting discussion involving beer, decided to bring her to Frances to tell her story.

Mrs Fisher had worked for Edwin Antrobus' uncle Mr Henderson up to the time of his death and thereafter for his heir. She had been in the house at the time of the unfortunate accident with the pistol, and it was a tale she was determined to tell to anyone who would listen and probably a great many others who preferred not.

'I shall never forget that day!' she declared, breathing beery fumes across the parlour table. 'The family was there for dinner, Mr Henderson and his old aunts, three of them, all long gone now, and Mr Edwin Antrobus and his intended and her family. Mr Henderson always had such lovely evenings. He used to play the piano after dinner while Mr Antrobus sang. He had a beautiful voice, very sweet and light, like a songbird. Good enough for the stage. If I got the chance I used to creep up into the hall to listen. That night I was just coming up from the kitchen, hoping to hear some music, when there was this terrible loud bang from upstairs and a big commotion.

'Mr Edwin, he come rushing out of the drawing room and goes running up the stairs, and two of the old ladies came out, but they stayed down in the hallway; they didn't dare go up.

'Then after a few minutes Mr Edwin came down and he was very upset and said there had been a terrible accident and Mr Henderson was dead and there was nothing anyone could do.'

She heaved a sorrowful sigh and hiccupped loudly, wiping her face with her shawl.

'There were rumours that Mr Henderson had taken his own life,' prompted Frances, 'and the inquest only held that it was an accident in order to spare the feelings of the family.'

'I don't know about no inquest. But he used to have a bad head sometimes, migraine he called it, and there weren't nothing that could take it away. So perhaps he couldn't stand no more of it and decided to blow his head off.' She shrugged. 'Or he might have been cleaning the gun and didn't see it was loaded.'

'Would a man go and clean his gun after dinner with guests in the house? Had he done such a thing before?'

'No, he used to clean it before he went out shooting and after he came back.'

'And of course, it was through his death that Mr Antrobus inherited his fortune.'

Mrs Fisher winced and rubbed her stomach. 'Poor man. He said he would have given it all away just to get that terrible sight out his head. But he never could.'

'Were he and Mrs Antrobus a contented couple?'

'Contented enough. You know about her ears, of course?'

'Yes.'

'She used to play the piano like Mr Henderson, only very quiet, but Mr Edwin never sang for her. I don't think he ever sang again after his uncle died. You know, my brother has the same thing as Mrs Antrobus. He was in the ironworks ten years, and all that banging and clanging of the hammers did for him. He can't even bear to hear birds singing now, and he used to like to listen to the birds,' she added wistfully.

'Did you ever see any reason to suppose that Mr Antrobus would desert his wife, or did he have any enemies who might have harmed him?'

'No.'

'There was a man who tried to get into the house, a ragged looking man, who he turned away. I was told you'd chased him off.'

She laughed. 'Oh yes, he had a cheek all right! I sent him packing more than once. Caught him trying to get in at a window and so I hit him with my broom, and off he went sliding down the drainpipe and jumped over the back wall like a rabbit. Lizzie told me he was Mrs Antrobus' cousin, but I didn't believe it. He was just saying that so she'd let him in.'

'But she thought he was? Why was that?'

'Can't remember now, something about Mrs Antrobus being unhappy at having such a bad man in the family.'

'Did he ever get in to steal anything?'

'Not that I know of.'

'When did you last see Mr Antrobus?'

'Oh, I didn't see him much at all because he was out at his business when I was there.'

'You don't know if he was wearing his signet ring when he left for Bristol?'

She shrugged and hiccupped again. 'You haven't got a bit of peppermint about you?'

'So,' said Frances to Sarah after Mrs Fisher had gone and the room had been sprinkled with lavender water. 'The man who said he was Mrs Antrobus' cousin Robert Barfield and tried but failed to get into the house, didn't limp. Indeed everything I have heard about Mr Barfield suggests that he was very agile. But who was the limping man? And do we have several limping men or just the one?' Frances opened her notebook and made a list.

'We first encounter a limping man in late September 1877 when he lodged in Redan Place. He is shabbily dressed, suffers from toothache and has no bag or ring. We next find a limping man on 3 October lodging with Mrs Eves, rather better dressed, no bag, probably no ring and no toothache.'

'The same man only with a bit of money?' suggested Sarah.

'Very possibly. On the 13th of October 1877 a limping man is seen with Mr Edwin Antrobus at Bristol station. Soon afterwards Mrs Eves' lodger is carrying a bag very like the one Mr Antrobus had and wears a signet ring.'

'Then he's the man on the train.'

'I think so. He then goes missing in November.'

'When did the man fall down into the cellar?'

'I don't know the exact date, but there is nothing to suggest that Mrs Eves' lodger cannot be the same man who tried to blackmail Dr Goodwin and the man whose bones were later deposited in Mr Whiteley's property in Queens Road. But he was not Mr Antrobus. Dr Goodwin is very certain that the man who tried to blackmail him was not Mr Antrobus, and it is clear from Dr Bond's recent examination of the remains that the limp was not feigned.'

'We still don't know for sure if Mr Antrobus was wearing his ring when he went away,' said Sarah. 'If it was too tight he might have taken it somewhere to get it made bigger, and then it got stolen. If that man had it how did he get it?'

Frances looked at her notes. 'You spoke to the parlourmaid Lizzie before the ring was found, so she was never asked about it. Perhaps we should see her again. She might remember something.'

Lizzie was about to enjoy a rare half-day holiday but was persuaded by Sarah to spare a short hour that afternoon as long as it involved a visit to a teashop. Frances met her there and found the maid dressed in some style, in a gown most probably given to her by her new mistress, cast off as unfashionable and made over with care. Her bonnet, which had started out quite plain, had been beribboned almost to the point of coquettishness. Many people were shocked at such displays, and newspapers often published letters of complaint, deploring the fact that it was becoming impossible nowadays to tell the difference between a lady and a servant.

Lizzie cheerfully ordered a pot of tea, with sponge cake, scones and strawberry tarts, and there was no question but Frances would be paying for the treat.

'I spoke to Mrs Fisher today,' said Frances as a cream tea sufficient for four people was brought to the table. 'She told me a very amusing story of how she chased off a ragged man from Mr Antrobus' house with a broom.'

Lizzie laughed, helped herself to a tartlet and spooned a thick layer of cream and jam on a scone. 'Oh, she wasn't a person to stand any nonsense!'

'I believe the man tried to get past you too, claiming that he was Mrs Antrobus' cousin, but you were too clever for him.'

'That's right, well cousin or not, I wouldn't let such a man into the house. He was up to no good, I'm sure of it.' She bit into the scone and wiped a blob of cream from the tip of her nose with a practised gesture.

'Did you think he was Mrs Antrobus' cousin?'

'He might have been. I know she did have a bad man in her family because I heard her talking to her sister about it. She'd read something in the newspapers that had upset her. I think he was in prison.' There was a brief lull in the conversation as Lizzie's scone disappeared in less time than Frances had thought possible. The girl scarcely paused for breath before busily attacking the tartlet. 'I don't want you to think I'm in the habit of listening at keyholes,' she went on, her voice muffled by pastry. 'That wasn't at all how it was. I only went in because Miss Pearce wanted to have a birthday tea for her sister and cook had sent me to ask what was wanted. They had the newspaper open in front of them, and Mrs Antrobus was crying.' Lizzie licked her lips and took a second tartlet. 'Mmmm. Strawberries. That was her favourite.'

'Not in February, surely?' said Frances, recalling that this was the month in which Barfield had last been incarcerated. 'A rare commodity at that time of year.' She appropriated a slice of sponge cake and a scone before Lizzie could finish the plateful.

'No, it was in the summer. Mrs Antrobus' birthday is June or July, I think.'

'Do you remember if this conversation occurred before or after the ragged man came to the house?'

'It would have been afterwards, because I remember thinking at the time that it was him they must have been talking about.'

'It wasn't just before Mr Antrobus went missing?' Frances wondered if the newspaper report might have stated that Barfield was to be released early, an understandable source of alarm, but on reflection realised that had that been the case Mrs Antrobus would have known he was free at the time her husband disappeared, which clearly she had not.

'No, it was a long while before that. A year or more.'

The summer of 1876, thought Frances, but that seemed unlikely as Barfield had already been in prison for several months then. The previous year, perhaps – maybe he had served a short sentence for a minor offence.

'Do you remember Mr Antrobus wearing a signet ring, the one he inherited from his uncle?'

'Oh yes, I remember that very well.'

'I don't suppose – and of course I will quite understand if you can't recall – if you happened to notice if he was wearing it when he went to Bristol that last time?'

Lizzie smiled, poured her third cup of tea and took the last piece of sponge cake. 'That's easy! He wasn't wearing it.'

'Really?' exclaimed Frances in astonishment. 'How can you be so sure?'

'Because I helped him take it off. Poor man, it was so tight and his finger was all sore. He said he thought he would have to have it cut off – the ring, I mean, not the finger – and he didn't want to do that because it was a memento of his uncle. So I said I knew a trick my grandma showed me, and if he had a nice bit of soap I might be able to help. And I did. He was ever so grateful.'

'What did he do with the ring? Did he put it in his pocket, perhaps? Or hang it from his watch chain?'

'No. He put it in the trinket box in his dressing room. He had all sorts of little studs and pins and things in there. He said when he came back from Bristol he would take it to a jeweller and get it made bigger.'

'This was just before he went away that last time?'

'The day before, I think.'

'So by rights it should still be there.' Unless, Frances thought, Mrs Antrobus had sold it and was unwilling to admit as much in case her brother-in-law discovered what she had done. It would take some delicacy on her part to tease out that piece of information, since Mrs Antrobus was undoubtedly afraid that her transgression would be met with an unkind response. It was, however, something the police ought to be told, and Frances wondered how she might best present the information to avoid unpleasant repercussions.

'Did you look in the trinket box after he left for Bristol?' she asked. It was just possible that Edwin Antrobus, not wishing to be parted from the cherished heirloom, had changed his mind and taken it with him just before he departed.

Lizzie dabbed crumbs from her lips and studied the menu card. 'Oh yes. I gave the ring a bit of a polish, which it needed. It came up lovely.'

Frances decided to pay a call on Mrs Antrobus to see if by any chance there was some error in the matter of the ring. She was met at the door by Charlotte, who was undeniably pleased to see her.

'Miss Doughty, we – that is, I – or perhaps it should be we – were thinking of making a call on you very soon.'

'Oh? Has there been some good news?' asked Frances as she removed her shoes.

'Well,' said Charlotte with a smile, 'not about Edwin I am sorry to say, but do come into the parlour and we will talk. Harriett is having her nap now, so I will not disturb her.'

'Before I do that, I hope you don't mind but I need to look at something.'

'Oh?'

'Could you conduct me to Mr Antrobus' dressing room and allow me to examine the trinket box there?'

Charlotte was surprised by this request but not discomfited, and she at once took Frances up to the little room. There, all the clothes and other items of gentleman's apparel were carefully stored against the owner's return, his hairbrushes, combs, soap and toilet water laid ready for his use.

'It looks as though he has just stepped out and will return at any moment.'

Charlotte gave a sad smile. 'That is how Harriett has always insisted it be kept. She never loses hope.'

There was only one small trinket box, and Frances opened it. It was empty. 'Might I ask who comes in here?'

'Only myself. I dust and clean, and keep it fresh.'

'Not the servant?'

'No, she does the heavy work of the house.'

Frances showed Charlotte the open box. 'I was expecting to find some studs and pins in here. Is that not where your brother-in-law kept them?'

Charlotte stared into the box, puzzled. 'I imagine he must have done, but let us look in case they are somewhere else.'

A quick search through some drawers revealed nothing more. 'Would your sister have sold any of these things?' asked Frances. 'The reason for my question is that I have just learned that Mr Antrobus removed his signet ring before he went to Bristol. It was last seen by the maid, Lizzie, in this box.'

Charlotte was astonished at this news. 'Oh no, she would never have dreamed of it. They were not hers to sell, but in any case, even if Edwin never returned she wanted his personal jewellery to go to her sons. I will ask her about it when she wakes.'

Frances did briefly wonder if Lizzie might have taken the items before she was dismissed but reflected that had the maid stolen the ring then she would not have revealed that it had left the owner's finger.

They were in the upper hallway when Frances said, 'You were here in this house when Mr Charles Henderson died, were you not?'

Charlotte paused. 'Yes, how did you know about that?'

'From my study of the newspapers. I was told that Mr Antrobus was greatly affected by the incident.'

'He was, as were we all.'

'Tell me about that night.'

'I don't understand. How can it be important?'

'Mr Luckhurst told me that even years later it weighed on Mr Antrobus' mind. Maybe what happened to him is connected in some way.'

Charlotte looked far away, seeing and not wanting to see. 'It was a terrible time. And it all began so pleasantly, never a suggestion of the tragedy to come. We had dined and then retired to the drawing room. Mr Henderson said he would show us his collection of snuffboxes and went to get the key, but he was gone a long time.'

'And all the company was in the drawing room when you heard the shot?'

'Not all. Aunt Lily had been exclaiming on how long it was taking him to find the key and said she knew where it was to be found; it was in a cupboard in the hallway, and so she went to fetch it. And mother was feeling very tired so Harriett took her into the parlour. There was a chaise longue where Mr Henderson liked to recline when his head ached and Harriett settled mother there and sat by her and bathed her temples with eau-de-cologne. I was in the drawing room with Edwin and the other two aunts and father.'

'So at the time you heard the shot the only person who was not in the company of anyone else was Aunt Lily?'

'Yes, but only because she was looking for the key.'

'Can you show me the study?'

'Of course. It is never locked nowadays.'

The study was smaller than Frances had expected, and she thought that had the house been occupied by a family then it might have served as a nursery. It was furnished with a desk and chair, and there were bookcases, some of which were secured with glass doors. A few volumes stood on the open shelves, but there was no sign of any snuffboxes or pistols.

'Lionel has taken all the items that might be of value to a collector and placed them in the bank,' explained Charlotte. 'He claimed it was to keep them safe, but we think it was to prevent us from selling them.'

'You did not witness the scene of death, I take it?'

'No, when we heard the shot Edwin told us to stay where we were and rushed out. Then when he came back – I shall never forget the terrible expression on his face – he said his uncle was dead, and he was sending for a doctor but there was nothing to be done. He told us all not to go upstairs. Then he went to fetch Aunt Lily and Harriett and mother and told them to join us. Aunt Lily had been in the hallway when she heard the shot, so she was nearer than anyone else and was in hysterics. She had been particularly fond of her nephew, and the shock turned her mind – she died not long afterwards.'

'Do you think Mr Henderson's death was an accident?'

'I cannot permit myself to think it was anything else.'

As they returned downstairs the servant creaked up to meet them.

'Mr Martin has come, I've shown him into the front parlour.'

Charlotte's serious face broke into a happy smile. 'Come, we will have tea.'

As Frances entered the parlour she saw the table already laid and her uncle Cornelius rose to greet her. Not only was he attired in the first new suit he had purchased in many a year but his hair was several shades darker than at their last meeting.

'My dear!' he exclaimed, beaming with delight, 'it is always a pleasure to see you but most especially so today of all days! Please join us and allow me to share our good news.'

Frances took a seat, and Charlotte managed the teacups and plates.

'You know of course that I have been a lonely man for many years, and after poor Phoebe passed away I never imagined that I would find contentment, let alone happiness, again. But how wrong I was! Miss Pearce – Charlotte I may call her now – has consented to be my wife.'

Frances had anticipated this development but perhaps not quite so soon. She reflected, however, as she offered her sincere congratulations, that neither her uncle nor his intended bride were of an age where waiting was normally advised. 'And it is our pleasure to invite you to a small gathering to celebrate our betrothal next Sunday afternoon.'

'We will only have a very few guests, as you may imagine,' said Charlotte, 'but it will be the happiest occasion this house has known for some little time.'

The servant arrived with the teakettle and Charlotte removed a cloth from a plate of bread and butter and unwrapped a plum cake that Frances felt sure was a gift from her uncle.

'Have you decided on a date for the wedding?'

Charlotte smiled. 'Not yet, but we do not plan a long engagement. It will be a small affair, as I hope that Harriett will be able to attend as matron of honour.'

'And I promise there will be no firework display afterwards,' said Cornelius solemnly. 'Really I think they should not be allowed if they can cause such unpleasantness as is Mrs Antrobus' daily lot, or if not then people who go to such things should be told to bring cotton to stuff their ears.'

'Where will you reside?' asked Frances. 'Does Mr Lionel Antrobus still intend to take the house for himself and his nephews?'

'I mean to speak to him on the subject. I think he and his nephews will be very comfortable if they take the ground floor and basement portions, and I will rent the upper floor. An investment I made many years ago has most fortuitously recently matured and will produce an income, and I will retain my present home and rent it out. There will be accommodation enough here for Charlotte and myself, and Harriett will live with us of course. I know I need to learn how to be very quiet around the house, but I am sure I can do so.' He glanced at Charlotte with an obvious expression of affection that was warmly returned.

'Do you think Mr Antrobus will permit this?' asked Frances. 'I do hope so, but he can be very unreasonable and has said he does not wish Mrs Antrobus to live under the same roof as her sons.'

'I think I can persuade him to agree. The house will be run as two quite separate establishments. He will be on hand to ensure that this is so and I will promise to respect his wishes. Once the boys are older they may make their own decisions, of course.'

Charlotte gazed at her betrothed with happiness and confidence. 'It will please Harriett so much to have them close and receive reports about their health and how their education is progressing. It is not, of course, satisfactory, but it is very much better than the present situation.'

'And perhaps in the fullness of time, Mr Wylie might make your sister a happier lady,' suggested Frances.

'I had hoped so, but I fear that may never be. I have just learned that he will shortly be leaving London to return to Bristol.'

'For a visit only, I would have thought?'

'No, he sent a note to say that he intended to reside there. It was very sudden.'

Frances was mystified. 'But I thought he was quite settled in London.'

'So we all thought, but something has happened to make him change his mind. Perhaps some family business that demands his presence.'

The peaceful celebration continued, and toasts to the happy couple were drunk in copious amounts of tea. Once home, however, Frances found the business card Mr Wylie had given her on which he had written the address of his lodgings.

'It might be nothing at all to concern me,' she told Sarah, 'but I need to know why he has so suddenly changed his mind, and if he is in a hurry then I ought not to delay.'

Chapter Twenty-Four

rances and Sarah went together to Mr Wylie's apartments and found him busy packing his possessions.

'Miss Doughty? Miss Smith? What can this mean? I am afraid I am in no position to entertain visitors as I am very shortly to depart, but if you have any news for me, please let me know it at once.'

He darted about the room as he spoke, a bundle of neckties in one hand and kerchiefs in the other.

'I have just come from the home of Mrs Antrobus,' Frances began.

'Ah,' was all he could say.

'I have received some very happy news. Miss Pearce has just become engaged to be married to my uncle, Cornelius Martin.'

'Rich gentleman is he?' said Wylie, bitterly. 'Does he have a fortune to squander in the pursuit of ghosts and skeletons?'

'I don't believe so, but I understand your annoyance. You have expended considerable funds on Mrs Antrobus' behalf and to no avail. I assume you will try to recover the cost of the court actions concerning the canal remains from the asylum company whose silence on the fate of Mr Dromgoole was so misleading.'

'I have given it my consideration, but it would be a tediously long affair and I fear that any damages I receive will pass straight into my solicitor's pockets. Then there was the second case, when – and I have to admit it – I did tell an untruth in what I thought was a good cause. And I am sure that when the next unnamed body is found it will start all over again. If I stay here any longer I will be a pauper or worse.' He dropped the ties on a chair and held the kerchiefs to his forehead. 'I have opened my purse for her, I have lied for her, what more she might ask me to do I cannot say.'

'I know I spoke harshly to you at the inquest,' Frances admitted, 'but I do see now that what you did was from the kindness of your heart.'

'Oh yes, she saw that I was an easy mark for her schemes,' he snorted. 'I am a single man, Miss Doughty, not because I cannot support a wife and family or because I have no wish to marry. I am single because I have devoted most of my life, from my early twenties, to caring for aged relatives. And I was glad to do it, make no mistake about that. When my dear mother finally passed away there was an empty place in my heart, and when I heard of Mrs Antrobus' plight that place was filled up. But there is only so much a man can do. And I can assure you that no member of my family ever asked me to commit perjury.' He threw up his hands in despair and frustration. 'What can I have been thinking of?'

'Surely that was your own idea, based on what you had learned?'

'Oh no, Miss Doughty, what do you take me for? Do I look like a man who would even think of standing up in court to tell a lie? No, I did it because Mrs Antrobus asked me to. She told me about the injured leg and the wisdom tooth when I went to see her to tell her about the discovery.'

'But that was before the bones had even been examined, and the statement Mrs Antrobus prepared for the court was vague enough that it could have applied to many men. It was your evidence that supplied the detail. If, as you say, she told you what to testify then how did she know about it?'

He gathered brushes and combs and pushed them into a toiletries case. 'I don't know and I have no intention of asking her. At the time, of course, I thought that the bones really were those of her husband and she was describing something she already knew about him and only asked me to say what I did in order to add verisimilitude to her story. Now I know differently. I have been made into a fool and a criminal. I have tackled her about it but she waves it away as if it is nothing, tries to persuade me it was just a mistake. And then —' he shook his head.

'And then?'

'Oh more funds needed for some other scheme she has, but I am finished with it now. The lawyers of Bayswater have had as much of my money as they are going to see.'

❦

When the two detectives returned home for what they hoped would be a quiet evening during which they could contemplate and discuss what had just been learned, there was a more serious concern, as they were greeted by a very miserable looking Dr Goodwin who had been waiting for Frances.

'I did as you suggested, Miss Doughty, I told the police about the man who fell in the cellar and how the boys helped to hide the bones, and I accepted that there would be a fine for concealing a death and offered to pay it, but now they have arrested Isaac for murder!'

Frances guided him to a seat and poured a glass of water. 'I am sorry to hear it. The police are sometimes a little eager to arrest the man nearest to the death, but they can have no evidence of wrongdoing. Dr Bond himself said at the inquest that a fall down a flight of stairs could have produced the injuries. If it is possible to show that the death could have been an accident, then I doubt that the matter will even come to court.'

'Please, Miss Doughty,' he begged, 'go with me to Paddington Green and speak to Inspector Sharrock. He won't let me help him question Isaac as he doesn't trust me to interpret the signs truthfully. Happily, a former teacher at the school has offered to help. But I know he listens to you. You might make him see reason.'

'I will come with you, and please do not give up hope. We may find that the Inspector is simply following a procedure that he is obliged to follow in order to clear your son's name.'

They were just about to leave by cab when Mr Candy arrived unexpectedly with another request, and Sarah stayed behind to interview him and find out what he wanted.

'I am afraid Isaac did himself no good when he confessed to the murder of Mr Eckley in a misguided attempt to save me,' said Goodwin dejectedly. 'Have you been engaged on that case?'

'No, it is solely in the hands of the police.'

'While I was at the station the Inspector asked me some more questions about it. I am very glad that you refused to work for Eckley in his attempts to blacken my character. I would have thought less of you had you done so, but there are others in Bayswater who are not so nice about how they earn their bread.'

'I cannot say I am surprised.'

'I was told that the detective employed by Eckley, thinking that his work might contain some clue as to the motive of the murderer, and probably hoping for a reward, has turned over his papers to the police. It seems he did rather well. Through means I do not pretend to understand, he was able to discover that it was I who placed Isaac with his foster parents when he was an infant. Really it seems impossible to have any secrets nowadays.'

Frances could not help smiling at this observation. 'Were you able to help the police?'

'I was obliged to inform them that I knew the identity of Isaac's mother but not the father, and they pressed me most strongly on the point. But I would not reveal what I knew except to say that while there may be ladies and gentlemen in the high life, who guard their reputations so jealously that they will commit murder to keep their secrets, I do not think that can be the case here.'

As soon as they reached Paddington Green Dr Goodwin approached the desk sergeant and asked if he might see his son. The sergeant gave a sideways look at Frances but regarded the doctor with more sympathy. 'He's being questioned now sir, so you'll have to wait. There's a lady in with him who knows all the –' he waved his hands in a rough approximation of sign language.

'Could you at least send in a note to say that Dr Goodwin is here?' asked Frances. 'We will wait until the interview is over, but we would very much like to speak to the Inspector and hope that we might be permitted to take Mr Goodwin home after his ordeal.'

'I don't know about you taking him home,' said the sergeant, gruffly, but he looked carefully at Dr Goodwin, who seemed to be about to break down. 'I'll get a note sent in to say you're here. You have a sit down now, sir. Will you stay with him, Miss Doughty?'

'Of course I will,' replied Frances, seeing that she was valued as a nurse if not a detective.

It was a lengthy wait and Dr Goodwin, looking like a man haunted by memories, said very little except to reiterate that Isaac was the best of sons.

'I am sure he has never forgotten that you rescued him from a life of destitution,' said Frances.

Goodwin refused to be cheered by this observation. 'My care is being used against him, now. The police have suggested that he is actuated by gratitude because his foster parents used him cruelly and turned him onto the street. It might prove necessary to tell them the truth.'

'The truth? How hard a commodity that is to come by.'

'We sometimes conceal it for the best of intentions, and then it comes back twisted by time and circumstance.'

Frances hesitated. 'I know you have been asked this before, and please forgive me for asking again, but I feel you are about to be open with me at last. Is Isaac your natural son?'

'No, he is not related to me by blood, but he is the son of a respectable person I cannot name. Soon after his birth I placed him with a good family who wanted a child, and he was well looked after, but when he was seven his foster parents died within a week or two of each other, the father in an accident and his wife after suffering a fit. There was no one to care for him. When I discovered his situation I adopted him. To anyone who asked I said that I had found him in the street, as I did not wish his actual parentage to become known.'

'If there is no crime involved then I doubt the police would be interested,' Frances reassured him. 'I am of course naturally curious, but if it has no relevance to any wrongdoing I will not enquire further.'

'I do not think revealing what I know would assist anyone.' His face was hard and shadowed with despair, and Frances felt sure that the truth had once again slipped away from her.

The Inspector appeared, followed by Isaac Goodwin, who was being comforted by a lady teacher and escorted by a constable. Dr Goodwin immediately leaped up and ran to him. The constable looked worried and was about to intervene but Sharrock waved him back and permitted father and son to embrace and wipe away each other's tears. There was a quick conversation in sign language, then Goodwin turned to the Inspector with an expression of horror.

'You are charging him with murder? How can that be?'

'No choice in the matter,' said the Inspector, 'and I've asked Dr Bond to have another look at the bones. Come into the office and I'll explain.'

Goodwin signed what Frances was able to recognise was his grateful thanks to the lady teacher, who patted his arm sympathetically before he followed Sharrock to his office. Isaac, with a look of heartfelt appeal in his eyes, was taken to the cells. 'Inspector, I wish to engage Miss Doughty to look into the matter and insist that she is present at our conversation,' declared Goodwin. 'One of us must have a clear mind to apply to the matter and I am afraid that today, under these terrible circumstances, it cannot be myself.'

'As you wish,' shrugged Sharrock. Once in his office he flung himself into his chair with an expression of extreme regret. 'Young Mr Goodwin is a better class of person than we usually have in here, and if it wasn't for all this business he'd be a credit to you.'

'He is, and will always be, a credit to me. But why do you believe him to be guilty of a terrible crime? There must be a mistake! What motive could he have to kill this man? He knew nothing of the fellow's threats against me.'

'I'm afraid that isn't the case. We have interviewed the school-boys who have admitted that they hid the bones on your son's behalf. It turned out that the victim was unwise enough to repeat his threats against you as he was leaving the school, and some of the boys were nearby. He made the mistake of assuming that as they were deaf they could not understand the conversation. In fact they could, as one of them can hear a little and they can all read speech by looking at the shape of the speaker's mouth. I don't know how they do it, I've tried but it's beyond me.'

A memory arose and flitted across Goodwin's features. 'I remember now. I thought I heard footsteps behind me, but when I turned around no one was there. Sometimes ...' He held a hand to his head. 'Sometimes it is hard to tell if the noise is from inside or out.'

'The boys think a lot of you, and they didn't want any harm to come to you or the school, so they went and told your son what they knew. So you see, when the man came for his second visit Mr Goodwin was very well aware that he had been blackmailing you.'

'But murder? You think him capable of that?'

'It's not what I think, Dr Goodwin. It's gone beyond that now.'

'I assume he has told you it was an accident.'

'Yes, he says he asked the man to wait in the visitors' room but he took the wrong door. Seems like a weak explanation to me.'

Frances decided to offer a suggestion. 'Perhaps he tried to trap the man in the cellar so he could call the police and have him arrested, which is a very commendable thing to do, but the man had a bad leg and stumbled and fell.'

'If he changes his story I'll let you know,' Sharrock grunted, 'but juries don't like it when the accused does that. It shows him to be a liar, and which story are they to believe? The first one, the second one, or neither?'

That, Frances was obliged to acknowledge, was very true. A change of tale was usually no more than the desperate attempt of a guilty person to escape justice by any means available.

Sharrock leaned forward. 'Dr Goodwin, did you ever wonder why the blackmailer never returned?'

'Naturally. He told me at the first visit that he would allow me some time to consider my position and accumulate the money he wanted and then he would come back. When I did not see him again I assumed that he had been arrested for some other crime. Ever since then it has been a constant worry to me that he might reappear.'

'Well, he won't do that now. And what about Mrs Antrobus? What did she think of it all?'

'This is nothing to do with Mrs Antrobus,' said Goodwin brusquely. 'I know the criminal sought to imply that I would do these terrible things because of some fancied connection, but there was no such connection.'

'But she was also accused, wasn't she?'

'Mrs Antrobus?' queried Frances, glancing at Goodwin.

'Wild foolish allegations, based on speculation. Really, these rumours about my private life are disgusting and intolerable.'

Sharrock looked unconvinced. 'Yes, the boys said that the visitor accused Dr Goodwin of murdering Mr Edwin Antrobus not so much for the sake of his wife but at her very specific request.'

'You can attach no importance to statements of that kind,' snapped Goodwin, flushing with anger. 'The man was a criminal and would say whatever he wanted in order to extract money from me. Why should I consent to such a thing, a thing quite against my nature, for someone who was no more than a patient?'

'He thought there was more.'

'I cannot help what he thought. He was wrong.' Goodwin rose. 'I have suffered these attacks on my good name for too long! Until now I have treated them with the silent contempt they deserve, but this cannot be permitted to continue. I will consult my solicitor at once, and you may expect a visit from him very soon.'

Goodwin was fuming as he left the station, but as Frances joined him in a cab home she was thoughtful. 'I believe that the blackmailer, whoever he was, is the same man who was seen in the company of Mr Antrobus at Bristol station. He was later seen with some of the missing man's property. I think he murdered Mr Antrobus but profited very little from his crime. Perhaps he imagined Mr Antrobus carried large sums of money on his person and was disappointed to find that he did not. So he tried to make further gains by using the rumours that have been circulating in Bayswater in order to blackmail you. He may have thought that if he made enough accusations then one of them would strike home.'

'He was mistaken. I have committed no crime and neither has my son.'

'Do you actually wish me to make enquiries concerning the deceased? Or was my name merely conjured to strike terror into the Inspector's heart?'

'Please do whatever you can. I have devoted a great deal of time to thinking about that unpleasant fellow, his appearance and his manner, and I can think of nothing that might help you other than what I have already said.'

Frances did at last have an explanation for something that had been puzzling her for some time. If Edwin Antrobus had been murdered by someone who had hoped to profit under his will, such as his brother Lionel or his partner Mr Luckhurst, then the murderer, impatient for his reward, would have taken steps to ensure that the body was found. Although Mrs Antrobus did very badly under the will, it was to her advantage to have her husband's death proved to enable her to challenge it. Any of those three people, had they been involved in the murder, would by now have found some way of making sure that the body was discovered, but clearly none of them had so much as attempted to do so. The mystery man, however, was a simple thief, with no interest in the will, and it had mattered nothing to him whether the body was found or not. Unfortunately, the location of Edwin Antrobus' remains was most probably known only to the man whose bones had been found in the brickyard.

With that question settled, many others remained unanswered, and there was something at the back of Frances' mind, something that Mrs Fisher had said to her, which was troubling, but she couldn't think what it was.

CHAPTER TWENTY-FIVE

Next morning, Frances was back at the *Chronicle* offices, working on Mr Candy's new commission to discover if an applicant for assistance had, as it was rumoured, previously attempted a fraud on another charity.

While there she decided to examine the newspapers for the summer of 1875 to see what article the Antrobus' parlourmaid, Lizzie, said had so distressed her mistress. Frances spent an hour reading closely every issue for June and July but saw nothing that could have had such an effect. Neither Mrs Antrobus' cousin nor anyone with whom she might have been connected had been imprisoned at that time, and there was no other item of news that might have upset her. Frances extended her search to May and August, since Lizzie's memory might have been at fault as to the month, but without result. She decided instead to try June and July of 1876, and she found it almost at once. In the last week of June, Robert Barfield, who sometimes went by the name John Roberts, also the soubriquet 'Spring-heeled Bob' because of his agility, had attempted to escape from prison, where he had been serving a term for theft. He had scaled a high wall but suffered a heavy fall onto some stones, and he had been taken to the prison infirmary with a badly shattered leg. He was expected to live, but his career as a window man was over.

When Frances came home, she took all her notes and spread them out over the table like the pieces of a jigsaw puzzle. They connected, she was sure, but the things that would link them were contained in secret conversations and meetings, what was believed or not believed and, in some cases, her own assumptions and suppositions. She knew that Edwin Antrobus was dead, she knew that he had been murdered and by whom and in all probability why. She was unable, however, to prove any of it.

One important piece of clarification could, however, be supplied by the missing man's widow.

Harriett Antrobus was delighted to see Frances; her features glowed with happiness and the light in her eyes testified to the compelling charm she must have exerted in her youth. 'My dear, dear Miss Doughty,' she breathed, 'what a pleasure it is that we are soon to be related! Please do call me Harriett and permit me to anticipate our connection by addressing you as Frances. What joy your uncle has conferred on dear Charlotte, and how well she deserves it!'

Frances sat with her future aunt and broached a difficult subject. 'I do hope that we may be very close in future, and to that end, I must implore you that there should be no secrets between us. Indeed, it is well known that sisters, or ladies who are affectionate friends and think of themselves as sisters, hide nothing from each other.' She felt a little stab of guilt as she said that, since she had imagined for some time that she had successfully concealed from Sarah the fact that she had been having nightmares. Her confession to Sarah, the appearance in her dreams of a shadowy rescuer and long energetic walks had at last consigned those terrors to the past.

'Why, whatever can you mean?' wondered Harriett, more amused than disturbed by the question. 'If there is something you wish to know, do by all means ask, and I promise to tell you everything.'

'I beg you not to be offended, but I think there are matters best resolved as soon as possible so that we may put all doubts behind us.'

'You have quite alarmed me, Frances,' teased Harriett with a friendly smile. 'But it is most intriguing too, and I am eager to discover what this is about.'

'Are you willing to admit to me that you asked Mr Wylie to lie at the inquest on your behalf so that the bones found in Queens Road would be identified as those of your husband?'

'Oh dear!' said Harriett with a soft little laugh. 'I am not at all offended, I do know that you must ask these difficult questions, and I agree that it is best to put an end to all doubts on this matter now. You will no doubt think me a very wicked woman, but I suppose, yes, I did suggest to him what he might say. After the terrible disappointment of losing the court case over the remains found in the canal, I thought this might be my last chance of setting my affairs straight. There – I have confessed my sin, and I am sorry for it. But I did it from desperation, in the hope of at last freeing myself from Lionel's clutches. Can you forgive me?'

'I am happy that you have made that clear to me,' said Frances, evenly, 'but it leaves me with another, rather harder question.'

Harriett smiled the untroubled smile of a woman with a clear conscience. 'Ah, so I am not yet forgiven. Do go on.'

'I have recently discovered that your cousin Robert Barfield attempted to escape from prison just over a year before your husband disappeared. He suffered a fall in which he was badly injured. A broken leg. I also know that he was released from prison the month before your husband disappeared. I think it is possible that he was the limping man last seen with your husband in Bristol and the same limping man who was later seen wearing your husband's signet ring. It leads me to believe that the bones found together with your husband's travelling bag were his.'

Harriett was silent for a time, her smile declining into a look of regret and sadness, then she rose and went to the piano, put aside the shawl that lay across the keys and started to play. She used only the low notes, her fingers moving very gently like the waves of a quiet sea. There was none of the emphasis that was often to be found in music, every note was the same degree of loudness as the others, monotonous and yet curiously soothing.

Frances went to stand by her.

'At the time the bones were found all the evidence we had suggested that they might be the remains of your husband. Yet, before any doctor had examined them, you knew at once they could not be his; more than that, I believe you knew that they had to be those of your cousin. Your description, the leg injury and the tooth extraction, the details you asked Mr Wylie to give in evidence, evidence you very carefully distanced yourself from by making your statement sufficiently vague to avoid all blame; I really do not think that was coincidence. Yet you told me yourself that you had not seen your cousin since he was a child.'

Harriett stopped playing, replaced the shawl across the piano keys and carefully closed the lid. 'I suppose that I could not persuade you that it was by chance?'

'You could not.'

'No, of course, you are far too clever for that. My poor, poor cousin, what a terrible fate.'

'I believe that you have been concealing from everyone that you saw him after he came out of prison in September 1877 and that he came to this house after your husband disappeared.'

Harriett returned to her comfortable chair and poured water for them both. She sipped slowly, her eyes misting as she did so. 'Yes, he had been watching the house. He knew he would not be allowed in, but he saw that I sometimes went to visit my father's grave. One day I found him waiting for me by the cab. He was in a pitiful state. His clothes were those of the gutter, his injured leg pained him with every step and he was in agony from an abscess on his wisdom tooth. I allowed him to join me and we rode up to the cemetery together. Of course he was desperate for money, and I gave him a brooch and a bracelet of mine. But there was a sense in which his injury was almost a blessing. You see, I dared to hope that if he was no longer able to make his living by thieving he might resort at last to honest work. I told him that if he was to get some better clothes and go to the baths and the barber, and find respectable lodgings, and see a man about the toothache, he might be able to present himself well. I even offered to recommend him to Edwin and Mr Luckhurst as a reformed character and ask if he might be given some employment.

Unfortunately, while he was happy to take my jewels, he did not approve of my plan since it involved actual work. His mind was only able to engage itself with criminal designs. Now that I think about it, it was a foolish idealistic plan. Had Robert gone to work for Edwin he would have stayed only long enough to discover how he might steal from him and then run away with a bundle of tobacco or boxes of cigarettes.

But Robert had much larger ideas. He entertained the wholly erroneous belief that if something were to happen to Edwin then I would be a wealthy woman. I could see where that was tending: he thought that if I was wealthy then he could live in idleness off my fortune. I disabused him of that assumption very quickly. I told him that I would not come into great wealth on Edwin's death, instead I would be forced to rely wholly on the generosity of my brother-in-law, who I was quite sure would not give him a penny piece.'

'Did your cousin actually suggest that he might cause some harm to come to your husband?'

'Not in so many words, it was more of a veiled allusion to judge me by my reply. But I knew what he meant. I said I would not listen to his foul schemes and had nothing more of value to give him and that was an end of it. I didn't think I would see him again.'

'But you did.'

She cradled the water cup in her hands and stared into it as if trying to divine her future. 'Yes.'

'When was this?'

'It was soon after Edwin had failed to return from Bristol. Robert, having improved his appearance as I had suggested, and had his bad tooth taken out, came to see me and claimed that he had been to Bristol and killed Edwin. I didn't know if he was telling the truth, one could never be sure of that with Robert, but he was carrying Edwin's bag with his card case, so I knew at the very least that he had robbed him. I begged him to let me know where Edwin was but he just laughed and said that all would become clear in time. He wanted me to sign an agreement to make over half my fortune to him should I become a widow. I said I would do no such thing. He said that if I did not he would make my life such agony that I would not want to live it. He went away promising that he would come back very soon and that I must do as he demanded or it would be the worse for me.'

'Do you know if he went up to your husband's dressing room during that visit?'

'He did, without my permission, look around the house, and he said what a fine place it was and how he would enjoy living here.'

'I think that was when he took the opportunity to steal some of your husband's trinkets, including the signet ring. Did he return?'

'No, I never saw him again. There was so much in the newspapers about Edwin's disappearance I assumed that Robert was keeping out of the way but would come back to torment me when he needed money. As time passed and he did not reappear I thought it very probable that he was in prison again.'

'Harriett – why did you say nothing of this? You have concealed the truth not only from me but the police too. They would see that as a crime.'

'Because I was afraid,' she pleaded. She put aside the cup, and taking Frances' hands, pressed them earnestly. 'I was afraid of Robert and what he might do to me. Until the bones were found I thought that he was still alive and could come back at any time. When they were found, I knew that I was finally free of him, free from fear, and at the same time I thought that if the bones could be identified as Edwin's then I would be free of Lionel too.'

'I understand. Your cousin knew that you would be powerless until your husband's body was found and used his knowledge of its whereabouts to try and force you to agree to make over the fortune of which he imagined you would become mistress. Unfortunately he died before he was able to reveal where he had hidden the remains.'

'Then you do think Edwin is dead?'

'I don't know for certain, but I fear he is.'

Harriett heaved a sigh that seemed to come from her soul. She picked up the water cup and drank again. 'Will you pursue your enquiries? I ask not as a client but a relation. It would mean so much to me if you did.'

'I will do what I can. I assume I am no longer engaged by Mr Wylie since he is gone back to Bristol.'

'So Charlotte has advised me. After the last inquest we found ourselves no further forward, and I hoped he would help me pay for some more searches to be done, but he would not. I think he is angry with me. He has never forgiven me for suggesting what he might say in evidence.'

'Did you know that a man has been arrested for the murder of your cousin?'

'No, I had not heard. One of his criminal associates, I suppose.'

'No, it is Isaac Goodwin, Dr Goodwin's son.'

'Really? How astonishing! But he is just a boy.'

'I believe and hope that your cousin's death will prove to have been an accident. A fall down some cellar stairs. But Mr Goodwin is under suspicion because your cousin had been trying his black-mailing tricks on his father, accusing him of being responsible for your husband's death. Now why should that be?'

'Why indeed?' responded Harriett. 'What possible reason could Dr Goodwin have to harm Edwin?'

'None, but your cousin may have fancied that Dr Goodwin wished to remove a rival for your love.'

'Oh that is absurd. We were doctor and patient, nothing more.'

'So Dr Goodwin says.'

There was just the smallest indication that, despite her words, Harriett was not flattered to know this.

Frances called on Dr Goodwin and, as was so often the case, was unsure as to whether the news she was bringing would please him or not. She found him not exactly cheerful but more optimistic than before.

'I have just come from a long consultation with Mr Rawsthorne, and I am encouraged to believe that no prosecution will be brought. He has advised Isaac to say no more than he has already said, and if he holds his nerve all will be well.'

'I am glad to hear it,' said Frances. 'Since we last spoke I have made a discovery which suggests to me that the man who called on you was none other than Robert Barfield, a cousin of Mrs Antrobus. He was the outcast of the family, more often in prison than out, a burglar who once rejoiced in the appellation "Spring-heeled Bob".'

'He had no spring in his heels when I saw him,' grunted Goodwin.

'He had injured himself attempting a prison escape, and his old profession was closed to him. When he came out of prison in 1877 he accosted Mrs Antrobus and offered to murder her husband, believing, despite her assurances to the contrary, that on his death she would become rich and he would live off her.'

Goodwin gave her a curious stare. 'Did he now?' He seemed about to say more but closed his mouth firmly.

'I think he followed Mr Antrobus to Bristol. Perhaps he hoped to find an opportunity to kill him there but failed, and the two were seen at the railway station together on their way back to Paddington. He was later seen in possession of Mr Antrobus' bag and signet ring.'

'So the body has not yet been found?'

'No, and it may never be.'

'Neither man was seen alighting from the train?'

'I believe not. Of course Paddington is such a very busy station.' She prepared to depart. 'I will let you know if I discover anything further. The case has become of greater importance to me now, in view of the fact that I will soon become related to the family.'

'Related?' he exclaimed. 'How so?'

'My uncle, Mr Cornelius Martin, a widower, is due to announce his engagement to Miss Pearce. It has all been a little sudden, but I am happy for them both.'

Dr Goodwin appeared anything but happy.

Frances faced him across his desk, placed her hands upon its surface and leaned forward to speak in a firm and earnest manner. 'I don't know what it is that you know, but I beg of you to reveal it either to me or to the police. I think that you are concealing something, not from a sense of guilt but out of a desire to protect a reputation. But think of this: murder has been done, and who knows but it might be done again? Imagine the guilt you will feel should a life be lost and you know that you could have saved it by speaking out. The choice is yours to protect either a reputation or a life.'

He was silent, but she had said enough and left him.

CHAPTER TWENTY-SIX

On Sunday afternoon, after the cool quiet of church followed by a simple luncheon, there was a family tea party at Craven Hill to celebrate the betrothal of Miss Charlotte Pearce and Mr Cornelius Martin. The happy couple were joined by Harriett Antrobus, Frances and Sarah in Mrs Antrobus' private parlour, and Cornelius had thoughtfully engaged a tidy little maid to fetch and carry so his affianced lady should not have to trouble herself.

There was quiet conversation over the wooden cups and plates, and Cornelius revealed that he had spoken to Mr Lionel Antrobus who had agreed to his renting the upper part of the house after the wedding. Only immediate family would attend the ceremony, and Harriett had consented to be matron of honour. Shyly, Charlotte asked Frances if she would be bridesmaid and hoped that Sarah would be one of the witnesses. After receiving their warm agreement there was much talk of gowns, Cornelius maintaining a cheerful silent smile, despite the inevitable expense that must follow.

The maid, who had been well instructed, moved about as if afraid to make any noise at all. Charlotte was just about to ring for the girl to freshen the teapot when she appeared at the door. 'If you please, Miss, I'm very sorry to intrude, but there's two policemen say they want to talk to you very urgent. I tried to put them off, but —'

Cornelius rose. 'I will deal with this,' he said, but before he could do so, Inspector Sharrock walked in.

'Oh,' gasped the maid, 'I am sorry —'

Sharrock looked about him at the company and the tea table. 'Well this is very nice.'

'Inspector, your visit is most inconvenient,' Cornelius protested. 'This is a family celebration. Can you not return another day?'

'Please can everyone moderate their voices,' asked Mrs Antrobus faintly, holding her hands over her ears.

'Yes, let us be calm and do as Harriett asks,' agreed Charlotte. 'Elsie, bring more hot water, please.'

'I don't think so,' said Sharrock, barring the maid's way. 'Elsie, you be a good girl and sit quiet in that corner. My business isn't with you, but I want you to stay here.'

Frances saw that he would not be deflected. The maid, who was retreating to a chair looking very frightened, had, she noted, announced the arrival of two policemen, yet only Sharrock had entered the parlour, and Frances wondered what the other one was doing. 'Might I at least request that your business be completed swiftly so we may continue our celebration?' she said. My uncle and Miss Pearce have just announced their betrothal.'

Sharrock did not share the joy of the company. He had not been offered a seat, but nevertheless he sat down. 'I am investigating the murder of Mr Jonathan Eckley and have made a list of all persons who might have had a motive to kill such a highly respected gentleman. You know of his quarrel with Dr Goodwin, however I am satisfied that the doctor has an alibi for the time of death. I have also interviewed all the teachers recently dismissed from the school by Mr Eckley, which was very interesting since they were all deaf. Funny business that. However, I have been able to eliminate all of them from my enquiries. Mr Isaac Goodwin is also not under suspicion for that crime. Recently I was supplied with some documents relating to work carried out for Mr Eckley by a private detective.'

Cornelius glanced questioningly at Frances, and Sharrock smiled wryly. 'No, on this occasion it was not Miss Doughty, but another, less illustrious member of that profession. Amongst those documents was a list of names: the persons he had interviewed on the subject of Isaac Goodwin, whose parentage he had been engaged to discover.'

'Then you will know that the detective came here and spoke to us,' said Harriett. 'He said that he was interviewing all former patients of Dr Goodwin and their families.'

'Indeed, and his account of that interview shows that while you believed your mother was once a patient of Dr Goodwin, you had no information to impart regarding Mr Isaac.'

'Yes, that is so.'

Sharrock pulled a notebook from his pocket and thumbed through the pages. 'Following that interview, however, Miss Pearce paid a visit to Dr Goodwin. Is that not the case?'

All eyes turned to Charlotte. 'Yes,' she admitted. 'I thought he should be warned about the enquiries, as it seemed to me that someone was attempting to defame him, and it has always been my belief that he is an honourable man.'

'During your conversation with Dr Goodwin, he mentioned to you that he knew who was employing the detective, in fact he told you that it was Mr Eckley.'

'Yes, he did.'

'But having warned the good doctor about the detective, and discovered that he already knew about him, I would have thought that you had done all that was required.'

'Inspector, where is this leading?' Cornelius demanded.

'All will be clear in a moment, Sir,' said Sharrock. 'The thing is that shortly after Miss Pearce called on Dr Goodwin, a lady who had taken care to wear a thick veil called on Mr Eckley and demanded a private interview. Now the maid who admitted her did not of course see her face, but the case being curious she took note of the lady's dress and height, and it was distinctive enough that she felt sure that she would be able to recognise her again.' He consulted his notes. 'Woven braid used to mend the cuffs of the gown and an unusual padded bag. I am in very little doubt that the lady in question was Miss Pearce.'

Charlotte took a deep breath. 'I do not deny it. I went to beg Mr Eckley not to continue his pursuit of a good and innocent man.'

'That was very kind and brave of you my dear,' soothed Cornelius, patting her hand.

'If the ladies would be good enough to let me know where they were on the night of the murder of Mr Eckley?' asked Sharrock. 'That would be a week ago last Wednesday? About eight o'clock?'

The sisters glanced at each other. 'I am sure we were at home here together as we usually are,' said Mrs Antrobus, 'but one day is so very like another.'

'It would have been the day after the investigator called,' Sharrock told her. 'The day after Miss Pearce made her visits to Dr Goodwin and Mr Eckley. That might help place it better in your mind.'

'You were ill all that day,' said Charlotte turning to her sister. 'I remember thinking at the time that it was because that man had upset you.' She addressed the Inspector. 'Harriett sometimes wakes up with a pain in her head and when she does it can last the whole day until she sleeps again. She usually retires to bed very early on those occasions.'

'So at the time Mr Eckley was being stabbed, Mrs Antrobus was in bed. And you, Miss Pearce?'

'I was here, doing some needlework.'

Constable Mayberry appeared in the doorway. 'Sir – I found these in the kitchen,' he said, handing over some cook's knives.

'Good work,' approved Sharrock, examining the knives closely. The metal blades clattered together as he did so, and Harriett flinched. 'Interesting. A matching set, I believe. Nice quality. Were these all you found?'

'That was all, sir.'

'Inspector, where is this questioning tending?' asked Cornelius, 'because I am finding it most objectionable. And please stop making so much noise.'

Sharrock said nothing but pushed aside some of the dishes on the parlour table to make a space and laid out the knives on the cloth in order. There were four of them, ranging in size from a small paring knife to a cleaver, but he then parted them to leave a space between the second and third. 'Something missing, I think: medium size, six inch blade. Something like this.' He took a paper-wrapped object from his pocket and laid it in the space, then opened up the paper. It was the missing knife, stained with blood and dirt.

Harriett uttered a little gasp and placed a hand over her mouth, and Charlotte recoiled in distaste. Frances and Sarah, who had seen worse sights, gazed at the object with interest. All the knives, including the one Sharrock had brought, had the same design of stout wooden handle stamped with the name of the manufacturer.

'Surely this is not an object to place on a tea table in front of ladies,' Cornelius objected. He made to cover it with a napkin, but the Inspector stretched out an arm and prevented him. 'You are not suggesting it is from the same set are you? The wear on the handle is quite different from the others.'

'The ladies might be able to enlighten me on this,' suggested Sharrock, 'but it is my belief that in a set of knives of different sizes the cook does not use them all the same amount, so some get worn more than others.'

Cornelius glanced at the ladies in the room. 'Miss Smith?'

Sarah nodded. 'The Inspector is right.'

Sharrock had that air of satisfaction that always preceded his making someone's day very uncomfortable. 'You see, I think that Miss Pearce's anxiety over Mr Eckley's enquiries was not so much for Dr Goodwin but for her own reputation and indeed, as I now see from this little celebration, her future prospects. I believe she made an appointment to see Mr Eckley in private, perhaps luring him with the promise of information for his pursuit of Dr Goodwin. She slipped out of the house when Mrs Antrobus was in bed, taking this knife, and stabbed Mr Eckley. As she ran away she bumped into the young person called Ratty. He saw no face, not even eyes as he might have done in the case of a masked robber. What I think he saw was a lady wearing a heavy dark veil. Not wanting to be seen running down the street with a wet bloodstained knife, or get blood on her clothes by putting it in her pocket, she pushed it into one of the flower urns near the school, hoping to recover it at her leisure.'

'This is outrageous!' exclaimed Cornelius, forgetting himself, and Mrs Antrobus whimpered in pain and covered her ears. 'Inconceivable! What possible motive could Charlotte have to do such a thing? She is a gentle creature and quite incapable of any such action.'

Charlotte took his hand and pressed it, laying a finger against her lips.

'As to motive, that is something that the lady might wish to discuss in private,' said Sharrock. He rose to his feet. 'Charlotte Pearce, I am arresting you for the murder of Jonathan Eckley. You are advised not to make any statement that might tend to incriminate you. I require you to accompany me to the station for further questioning.'

Cornelius made to protest, but Charlotte silenced him and rose. 'I will go. Miss Doughty – Frances – would you be so kind as to stay here with Harriett?'

'And I will accompany you, my dear, and do everything necessary to resolve this dreadful mistake,' Cornelius assured her.

The unfortunate maidservant was sitting in a corner, sniffling with fright. 'Please, everso please, can I go home now?' she whispered.

Cornelius pressed a coin into her hand. 'And not a word to anyone of what has happened here.' She looked at the coin, gasped, nodded and hurried away.

Charlotte departed soon afterwards, leaning on Cornelius' arm, the couple flanked by the two policemen. Frances and Mrs Antrobus were left with the dismal remains of the celebration. Frances did what she could to console the lady in her misery, but at length the conclusion was that the only thing that would mend the situation was Charlotte's return.

'I have every confidence in my uncle,' said Frances. 'He will leave nothing undone to assist, I know it.'

'I am sure of it. He is a true gentleman and a good friend.'

'Perhaps if you were to tell me everything you know, I might be able to find some way in which I too can help. Is it true that Charlotte went to see both Dr Goodwin and Mr Eckley?'

Harriett nodded.

'What do you think Inspector Sharrock meant when he referred to Charlotte wanting to protect her own reputation and prospects? Is he just guessing at something?' Frances' mind went back to her conversations with Dr Goodwin, the fact that he had admitted he knew the identity of Isaac's mother and her own firm exhortation to tell the truth, however upsetting. 'Or has he learned that Charlotte is Isaac Goodwin's mother? I think he has.'

'All is now ashes!' moaned Harriett. 'My poor sister! I am told the boy is handsome and the image of his father. I hope he is never so cruel as to deceive an unfortunate girl. The man came to the shop – Charlotte assisted our father there sometimes – he represented himself as single and offered her marriage. But we found out too late – far, far too late – that he already had a wife and children.'

'And Dr Goodwin, who knew your mother since she was a patient of his, helped find a family to care for the child.'

Harriett clasped Frances' hands. 'We were so nearly sisters, I think of you still as a kind sister. I know you will not broadcast poor Charlotte's shame.'

'No, of course not. I can see why someone might suppose she had good reason to try and stop Mr Eckley from making his enquiries, but from pleading with him to taking violent action against him is a long step which I cannot believe she would take.'

They were expecting a message from Cornelius, but in the event he returned to the house alone, looking like a man crushed by fate. 'She has been charged with murder,' he told them, quietly. 'I have procured the services of a solicitor to stay by her side while Inspector Sharrock speaks to her, but he would not permit me to be present. And would you believe, my poor dear Charlotte never for one moment thought of herself, only you, Harriett. She could not be easy in her mind until I assured her that I would engage a competent servant to care for you, which I have done, and she will be here directly. But you have my solemn promise that I will not rest until Charlotte is free again. Frances, you must instruct Tom Smith's boys to carry messages to me from the police station every hour of the day, every minute if need be.'

'Of course I will.'

He shook his head in disbelief. 'They really have no evidence. There must be a thousand knives like the one the Inspector had all over London. It is outrageous that the police should be going about arresting respectable people – are there no criminals in Bayswater?'

'There are any number of desperate persons willing to stab a man to death for the sake of his watch,' said Harriett. 'One reads about them in the newspapers all the time. The Inspector must be urged to look for them. Frances – will you try to convince him?'

'I will do what I can.'

Within the hour a large comfortable-looking nursemaid had arrived and taken charge of the patient, and Frances went home to reflect on the events of the day.

CHAPTER TWENTY-SEVEN

Next morning Frances, with a firm sense of what she must do, returned to Craven Hill to see Harriett Antrobus. She found the lady in a better state than she might have been under the circumstances, declaring that the nursemaid Cornelius had engaged to care for her was 'a treasure and a miracle. Nothing is too much for her, and she even has a gruff voice. Your uncle is so very kind to me.'

'I will reassure Charlotte that you are well looked after and keeping in good spirits,' Frances promised. 'I was able to see her just now, and she is hopeful that all will be resolved happily very soon. There is no further news on the case, but I did speak to Inspector Sharrock, and I think I have made good progress towards persuading him to direct his enquiries another way.'

'Oh, but that is wonderful!' breathed Harriett. 'I am sure no one but you could have achieved so much.'

'There is still a great deal to be done before Charlotte can be declared innocent of all blame, but I have given the matter careful thought, and I think I can see a way of further influencing the Inspector. I have come to know his ways and character very well in the last year or so. Despite his harsh manners and rough exterior, Inspector Sharrock does have a sympathetic nature, and I think he might respond to an appeal made by two ladies together with my uncle, who I believe has impressed him as a respectable gentleman incapable of untruth.'

'But you cannot expect me to go to a police station,' Harriett objected. 'There would be crowds of noisy people there. I could muffle my ears of course, but how might I then hold a conversation?'

'No, I understand that and would never ask you to do such a thing, which is why I have asked both the Inspector and my uncle to come here today.'

'Today?'

'I know I have taken a liberty by inviting guests to your home, and I beg your forgiveness, but I thought you would not wish your sister to remain in custody for a moment longer than is necessary.'

'Not a single moment,' Harriett agreed. 'What a surprising and energetic young woman you are; I can see why the newspapers praise you so.'

Soon afterwards Cornelius and the Inspector arrived as arranged, Sharrock looking grim and Cornelius weary but resolute.

When they were all assembled in the little parlour Frances addressed the Inspector. 'I have asked you to come here today to listen to the very earnest entreaties of Mrs Harriett Antrobus on behalf of her poor sister. You will, I am sure, admit that she knows her own sister better than anyone and can give you a full understanding of her character. When you have heard what she has to say you will see that it is quite impossible for Miss Pearce to have acted in the manner of which she has been accused.'

Cornelius nodded emphatically. 'Well said, my dear. Inspector, I beg you to listen and take good note of what both my niece and Harriett have to tell you.'

'We also feel very strongly that the police have been hasty and presumptuous, and ignored other far more obvious avenues of enquiry,' added Frances, glancing at Harriett, who nodded emphatically.

'Oh we have, have we?' growled Sharrock. 'Well let Mrs Antrobus speak for herself.'

Harriett turned her bright, luminous eyes to the policeman. 'I am so grateful that you have taken the trouble to listen to me. My poor sister is a gentle selfless creature, who has laboured all her life in the interests of others but has never committed an act that would harm another. She would be quite incapable of doing so.'

Sharrock remained unconvinced. 'People have surprised me before with what they are capable of; they've surprised their nearest and dearest too.'

'But your actions are so blinkered!' exclaimed Cornelius, loud enough to make Harriett wince. 'First you arrest a respectable doctor and then a virtuous lady! Who will be next? The Lord Mayor of London?'

'Indeed,' continued Harriett. 'Why cannot you look for some common street thief – every day the newspapers tell of desperate creatures who commit the most terrible crimes for next to nothing. Mr Eckley was surely lured into the Mews and murdered by a robber for the sake of his watch.'

Sharrock shook his head. 'Street robbers act on the moment, they see something and they snatch it or they follow their mark to a quiet place. They don't make an appointment by letter. We know that Eckley received a letter that day and took it with him to meet his murderer. We found a fragment of it in his hand.'

'But you don't know what the letter said,' reasoned Harriett. 'It might have had nothing to do with the case.'

'Then why would the killer take it away? It makes no sense. People don't steal letters. No, the killer took it because it made the appointment and was incriminating. Eckley must have been told to bring it to the meeting. The watch was only taken to make it look like a robbery.'

'Harriett,' interrupted Frances, softly, 'how did you know that Mr Eckley's watch had been stolen?'

Harriett looked startled, but recovered. 'The Inspector has just said so.'

'Yes, but you mentioned it before he did.'

'Did I? Then you must have told me about it.'

'I did not.'

'In that case I must have read it in the newspapers, in the account of the inquest.'

Frances shook her head. 'I was at the inquest. It was never mentioned.'

Harriett turned to Cornelius. 'Then you must have told me, I am sure that someone did.'

'I didn't even know that his watch had been taken,' protested Cornelius.

Sharrock gave Harriett a penetrating stare. 'Very few people indeed know of it apart from the police.'

'Then I must have been mistaken,' said Harriett, lightly. 'Perhaps I was confusing it with something else.'

'Oh but you seemed very certain of yourself just now,' Sharrock persisted. 'You've been caught out, Mrs Antrobus. Just as we hoped you would be. All credit to Miss Doughty for spotting your little mistake yesterday and also for realising that it would be better evidence if spoken before a police witness. You see, to my mind there are only two ways that you could have known that Mr Eckley's watch had been stolen. Either you were there yourself and took it or you were told about it by the person who did. It's one of the two. Now which is it to be?'

Harriett looked about her, suddenly afraid, but there was no sympathy to be had from Frances.

Cornelius was astounded at the sudden turn in the conversation. 'Have you taken leave of your senses?' he exclaimed and then looked at Frances appealingly. 'Say something!'

'I'm sorry uncle, but I agree with the Inspector. I am waiting to hear what Harriett says.'

There were a few moments of quietness, broken only by the sound of Harriett trying to stifle her tears. 'I'm so sorry,' she told them, 'I admit that I have been telling untruths, but it was for the best of reasons, to save my poor sister. Can that be wrong? Does she not deserve to be happy? Perhaps I was selfish, wanting her always to be by my side. But she has done a terrible thing and I suppose she must suffer for it now. Charlotte wanted to stop Mr Eckley's enquiries because she knew,' Harriett took a deep shuddering breath, 'she knew that Mr Martin would abandon her when he found out that she was the mother of Isaac Goodwin.'

'What?' cried out Cornelius, aghast, and Harriett flinched at the stab of sound. He looked contrite and allowed her to recover before she went on.

'That day, when I woke with one of my headaches, Charlotte must have known that I would be retiring to bed before my usual time. We went out for an early walk in Hyde Park to get some air. The streets are at their quietest then, and when we passed the pillar letter box by the church she posted a letter. She tried to distract me by drawing my attention to the flower beds but I saw what she did, and when I asked about it she said it was a note to Mr Martin. That night I retired to my room at six o'clock and did not rise again until six the next day. I did not see Charlotte in all that time, but next morning she was so upset that she confessed what she had done. She told me she had put the knife in the flower urn, she said it was covered in blood and she dare not put in her pocket or she would stain her clothes.'

Cornelius hid his face in his hands and groaned.

'And she took the watch so the motive of the crime would appear to be robbery?' asked Sharrock.

'Yes.'

'What did she do with it?'

Harriett fidgeted and her eyes flickered nervously about the room. 'She knew she could not sell or pawn it. She threw it away.'

Frances had been watching the eyes of the trapped woman. She rose and went to the writing desk and tried to open the drawer, but it was locked. 'Please let me have the key to this drawer.'

'I don't have it. Perhaps Charlotte has it.'

Frances turned about and came to face her. 'I'm afraid I don't believe you. In fact I don't believe most of what you have been saying to me for the last month. I am going to have to search you.'

Harriett recoiled. 'Please, no,' she whispered.

'I think you would prefer it to the Inspector searching you, which I am sure he is prepared to do.' Sharrock looked alarmed at the suggestion but said nothing. 'Or to avoid any searches, kindly give me the key.'

'Harriett, I beg you,' said Cornelius, 'we must have this resolved. For the sake of decency give Frances the key to the desk. If you cannot then I will force the lock myself.'

Harriett hesitated and, without meeting the gaze of anyone in the room, took a key from her pocket and handed it to Frances. Cornelius smiled in relief, took Harriett's hand and patted it gently. 'Don't worry; all will be well, I am sure of it. There has been a terrible mistake. Frances will find the answer, she always does.'

'You are such a good kind man,' murmured Mrs Antrobus, gazing up into his face, her eyes bright with tears, and Cornelius, like so many men before him, was unable to do anything but melt in sympathy.

As Frances unlocked and opened the drawer the Inspector hurried to her side and peered in. 'Aha!' he said, loudly enough to make Mrs Antrobus wince.

Cornelius cupped his hands protectively over Harriett's ears. 'Please – this lady has suffered enough.'

Frances stood back, and Sharrock delved into the drawer, removed a silver watch with a broken chain and held it up. 'That should match the portion of chain found on the body, and if I am not mistaken, we have an engraving here – J.E.'

'Charlotte gave it to me, she told me to hide it,' whispered Harriett.

'Was that before or after she threw it away?' retorted Sharrock sarcastically. 'Mrs Antrobus, I am arresting you for the murder of Jonathan Eckley —'

'No,' Harriett wept. 'Please don't put me in a cell, I couldn't bear it.'

Cornelius stared at her in horror. He let go of her hand, rose and looked at the watch. 'There can be no doubt?'

'None,' Sharrock assured him. 'This is the murdered man's watch. If Miss Pearce didn't kill him then Mrs Antrobus did, and my money is on this lady here. Why don't you call a cab, sir, and we can take her to the station?'

'Please — no,' begged Harriett.

'Inspector — Uncle — might I suggest something?' Frances interrupted. 'I think in this very particular and unusual case it would be better if Mrs Antrobus was not taken to the police station but placed in some other secure custody, somewhere that would not be torture to her. A sanatorium, somewhere quiet. You could employ suitable women to guard her.'

'I don't have armies of women at my beck and call to guard special prisoners,' argued Sharrock, 'neither do the police have limitless monies for fancy sanatoriums.'

'I am sure some arrangement could be made. Would you consider it? Uncle, can you help?'

Cornelius hesitated and then gave in. 'Very well, for Charlotte's sake, I will see what I can do.'

'I don't know, it's very irregular,' Sharrock grumbled.

'Please,' Harriett begged again, 'please don't take me to that awful place.'

Sharrock looked dubious.

'Perhaps,' Frances went on, 'the police would be willing to make a special case if, in return, Mrs Antrobus was to make a full confession of her crimes — all of them?'

'All of them?' bellowed Sharrock. 'How many are there?'

Harriett, with her hands over her ears, moaned 'Yes, yes, I will confess, only please everyone be quiet.'

'Let us all calm down and sit quietly,' agreed Frances.

The company was seated but no one in the room rested easy. Cornelius dragged his hands distractedly through his hair. 'What other crimes?'

'The murder of Charles Henderson and the murder of her husband.'

Harriett wiped her eyes. 'Please fetch me some water. I will do as you say.'

'I don't understand this at all,' sighed Sharrock, 'but I am sure Miss Doughty will explain, as she usually does.'

When Mrs Antrobus was given a refreshing drink, and the Inspector and Cornelius were quiet and attentive, Frances began.

'This is what I think happened. The two misses Pearce, Harriett and Charlotte, were the daughters of the Antrobus brothers' senior assistant, and when Mr Edwin became fascinated by the younger sister it was very good fortune for her. But his brother, Mr Lionel, was unhappy about the match. It would be some years before Edwin Antrobus could make a sufficient fortune to marry, and Miss Harriett must have feared that his brother would find some way of preventing it. Mr Edwin was, however, the principal heir of his uncle, Charles Henderson, who had willed him this house and its furnishings and some investments. With such a handsome legacy the couple would be able to marry at once. But Mr Henderson was only thirty-seven and, apart from his headaches, in good health.

'On the night of Mr Henderson's death he had gone to get a key to his study to show the company his collection of snuff-boxes. Mrs Pearce was feeling unwell, and Harriett took her mother into the parlour to look after her, but having settled her mother there, I think she hurried up to the study where she flattered Mr Henderson into showing her the pistol and how it was loaded. She must have been shown the study on an earlier visit and knew the gun was kept there. I expect she asked to hold the gun, promising to be careful. Then she shot him. She had only time to run into the nearest room, the bathroom probably, to hide, which was why the study door was found open. Edwin Antrobus rushed up the stairs and found his uncle's corpse. Harriet stayed in the bathroom until he had gone down to tell the others what had happened, and while he was so engaged she managed to creep downstairs to rejoin her mother in the parlour, who was sufficiently unwell that she was easily persuaded that her daughter had never left her side. I do wonder if Mr Henderson's Aunt Lily, who had gone to look for the key and was in the hallway at the time her nephew was killed, knew more than she was able to say. Perhaps she saw the murderer creeping downstairs. But the shock was so great that she was a broken woman and died soon afterwards.' Frances glanced at Harriet, who was icily calm. 'How did Aunt Lily die?'

'Peacefully, in her sleep,' said Mrs Antrobus, without a flicker of expression. 'She was very old.'

'I see. But there was one unforeseen result of the murder, was there not? A gun fired in a small space like a room is very loud indeed. Your ears were never the same afterwards. Mrs Fisher told me that your husband used to sing when his uncle played the piano and had a voice like a songbird, but he never sang again after his uncle's death. She must have thought it was because he did not have the heart to do so, but maybe there was another reason, maybe it was because his voice hurt your ears. The condition became worse over the years until it was impossible for you to live a normal life, but to avoid suspicion you were able to blame it on the firework display.'

Harriett sipped her water but said nothing.

'Your husband never suspected you of murdering his uncle until shortly before his last journey. He had a conversation with Dr Goodwin, who is an otologist, an expert on afflictions of the ears, unlike the other men who saw you. Your husband expressed the opinion that your condition could not have been caused by the firework display, and Dr Goodwin advised him that even if that was so, there are many other causes.' Frances took from her pocket Dr Goodwin's booklet on ear pain. 'He lists them here: a blow to the head; loud music, such as the sound of an orchestra which can affect the players; the noise of heavy machinery; loud explosions; even a single gunshot if close by can all produce the condition known as hyperacusis.' She closed the book. 'Did he realise then? Did you know before he went away that he planned to have you put in an asylum? Not because he thought you were mad but because he knew you to be a heartless murderer and wanted to avoid a trial that would distress his sons. There was nothing you could do until a suitable instrument arrived in the shape of your cousin Robert Barfield. He was in a sorry condition, ragged, limping from a poorly healed leg injury and in pain from a toothache. You were able to provide him with what he needed to appear respectable and engaged him to murder your husband. Even though you knew the will would be unkind to you, you felt sure that as a widow you would be able to challenge it. The plan, I think, was for Barfield to go to Bristol and kill your husband there, to place the crime far from home, but somehow he failed. Your husband, despite your cousin's protests that he was a reformed man, never gave him the opportunity. And so they returned to London. How and where the murder took place I don't know, but Barfield now only had one hold over you, he knew the location of the body. He tried to blackmail you by making you sign over the inheritance he thought you would receive before he would reveal it, but you refused. He stole your husband's ring and other trinkets from his dressing room and then tried, unsuccessfully, to blackmail Dr Goodwin by alleging that he had murdered your husband. When he failed to reappear, both you and Dr Goodwin were afraid that he would come back, but he was in fact dead, having fallen down the cellar stairs at the school.'

Inspector Sharrock and Cornelius listened to the long tale in silence.

'And now we come to the murder of Mr Eckley, whose enquiries threatened the happiness of your sister, her marriage representing your best escape from the tyranny of your brother-in-law. On the day of the murder you pretended to have a headache and wrote and posted the letter making an appointment, then when your sister thought you were asleep, you were able to closely muffle your ears and creep out of the house, going by the quietest route to meet him. Your guilt of the murder of Mr Eckley can be proved. The murdered man's watch and the knife that killed him are tied to this house. There is also your knowledge of the theft of the watch that you revealed before three witnesses and your lies to try and save yourself by incriminating your sister. How heartlessly you turned on her when you were finally cornered, and then, almost in a breath, you fastened your sights upon my uncle.'

Frances kept her eyes on Mrs Antrobus but heard Cornelius utter a groan. She pressed relentlessly on. 'Your guilt of the other two murders – or possibly three, as I suspect that Mr Henderson's Aunt Lily was hurried to her death so she could not reveal what she saw – cannot be proved, but it might make a difference to your fate if you were to confess to them. Will you do so?'

Both Frances and Harriett looked at Sharrock. 'I can't make any guarantees,' said the Inspector, 'but if this lady was to confess to a catalogue of crimes so horrible that no one would think a woman would even be capable of them, then she might well be able to convince a court that she is someone who can't tell right from wrong.'

Harriett rose gracefully from her chair and went to sit at her desk, then took a fresh pen, ink and a sheaf of paper. 'I will write it all down.'

'Does Miss Doughty have it right?' Sharrock asked her.

Harriett smiled calmly. 'She does, except in one respect. Robert did not blackmail me concerning the location of Edwin's body. He himself did not know where it was, and neither do I.'

'I don't understand,' said Cornelius. 'Is your husband dead?'

'I expect so, yes,' said the would-be widow, without a trace of emotion.

He looked appalled. 'You seem not to mind.'

'I mind not knowing.'

'I think I might be able to guess at what happened,' said Frances. 'Since Mr Barfield was unable to walk fast on his injured leg, he would have found it hard to commit murder in the street or in any place where his victim could run away. He had to get him in a small space, a hotel room perhaps, but Mr Antrobus didn't trust him enough to agree to a private meeting. Barfield attacked him on the train, didn't he? And he was very strong in the arms and upper body, so he would have prevailed. Did he throw Mr Antrobus from the train?'

Harriet nodded, her pen moving smoothly, without pause. 'So he said.'

'And you both simply had to wait and hope that the body was found, but it never was.'

'That can't be right,' objected Sharrock. 'The track was searched, but nothing was found.'

'You were looking for a man who might had fallen from the train,' Frances reminded him. 'If he was pushed by someone very strong the body might not have landed on the track.' Frances searched the bookcases in the room and found a directory with a railway map. 'Did he say whereabouts on the journey it happened?'

'Robert was always a coward in such things,' said Harriett disapprovingly. 'He was still very shaken when he came to see me and confessed that he had not thought to make a note of the location until it was too late. All he could tell me was that the train had been travelling for at least half an hour out of Bristol and had not yet arrived at Reading.'

'I suppose fifty miles of railway is better than a hundred,' grunted Sharrock. 'It'll be a long job, mind.'

Cornelius was visibly trembling as he went to stand by Mrs Antrobus, who continued to write unconcerned. 'And is Charlotte innocent? Tell me that!'

The pen flowed swiftly on. 'She is innocent of murder.'

'And the other thing? Please tell me she is innocent of that also!' he begged.

'You must ask her yourself. She will tell you the truth.'

Frances saw her kind uncle's face crumple with grief.

CHAPTER TWENTY-EIGHT

'So,' said Dr Goodwin, when Frances paid him a visit a week later, 'they have found the body at last.'

It was a happier occasion than when they had last met, and she, the doctor and young Isaac, who had been released when the charge of murder against him was dropped, were enjoying a pot of tea and some fancy cakes topped with strawberries.

'They have. The railway men made a thorough search of the line between Bath and Reading, and the police interviewed the farmers. One man with a farm near Didcot had found a hat lying in his field and assumed that it had been blown from the head of a gentleman looking out of a train window. He still had the hat and wore it to church. Mr Antrobus' hatter was able to identify it. Some bones were found in a deep ditch where the body must have rolled out of sight.'

'No wisdom teeth, I assume?'

She smiled. 'Not one. The inquest opened this morning, and the remains have been formally identified as those of Edwin Antrobus. Of course his widow is now in no position to contest the will.'

Dr Goodwin signed the conversation to Isaac, who replied.

'Isaac says you are the cleverest lady in all Bayswater,' Goodwin translated. 'You will also be pleased to hear that he has recently had a very affectionate interview with his mother. Poor lady, she has suffered much, and he has been a great comfort to her.'

'I was hoping,' ventured Frances, 'although this will make no difference now, if you could enlighten me on a number of things. In particular your dealings with Mrs Antrobus.'

'Ah, yes,' he said thoughtfully and refreshed his teacup.

'If you are in any doubt about how much to tell me, my advice is – everything.'

Isaac tapped his father on the shoulder and signed anxiously. Goodwin made a reply. 'My son hopes that you will not accuse me of anything,' he told Frances. 'I have reassured him that I have nothing with which to reproach myself.'

'I am quite certain that you do not.'

Goodwin sipped his tea thoughtfully and put the cup down in a calm and deliberate fashion. 'I will conceal nothing from you Miss Doughty, a vain exercise, as so many others have found to their cost. On my last professional visit to Mrs Antrobus, she appealed to me to make her husband understand that her illness was of the ears and not the mind. As she requested, I spoke to him again, but he adamantly refused to believe it. His grounds were that she had always attributed the illness to the noise of a firework display, but he was certain that this was untrue. He said that she had imagined noises to be loud before then, and he had persuaded her to attend the display with him to prove that it was all in her mind, but soon after it began she said that the noise was too much and retired indoors. There was one firework that exploded close to the ground, but she was not present at the time and he had told her about it afterwards.

'I suggested to Mr Antrobus that even if the fireworks were not the cause of her hyperacusis it could have been another event that she had not realised was harmful at the time. I described the kinds of noises that have resulted in ear pain for my other patients and he denied she had ever been subjected to any of them except one. The sound of a gunshot.

'As I said it a look passed across his face, like that of a man who had seen a ghost and was struck with horror. I thought that he must have taken her shooting and had discharged a gun close by and suddenly saw that her affliction was his own fault. I asked if he went shooting, and he said no but his late uncle had. I tried to question him further but he was obviously distressed and would tell me no more.

'The next day I received a letter from Mrs Antrobus asking if I might meet her at Kensal Green. I did so and we discussed my conversation with her husband. She mentioned the death of Mr Henderson and admitted to me that she had been in the room when he had shot himself. She said she had been so frightened that she had rushed out of the study and hidden in the bathroom. Her husband, she said, was now accusing her of having shot Mr Henderson in order that he might inherit his fortune. She told me that her husband treated her cruelly and she almost

wished that he would suffer some accident and expire but providence had not granted her wish. She said that all she wanted was
to be happy and share her fortune with a man who would be
kind to her. She wept a great deal, but I have seen her weep many
times before, and I believe she may do it at will, without emotion.
I have encountered people before who have this singular ability.'

'What did you say to her?'

'I was naturally confused. It was as if she was asking me to
commit some violence on her husband. She reached out and tried
to take my hand but I could not allow it, not after what she had
said. I replied that she could not possibly mean what her words
seemed to suggest. She gave that little smile of hers. I think you
know the one. I told her that it would be best if we never met
again, and that as long as she promised to forget the terrible things
she had said then I would be prepared to forget them also.'

'That would have been very shortly before Mr Barfield
approached her.'

'Yes, and when he confronted me he used the same words she
had spoken, the same sentiments she had expressed. I knew that
he had seen her, and I believed she had made him her creature,
but of course I had no proof. I only saw her once more, after her
husband was missing. I suppose I was curious to find out if she
had had anything to do with it. She denied any knowledge of his
fate and also claimed that I had not recalled our last conversation
correctly. I thought it best not to seek her society again.'

Goodwin turned to Isaac and signed. The boy nodded, his large
hands wrapped around his teacup making it look like something
out of a doll's house.

'I have told him,' explained Goodwin, 'that there was a cruel
lady who had done some bad things but because of the clever Miss
Doughty she is now in a place where she can do no more harm.'

Father and son looked at each other with an expression of
warmth that could only give pleasure to anyone seeing it. Frances
knew that she could destroy that happiness, or at least cast a terrible shadow on the future lives of Dr Goodwin, Isaac and his
mother, but she could not bring herself to do so.

❧

'When Mr Barfield attempted to blackmail Dr Goodwin he made a singular error,' said Frances to Sarah later that day. 'He thought that because the children could not hear they could not understand what he was saying. Today Dr Goodwin and his son made the same error. They thought that because I can hear that I cannot understand a conversation in signs, but our study of them in the last weeks has been most illuminating. Isaac was extremely anxious in case I had discovered his secret, and I was for a moment tempted to sign to him that I knew it. But I did not. If I made an allegation I doubt that I could prove it, in any case, and I do not wish to be seen as a threat to a youth who I now know to be both capable of and willing to break a man's neck with his bare hands.'

Lionel Antrobus had been busy with all the duties attendant on him as executor of his brother's will, so it was not until a week after the inquest that he came to finally settle his account with Frances for the work she had commissioned with Tom on his behalf.

He examined the invoice without a change in expression and handed her an envelope. She expected him to take his leave as soon as the business was done, but he did not.

'A few days ago,' he announced, 'I had a conversation with Dr Goodwin.'

'What, the Don Juan of Bayswater?' said Frances teasingly.

He gave her a cold stare. 'You taunt me, Miss Doughty.'

'Yes, I do,' she retorted, staring back at him unflinchingly. 'But tell me, has Dr Goodwin finally succeeded in convincing you that Mrs Antrobus has an affliction of the ears?'

'It is clear to me now that something occurred from the sound of the gunshot with which she killed Mr Henderson which has affected her hearing. I already knew that persons can become deaf from such insults, and Dr Goodwin assures me that the opposite may also be the case.'

Frances had been pondering something. 'At our first conversation when I said I believed Mrs Antrobus to be genuine you disagreed very strongly, saying that you knew her better than I did. I now see that you were, in a sense, right, but it was for the wrong reasons. You knew, you somehow felt from the start of your acquaintance with her, that she was not to be trusted. It was this that made you believe that her hearing condition was a mental affliction.'

'So the great detective can be wrong?'

'I can be wrong about many things,' she replied. There was a moment's silence.

'Dr Goodwin suggested that it would be for the best if Harriett did not come to trial. If she did she would evoke sympathy and would no doubt be imprisoned rather than hanged. Under those circumstances it would be very probable that she might try to take her own life. It is hard enough for the boys to have a mother in prison for such terrible crimes, but the additional taint of suicide would be insupportable. It would be better therefore if she was adjudged unfit to plead and placed in a secure situation.'

'An asylum? But she is not insane.'

'I really do not care whether my brother's murderer is insane or merely wicked. But I think you would agree that it is better if she is allowed to live out her days in some quiet location. She is an evil woman, but I do not think it is justice that she should endure the torments of the abyss, at least, not while she is still living. The hereafter will judge her in due course. I have therefore taken the necessary steps, and Dr Goodwin supports the arrangement. Not the public asylum, but a place with respectable females to care for her. She would even be permitted to receive visitors and play her piano.'

Frances could see the sense of his argument and had to admit that it was probably for the best. 'Who will pay for this?'

'Mr brother's estate. I act wholly for my nephews now. I have discussed the question with young Edwin, who is a sensible boy, and he agrees with my course of action. He wants to be able to visit his mother, and I do not intend to prevent him.'

He rose to leave, but there was something else on his mind, and he hesitated for a while, then addressed her again. 'Miss Doughty, you strike me as a capable and intelligent young woman. I have never opposed the idea of women in the professions, or in honest trades; I believe there may be as many women so suited as there are men, but I cannot help thinking that you have chosen unwisely.

'It is my intention to open another tobacconist's shop on Westbourne Grove. If you are interested I can offer you a position there where you would be able to learn the business. In time, I have no doubt that you would be able to progress to manageress.' He paused. 'In fact, you might well be able to aspire further.'

Frances thanked him but her first impulse was to decline. He was not, after all, a bad man, merely one in whose company she did not feel easy.

'I do not expect an answer at once. Will you consider it?'

Frances promised that she would, and over the course of the day the more she thought about it the more attractive the prospect appeared. The tobacco trade, she reflected, was not so very far different from the work she had undertaken in her father's chemist's shop. She could undoubtedly make a success of it, and the position of manageress was tempting. She found herself wondering what Lionel Antrobus would be like as an employer and whether that stiff formality ever unbent.

Her thoughts were interrupted by the arrival of a tearfully grateful client, pressing rewards upon her for finding a missing child, who had been discovered by Tom, muddy, cheerful and unharmed, having sought an afternoon of excitement with a little band of street urchins. The joy of the happy mother was enough to decide Frances. There could be no comparable satisfaction to be gained in selling cigars. She decided to write a polite letter to Lionel Antrobus thanking him for his kind offer but saying that she could not accept.

As to the further aspirations he had hinted at she could not imagine what that could mean. It was only after she had discussed the conversation with Sarah and seen her assistant's horrified reaction that Frances realised that she had just received a proposal of marriage.

It was an autumn wedding; a quiet affair in which it was possible for old differences to be settled and new connections forged. The bride had never looked so well, and the groom was happier than he had been in many a year. Frances was glad to see Lionel Antrobus shake hands with her uncle and genuine good wishes exchanged. Sarah was a witness, as was Mr Luckhurst, who arrived with a handsome new ring sparkling on his finger and a merry twinkle in his eye. Dr Goodwin stood in place of the bride's father, while Isaac, all smiles, was the perfect usher.

Nothing was said of what had recently passed, and no mention was made of those who perforce were absent.

The ceremony over, Frances embraced her aunt, the former Miss Charlotte Pearce, now Mrs Cornelius Martin. Her uncle was kind and forgiving, and had not allowed the youthful error of his intended bride to affect his love for her. 'Who amongst us is without fault?' was all he had said to Frances when telling her that the wedding would take place as planned. 'We all make mistakes when we are young, and why should we suffer for them our whole lives? In my dear Charlotte's case I am inclined to think that the man was a scoundrel and, as a man of the world, far more to blame than she.'

After the wedding breakfast the happy couple were due to depart for a week's honeymoon at a quiet hotel on the south coast, and they would then take up residence in Craven Hill. Though the house held many unhappy memories both seemed determined to populate it with new and better ones.

'So,' smiled Cornelius to Frances and Sarah as the carriage arrived to bear the newlyweds away, 'which one of you will be the next to marry?'

'Not me!' said Sarah, robustly. 'It wouldn't suit at all.'

'And you, Frances, do you not have a sweetheart?'

Frances smiled and assured him that she did not. There was a sudden laugh and an exclamation, and she saw a posy of flowers, the bride's bouquet, flying high into the air. Without effort, she reached out and caught it.

※ END ※

Author's Note

The author has suffered from both hyperacusis and tinnitus for many years and is the founder of a support group on Facebook for people with hyperacusis. The main symptom of tinnitus is a constant noise in the ears that comes from no external source. Hyperacusis is a reduced tolerance to sound, which means that the noises of everyday life, especially if high pitched, cause pain. The earliest reference to the term hyperacusis the author has traced so far dates to a medical volume published in 1873.

For more information see:

www.tinnitus.org.uk

www.hyperacusisresearch.org

The Facebook support group is Hyperacusis Sufferers at www.facebook.com/groups/2414964219/

The Paddington Canal Basin was drained in November 1880 following complaints about pollution and smell, and some human bones were found. The event is recorded in the *Bayswater Chronicle*.

In 1880 Mr William Whiteley purchased properties in Queens Road (nowadays Queensway) in order to erect new warehouses. More details about Mr Whiteley's character and career are in the author's *Whiteley's Folly: The Life and Death of a Salesman*.

Gilbert and Sullivan's comic opera *Patience* opened at the Opéra Comique in April 1881 and played there until October.

Ignatius 'Paddington' Pollaky was a private detective known for his keen questioning. He retired in 1882. For more information see *Paddington' Pollaky, Private Detective: The Mysterious*

Life and Times of the Real Sherlock Holmes, by Bryan Kesselman. (The History Press, 2015)

In 1881 American inventor James Bonsack patented a machine for the mass production of cigarettes. It was introduced into the UK in 1883.

Following the Milan conference of 1880 many schools for the teaching of deaf children converted to the German 'pure oral' system, banning the use of sign language. Children sometimes had their hands tied together to prevent them signing. More information can be found at http://deafness.about.com/cs/featurearticles/a/milan1880.htm.

This pivotal event in deaf history is thought to have set back the education of deaf children by about 100 years.

In the
Frances Doughty
Mystery Series

The Poisonous Seed: A Frances Doughty Mystery
The Daughters of Gentlemen: A Frances Doughty Mystery
A Case of Doubtful Death: A Frances Doughty Mystery
An Appetite for Murder: A Frances Doughty Mystery

PRAISE FOR THE FRANCES DOUGHTY MYSTERY SERIES

'If Jane Austen had lived a few decades longer, and spent her twilight years writing detective stories, they might have read something like this one'

   Sharon Bolton, author of the best-selling Lacey Flint series

'A gripping and intriguing mystery with an atmosphere Dickens would be proud of'

   Leigh Russell, author of the best-selling Geraldine Steel novels

'I feel that I am walking down the street in Frances' company and seeing the people and houses around me with clarity'

   Jennifer S. Palmer, Mystery Women

'Every novelist needs her USP: Stratmann's is her intimate knowledge of both pharmacy and true-life Victorian crime'

   Shots Magazine

'The atmosphere and picture of Victorian London is vivid and beautifully portrayed'

   www.crimesquad.com

'Vivid details and convincing period dialogue bring to life Victorian England during the early days of the women's suffrage movement, which increasingly appeals to Frances even as she strives for acceptance from the male-dominated society of the time. Historical mystery fans will be hooked'

Publishers Weekly

'[Frances'] adventures as a detective, and the slowly unraveling evidence of multiple crimes in a murky Victorian setting, make for a gripping read'

Historical Novel Review

'The historical background is impeccable'

Mystery People

Visit our website and discover thousands of other History Press books.

www.thehistorypress.co.uk